The Mammo

# Vampire Romance

Also available

# The Mammoth Book of

# Vampire Romance

### Edited by Trisha Telep

RUNNING PRESS
PHILADELPHIA · LONDON

Constable & Robinson Ltd
3 The Lanchesters
162 Fulham Palace Road
London W6 9ER
www.constablerobinson.com

First published in the UK by Robinson,
an imprint of Constable & Robinson, 2008

A copy of the British Library Cataloguing in Publication
Data is available from the British Library

UK ISBN 978-1-84529-859-3

3 5 7 9 10 8 6 4

First published in the United States in 2008
by Running Press Book Publishers

9 8 7 6 5 4 3 2
Digit on the right indicates the number of this printing

US Library of Congress number: 2008927573
US ISBN 978-0-76243-498-5

Running Press Book Publishers
2300 Chestnut Street
Philadelphia, PA 19103-4371

Visit us on the web!

www.runningpress.com

Printed and bound in the EU

# Contents

# Acknowledgments

# Introduction

## Trisha Telep

On any given day at Murder One in London, the crime and romance bookstore (where I work as the romance book buyer), you might come across romance regulars clutching recent but dog-eared copies of the *Romantic Times* magazine, the pages marked up to show new romance titles they want ordered and the authors they follow religiously with standing orders in the shop. You will also see readers browsing the romance shelves (stacked to the roof – and more – with books) and, although the romance room is a tad small, hanging out and talking among themselves, reading back covers and first pages and getting advice from other readers before making final purchases. And you'll certainly see die-hard customers leaving with stacks of all types of romance, but mainly, at the moment, with paranormal romance. The massive demand for paranormal romance these days means that every month there is an avalanche of new titles from publishers for romance readers to keep up with. Yet – somehow – romance readers seem to manage.

In this celebratory spirit, *The Mammoth Book of Vampire Romance* brings together the largest number of new paranormal romance stories ever assembled under one cover. The collection focuses on one of the original, most ancient characters of this genre – the vampire – and includes not only those authors who have built their writing careers on bloodsuckers, but also great writers from elsewhere in the paranormal genre for whom this is their first vampire outing. This means that you'll find a fun, broad range of stories of all kinds of unexpected vampires, from the traditional worlds of horror to gothic-romance and historical, to contemporary urban fantasy, fang-in-cheek comedy and the hottest erotica, all the way to the downright romantic, boy-meets-girl, sweetheart stories from tried-and-true romances (albeit with a bite ripped out of the heart and a vase full of blood for the flowers).

Also, keep an eye out for the smattering of stand-alone stories that feature connections to a particular writer's existing series, or that follow an intriguing character who didn't get a chance to realize their full potential in a previous book and whose story may be being told here for the very first time (see the story of Dante Valentine's foster daughter, Liana, in Lilith Saintcrow's "Coming Home", Tomas the vampire in Karen Chance's "The Day of the Dead" and the story of Viper's beginnings in Delilah Devlin's "Viper's Bite"). And, if you find yourself hooked on a particular writer after reading one of their stories, you can always get a quick fix by going out and scooping up their trademark series to tide you over until the next instalment! But the real question that you'll find cropping up again and again within these pages is this: is being a vampire all it's cracked up to be? Sure, you get to live forever and never age, sure you get powers of sexual magnetism beyond any human's wildest dreams, but is it worth it? This question is like an echo through many of these stories. So go for the jugular ( . . . and the carotid, the femoral artery at the inner thigh, the soles of the feet, the bend at the elbow, the ankle . . .) with this motley crew of *Mammoth* vampires and find out.

# Fade to Black

## Sherri Erwin

My mind wandered through a mental inventory of my life as I felt his teeth sink into my skin.

About to turn 30, I lived in a one-bedroom apartment that I could barely afford, even with the reduced rate of rent from my employer. Between my car bill, credit card debt and student loan payments, I could barely afford any luxuries, and that was only if I left necessities behind in the grocery aisles. I lived for invitations to dine with the students in the dorm: free food.

And now? I had probably risked the career I'd come to resent, the only thing I had going in life, by accepting an invitation from Connor Black (my sole male student) to go out for a drink – only to find he was a card-carrying member of Bloodsuckers Anonymous. *A vampire.*

Risked my career? It should have been the least of my worries as I prepared to be dinner for one. What the hell, though, right? Could he suck me any drier than my creditors, who apparently thought I bled cash?

Oh, no. I bled blood, confirmation of which came as his fangs made their introductions to my veins via the tender flesh at the base of my neck. A dribble rolled down my bare shoulder to pool in the lace edging of my shell-pink bra, a purchase that had sat in my drawer long after Victoria's Secret had closed my account. Hopeful for a chance to show it off, I'd put it on this morning for the first time. And here I was.

"You taste like the wine," he said, coming up for air. His palm grazed my nipple through the silk. It reacted, hardening under his touch with traitorous speed.

I met his gaze, cobalt eyes set in a face more inspiring than anything painted by Botticelli.

"It doesn't hurt." Surprised, I reached up to stroke the puncture wound.

He smiled, beatific despite the sharpened canines. "We pack a sort of numbing agent. Localized."

"Like mosquitoes? You don't know they're sucking until they've almost fed."

He laughed, a low chortle, much deeper and richer than any sound I'd heard from him in the classroom, where he'd managed to pass himself off as an ordinary young man, albeit a fascinatingly beautiful one.

A fascinatingly beautiful one who had captured the attention of every woman in the room, even the self-proclaimed lesbians. Rumour had it that he'd slept with every student in my Romantic poets class. From the way they looked at him, with the tight focus of famished animals desperate to get a bite, I didn't believe it. They hadn't had a taste. Not one of them. Not yet.

We'd all seemed to think *we* were the hunters and he our prey. Fools. Today, I'd worn a thin blouse over my new bra, unbuttoned further than usual, and I'd leaned low over his desk, on purpose, when handing back his paper. *The better to tempt you with, my dear*. And when he'd asked me out for a drink after class "to discuss his grade" (a solid A), I'd thought my little plan had worked. *I had him right where I wanted him*. Hard to believe I'd been so clueless just a few short hours ago.

Truth be told, I'd had a moment of reservation. I couldn't date a student. It was wrong. What if someone saw us? But my libido had won out. I wanted him. I wanted him like I'd never wanted a man in my life. And the fact that he seemed to want me – the oldest woman in the room next to all the lithe young coeds? Too tempting to pass up.

"That's it, love." He leaned in for a kiss, the tang of my blood on his tongue. "Give in. I can make you feel so good."

The erotic drag of soft lips against skin as he dropped a trail of kisses down the valley between my breasts convinced me he was right. He could make me *feel*. Good, bad, it hardly mattered. It had been so very long since I'd felt anything.

A lifeless drone, so steeped in debt and disappointment that I'd stopped allowing any reactions; I simply carried on. Work. Home. Eat. Sleep. Lather. Rinse. Repeat.

He recaptured my attention as his teeth tugged at the lace of my bra, his mouth begging entry to the silken cups. I slipped my hands up to tangle in his dark hair, slightly in need of a trim, and down to caress the corded muscles of his bare back. Caught in the throes of fresh passion, we'd stripped down almost as soon as we made it back to my apartment. His Stones concert T-shirt was still in my doorway, my skirt and blouse not far ahead to mark the trail that led from hall to kitchen.

He cradled my buttocks in his hands, lifted, and rested my bottom against chipped Formica before forming his tongue around my bare nipple and sucking it in for a long, hot pull. My knees would have buckled if I wasn't already balanced on the counter.

Had he broken the skin on my neck with his bite? I couldn't tell. His tongue stroked and laved, drawing me in. He suckled, as greedy as a newborn. But *I* was the mere babe.

Over the second glass of wine, he'd confessed to being nearly 600. I'd laughed, not yet moving past the state of disbelief. It took his confession to having been an intimate of the Shelleys to push me into the realm of acceptance. His explanation of Mary's belief that she had failed her husband struck a chord and felt so real.

He knew things that only years of study and access to sealed documents at the Bodleian Library would have confirmed. Mary's private letters, many lost, came to life in Connor Black's descriptions. He would be far too young to know so much, unless . . . *600 years old? Really?*

What drew him to me, he claimed, was reading my dissertation on Mary Shelley's yearning for immortality as expressed in her novels. I'd apparently captured such a sense of the real Mary that he wanted to meet me, and became a student to do so. He'd been close to her after her husband's death, but she'd refused to let him turn her.

"Because it was too late for her," I interjected, downing my third glass. Good Cabernet. "Why would she want to live when everyone she cared about had died?"

"The very reason she refused me," he confirmed, with a lift of his glass. "But you won't refuse me, will you?"

"Immortality doesn't hold a lot of appeal right now." Life being such a joy and all.

"How about a sharpening of your senses, all of them? Sounds, smells, tastes. You can't imagine what chocolate tastes like to me. And this wine, oh." He rolled his eyes back in his head as if the wine was ambrosia of the gods.

"I can still eat chocolate, then?" I tingled with curiosity. "It's not all about the blood?"

"The blood fortifies, it sustains you. But the food? Eat anything you like. You won't gain a pound."

I laughed. He had to be kidding.

"I'm completely serious. You'll remain as you are now, perhaps a little leaner."

"Only a little?" I raised a brow. "Perhaps I'll call you after I lose another ten pounds."

"No." There was an edge in his voice. He grew insistent. "Now. We'll go back to your place now. Let me show you."

"Show me?" My nerves skittered with curiosity mixed with a hint of fear.

"What I can do to you. For you," he corrected. "Tell me to stop if I make you uncomfortable. You're in control."

"I'm in control," I echoed now, as if suddenly remembering. My nerves no longer skittered, but were as taut as violin strings. And how they sang.

"Mm." He looked up, a drip of blood trailing down his stubble-dotted chin. "Your wish is my command."

But he didn't stop to take commands. He dropped to his knees, tugging the underwear that matched my bra down my hips and dipping his head between my thighs before I had a chance to protest. I shifted, leaning back to allow him better access. He drank deeply, and for so long that I lost all thoughts of control. I lost my mind. I barely remembered my name.

And then, I nearly lost consciousness. I tingled all over, felt light-headed, euphoric. I'd never felt so at peace, and yet so high. So very high. I drifted in the air, hovering over the scene. I looked good stretched out along my kitchen counter, my torso elongated to best advantage for my slightly rounded abs. My stomach looked flat, lovely. My breasts, firmer than I remembered. My legs, longer than I ever imagined, and perfectly shaped as they wrapped around him, pulling him tighter, before they went quite limp.

He rose, wiping his mouth with the back of his hand. Wait, how was I watching? Was I – realization dawned. I was dead?

He left me there, an abandoned rag doll, and went off in search of something. A knife. He stripped off his shirt and sliced a red welt along his well-honed shoulder blade. He leaned in for a kiss. "Your turn. Drink."

I didn't know how I could comply with his orders from way up in the ether, but I tasted brine, like seawater, on my tongue as he pressed against my mouth. Drowning, I drank him in, unable to hold back, and I gasped, coming to the surface at last.

"That's it." He cradled my head in his hands.

The blue of his eyes shone through my haze to guide me, stars in a midnight sky. I dipped my head again and darted my tongue along the tangy red welt. Now I tasted the wine, the Cabernet we'd had earlier, the rich berry essence with a hint of tobacco, earth and salt. Connor's blood. Clarity returned with every taste. I became all too aware of my fingers sliding over his bare chest, down his arms, and up again, pausing at every sinew and cord. He was real, no figment of my imagination. I slid my bottom down off the cabinets, cold linoleum under the balls of my feet as I rose up on tiptoe to kiss his lush, quivering mouth.

My hands strayed to the button of his jeans, too much clothing. I wanted to feel him against me, inside me. I felt so new, so alive, aware of every little thing: my nerves pulsing under the skin, blood thrumming through my veins, the tick of the clock in my bedroom, a soft mewling yawn from the baby next door. Next door? Could I hear that far?

"Your senses sharpen," he said, as if he could hear my thoughts. And then I realized that he hadn't spoken aloud. I could hear his thoughts, and he mine. *We're connected now.*

"For life?" Not used to telepathy, I'd asked it aloud.

He laced his fingers with mine. *For eternity. My epipsychidion.*

Soul of my soul. I knew the Shelley poem, the poet's fixation with a lover. I also knew the reality behind the poem. Shelley had fallen for a phantom, his own idealized version of what love should be. Was I, in fact, a phantom now? Or was I waking from past disillusionment, ready to accept a whole new life?

With my newly sharpened senses, I assumed the sound of breaking glass was the shock of my own realization. It took a second to comprehend that it was my actual window breaking. A man was climbing in through the broken glass, and another two coming in the door I'd left unlocked. I assumed they were men, larger than life in dark jumpsuits and helmets, faces covered with masks. Gas masks.

Connor shoved me behind him as if about to defend me. I was touched by the gesture until he fell at my feet. A heartbeat later, my shouts of protest echoing in deep-throated slow motion, I fell atop him and into the black fog of my own mind.

I woke up in the dark. So dark I couldn't see. I could feel that I was in bed, in a cotton gown, but not my bed and not my gown. Hospital? I sat up. Hospitals had those infernal fluorescent lights, always on. I couldn't see any cracks of light to indicate a window or a door. I inhaled, rubbed my arms, and discovered an IV jabbed into the inside of my left elbow. Hospital, I reaffirmed, and tried to feel better about it.

Hospital. I squinted into the darkness. Had I gone blind? Panic set in. I was blind! Lord, I hoped it was only a temporary condition. I reached out at my sides, fingers meeting metal rails.

"Hello?" If I couldn't see, how would I know if there was someone in the room? "Hello?"

No answer. I sighed, reached over, and worked my hand up the IV tube to a box-like machine. My finger hit a button, something. A buzz went off, and stopped, followed by a soft whir, and what felt like a pulsing down the tube. Maybe I was getting more drugs, whatever had knocked me out. Maybe I didn't care. But I did care. I struggled to remember what had happened, why I was here. And then my mind found Connor.

*I'm here.* Connor Black's voice in my head, as if he were speaking to me.

*Where?* Whether I was crazy, dreaming or drugged, what did it matter? I may as well answer.

*You have to find me*, he said. *Find me.*

I preferred to find *me* first.

Deductive reasoning had never been my strong point, which was why I'd gone into teaching literature. *Teaching.* The Shelleys. I'd been having wine with Connor. It all came flooding back to me. The wine. The apartment. His mouth on me. My wrist flew up to stroke my neck. My breath caught up with me a second later. Vampire? It couldn't be.

My blood pounded in my veins so hard I could practically hear it. I remembered the window shattering, three men in jumpsuits and masks, my falling at their feet, and the world fading to black. I sat up fast, the tubing ripping from my skin on a snap of pain that faded as realization dawned. Hospital? Or had I been abducted?

The world came into focus, a dim glow lighting the room, or were my eyes finally working? I squinted in the darkness until I realized that I didn't need to squint. I could see everything fine, even in the dark. The machinery at my side, a medical-looking box with two bags hanging suspended – one as clear as water, the other as opaque as blood – both feeding in to the tube that had been stuck in my veins. The bed, covers rumpled at my feet, the walls covered in what looked to be watered silk, there were gilded wall sconces, tasteful paintings of flowers in vases, two dressers, a vanity with an enormous mirror, a chair, and doors – a bathroom? Closet? Hall? No curtains, no windows. My bare feet found the soft, woven carpet, not exactly standard hospital issue.

The doors should have been my target. Which one to exit? Where to call out? I headed for the mirror, my breathing suspended. I feared what I might, or might not, see but there I was, bathed in a golden glow as if kissed by the dawn, lovelier than I'd ever appeared. My hair hung in soft, honeyed curls to my shoulders. I stroked my cheek, pale or simply an effect of the darkness? My eyes glowed, cat's eyes, predatory and shrewd. Me, but not me. What had happened? Where was I?

Again, I left the doors unchecked in favour of sifting through the dresser drawers. My favourite jeans, a not favourite sweater. My clothing was here, and what else? I pulled the jeans on, not bothering to look for more. The jeans hung, just barely staying around my hips. The sweater had been nearly too tight, but now it draped my frame. No time to think. Shoes. I needed shoes and I could walk out of here and into the night. Something told me not to call out, not to stay. A voice in my head, not my own. *Connor.*

A sound caught my attention, a rustling from the direction of the door at the far end of the room. A heartbeat later, the door swung open.

A man stood outlined in a halo of light. Once he stepped inside, I could see that he looked something like an angel. Blond curls, structured cheekbones. I met his gaze as he stepped inside and closed the door behind him. I didn't know how I could so clearly make out the colour of his eyes through the dark, but they shone amber, warm as candlelight diffused through a glass of Irish whiskey.

He held a clipboard, his arms crossed over his white coat, which reminded me of folded wings.

"Luke." He held out his hand and smiled, straight white teeth, no fangs. Another good sign. Not that Connor had appeared to have fangs until he'd been about to bite. "Luke Jameson."

"Doctor Jameson?" I asked, hesitant, as I placed my hand in his soft, warm grip.

He nodded. "I'd prefer that you call me Luke, but whatever makes you comfortable. The whole suite—" he gestured around us "—was designed for your comfort. I'd prefer you thought of it as home."

"I'd like to go home." To my real home. Not that my shoebox apartment had ever felt much like home.

"Why don't we go have a seat? We've a lot to discuss." He opened the door adjacent to the one he'd come in, the one I'd assumed was a closet but turned out to be a sitting room. I followed him into the light, to an overstuffed lavender sofa in front of a brick hearth with a walnut mantel. A pastel woven rug covered a bare wood floor. Heavy curtains covered a back wall.

Windows? He settled on the ottoman of the chair that matched the sofa, set the clipboard on a side table, picked up a remote control and lit the gas-fuelled fireplace.

"Very cosy," I said to break the silence. I curled up in the corner of the couch.

"I'm glad you like it." He leaned forwards. "It is your home now."

A prickle of foreboding ran up my spine. I narrowed my eyes. "Is that a threat? Are you saying I don't have the freedom to leave?"

I struggled to hear Connor's voice in my head, but there was no sign of him.

Luke sighed and tented his fingers, elbows resting on the knees of his long slender legs. "It's not that complicated, but it may be hard to get used to at first. You've been given a virus."

"A virus?" I stood quickly, but didn't miss that his gaze lingered on my braless breasts bouncing under my sweater. He cleared his throat. I crossed my arms and sat down again.

"Vampirism is caused by a virus," he said, meeting my gaze again, warmth in his amber eyes. "Infectious. Passed through body fluids."

"Blood." I felt it rush to my cheeks at the memory of drinking from Connor. "I'm infected."

"It's more than vampirism. There's also hypertelomerase at work, the excess production of a hormone that halts the ageing process. It's not a death sentence. We're working to find a cure."

"So it's more of an eternal-life sentence?" I smiled so he could see that I was joking. I tried to relax.

"It's true that the bearers of the virus don't seem to die from natural causes. The body ceases to age. That's not a bad thing. In fact, it's one of the properties of the virus that we're fighting to preserve."

"But there are properties you would rather eliminate?" I raised a brow. "The blood-sucking?"

His turn to stand. He began pacing in front of the fireplace. "I don't think it's fair for some of us to spread our disease to the unsuspecting."

"Disease." It was the first I'd thought of myself as diseased, though he had referred to it as a virus. "But I was given a choice."

He shook his head. "Not without understanding the full implications. The need to hunt. The powerful urges to mate. The restlessness." His voice broke.

"The loneliness." I had no idea yet, having been infected such a short time and most of that spent unconscious, but I did know about being alone and the suddenly sad look in his eyes clued me in to the rest. I thought of the Shelleys, of Mary's refusal to let Connor turn her. "You're infected, too. Aren't you?"

"I am." His arm rested on the mantel and I could see his hand curl into a fist. "But I would never be so callous as to bite another human being. We've taken an oath here."

"We?"

"Back to you." He tipped his perfect, chiselled chin in my direction. "For all intents and purposes, you're dead. Your family, your friends, your work, everyone believes you to be gone."

"Without a body?"

"All signs led to abduction and murder. It was a logical conclusion."

"All signs. *Planted* signs. Who are you people? How long have I been here? Where are we, for that matter?" I stood and walked to the curtains behind us, opened them and looked out. I gasped. It wasn't night, but midday. The most beautiful band of coastline met my eyes, pristine sand, crystalline blue waters lapping to the shore in waves. "Palm trees. There are palm trees, for God's sake. Where have you taken me?"

"It's an island. All ours. You've only been here for two days now."

"Ours?" Two days. Two days of my life gone. But how many gained? Eternity?

"SPAHC's. The Society for Prevention of Advanced Hypertelomeric Cruorsitis.'

"That's what I have? The full name for it? Advanced Hypertelo-whatsis Cru-oh-who?"

"Hypertelomeric Cruorsitis. Yes."

"And you want to make it go away? That's why we're isolated here? On an island?"

"We have a full research facility. State of the art. Complete with luxurious living quarters, private beach—"

I held my hand up, interrupting. "I'll grab a brochure on the way out."

"You are free to leave. Please, don't be frightened. We're all here by choice. It might be awkward for you to try to go home again, but if you wish it."

I didn't wish it. He probably knew as well as I did that there was nothing left for me there. "I've always wanted to travel."

"We can arrange it. All I ask is that you stay here for a period of time. We like to get a full study of all the infected, to see if there's a mutation or something we may have missed along the way."

"Something you can use to find a cure?"

"Exactly."

I thought about it for a moment. "What if one doesn't want to be cured?"

"Everyone wants to be cured." He looked at me, his eyes wide with incredulity. "If not right away, they come to it eventually."

"Eventually," I echoed. I had no idea how I felt about who I was, what I'd become. Until I understood what the disease was all about, how would I know if I wanted to be cured?

"You'll stay then? A month or two?"

I had no idea where else I would go. No job, no money, no identity. "I'll stay. For now. Until I can investigate some job possibilities, see who's hiring."

He reached for my hand, a tender look in his eyes. "I'm sorry, Miranda. You can't go back to teaching. You have no credentials."

My lungs constricted with sheer panic. "All my years in school? All that time?"

"Gone." His lips drew to a tight line. "It's like witness protection. You have to leave everything you knew behind and start fresh. Clean slate. In the process, you discover things about yourself that you never even knew existed." His lips curved as if to show it was a good thing, but the smile never reached his eyes. It made me wonder.

I looked out of the window to the sand, the ocean and the horizon stretching endlessly beyond. I thought of my mother, ice clinking in her old-fashioned glass as she raised it for my stepfather to refill. "*I always told her she would come to no good.*" I thought of my sisters, probably bitter that I went first and left them to deal with Mother. I thought of my students marvelling at the juicy scandal of Connor Black attacking their dowdy old professor instead of choosing a tempting, ripe, youthful victim from among them. Would they all score an automatic A? Or would Beth Hinkle, the department head, step in and take over the class, business as usual?

It made me suddenly giddy to think of all I'd left behind. All that, gone. Gone. My nerves hummed with excitement. Or was it hunger?

I turned to Luke. "So, what have you got to eat around here? I'm starving."

Over a large meal of steak (rare) and potatoes (garlic mashed) hand-delivered by Luke to my room, he explained the vampire myths that weren't true. Garlic wasn't anathema, as evidenced by the delicious potatoes. Sunlight didn't burn us to a crisp. We weren't immune to death or invincible to injury. We didn't age, true enough, and our cells had remarkable resilience, but we could bleed and we could die given the right damage. As for our souls, who could tell? Who could tell what happened to any man's soul? Why should we be any different?

"Fair enough." I wiped my mouth after the last bite of steak and leaned back in my chair. "So, we're just like ordinary people except—"

"For the lack of ageing. And the fact that we do crave blood." Luke used a crusty bit of bread to wipe the excess juices from his plate, then popped it in his mouth and smiled, savouring it, as if to prove a point. "A desire we try to keep in check with a limited diet."

"Rare meat?" I raised a brow.

He shook his head. "Breakfast. Oatmeal. With blood."

"Ew." I recoiled.

"You'll get used to it. Trust me." His eyes crinkled at the corners when he smiled. Just a hint of age?

"I do. So tell me." I leaned forwards, my chin on my hand, suddenly interested in all things Luke. Appetite sated, I began to crave something else. "How old are you, Doctor Jameson?"

"Old enough to know the signs."

"Signs? What signs?"

"Your body's sending you signals. For all our advancement, we're still so primitive under the skin."

I didn't mind the idea of getting primitive with Luke.

"Aha, see? The gleam in your eye. You're feeling the effects." He got up, crossed over to the side table, picked up the opened bottle of wine, and returned to pour more into my glass, then his. "You're too new to control it. It's about to overwhelm you."

"I'm hardly overwhelmed." But even as I said it, I felt my lips curl in wily ingénue fashion. "I'm just trying to get to know you better, Luke."

"I can see that." His gaze followed to where my hand toyed with the neckline of my sweater. "I'm sure we could know each other quite well by the time the sun sets."

He stood confident in front of me, his hands resting in the pockets of his khaki trousers as he allowed my gaze to run over his lean, muscular form. He'd removed his white jacket before dinner. Blond curls grazed the collar of a button-down blue oxford shirt that hugged broad shoulders. A powerful chest narrowed to a slender waist, probably washboard abs, and the fit of his pants left no doubt about the muscular thighs beneath. And in between? My glass in one hand, I rose and approached, the index finger of my other hand extending to make friends with the skin between his collar and hairline. His pulse worked a fierce tattoo under my finger pad. He backed away.

"This is why we keep the newbies isolated." He stepped around me to pick up his glass, downed half the contents and set it back on the table. "You're all so eager to test your skills."

"My skills? So I do have superhuman powers?"

He laughed, a low rich chortle that hummed in echo through my bloodstream. "Superhuman urges, perhaps."

"And we're discouraged from indulging?" I pouted, a recalcitrant child.

He faced me. "For now." His words indicated a delay but his heavy-lidded gaze, dropping down the length of me, indicated anything but rejection. "Until you know yourself a little better."

I hazarded contact, stepping right up so that the tips of my breasts brushed his chest as I looked up into his arresting amber eyes. "Perhaps I could find myself through knowing you better first."

"You want to know me?" I could feel him breathe. "I was just a lad. Not even thirteen when he took me."

"He?" My gaze caught on his. "A man turned you?"

"Mm." He nodded. His hands ran up my arms. "It happened in the Sun King's court."

"Louis XIV?" My momentary distraction from the heat of his touch made me wonder if I'd got it right.

"My father, a devoted courtier to England's Charles II, died some six months before the marriage was arranged between Charles' sister Henrietta and the King's brother Philippe, Duc d'Orleans. It was decided that Henrietta needed some more experienced women among her entourage and my mother, a widow, was enlisted. I was an only child. She brought me along."

"To the court of Louis XIV?" My heart raced. How exciting! I always loved to find good primary sources, and I had one standing right in front of me. "You were there?"

He stepped back, his hand reaching up to rumple the back of his hair. "Mother lost herself in intrigues and affairs, all the while forgetting that she'd brought me along, or so it seemed. She found me a position in Philippe's service: glorified footman. It wasn't long before I graduated to favourite plaything."

"Oh, Luke." I ached for him. A boy left to fend for himself among the fondling of jaded courtiers?

"Philippe's favourite, the Chevalier de Lorraine, was kind to me at first. He plied me with wine, whispered that it wouldn't hurt, that it would make me stronger. I wanted to be stronger to be able to fend off some of the more forward members of Philippe's entourage. Philippe eventually joined us, but he apparently didn't know."

"That the chevalier was a —"

"A vampire, yes. Or that he had made me one. Philippe had been drinking heavily. Lorraine convinced him I was dead, that he had somehow killed me accidentally, and he talked Philippe into letting him do away with my remains before a scandal could erupt."

"But you were just a boy." And now he was clearly a man. I grew confused. How had he aged?

"I was. They claimed I'd fallen down some stairs. They told my mother I was dead. The Chevalier de Lorraine told me *I* was dead, that I was no more than a phantom and I would have to find my own way in the world."

"He turned you out with nothing?"

"With a few baubles, actually. Things I could sell on the street, and I did. I made enough to earn passage back to England and I went to my father's estate. The servants, having heard of my death, were convinced I was a ghost. Rumours of my haunting the place persist until this day." He laughed now, his mood growing lighter. "I took more things to sell so I could live, and I disappeared. I didn't know what to do. I ended up on a merchant ship to Barbary, where I fell victim to slave traders."

I gasped. "Slave traders?"

"My blond hair and pale skin made me a desirable item for any sheik's private collection. Fortunately, a Persian doctor rescued me and brought me to live with his family."

"Amazing."

"Lucky. He knew a few things about my condition." He stopped talking and stared out of the window, at the sky growing darker over the rolling waves.

His back to me, I risked getting close to him again, this time to comfort, not to seduce. I pressed myself to his back and gave a light squeeze, my hands cupping his shoulders.

He spun around to face me. "He cured me. The Persian. Or so I thought. He made potions that he encouraged me to drink. I

still don't know what was in all of them, but I've tried to
duplicate most of them from memory." He laced fingers with
mine. "I aged. I grew up. Cured. Or so I thought. And then –"
   "Then?"
   "He died. He died, and his secrets died with him. I realized
that without his medicines, my symptoms were coming back
and I moved on."
   "Where? Back to England?"
   "I banged around the Barbary Coast for years as a pirate."
   "Of the eye-patch-wearing, peg-leg, shiver-me-timbers variety?" I crossed my arms over my chest. I imagined him in tawny
leather breeches, a billowy shirt opened to his navel. Maybe not
such a stretch.
   "A pirate. Of the bloodthirsty, treasure-pillaging variety."
He nodded, apparently not about to offer more proof than his
word. "A damn good pirate, too. They called me Goldbeard. I
was feared around the globe. All right, at least around that
particular coastline. I set my sights on raiding all French ships
that came into range. There was a price on my head for many
years. I eventually got tired of the lifestyle and decided to try
my hand as an explorer."
   "Of course. And what did you explore? Mayan ruins? Perhaps you discovered the Fountain of Youth?"
   He shrugged. "Who needed it? I explored the colonies.
America. I settled with some displaced Huguenots along the
coast of Maine."
   I cocked a brow. "I suppose you also fought in the Revolu-
tionary War?"
   He shook his head. "I'm not a fan of war. I was off on new
adventures by then. Adventures in botany, actually. Still looking
for the right combination of herbs and roots to make the cure. It
wasn't until the sixties that I finally attended med. school."
   "The 1960s?" He nodded. I needed to make sure. "Wow. So,
when in all that time did you come across Connor Black?"
   His sharp intake of breath indicated his displeasure with the
change of subject. No, I hadn't forgotten Connor, though I
could no longer hear him in my mind.
   "We've crossed paths through the centuries." He met my

curious gaze, the amber of his eyes as intense as a gold-tinged flame. "We're brothers of a fashion."

"Brothers?" My hand flew to my neck. I knew he didn't mean actual brothers. "The Chevalier de Lorraine? But Connor doesn't support your cause?" An innocent question on the surface, but I had a feeling it went deeper between Luke and Connor. Way deeper.

"We'll never be in agreement on the ethical responsibilities of our condition. I've given up on Connor Black."

"And he would rather not see you, either, I'm guessing. So why were you there that night? Why track him down?"

"He's spreading the infection. It goes against everything we believe in here."

A pain stabbed deep in my chest. "Where's Connor now?"

He reached out to stroke the hair back from my face, a tender gesture that felt all too protective. "You need rest. Your system still hasn't adjusted."

"I don't want to sleep, Luke. I want to know the truth."

"You will. In time. But trust me on the sleep thing. I know what you need."

And suddenly, as if his voice registered a hypnotic suggestion, I could hardly keep my eyes open.

"Sleep," I echoed. "Yes. I need sleep." And before I could blink, I felt myself sliding to the floor. The last thing I knew was the feel of Luke's arms around me as he carried me to my bed.

I woke breathless, buried under the sea, paralysed by the weight of water pummelling, pummelling, even as the waves brought me closer to shore. I could see the light beyond white crests but couldn't reach it, too far, so far away. I told myself not to breathe, that breathing would be death, but I couldn't fight the urge. I sucked in, like breathing through a velvet curtain then swallowing said curtain whole. Too thick, it caught in my throat. Connor grabbed the end and pulled.

"Breathe, Miranda. You have to breathe!"

I sat up choking and grasping at my throat. It was all a dream. But Connor's voice still lingered.

"I. Can. Breathe," I whispered into the night air, taking great gulps between words.

*Now find me.* Connor's voice stayed with me. *Walk towards the shore.*

Barefoot, still in my cotton nightdress, I walked to the sitting room and slipped out through the patio doors. The night was warm and still, no trace of a breeze. The moon hung low over the water. I headed towards it, wood patio slats giving way to soft sand. Waves caressed the shore with a sound as light as a lover's touch. When I got closer to the water, I turned back to look at the house.

It was larger than I imagined, too big for one or two people. An enormous stone mansion that could have come straight out of a film version of *Pride and Prejudice*, Mr Darcy's Pemberley. He'd said the lab, research facility and dorms were in another building, so why all the space? There was more to Luke, and this little island retreat, than he'd let on. Suddenly I wondered how he would react to know that I was awake and walking around. Had alarms gone off? Would he come looking for me? Or was I truly as free to come and go as he'd said I was? I had my doubts.

I forgot the waves and the beauty of the night and returned to the house. My little suite of rooms didn't show through the trees, but there were lights on in what looked to be the main part of the house, an enormous central room lined with windows looking out to the sea. The room took a clearer shape as I approached. It was a library, rows of books lining shelves around the room, tables and chairs in the centre. I saw Luke on a ladder, his back to me.

As I neared a row of stone steps, something beckoned off to the side, and a voice in my head said: *Stay low.* Low? I crouched, an instant reaction, and ducked around the wall. A light in another window caught my gaze. I headed for it and found that it was open. I shimmied across the window sill carefully, the coolness of the stone against my thinly clad bottom reminding me I probably should have dressed before heading out for an adventure. My feet touched down on smooth tile in a room with steel tables, glass tubes, vials, burners and sinks. It looked to be some sort of lab, probably where Luke did some of his more private research. I walked out of a side door and into a dark corridor. *Find me.* Connor's voice became louder, as if perhaps I'd got close. I opened a door, some sort of bedroom with an antique canopied bed at the centre. Heavy velvet linens draped a matching wine-coloured duvet. No sign of Connor, but there were pictures everywhere.

A painting of a lovely woman in a 1970s-style gown, pink chiffon, graced the wall opposite the bed. There were photos of the same woman under the painting in various poses and outfits, different days, celebrating different black-and-white moments in her life: having a picnic, walking on the beach, holding a baby and standing under an arch of flowers at what had to be a wedding. She looked a decade older than Luke, who stood beaming at her side, so handsome in black tie.

She looked familiar somehow, but it took me several stilted heartbeats to figure out why. She could have been me. We looked a lot alike. Had this been her room? What about the baby? *Find me.* My attention flew to the door opposite the bed. Connor.

I opened the door. No sign of Connor, but I knew the baby had been a girl, and this had been her room, next to her mother's. It must have been a lovely child's room, all pink and lace, but it hadn't translated well to a young woman's private domain. A do-not-disturb sign hung from the knob, heavy-metal posters on the back of the door of Van Halen, The Who, AC/DC. Maybe some of them were vampires. Who knew? The fact that Connor didn't believe in Luke's mission meant that there were probably plenty of vampires out there, feeding among the masses, spreading their disease.

"Our blessing," he said, muffled but distinctly out loud.

I looked around. "Where are you?"

"Open the closet. I'm locked in. It opens from the outside."

I opened it quickly. Connor squinted into the night. "Thank God, you finally found me. It's like a coffin in here. I can hardly move. Lend a hand."

I helped him climb out of the empty, rectangular darkness.

Much like a coffin, I agreed. Only he'd been left standing up. "Poor thing. Can you walk?"

He stretched, squatted down on his haunches and stood back up again. He wore the Stones T-shirt and the same jeans I'd been ready to slide off him on that fateful night in my apartment. The night we'd both been taken. Taken, I realized at last. No one had asked my permission.

"I can walk." He took my hand. "Come on. We have to move fast. I know where we can find a boat."

"A boat? You think we should just leave?"

He turned to me, such a look in his eyes. "I haven't exactly been kept in luxury accommodation. I have a house in the Keys. We could make it by daylight if the weather cooperates."

"Daylight," I echoed, following after him to the next room. I tugged him back. "Why don't we go out a window? We're on the ground floor."

He gestured to the windows. Barred. Apparently, Connor wasn't the only one to be held against his will. "Oh. God. Why?"

"Later. Come on." He led me back to the lab where I'd come in. He helped me through the window first, then followed me out. "Down the beach. There's a boathouse."

He moved faster than I could have imagined, as if he had wings on his feet. What should have been more surprising was that I'd kept pace with him without losing my breath. But I pulled back as we neared the boathouse, a small storage area with a dock at the end of the sand.

"No. He's there."

"Luke?" Connor looked at me with concern. "How do you know?"

"I can feel him."

"Like you can feel me?" He seemed to be hurt, as if he hadn't even considered the possibility. I hadn't realized it myself until now.

"The same way."

He dropped my hand as if scorched. Luke appeared in the doorway.

"I thought you were going to stay?" He ignored Connor in favour of questioning me.

"I thought I was free to make up my own mind." I could imagine how he must have looked as Goldbeard, terror of the sea. The firm line of his jaw and the fire in his eyes made me afraid I'd be forced to walk the plank, and then glad of it. Better to face the sharks than to have a go with an angry Goldbeard.

"You are free. I'm asking, not demanding. Please stay."

"What about Connor?"

Connor laughed. "He's not about to challenge me now that I'm not locked up. I'm taking a boat and I'm going. Are you staying or coming with me?"

I looked at Luke. Was it true? He wouldn't challenge Connor? Fight him? Force him to stay? The men looked at each other as if they could gleefully go at it to the death. Perhaps they had, and more than once. Perhaps that's why neither one of them made a move now. "I'm not sure."

"Christ," Connor swore and looked at the heavens. "Miranda, look at me. You know we belong together." Something in his gaze made me certain he was right. But something about Luke made me wonder if I should stay. I felt suddenly torn, oddly connected to both men.

Luke held his hands out to his sides. He wouldn't try to pressure me.

Connor closed the distance between us and stroked my cheek. "You should know who you are before you seek a way to eliminate that part of you."

"But Luke's research is important."

Luke smiled, just a little too boldly for Connor's taste.

"Luke's research," Connor scoffed. "Did he tell you what his research did to his daughter, Kelly?"

"Don't speak of her. You don't deserve to speak her name." Luke was on Connor in seconds, holding him up by the throat. "Kelly was the daughter of my heart, my wife's child from a previous marriage. He convinced her to run off with him. He turned her." Luke let Connor drop to the sand. There was no longer any question who could prevail in a fight.

My eyes went wide as the moon. "*You* turned her?"

"She wanted to know what it was like." Connor sat up, propped on his elbow. He didn't stand. "I did her a favour. We could have lived forever, together. But he found us. He poisoned her against me. And then he killed her."

Luke's eyes darkened to black. He ran his hand through his hair, turned away as if gaining control of his emotions, then turned back to me. "I did. It was a mistake. I was trying to save her."

"To turn her back." Connor stood up. "But he ended up killing her with a virus of his own."

"A mutation," Luke clarified. "It should have cured her but—" His voice broke off.

I felt for him, went to him, took his hand, and filled in what was left unsaid. "It didn't work. Luke, I'm sorry."

"Miranda." His eyes held that mysterious golden light as he met my gaze. "Please stay. We can find out so much more, save more of us."

I stepped back. "I'm not ready, Luke. I don't want to be cured. Not now."

I wasn't sure how or why I'd come to such a conclusion, but I knew that Connor was right about me. I needed to explore what it was I had before I cut that part of me away. "I'm going with Connor. Just for a while. But I'll be back. If you let me go. Don't try to stop us or force me to come back before I'm ready. Promise me."

Luke sighed, then took me in his arms and held me tight. "Please come back. Come back soon."

"I will," I said, and reached up to stroke his stubble-dotted cheek. "Goldbeard."

"My fair Miranda." He bowed his head and kissed my hand, very gallant and old-fashioned but so sweet.

A shiver ran up my spine but I tore my gaze from him and turned to Connor. "I'm ready. Let's go."

Connor smiled wide, triumphant and dazzling in the moon-light. "Let's go."

Luke left us while Connor readied the boat, a small motor-powered skiff that he assured me would get us away safely. I believed him. I trusted him.

I belonged with him.

But somehow, as I got into the boat beside him and took one last look at the sun coming up behind the magnificent house, I wondered if I wasn't about to make the biggest mistake of my life.

# Ode to Edvard Munch

## Caitlín R. Kiernan

I find her, always, sitting on the same park bench. She's there, no matter whether I'm coming through the park late on a Thursday evening or early on a Monday evening or in the first grey moments of a Friday morning. I play piano in a Martini bar at Columbus and 89th, or I play *at* the piano, mostly for tips and free drinks. And when I feel like the long walk or can't bear the thought of the subway or can't afford cab fare, whenever I should happen to pass that way alone in the darkness and the interruptions in the darkness made by the lamp posts, she's there. Always on that same bench, not far from the Ramble and the Bow Bridge, just across the lake. They call that part of the park Cherry Hill. The truth is that I haven't lived in Manhattan long enough to know these things and, anyway, I'm not the sort of man who memorizes the geography of Central Park, but she *told* me it's called Cherry Hill, because of all the cherry trees growing there. And when I looked at a map in a guidebook, it said the same thing. You might mistake her for a runaway, 16 or maybe 17; she dresses all in rags, or clothes so threadbare and dirty that they may as well be rags, and I've never seen her wearing shoes, no matter the season or the weather. I've seen her barefoot in snow. I asked her about that once, if she would wear shoes if I brought her a pair, and she said no, thank you, but no, because shoes make her claustrophobic. I find her sitting there alone on the park bench near the old fountain, and I always ask before I sit down next to her. And always she smiles and says of course, of course you can sit with me. You can always sit with me. Her shoulder-length hair has been dyed the colour of pomegranates and her skin is dark. I've never asked, but I think she may be Indian. India Indian, I mean. Not Native American. I once waited tables with a girl from Calcutta and her skin was the same colour, and she had the same dusky brown-black eyes. But if she is Indian, the girl on Cherry Hill, she has no trace of an accent when she talks to me about the fountain or her favourite paintings in the Met or the exhibits she likes best at the Museum of Natural History. The first time she smiled . . . "You're a vampire?" I asked, as though it were the sort of thing you might ask any girl sitting on a park bench in the middle of the night. "That's an ugly word," she said and scowled at me. "That's a silly, ugly word." And then she was silent a long moment, and I tried to think of anything but those long incisors, like the teeth of a rat filed down to points. It was a freezing night near the end of January, but I was sweating, nonetheless. And I had an erection. And I realized, then, that her breath didn't fog in the cold air. "I'm a daughter of Lilith," she said. Which is as close as she's ever come to telling me her name, or where she's from, or anything else of the sort. *I'm a daughter of Lilith*, and the *way* she said it, with not even a trace of affectation or humour or deceit, I knew that it was true. Even if I had no idea what she meant, I knew that she was telling me the truth. That was also the first night that I let her kiss me. I sat with her on the bench, and she licked eagerly at the back of my neck. Her tongue was rough, like a cat's tongue. She smelled of fallen leaves, that dry and oddly spicy odour that I have always associated with late October and jack-o'-lanterns. Yes, she smelled of fallen leaves, and her own sweat and, more faintly, something that I took to be wood smoke. Her breath was like frost against my skin, colder even than the long winter night. She licked at the nape of my neck until it was raw and bleeding, and she whispered soothing words in a language I could neither understand nor recognize. "It was designed in 1860," she said, some other night, meaning the fountain with its bluestone basin and eight frosted globes. "They built this place as a turnaround for the carriages. It was originally meant to be a drinking fountain for horses. A place for thirsty things."

"Like an oasis," I suggested, and she smiled and nodded her head and wiped my blood from her lips and chin. "Sometimes it seems all the wide world is a desert," she said. "There are too few places left where one may freely drink. Even the horses are no longer allowed to drink here, though it was built for them."

"Times change," I told her and gently touched the abraded place on my neck, trying not wince, not wanting to show any sign of pain in her presence. "Horses and carriages don't much matter any more."

"But horses still get thirsty. They still need a place to drink."

"Do you like horses?" I asked, and she blinked back at me and didn't answer my question. It reminds me of an owl, sometimes, that slow, considering way she blinks her eyes. "It will feel better in the morning," she said and pointed at my throat. "Wash it when you get home." And then I sat with her a while longer, but neither of us said anything more.

She takes my blood, but never more than a mouthful at a time, and she's left me these strange dreams in return. I have begun to think of them as a sort of gift, though I know that others might think them more a curse. Because they are not entirely pleasant dreams. Some people would even call them nightmares, but things never seem so cut and dried to me. Yes, there is terror and horror in them, but there is beauty and wonder, too, in equal measure – a perfect balance that seems never to tip one way or the other. I believe the dreams have flowed into me on her rough cat's tongue, that they've infected my blood and my mind like a bacillus carried on her saliva. I don't know if the gift was intentional, and I admit that I'm afraid to ask. I'm too afraid that I might pass through the park late one night or early one morning and she wouldn't be waiting for me there on her bench on Cherry Hill, that asking would break some brittle spell that I can only just begin to comprehend. She has made me superstitious and given to what psychiatrists call "magical thinking", misapprehending cause and effect, when I was never that way before we met.

I play piano in a Martini bar and, until now, there's never been anything in my life that I might mistake for magic. But there are many things in her wide burnt sienna eyes that I might mistake for many *other* things, and now that uncertainty seems to cloud my every waking thought. Yet I believe that it's a small price to pay for her company, smaller even than the blood she takes. I thought that I should write down one of the dreams, that I should try to make mere words of it. From this window beside my bed, I can see Roosevelt Island beyond the rooftops, and the East River and Brooklyn and the hazy blue-white sky that can mean either summer or winter in this city. It makes me think of her, that sky, though I'm at a loss to explain why. At first, I thought that I would write it down and then read it to her the next time I saw her. But then I started to worry that she might not take it the way I'd intended, simply as reciprocation, my gift to repay hers. She might be offended, instead, and I don't think I could bear the world without her. Not after all these nights and mornings and all these dreams. I'm stalling. Yes, I am.

There's the silhouette of a city, far off, past the sand and smoke that seem to stretch away in all directions except that one which would lead to the city. I know I'll never go that far, that going as far as that, I'd never again find my way home. The city is for other beings. I know that she's seen the city, that she's walked its streets and spoken all its dialects and visited its brothels and opium dens. She knows the stink of its sewers and the delicious aromas of its markets. She knows all the high places and all the low places. And I follow her across the sand, up one dune and down another, these great waves of wind-sculpted sand that tower above me, which I climb and then descend. In this place, the jackals and the vultures and the spiny black scorpions are her court, and there is no place here for thirsty horses. Sometimes I can see her, through stinging veils of sand. And other times it seems I am entirely alone with the wailing sirocco gale, and the voice of that wind is 1,000 women crying for their men cut down on some Arabian battlefield 1,000 years before my birth. And it is also the slow creep of the dunes across the face of the wasteland, and it is my heart pounding loudly in my ears. I'm lost in the wild, and I think I'll never see her again, but then

I catch a glimpse of her through the storm, crouched in the lee of ruins etched and defaced by countless millennia of sand and wind and time. She might almost be any animal, anything out looking for its supper or some way to quench its thirst. She waits there for me in the entrance to that crumbling temple, and I can smell her impatience, like dashes of turmeric. I can smell her thirst and her appetite, and the wind drives me forwards. She leads me down into the earth, her lips pressed to my ear, whispering so I can hear her over the storm. She tells me the name of the architect who built the fountain on Cherry Hill, that his name was Jacob Wrey Mould, and he came to New York in 1853 or 1854 or 1855 to design and build All Soul's Church. He was a pious man, she tells me, and he illustrated Thomas Gray's "Elegy Written in a Country Church-Yard" and *The Book of Common Prayer*. She says he died in 1886, and that he too was in love with a daughter of Lilith, that he died with no other thought but her. I want to ask where she learned all these things, if, perhaps, she spends her days in libraries, and I also want to ask if she means that she believes that I'm in love with her. But then the narrow corridor we've been following turns left and opens abruptly on a vast torch-lit chamber. "Listen," she whispers. "This is one of my secrets. I've guarded this place for all my life." The walls are built from great blocks of reddish limestone carved and set firmly in place without the aid of mortar, locking somehow perfectly together by a forgotten Masonic art. The air reeks of frankincense, and there is thick cinnamon-coloured dust covering everything; I follow her down a short flight of steps to the floor. It occurs to me that we've gone so deep underground that the roar of the wind should not still be so loud, but it is, and I wonder if maybe the wind has found its way *inside* me, if it's entered through one of the wounds she leaves on my throat. "This was the hall of my mother," she says. And now I see the corpses, heaped high between the smoky braziers. They are nude, or they are half-dressed, or they've been torn apart so completely or are now so badly decomposed that it's difficult to tell whether they're clothed or not. Some are men and others are women and not a few are children. I can smell them even through the incense, and I might cover my nose and mouth. I might begin to gag. I might take a step back towards the stairs leading up to the long corridor and the bloodless desert night beyond. And she blinks at me like a hungry, watchful owl.

"I cannot expect you to understand," she says.

And there are other rooms, other chambers, endless atrocities that I can now only half recall. There are other secrets that she keeps for her mother in the deep places beneath shifting sands. There are the ghosts of innumerable butcheries. There are demons held in prisons of crystal and iron, chained until some eventual apocalypse; their voices are almost indistinguishable from the voice of the wind. And then we have descended into some still greater abyss, a cavern of sparkling stalactite and stalagmite formations, travertine and calcite glinting in the soft glow of phosphorescent vegetation that has never seen and will never have need of sunlight. We're standing together at the muddy edge of a subterranean pool, water so still and perfectly smooth, an ebony mirror, and she's already undressed and is waiting impatiently for me to do the same.

"I can't swim," I tell her and earn another owl blink.

If I *could* swim, I cannot imagine setting foot in that water, that lake at the bottom of the world.

"No one has asked you to swim," she replies and smiles, showing me those long incisors. "At this well, men only have to drown. You can do that well enough, I suspect."

And then I'm falling, as the depths of that terrible lake rise up around me like the hood of some black desert cobra and rush over me, bearing me down and down and down into the chasm, driving the air from my lungs. Stones placed one by one upon my chest until my lungs collapse, constricting coils drawing tighter and tighter about me, and I try to scream. I open my mouth, and her sandpaper tongue slips past my lips and teeth. She tastes of silt and dying and loss. She tastes of cherry blossoms and summer nights in Central Park. She wraps herself about me, and the grey-white wings sprouting from her shoulders open wider than the wings of any earthly bird. Those wings have become the sky, and her feathers brush aside the fire of a hundred trillion stars. Her teeth tear at my lower lip, and I taste my own blood. This wind howling in my ears is the serpent flood risen from out of that black pool, and is also icy solar winds, and the futile cries of bottled demons.

"Don't be afraid," she whispers in my ear, and her hand closes around my penis. "One must only take very small drinks. One must not be greedy in these dry times."

I gasp and open my eyes, unable to remember having shut them, and now we're lying together on the floor of the abattoir at the end of the long corridor below the temple ruins. This is the only one of her secrets she's shown me, and anything else must have been my imagination, my shock at the sight of so much death. There is rain, rain as red and sticky as blood, but still something to cool my fever, and I wrap my legs around her brown thighs and slide inside her. She's not made like other women, my raggedy girl from Cherry Hill, and she begins to devour me so slowly that I will still be dying in 1,000 years.

She tells me she loves me.

There are no revelations here. My eyes look for the night sky somewhere beyond the gore and limestone and sand, but there are only her wings, like heaven and hell and whatever might lie in between, and I listen to the raw and bitter laughter of the wind . . .

Some nights, I tell myself that I will walk around the park and never mind the distance and inconvenience. Some nights, I pretend I hope that she *won't* be there, waiting by the fountain. But I'm not even as good a liar as I am a pianist, and it hardly matters, because she's always there. Last night, for instance.

I brought her an old sweater I never wear, a birthday present from an ex-girlfriend, and she thanked me for it. I told her that I can bring her other things, whatever she might need, that she only has to ask, and she smiled and told me I'm very kind. My needs are few, she said and pulled the old sweater on over whatever tatters she was already wearing.

"I worry about you," I said. "I worry about you all the time these days."

"That's sweet of you," she replied. "But I'm strong, stronger than I might seem."

And I wondered if she knows about my dreams, and if our conversations were merely a private joke. I wonder if she only accepted the sweater because she feels sorry for me.

We talked, and she told me a very funny story about her first night in the park, almost a decade before I was born. And then, when there were no more words, when there was no longer the *need* for words, I leaned forwards and offered her my throat. Thank you, she said, and I shut my eyes and waited for the scratch of her tongue against my skin, for the prick of those sharp teeth. She was gentle, because she is always gentle, lapping at the hole she's made and pausing from time to time to murmur reassurances I can understand without grasping the coarser, literal meaning of what she's said. I get the gist of it and I know that's all that matters. When she was done, when she'd wiped her mouth clean and thanked me again for the sweater, when we'd said our usual goodbyes for the evening, I sat alone on the bench and watched as she slipped away into the maze of cherry trees and azaleas and forsythia bushes.

I don't know what will become of these pages. I may never print them. Or I may print them out and hide them from myself. I could slip them between the pages of a book in the stacks at NYU and leave them there for anyone to find. I could do that. I could place them in an empty wine bottle and drop them from the Queensboro Bridge so that the river would carry them down to the sea. The sea must be filled with bottles . . .

# Fangs For Hire

## Jenna Black

*I* met my client at a seedy, unpleasant bar. Not because I liked such places, but because it's what clients usually expect when they hire a hit man – or, in my case, a hit woman.

My nostrils flared as I opened the door and stepped inside. The place stank of stale beer, stale sweat, stale cigarettes and stale lives. Even though it was late on a Saturday night, prime bar hour, the place was practically empty. As advertised by the hogs parked outside, there were a handful of biker dudes and their slutty chicks hanging out at the pool table. At the bar itself, there were a couple of men who might as well have had "loser" tattooed on their foreheads. They both looked unhappily drunk.

Remind me why I chose this place for a rendezvous? Oh, yeah. The atmosphere.

I could smell my client from clear across the room. Not because he stank, but because he smelled like he'd had a shower within the last week, which was more than I could say of the other patrons of this fine establishment. Being a vampire has its advantages, but the enhanced sense of smell is something I would happily do without.

My client occupied one of the bar's rather unsanitary booths. He was much younger and much softer looking than I'd expected. I guessed his age at about 22 or 23 and, though he'd dressed down to meet me here, his jeans looked like they'd been artificially aged and the plain white T-shirt still had creases from being in its package. I'd bet he usually wore suits, or at least designer grunge wear.

His scent changed when he saw me coming: a delicious bouquet of fear and musk blending with his expensive after-shave. No doubt if he'd known I was a vampire, rather than your run-of-the-mill hitter, he'd have run screaming from the room. I had, of course, dressed the part. No reason to pick an atmospheric dive and then go in looking like Jane Normal. If I hadn't been broadcasting that special vampire don't-notice-me vibe to everyone but my client, all the guys in the bar would have been after me in the vain hope of getting lucky.

Leather pants, stiletto heels and some nice cleavage. Gets 'em every time. My client – or really, I should say my potential client, because he hadn't officially hired me yet – swallowed hard when I slid into the booth across from him. I wasn't sure if that was from lust or fear.

I smiled pleasantly and reached my hand out across the table. "Gemma Johanson at your service," I said, and like a good little boy he shook my hand. I could have gone for the stereotypical cold, psychotic stare, but I thought this kid was already shaken up enough. Wouldn't do to scare away a customer!

He cleared his throat. "Hi. I'm Jeffrey. Reeves."

I arched an eyebrow. "I rather figured you were."

Even in the darkness of the bar, I could see the blush that crept up his neck and flushed his cheeks. "Sorry. I've never, uh, done this before."

No kidding? "Why don't you tell me about the job?" I prompted, because if I waited for him to get around to it, I'd have been there all night.

Jeffrey's eyes darted nervously around the bar, but no one was paying any attention to us. He leaned over the table and whispered. "I want to hire you to kill someone."

Apparently, my would-be client had a special talent for stating the obvious. I made a "keep talking" gesture.

He licked his lips, then took a deep breath. That seemed to settle him down some. "It's my stepfather," he said, his lips curling – unconsciously, I think – with distaste. "His name is Ross Blackburn, and he's a murdering son of a bitch who deserves to die."

Jeffrey's body language changed completely, his fear and uncertainty buried beneath the rage that now filled him. His hands clenched into fists, his shoulders stiffened and I could hear the angry thump of his heart. I have to admit, it was rather disconcerting. He'd looked so soft and harmless when I'd first caught sight of him. Now he looked like someone who'd seriously considered doing the job himself.

"OK," I said, not really caring if Ross Blackburn deserved to die or not. I had yet to be hired to kill someone who didn't have it coming, one way or another. I'd made it very clear to Miles, my handler – or my pimp, as he laughingly called himself – that I wasn't hitting any innocent bystanders who just happened to be at the wrong place at the wrong time. I'm sure he farmed out jobs like that to someone else, but as long as I didn't know about it, I could justify letting him live.

Jeffrey seemed surprised by my easy agreement.

"You, uh, don't need to know any more?" The anger had drained away as quickly as it had come. He now had that lost and vaguely pathetic look he'd worn when I'd first caught sight of him.

"I'll need an address. And, of course, a deposit."

He swallowed hard again. "Yeah. Sure." He leaned forwards as he dug his wallet out of his back pocket. "When will you . . . do it?"

I was pretty sure Miles had explained my modus operandi when Jeffrey had contacted him. (How this kid had managed to find Miles in the first place might be an interesting story, if I were nosier.) But he seemed too rattled and nervous to remember, so I generously answered him anyway. He slid a slim envelope across the table to me.

"Within the next two weeks he'll disappear, never to be seen again." I verified the amount on the cashier's cheque inside the envelope, then looked up and caught Jeffrey's eye in one of my more menacing stares. "If you're killing him for an inheritance, you'll have a long wait before he'll be declared dead. His body will never be found."

He shivered. "I don't care about the money. I just want him dead." There was a sheen of tears in his eyes, though none fell.

Generally, I don't like to ask my clients any questions. I trusted Miles – sort of – not to give me innocent victims, and, hey, since I had to eat anyway, I might as well get paid for it. But maybe I was getting soft in my old age. I couldn't help being just a little curious, seeing as this kid was nothing like my usual clients.

"What'd he do?" I asked. I think Jeffrey was relieved to be able to tell me.

"He killed my mother." The anguish in his voice told me that his grief was still fresh and raw. "He married her for her money because he knew she was already sick. Then when the cancer didn't kill her quickly enough, he poisoned her."

OK. This was definitely not sounding like my usual case. I know I said I didn't care about the details, but I couldn't help prodding just a little bit. "And have you told this to the police?"

He waved his hand dismissively. "Everyone says she died of natural causes, but I know better. She was supposed to have another couple of years, and then six months after she married this asshole, she's dead. And he's got half her estate."

I supposed it did sound kind of suspicious, at least to a grieving son. I tucked the envelope with the cheque into my pocket book, wondering if I was going to end up killing an innocent person after all.

But then I brightened. I had two weeks to make the kill, and I had an (admittedly) almost feline enjoyment of playing with my food. With a little clever investigating, I could find out for myself whether Ross killed his old lady or not. If it turned out he didn't, then Junior here could be my flavour of the month. I don't make a habit of killing my clients – Miles rather frowns on that – but I thought I could make an exception if it turned out that Jeffrey had hired me under false pretences. It wasn't like Jeffrey's death would ever be attributed to me.

"Give me two weeks," I said, reaching across the table to shake his hand again. "After that, you won't have to worry about him any more."

After Jeffrey left, I slipped back inside and took a seat at the bar beside one of the drunken losers I'd noticed earlier. He was such a sorry specimen, I might not even have needed my supernatural powers of persuasion to wrap him around my little finger, but I didn't want to hang around this dive any longer than necessary. The moment I managed to catch his attention – not easy when his tequila was so much more interesting – I mesmerized him with my gaze. No one paid any attention to us as I led him back to the grimy, unisex bathroom. Based on the taste of him, there was more alcohol than blood running through his veins and I swear I felt a bit tipsy after I drank. No, I didn't kill him. While I need to feed every night, I only have to make a kill every few weeks, to recharge my psychic battery. If I don't recharge it, my body will slowly wither and die, and that's where my line of work comes in handy.

After I left, and had a short, dark and disgusting nap to sleep it off, I decided to take a first pass by my target's house. It was well after midnight by now, so I didn't expect to do more than a drive-by, just to familiarize myself with the neighbourhood, but when I got there, it was to see lights blazing all through the house.

I parked my car (an intentionally nondescript brown Camry) by the side of the road and took in the sights.

It was a nice neighbourhood, a typical example of wealthy suburban America. Houses on what I'd estimate were one-acre lots, many of them hidden from the road by generously wooded front yards. Wealthy, but not ultra-wealthy, if you know what I mean. These were houses, not mansions. I frowned a bit and wondered whether someone living here really had enough money to tempt a man to marry and then murder her. I wouldn't have thought so, but then money makes people the world over act like idiots.

It started raining, a hearty summer downpour that could last for five minutes or five hours. I made an impulsive decision to meet my soon-to-be victim this very night.

No way was I going out in the rain in my expensive leather pants. Luckily, I was in the habit of keeping a duffle bag with a change of clothes in the back seat. Comes in handy when my meals aren't as . . . tidy as they should be.

The street was deserted, everyone with any sense asleep snug in their beds, so I didn't worry about being observed as I changed into jeans and a T-shirt. The T-shirt had been a gag gift from Miles. It was white, with the words "BITE ME" emblazoned in bold black letters across the chest.

I pushed open the car door and stepped out into the rain. I was soaked through before I'd closed the door behind me. Luckily, it was a comfortably warm night.

I splashed my way down the driveway towards the Blackburn house, stealing glances at the lighted windows as I approached, but I didn't catch sight of my quarry. I was going to be pissed if I'd got drenched only to find him not home after all. I rang the doorbell, then took advantage of the covered front porch to wring some of the water out of my hair. The porch light flicked on, and I noticed that my white T-shirt had, predictably, gone see-through in the rain. My sheer lace bra ensured that my assets were plainly visible. I'm not what you'd call modest, but I figured it would enhance my disguise as a helpless damsel in distress if I pretended to be, so I crossed my arms over my chest as footsteps approached. I even hunched my shoulders a bit as if I were cold.

The door swung open, and I caught my first sight of Ross Blackburn.

My immediate impression was that he was far too young to have been married to a woman old enough to be Jeffrey's mother. I wouldn't have put him at a day over 30. My second impression was . . . hubba hubba! If I were in the market for a toy boy, I'd have been wiping the drool from my chin. The look he gave me – a long, slow, up and down, followed by a frown and a disdainful sniff – suggested I was not making a similar impression. I unfolded my arms, ostensibly to free my hand to brush my hair out of my eyes. I have to admit, though, I was a little miffed when he didn't even glance at my chest.

"Yes?" he prompted, because I'd apparently stood there gaping too long.

"My car broke down," I told him while batting my eyelashes. "May I use your phone to call a tow truck?" The batting eyelashes didn't seem to make any more impression than my boobs. I must have been losing my touch.

"No cell phone?" Blackburn asked with a raised eyebrow.

What an asshole! Here was this helpless, drenched, sexy woman standing on his doorstep at an ungodly hour and he'd so far shown no inclination to invite me in out of the cold. OK, so it wasn't actually cold, but it's the principle of the thing.

"I left it at home," I said, and I let him hear the edge of annoyance in my voice. "Look, yours is the only house with lights on. Sorry to bother you, but if you'll just let me make a quick call, I'll be out of your hair in no time."

The corners of his mouth tightened in displeasure, but he stepped aside and opened the door wide enough to let me in. A spoken invitation would have been much nicer, but it seemed I wasn't getting one. I gritted my teeth against the painful resistance as I crossed the threshold. His non-verbal invite was enough to get me through, but not enough to make it a pleasant experience. Luckily, either I was a good enough actress to hide my discomfort, or he was sulking over my unwanted intrusion, since he didn't seem to notice the effort it took me to come inside.

"Wait here," he ordered me, and I wanted to smack him. Where did he get off giving me orders? It wasn't like I was the hired help! I thought about dear little Jeffrey and let a small smile curl my lips. In a manner of speaking, I was hired help after all.

Blackburn wasn't gone long. Before I'd even had a chance to look around, he emerged from what I presumed to be a powder room, carrying a fluffy white hand towel. For the first time, I realized that the foyer was made of beautiful, shiny hardwood, and that I was so wet I was dripping on the small rug that fronted the door.

I took the towel from him almost gratefully. I supposed I couldn't blame him for not wanting me to drip all over his hardwood.

"Thanks," I said as I began to blot water from my hair.

"No cell phone and no umbrella," he mused. "It appears you were ill-prepared for this evening's outing."

I glanced up at him from under my fringe. I honestly couldn't tell if he was being a jerk or if that was supposed to be friendly banter. I'm usually better than that at reading people.

"I also didn't bring a spare car, a hairdryer or condoms," I quipped. "I'm ill-prepared for just about anything except a quiet evening at home."

For the first time, a hint of humour glinted in his eyes. Eyes, I might add, that were the kind of smoky grey hue that would look blue if he were wearing a blue shirt. Yum.

"I can't help you with the car or the hairdryer, but if you need condoms, feel free to ask." The humour had drifted down to his lips, which were now curved into a faint, but truly sexy, smile. As far as I could tell, he still hadn't taken in the view my wet T-shirt offered.

I let the towel settle around my shoulders and peered up at him, trying to get a read on him. I noticed the gold band that circled his ring finger. I'd neglected to ask Jeffrey how long ago his mother had died, though I knew from his fresh grief it had been recent. I thought it notable, however, that Blackburn still wore the wedding band. If he'd married and murdered her for her money, it seemed like he'd dispense with the ring while in the privacy of his own home.

He saw the direction of my gaze, and the smile faded. "Please forgive my . . . erratic manners. My wife passed away last month and I'm not quite myself yet."

"Oh!" I gasped in feigned surprise. "I'm so sorry!" I reached out to touch his arm in a gesture of feminine sympathy.

He looked appropriately sad, but it was hard to see that crack about the condoms as anything but flirting. Of course, some men flirt by instinct. It doesn't necessarily mean anything.

"Thank you," he said, gently extracting his arm from my grip. "The phone is this way."

I prised my wet sneakers off and left them on the doormat, then followed Blackburn through the dining room and into the kitchen. He indicated the phone on the wall, then settled his butt against the butcher-block counter across from me and watched with unnerving intensity as I dialled.

"You must not be new to car trouble," he said.

I frowned at him as the phone began to ring. "Why do you say that?" As soon as the words left my mouth, my brain caught up and I knew what he was about to say.

"You've memorized the number for the tow truck."

I grinned ruefully. I was letting myself get too hot and bothered by Mr Ross Blackburn. Hormones and clear thinking don't go together. "My car's a piece of shit," I confided. "Pardon my French."

Finally, Miles answered the phone with his usual brusque "Yeah?"

"Hi," I said. "This is Gemma Johanson. I need a tow truck at . . ." I gave Blackburn a raised eyebrow, and he told me the address, which I dutifully repeated.

"That so?" Miles asked. He was used to calls like these, though usually I warned him in advance that I'd be calling and let him know who he was supposed to be.

"How long will it take?"

"How long do you *want* it to take?" he countered.

"An hour!" I wailed in mock dismay, and Miles snorted with laughter at my acting. "It's after midnight, and I'm stuck in some stranger's house. Can't you get someone here faster?"

"An hour, eh? I take it this one is going to die with a smile on his face?"

I sighed dramatically, wishing Miles would get his mind out of the gutter. Never mind that mine was there right with him. "Oh all right!" I said with exaggerated patience. "But I'm not keeping my host up for a whole hour."

Another snort of laughter. "I'm sure you're quite capable of it."

"I'll be waiting outside on the porch. In the rain. So if he can come faster, I'd really appreciate it." I'd been an actress back in the days when "actress" was often a euphemism for something entirely different. However, my acting skills were enough to keep me from bursting into laughter at the repeated innuendo.

I hung up before Miles could deliver another one-liner. I was good, but I wasn't cocky enough to think I'd be able to hide my amusement forever.

Across the kitchen from me, Blackburn was watching me with a curious half-smile on his lips and a twinkle in his eye. It was almost as if he'd heard both halves of that conversation, but I was sure the volume on the phone hadn't been high enough for that. The half-smile broadened into a full-out smile.

"I suppose you expect me to feel properly guilty and not make you wait out on the porch as you suggested to the towing company."

Well, yeah. If he was going to make a woman wait alone outside on a dark and stormy night, then I was going to play with my food more than usual. And he wouldn't think my games were fun.

"Well, Mr . . . ?"

"Blackburn," he supplied obligingly.

What? No invitation to address him by his first name? Wife-killer or not, he was one hell of a jerk.

"Well, Mr Blackburn," I started again, and even to my own ears my voice sounded a bit brittle, "I won't be telling everyone about your kind heart and generosity if you make me wait outside. However, it's your home and your prerogative." I gave him a challenging stare, daring him to prove how ungentle-manly he could be.

To my shock, he obliged me. "I'm glad you're so under-standing," he said. "I was about to turn in." He yawned, though I'd bet he was about as tired as I was – which is to say, not at all. "Although it is not my usual practice to leave beautiful women out in the cold, as it were, I have to get up early tomorrow morning. However, there's a rocking chair on the porch, and I assure you, it's quite comfortable. Would you like a cup of coffee while you wait? I believe I can keep my eyes open long enough to brew some."

I had the distinct impression he was mocking me, though it didn't show in his expression. I considered the possibility of ramming my fist through his teeth. Then I considered the possibility of killing him right there and then. But a quick death was too good for him.

"Sorry to turn down such a generous offer," I said, sneering to make doubly sure he caught my sarcasm, "but I think I'll skip the coffee. I'd hate to keep you from your beauty sleep any longer." I turned on my heel and stalked out of the kitchen. Although his footsteps were quiet and stealthy, I knew he was following me to the door. The better to kick me out on my ass, I suppose. Bastard.

I hoped steam wasn't coming out of my ears as I bent to snatch my wet shoes from the doormat. "It's been a real pleasure meeting you, Mr Blackburn," I said.

"The pleasure's been all mine," he responded smoothly.

I didn't dare turn to look at him as I jerked the door open and stepped outside. I was so pissed my fangs were extending. Normally, it's not that easy to get a rise out of me, but there's nothing like a good-looking man behaving badly to set my blood boiling. Such a waste of good beefcake.

The door closed behind me, Blackburn not bothering with a goodbye, and moments later, the porch light clicked off. My fists clenched at my sides. Not only was the asshole going to leave me waiting outside in the rain in the middle of the night, he wasn't even going to leave the light on for me.

Resisting the urge to bash the door off its hinges and sink my fangs into Ross Blackburn's despicable throat, I plopped down on the rocking chair and settled in to wait the hour it was supposed to take for the tow truck to get here – just in case Blackburn had a guilt-induced bout of insomnia, I didn't want to blow my cover story. But I hadn't been sitting there more than about ten minutes when the lights in the house flicked off one by one.

It's very easy for a vampire to be overwhelmed by ennui as the years, decades and even centuries roll past. Those of us who've seen multiple centuries and still enjoy our lives do so by continuing to learn, grow and change, which was why over the last ten years or so I'd been teaching myself to be an Internet expert. It also came in handy in my line of work.

I spent the remainder of my "day" (i.e. the hours of darkness) finding out everything I could about Ross Blackburn. Some of my methods were highly illegal, but by stealth and creative storytelling (also known as lying), I'd got access to a lot of databases meant only for law-enforcement personnel. I used those resources ruthlessly and – since several of them actually cost money – rather recklessly as well.

Through my prying, I determined that Mrs Blackburn's estate was probably worth about a million dollars, including the house. On the one hand, yes, that's a lot of money. On the other hand, Blackburn was only getting half of it. It seemed like if he were targeting rich women to marry and murder, he could have found someone considerably richer than that. And with his looks, he'd be a definite candidate for the position of trophy husband. Of course, he didn't exactly have the personality to go with it.

But what really convinced me he hadn't been after her money was that Blackburn himself was worth at least ten times as much. Hell, he was practically slumming. I'd wager neither Jeffrey nor the late Mrs Blackburn had had any idea how money Ross Blackburn was worth. Of course, money was only one possible motive for murder and, while I couldn't say I'd got a very good read on his personality, there was nothing about Blackburn that made me doubt he was capable of killing his wife. And Mrs Blackburn's death did seem sudden, or unexplained. According to the autopsy that Jeffrey had insisted upon, the cause of death was complications related to chemotherapy. But that sounded a bit like "we have no clue" to me.

The police had dutifully investigated Jeffrey's charges that his mother was murdered, but the case had been dropped for lack of evidence. Luckily, I had some resources – and some abilities – that the police lacked. After his behaviour earlier, I'd have been more than happy to kill Ross Blackburn whether he was a murderer or not. But I'd have a hell of a lot more fun if he was.

After a restful day's sleep, I made my way back to Blackburn's house with a fresh set of false pretences at the ready. I was annoyed to find the lights off when I arrived. The nerve of the guy, not to be home when I wanted him to be! I parked my car and, while I was debating whether I should wait, come back later or take a look around the house in its owner's absence, a black BMW turned into the driveway. The headlights illuminated a "FOR SALE" sign in the yard. Either I'd been terribly unobservant last night, or Blackburn had just put the place up for sale today. Interesting.

I waited ten minutes after the lights in the house went on before I slid out of my car and headed for his door. I preferred for him not to know I'd been staking out his house, even though my pretext for the evening was that I was a private investigator.

He took his own sweet time answering the door. I fumed a bit, just because it felt good to fume. But when the door swung open, I almost forgot what I was fuming about.

I'd halfway convinced myself that he couldn't possibly be as gorgeous as I remembered, but he was. His thick black hair was still damp from a recent shower – perhaps explaining his delay in opening the door – and he smelled of Ivory soap and minty toothpaste. His white shirt was untucked, his feet were bare and I doubt he could have looked any sexier had he tried.

There was still that personality problem, though. He didn't say a word, just stared at me with raised eyebrows and a faintly mocking grin on his lips. I waited a beat to see if he was going to at least say hello, but he didn't.

"Remember me?" I asked – rather inanely, I'm afraid.

"Indeed. How could I forget?" He was still grinning.

"May I come in?" I asked with a smile that was supposed to be pleasant. I'm not sure it was.

"What would you do if I said no?" he responded, and for a moment I had the crazy thought that he was on to me. But no, that really *was* crazy. Normal people don't even believe in vampires, much less think there's one standing on their doorstep.

"Probably something really childish, like ring your bell for four hours straight. Or maybe toilet paper your yard." Among other things.

"Well by all means then, come in."

He stepped back, making a sweeping invitation with one arm. Corny as hell, but I refrained from telling him that. I noticed that, while he'd left enough room for me to come in, he wasn't exactly being generous with the personal space. Even when I stepped forwards and crossed the threshold, he was uncomfortably close and didn't back away.

It wasn't until he'd closed the door behind me that I noticed it. Hidden beneath that strong, minty toothpaste. The faint scent of blood.

I felt my heart speed with sudden panic. If I could smell blood on his breath, that meant I wasn't trapping myself inside this house with a helpless human after all. It also meant that Jeffrey was right, and Ross Blackburn was a murderer (says the pot calling the kettle).

I took a deep breath, trying to calm my heart. He could no doubt smell my fear and, unless he'd figured out what I was, he'd have no good explanation for it.

Could he have figured it out? Had he smelled it on my breath last night? Had he noticed my hesitation crossing the threshold?

All these thoughts flitted frantically through my head in the half a second it took for him to close the door, then suddenly whirl on me. Before I could dodge, he'd grabbed hold of both my arms and shoved me face-first against the wall. I let out a gasp of pain as he then wrenched one of my arms up behind my back.

All my superior vampire strength was doing nothing for me. Ross Blackburn was flat-out bigger and stronger than I was, and my being a vampire didn't change that. Dammit!

His manhandling did have one positive, if perhaps paradoxical, effect: my fear dissipated, being replaced by anger. I forced myself to stop struggling.

"I thought you were just an asshole," I said, somewhat breathlessly. "I didn't realize you were a psycho, too."

He pressed his body against my back, pinning me even more firmly to the wall as he chuckled in my ear. "Brave words for a woman alone in a house with a presumably hostile psycho," he said.

He trailed his nose along the length of my neck, and I assumed he was taking in the scent of my blood. It was going to hurt like hell if he bit me, but I knew it wouldn't kill me. What I didn't know was if he'd be able to tell from the taste of my blood that I wasn't human. I intentionally bit my lip, hard enough to draw a little blood. Perhaps not smart, when Blackburn would be able to smell it, but too late to turn back now. I swirled that single drop of blood around my mouth, trying to determine whether I tasted human or not. I thought so, but then perhaps my own blood was too familiar.

"I'm waiting for your witty repartee," Blackburn said, nudging my arm up a little higher behind my back.

I hissed at the sudden flare of pain, but he must not have been much of a sadist, because he immediately backed off on the pressure.

"I'm wittier when my face isn't mashed up against a wall," I said, wondering why he didn't just get on with it and bite me.

He laughed softly and, this time instead of his nose sweeping over my carotid, it was his tongue. It should have been a disgusting, slimy feeling, but I found it vaguely erotic. I tried to tell myself it was just vampire mind-tricks. But those weren't supposed to work on other vampires.

"Tell me why you're here," he said. "If I like your answer, I might just let you go."

*And wouldn't that be a shame*, a little voice whispered in my head. I was appalled at myself. This was *not* a sexy situation!

"Did you kill your wife?" I found myself blurting. So much for playing the part of the smooth, sophisticated private investigator.

"*That's* why you're here?" he asked incredulously. "To find out if I killed my wife?"

I tried to nod, but that was hard to do in my current position, so I mumbled a "Yes," instead.

"And what were you going to do if you found that I did?"

I figured, "Kill you," probably wasn't a good answer.

"Call the police," I said instead.

He snorted. "A likely story. Is that why your 'towing service' asked if I was going to die with a smile on my face?"

Oops. I'd forgotten that with his superior senses, he would have heard both sides of my conversation with Miles. No wonder he hadn't let me hang around the house afterwards. I frowned. Why hadn't he killed me – or at least *tried* to kill me – last night?

"If you're going to kill me, just get on with it," I said. I wasn't making any progress in my current position, which meant I had to inspire him to lower his guard. If he bit me, maybe I could lull him into a false sense of security.

"Tempting," he murmured, then grazed my skin with his teeth. Teeth, not fangs. "But I want to know more. Did Jeffrey hire you?"

Due to factors beyond my control (i.e. a need to eat), there were times when I was forced to purposely misplace my conscience. However, it always seemed to find its way back to me. I didn't want to get Jeffrey killed, not when he'd obviously been right about Ross Blackburn.

"Who?" I asked, hoping I sounded convincingly clueless.

"I know he was very upset about his mother," Blackburn said, ignoring my question. "I don't blame him. Elizabeth didn't deserve to die so young, but her cancer had other ideas. Whether he knows it or not, he's better off not having had to spend the next year watching her suffer."

"So you're admitting you killed her?"

I felt him shrug. "Not that it does you any good, but yes. At her request, I might add. She was already beginning to decline. Now tell me, did Jeffrey hire you?"

"I don't know anyone by that name." I'm a good liar, but I didn't think I had much chance of pulling this one off. Blackburn obviously had reason to believe his stepson had hired me. Still, I had my professional pride and I wasn't giving up my client. I decided I'd try to distract him. "How did you know what my handler said on the phone?" I asked. "There's no way he was talking loud enough for you to hear him across the room."

To my shock, he laughed and let go of me, though he still hovered uncomfortably close, his palms pressed against the wall on either side of my head. Slowly, I turned around to look into those smoky eyes. He was grinning at me, making no attempt to hide his fully extended fangs.

"You're still under the impression I don't know what you are?" he asked. "I thought you were quicker on the uptake than that. If you could smell the blood over my toothpaste, what makes you think I couldn't smell it over your whisky, or whatever it was you used to try to cover it up."

Well, so much for lulling him into a false sense of security. Of all the shitty luck! Why did I have to take a contract to kill someone who turned out to be a bigger, stronger vampire?

I sighed and would have crossed my arms if he weren't invading my personal space so much. "I didn't try to cover it up. The guy I drank from was drunk out of his mind. So you know what I am, and I know what you are. Where does that leave us?"

"With me thirsting for Jeffrey's blood."

I opened my mouth to continue my charade that Jeffrey didn't hire me, but Blackburn shut me up by planting his mouth on mine. I struggled pointlessly for a moment, then let myself go limp and passive. The touch of his lips and tongue did sinful things to my insides, but I had no inclination to give in to my lustful desires. Hormones be damned, I wasn't letting him get away with being a sexual bully.

Blackburn quickly grew bored with my passive resistance and pulled away. He smirked at me, and I was sure he knew he'd aroused me. Apparently, even centuries of experience didn't stop me from being attracted to bad boys. They *did* give me enough experience to keep myself from acting on those desires, though.

"I have no intention of killing Jeffrey," he told me. "He's hated me since the first time we met, but even though he hired you to kill me, I don't hold it against him. Grief will make men crazy." '

"OK, so you're not going to kill Jeffrey. What about me?"

His grin was positively wolfish. "I'd rather fuck you than kill you."

Frankly, I'd prefer that, too. But since, regrettably, the two were not mutually exclusive, my fangs extended and I prepared for battle. "Try it, and you'll lose body parts."

His eyebrows lifted. "I didn't mean to imply I'd take you without your consent." He dropped his arms back to his sides and gave me space.

I glanced at the door, so tantalizingly close.

"I'm not particularly vengeful," he said, taking yet another step back. "I won't kill Jeffrey, because he had good cause to hire you. I'll merely disappear from his life so that he will not succumb to temptation again. And I won't kill *you* because you cared enough to find out whether I really killed my wife before completing your contract. I clearly won't be releasing an indiscriminate killer out into the world if I let you go."

I frowned. "And what will I be releasing if I let *you* go?"

He had now crossed all the way to the opposite side of the foyer, and leaned against the wall. There was no question in my mind that I could beat him to the door at this point, which calmed my fight-or-flight instincts enough to make me stay put.

"Elizabeth and I met because we were both volunteers for a hospice," he said, and his smile now was wry. "Does that give you a clue as to how I fulfil my needs?"

I grimaced. "You prey on helpless, innocent victims."

"No, I prey on dying, suffering victims. More specifically, on suffering victims who would prefer not to suffer any longer."

My conscience rolled that one around for a while, but I couldn't quite figure out what I thought of it. I tentatively decided it wasn't much worse than what I did, if indeed it was worse at all.

"And what about Elizabeth?" I asked.

Something that looked like it might be genuine grief crossed his face. "Elizabeth had ovarian cancer. She had some particularly brutal surgery, and then she started chemo. The side effects of that form of chemo can be excruciating, and she seemed to have every one. Her future would have been filled with pain, more surgery and long hospital stays. She'd loved me for quite some time, and I was fond enough of her to want to give her some happiness before she died. So I married her shortly after she was diagnosed, cared for her and eased the way when she was ready to call it quits."

I stared at him sceptically. "And convinced her to leave you half her estate."

He waved that off. "That was her decision, and I didn't know about it. I'd have stopped her if I had. I don't need the money, and I certainly didn't need to give Jeffrey any more reason to hate me."

Call me an old softie, but I believed him. Mainly because of all the bad things he could have done to me by then but hadn't. I hoped that the fact that I lusted after him wasn't any factor in my decision, but I can't say for sure.

"So you're just an all-round nice guy, huh?" I said.

"Something like that. Now are you leaving or staying? Because if you're staying, I'm sure we can find somewhere more comfortable than the foyer."

The glint in his eyes told me just where he had in mind for us to go. Temptation swamped me, though I figured it wasn't exactly professional for me to sleep with my supposed target.

A smile curled my lips as a thought occurred to me.

Blackburn's eyes widened. "Now *that* is a truly evil smile," he told me. "Do I want to know what you're thinking?"

"You said you were planning to disappear from Jeffrey's life."

He blinked at what must have seemed like a non sequitur. "Yes,' he answered cautiously.

"Would you be willing to do your disappearing within the next two weeks?"

He cocked his head at me, brow furrowed in puzzlement. "May I ask why?"

"My agreement with Jeffrey was that you would disappear, never to be seen again. And that your body would never be found. I didn't actually say I would kill you."

Blackburn threw back his head and laughed. "So you'll claim to have 'taken care' of me, and you'll take Jeffrey's money."

"I get my money, Jeffrey gets his revenge and neither one of us has to die. What more could you ask for?"

He was no longer leaning against the wall. Now, he was stalking across the foyer towards me in his full predatory glory. The door no longer seemed even remotely tempting.

"Oh, I can think of a few more things to ask for," he murmured as he took up his former position, crowding into my personal space.

"What makes you think I'd give them to you?" I asked. "You were a total asshole last night, and you've been an insufferable bully so far tonight."

His crooked grin made my libido dance a jig. "Oh, and you would have been the soul of courtesy and hospitality if you'd found an unfamiliar vampire on your doorstep? And then discovered she meant to kill you?"

I had to grant him that. "I still don't get why you let me go last night."

He shrugged. "I found you entertaining. And I knew you'd be back."

Arrogant bastard! "It would have served you right if I'd staked you as soon as you'd opened the door," I grumbled.

He pressed up close against me, letting me feel his own, er, stake. I guess death threats were a turn-on for him. "If you find me so terribly unappealing, you could always leave," he said. "I won't try to stop you, and I'll even disappear for you so you can collect on your contract."

I glanced pointedly at his ring, though I made no attempt to move away. "Aren't you in mourning?"

A shadow of grief crossed his face. "When I lost Elizabeth, I lost a dear friend. But not a lover. If we were to explore our mutual attraction, I would not feel it disloyal to her memory."

I was running out of reasons to turn him down. And truthfully, there were many advantages to having a vampire lover. Especially one as smoking hot – and relatively decent (if such a term could be applied to any vampire) – as Ross Blackburn.

"OK," I said. "I'll take you for a test drive."

He smirked at me in a way that would have infuriated me if he weren't so damn sexy. I grabbed double handfuls of his hair and pulled his head down to mine. And believe me, that smirk died a quick and glorious death.

# The Righteous

## Jenna Maclaine

### Castle Tara, Ireland, 1675

*T*he warrior stood with his hands braced on the huge oak table, his brow creased in concentration as he studied the map laid out before him. The flickering flames of the firelight played over the thick muscles of his chest and cast his face into shadows. As she watched, he tucked a lock of hair behind one ear. How she longed to reach out and brush his hair back, to feel the soft strands that changed from black to brown to a coppery blond between her fingers. He looked so very young tonight and yet centuries had passed since he'd been born into this world. Physically, he appeared as though he'd seen no more than 25 years, but his age showed in the hardness of his eyes and the sharpness of his tongue.

"Morrigan, if you must be here the least you can do is not skulk about in the shadows," he snapped.

The goddess sighed and stepped into the room. "Good evening, my love."

He raised his dark, angry eyes to hers. "I am not your love."

She felt a surge of pleasure as she noted the way he watched the sway of her hips as she walked towards him. "Such harsh words from lips that used to speak naught but tenderness to me," she said.

He grabbed her wrist as she reached to lay her hand against his cheek. "Any tenderness I felt for you died when you killed me."

She cocked her head to one side. "Do not act as though you were not complicit in your own downfall."

"You deceived me," he growled.

"And you betrayed me," she pointed out. "And yet I have made you a king."

He released her wrist suddenly and turned his back to her, surveying his map once more. "I grow weary of this argument, Morrigan. I will not have it with you again."

She nodded. "Fine. I didn't come to argue with you."

"Then why are you here?"

"Your vampires are killing my humans, even though you have forbidden them to do so."

"*My* vampires? They are your creation. Why is it that when they misbehave they are *my* vampires?"

"Because you are their king. You have set down their laws and now you must make them abide by those laws."

He made a sweeping gesture towards the map. "I rule two kingdoms, Morrigan. My lands encompass the majority of the known world. I cannot be everywhere. I am not a god."

She laughed. A man who didn't think he was a god. What a novelty. "May I make a suggestion?" she asked, sweetly.

He gritted his teeth and nodded.

"My creatures of the night fear nothing and it has made them overbold. I would now give them something to fear, as humans fear the Wild Hunt on a moonlit night."

"And what exactly would put that kind of fear into the undead?"

"I want you to create two groups of slayers, one here in the west and another in the east. They will be judge, jury and executioner among our vampires. So that they are free to travel at will their rank will be above that of any king or regent. They will be answerable only to you."

He considered it for a moment and then asked, "I suppose you have someone in mind for this Herculean task?"

She looked down at the map, tapping her finger over the city of Vienna. "The King of the Eastern Lands already has a trio of warriors that will suit our needs but he keeps them in his capital as his own personal guard. I want them to travel through his lands and execute any rogue vampire who does not adhere to our laws."

"Drake will not like the removal of his personal guard."

She arched one black brow. "You are the High King and he is your vassal. Make it so."

"Do you truly believe that three vampires can control the entire population of a kingdom?"

She laughed. "It has been too long since you have moved in the human world, my love. Humans are ruled by words in books. They follow the laws of their gods, against their baser instincts, because they fear punishment in the next world."

"But you've created vampires to be almost immortal. They have little fear of what comes in the next life."

The goddess smiled. "So we will give them something terrible to fear in *this* life."

He ran his hand over the map of his kingdoms. "It could work. I will send a messenger to the Eastern King. And what of my western lands?"

She walked around the table, trailing her long, shiny black fingernails across the wood. On the far side of the room, next to the King's bed, stood a white marble pedestal and on that pedestal rested the great Book of Souls. She made her way to the book, her book, and reverently touched its solid gold binding. It contained the names of every vampire who owed fealty to the High King. Opening it, her hand hovered over the pages and they turned without a touch until she found the name she sought.

"This one," she said, tapping the page.

Curious, the warrior king came up behind her and peered over her shoulder. "What makes this knight so special?" he asked, hating himself for the trace of jealousy he heard in his own voice.

"He is a good man, a righteous man, and he will make fine warriors for my cause."

"I will summon him."

"No," she said quickly. "Not yet. There is something he must do before he is ready."

He glanced sideways at her, frowning. "Are you matchmaking again, Morrigan?"

She smiled. "Send him to Paris. There he will find what he needs to become the man we wish him to be." She turned quickly and he reached out, grabbing her shoulders to steady them both. "Now, why don't you let me give you what you need," she purred.

"I want nothing from you," he spat, yet he didn't drop his hands or turn away.

"You need my blood," she murmured, running her fingertips over his bare chest, then down his stomach. She lingered over the bulge where his body strained against his breeches. "You may not want me but your body tells me a different tale."

He closed his eyes, trying to ignore the throbbing that only she could cause. "Do you really want this, Morrigan, knowing how much I hate you?"

She leaned into his body. "There is such a fine line between love and hate, my King. This will do . . . for now."

He opened his eyes and looked down into her strong, almost masculine features. Her black eyes flashed with triumph and her sharp, high cheekbones were flush with the lust she felt for him. Her full lips parted on a sigh as he grabbed a fistful of her jet-black hair.

"I hate you," he whispered, though the words held less conviction than he would have liked.

"I know," the goddess whispered back. "But you will always love me."


## Paris, 1675

The woman was dead before he found her. A vampire cannot drain a human in one feeding but this poor soul had run afoul of three of them and together they had bled her dry. He crouched on the rooftop, waiting. The girl he had been following, rooftop to rooftop through the winding streets of Paris, would happen upon this massacre at any moment. He shifted his weight to the balls of his feet and watched.

She was tall for a female, perhaps only six inches shy of his six foot four. He had laughed when he'd first caught sight of her tonight, clad in her dark, unadorned man's attire. She wore her pale wheat-coloured hair pulled back in a ribbon at the nape of her neck and the features of her face were partially obscured by

the wide-brimmed hat she wore. He could make out her aqui-
line nose and full, sensual lips but not the colour of her eyes.
How he wished he could see her eyes now as she stepped from
the shadows of the alley and came upon the three vampires
finishing off their victim.

She swept her coat back and from somewhere under its black
folds produced a long-handled axe fitted with a wooden stake on
one end. She swung and the vampire feeding from the woman's
wrist lost his head in the first stroke. He was old and with his
death his body turned to little more than dust and bone. The
other two looked up in surprise and the girl's foot shot out,
sweeping the legs out from under the vampire closest to her. He
went down with a shout and she twirled the axe around,
impaling the stake in his chest with one thrust. This one was
young and there was no dust, only a dead body on the ground.
The man on the rooftop figured that the older vampire was
probably out teaching two newly-made vamps to hunt. He
figured this because the last vampire standing didn't have
the sense to run.

"Slayer," the vampire sneered. "There's a price your head.
The Regent will pay me well for your lifeless corpse."

She dropped the axe on the ground and the man on the
rooftop tensed. He watched, ready to intervene, as the vampire
rushed her. She didn't panic. She took two deliberate steps
towards him, grabbed him by the front of his coat as he reached
her and pitched backwards, using his momentum against him.
The vampire went sailing through the air and the girl ended up
on her back on the cobblestones. As the vampire gained his feet
and strode back to her she rolled, flipping herself up and into a
crouch in one smooth movement. Her hand snaked out and
grabbed the handle of her axe, as if she'd known exactly where it
would be, and she sliced upwards with it as she spun around to
face her attacker. She caught him cleanly in the neck and his
disembodied head hit the street with a thump.

The man on the rooftop let out the breath he had been
holding. She was amazing. No wasted movements or unnecessary commentary, just a clean execution. By God, this girl
fascinated him. After three-and-a-half centuries on this earth

and a well-deserved distrust of the female gender, that in itself was quite an achievement. He watched as she knelt down to make certain that the vampires' victim was dead. She sighed and he thought he heard a prayer on her lips as she closed the woman's eyes. Getting to her feet, she stepped over one of the vampire bodies and swooped down to retrieve her fallen hat. She paused and glanced up, almost as if she could sense him. He slid back into the shadows and smiled. Her eyes were the colour of Louis XIV's great blue diamond. She slapped the hat onto her head and stalked off. He followed, his mind filled with plans of when and where he would finally meet her.

There were many things she loved about being the reigning darling of the Paris Opera: the stage, the costumes, the music. She loved to sing and she had a voice that was considered by many, including the great Jean-Baptiste Lully, to be unparalleled across Europe. It had brought her fame and fortune and the attention of kings. It had brought her up from the gutter to the glittering world that now surged forwards to offer its congratulations at yet another stellar performance at the Palais des Tuileries.

This was the only part of her life that she hated – the long walk from her dressing room to the carriage that awaited her. At one time it had been a heady thing, to have rich and powerful men offering her anything she desired for her favours. She had become the mistress of the Sun King at the tender age of 17. A few years later she had enjoyed the generosity of England's Charles II. That she had been the mistress of kings had only increased her value to the men who moved in Louis' privileged world and she had used their ambition to her advantage. She had chosen her few lovers with discrimination, selecting only those who would bring her closer to her goal. She now possessed her own house, casks of jewels and enough money to live comfortably for the rest of her life, if she was frugal. Most importantly, she was able to care for the only thing that truly mattered in her life: her sister.

And so she smiled and nodded and politely declined the offers made to her by the gentlemen of the court. She had thought that eventually their attention would wane but the fact that she had not taken a lover in over two years had only fuelled their interest in her. Briefly she wondered how much they were now wagering on who she would chose as her next protector.

In truth she missed having a man in her bed but she could not tie herself to another aristocrat who would expect her to be available whenever he wished. Her nights were now filled with darker things than illicit rendezvous with powerful men. The denizens of Louis XIV's court would leave the opera tonight and spend their evening drinking and gambling and speculating as to why one of the most desirable women in Paris would choose to go to her bed alone. But Justine Rousseau would not be found, this night or any other, in her bed. While darkness blanketed the city there were more important things to do than sleep. There were vampires to hunt.

As her carriage crossed the Seine at the Pont Neuf, Justine pulled the powdered wig from her head and ran her fingers through her long, pale-blonde hair. She noted the grand, awe-inspiring silhouette of Notre Dame cathedral looming in the distance as the carriage turned to go deeper into the city, as it did every night. Rolling to a stop in front of the Ursuline convent of Rue Saint-Jacques, the carriage would wait until she tapped on the roof and then it would return her to her house on the Rue des Tournelles.

Her sister Solange had been a boarder at the convent school for the last ten years. Their parents had died of smallpox when Justine was only 16. She often wondered if she had done right by Solange. It had been her intention to keep Solange with her but she hadn't known, in the beginning, what kind of life she had chosen for herself. She hadn't wanted her sister to grow up learning to be a courtesan, so she had enrolled her in the convent school at the first opportunity. It had been the beginning of the end of their relationship.

Solange was young. She didn't fully appreciate the fact that the money her sister had made with her body had kept them from starving on the streets, and had given her the luxury of being disdainful of the fact that her older sister was a woman of questionable virtue. Solange would no longer see her and that was, Justine supposed, the way things should be. But that didn't stop her from driving past the convent every night and stopping to say her silent prayer for her sister's happiness and well-being.

"God be with you," she whispered, as she rapped on the polished wood of the carriage to signal the driver. She closed her eyes and leaned back into the velvet cushions.

The carriage door flew open and a man's plumed hat sailed through the opening to land on the seat across from her. Justine sat upright, clutching at the velvet squabs, when the whole conveyance tipped wildly as the biggest man she had ever seen climbed in. He sat down on the seat opposite her and crossed his arms over his chest.

"Get out!" she yelled. "Henri! Henri!"

"He can't help you," the man said.

"What have you done with him?" she hissed.

"Ah good, you speak English. The boy is fine. He's taking a walk."

"Henri would not abandon his post."

"To be fair to the lad I did suggest it rather . . . forcefully."

She sat back and studied him. He wasn't just tall, he was broad. His dark-blue coat and vest covered wide shoulders, which seemed to fill her small carriage. His hair was black and cut short, so unlike the long, curly wigs which were fashionable for men these days. Black leather riding boots covered his long legs and she had to shift to make room for them.

"What the devil do you want?" she snapped.

He leaned forwards, his dark eyes glittering, and rubbed the stubble which covered his very square jaw. "I want to see the woman who brought me all the way from England."

She frowned. "I don't even know you."

"You are correct but you will know me well by the time this dance is done."

"You speak in riddles."

He leaned back and smiled. "Then let me make it plain to you. You have made a nuisance of yourself among some very powerful people."

Her eyes narrowed. "What people?"

"Namely, François, the Regent of Paris. It seems that you keep killing his vampires."

Her body tensed and she wondered if she could make it to the wooden stake that was tucked between the seat cushions in time. Careful not to draw his attention to her hand, she laid her palms on the seat and leaned forwards. There were, she realized, as his gaze was drawn to the swell of her breasts, things that being a vampire did not change. She took a deep breath, straining the limits of the pale-blue dress.

"I am not a murderer, *Monsieur*. If François would keep his vampires from killing humans, then I would not hunt them."

"It is against the High King's law to kill humans. How can you be certain they are doing this?"

"Because five of them nearly killed me two years ago."

"Are they dead now?"

She smiled. "They were the first ones I killed. I execute only the guilty."

He arched a brow at her. "And you decide who is innocent and who is guilty."

She shrugged. "Someone must."

He again crossed his arms over his massive chest. "I must say, my dear, you are quite impressive for a human woman. François says that you have nearly a hundred kills to your credit."

"Obviously it is not enough. One of his vampires murdered a woman near the Bastille two nights ago. But you did not cross the Channel just to congratulate me."

"No," he said, his eyes raking hotly over her. "I've been hired to kill you."

She jerked the stake from its hiding place and lunged at him. His hand caught her wrist like a vice and they both looked down to see the tip of the stake lost in the fabric of coat and vest.

"By God, you are a bloodthirsty wench," he muttered and grabbed the back of her head with his free hand, pulling her mouth down to his.

The stake in her hand was all but forgotten as his lips met hers. Before she knew how it had happened her body was flush against his and the hand that had held her wrist was pressing against the small of her back. She had no idea where her stake was and at the moment she didn't care. His tongue swept into her mouth and she melted into him, her body quivering. It had been years since she'd been kissed and longer still since she'd been touched by a man she felt any sort of passion for. This man, God, he fired her blood. She curled her fingers into the fabric of his coat and wondered what that wide chest would feel like if it were bared to her hands.

Abruptly he turned her loose, unceremoniously dumping her back into her seat. While she was still trying to get her bearings he scooped his hat up and bounded out of the carriage. He paused outside the door and swept her a low bow before placing the plumed hat back on his head at a rakish angle.

"I thought you were going to kill me," she said, inwardly wincing at the tremor and the faintest sound of disappointment in her voice.

"No, I said I've been *hired* to kill you," he replied with a smile. "Don't worry, I'll most likely get to it tomorrow."

And then he was gone, as if he'd been nothing more than her imagination. Justine blew out a breath. Her hands were shaking and she didn't think it was from fear. Perhaps it hadn't been such a good idea to be celibate these last few years. Perhaps then she wouldn't have found herself in a torrid embrace with a vampire. In a carriage, she thought with disgust. While sitting in front of a convent.

"*Mon Dieu*, I am going to hell."

But it would almost have been worth the trip.

The next night the theatre at the Tuileries Palace was filled to overflowing and Justine could not escape an invitation from the Duc d'Orleans to join his party at the neighbouring Palais Royal. For two hours she watched the clock, counting the minutes until she could make a graceful exit. Her thoughts completely revolved around the vampire in her carriage as she drank and danced and managed to successfully avoid the wandering hands of Monsieur La Fontaine. She was so preoccupied that, when the Duc d'Orleans loudly hailed her from across the room, someone had to grab her by the sleeve to get her attention.

"It looks as if the King's brother is bringing you a present," Madame de Montespan, Louis' current mistress, informed her with a sly smile.

"Oh dear God," Justine moaned as she stood rooted to the floor, watching the Duc cross the room with her vampire in tow.

Madame de Montespan chuckled and patted her on the arm. "Good luck, dear," she said with a wink, before blending back into the crowd.

Justine had to admit, in the moments before Philippe descended on her, that the vampire was quite a fine figure of a man. Tall and broad, every inch of him was overpoweringly male. No wonder he had caught Philippe's eye. Despite two marriages and five surviving children, the Duc d'Orleans was unashamedly, and quite flamboyantly, a lover of men. At any given time he wore more perfume than Justine had ever owned, and just about as much lace. It had come as quite a surprise to everyone when he had proven himself to be an excellent military commander. For all his foppishness though, Justine quite liked him.

'*Chérie*!' he greeted her. 'I have met the most charming man. Allow me to introduce to you to John Devlin, Earl of Falconhurst. He is newly arrived from King Charles' court.'

Justine arched a brow at the vampire's title but made her curtsey nonetheless.

"Yes, the Earl is an old acquaintance," she assured Philippe.

The vampire inclined his head. "It is lovely to see you again, *Mademoiselle*."

The stared at each other for a long moment until the Duc loudly cleared his throat. "Then I will leave you alone to renew your acquaintance," he said with a wink.

When Philippe was out of earshot Justine looked the vampire up and down. The silks and lace which looked so elegant on Louis' courtiers seemed out of place on him. His broad, muscular chest appeared more suited to chain mail than velvet. "You look ridiculous," she said.

He frowned, glancing down at his dark-blue velvet coat, heavily adorned with braiding and lace, the silk vest and knee breeches beneath it, and his silk hose and high-heeled shoes. "I look like everyone else," he protested.

"You still look ridiculous."

He shrugged. "Well, the fashions today are rather absurd. To tell you the truth, I've worn suits of armour more comfortable than these shoes."

Unable to help herself, she laughed. "Do you know the punishment for impersonating the nobility?"

"And what makes you think my title is not my own?" he asked with an arrogance in his voice that made her pause.

"How long have you been a vampire?"

"Over three hundred years."

"Well, then the title is no longer yours, if it ever was to begin with."

He shrugged. "I left no heirs so I feel justified in using it when I see fit."

She cast him a look which clearly said that she didn't know whether to believe him or not. "Why are you here, vampire?"

He winced and glanced around. "I have been called many things, including the Devil himself, but I would appreciate it if you would call me Devlin instead of 'vampire'."

She inclined her head. "Devlin, why are you here? Surely you do not plan to kill me in front of the King's brother and half the court?"

"Research, my dear," he said simply. "It is always to one's advantage to know as much as possible about your enemy."

"And what have you learned in this room full of gossips?"

"Well, they –" he started, but his attention was quickly drawn by something across the room. "Why is that young man glaring at me?"

Justine turned and promptly let out an embarrassed chuckle. "That is Philippe de Lorraine, the Duc's lover. Be careful of that one. He's beautiful but just as immoral and dangerous as any vampire in this city."

"Perhaps we should take a stroll through the gardens? I fear it would complicate my time here if I was forced to kill the King's brother's jealous lover."

She stared at him, incredulous. "Do you think I've taken leave of my senses, *Monsieur*? I will not be taking a stroll in the gardens with a man who has been hired to kill me."

He leaned in close to her, until his dark eyes filled her vision. "Ah, but I promise not to kill you tonight."

She pursed her lips. "That is hardly comforting."

He laid one hand on his heart. "My word of honour as a knight, no harm will come to you."

"I must be mad," she muttered, but allowed him to take her hand and place it on his arm.

When they were free of the prying eyes and the gilded confines of the Duc's apartment, the tension in Devlin's body began to ease. Justine was almost disappointed. She had been enjoying the taut feel of his biceps under her hand.

Devlin closed his eyes and inhaled the warm spring air. "They call you '*le chardonneret du Roi*', the King's goldfinch."

Justine nodded. "Your English king called me his 'French canary'."

He rolled his eyes. "Charles, on occasion, lacks imagination. You are much more than a pretty voice."

"Am I?"

"You are, I think, a woman of great fortitude. When your parents died, leaving you with the care of a baby sister, you could have scraped out a living doing any number of things. Instead you ended up the mistress of the King."

She snorted. "That was not my intention, I assure you. All I wanted to do was sing."

He smiled. "They say you stole a dress from some mantua-maker . . ."

"From the finest dressmaker in Paris," she assured him.

"And then you ambushed poor Lully outside the Tuileries one afternoon and convinced him to let you sing for him."

She stiffened. "I do not know this word 'ambush'."

He laughed, knowing that she knew his meaning exactly, and continued on. "And when the King first saw you and heard your voice, you and your sister never wanted for anything again. It is an amazing story."

"And do you not think less of me for making my fortune in such a way?" After all, her own sister did.

He gave her an odd look. "There is no shame in being the mistress of a king. It's a position of great power and influence. I think less of Louis for letting you go."

"He needed a spy at the English court. When he asked me if I would go, I could hardly decline."

"And Madame de Montespan?" he asked.

"When I returned, she had taken my place."

'Did that not sting a bit?'

Justine shrugged. "When a woman is out of sight, she is out of mind. It is the way of kings . . . and men."

He stopped and turned to her. "You have not been out of my mind since last night."

"Such attentiveness must be quite useful for an assassin."

He ignored her waspish comment and instead reached out to touch her hair. She had abandoned her wig after the opera and instead wore her own hair pulled back in loose curls. "Your hair is nearly silver in the moonlight," he said, twining one long curl around his finger.

She looked up at him, not knowing what to say to that. He took advantage of her silence by leaning in and brushing his lips to hers. She sighed against his mouth and he accepted the invitation, pulling her into his arms. Her head whirled with the feel of his hard body against hers as he kissed her lips, her cheek, as his tongue stroked down across the pulse hammering in her throat. She was completely lost to him until she felt the sharp scrape of teeth against her neck. Suddenly she was no longer in Devlin's arms. In her mind she was transported back to that night two years ago, the night when five vampires had caught her alone in the gardens of the Tuileries Palace. She pulled herself from Devlin's embrace and hit him on the jaw as hard as she could.

His hand flew to his face as he stumbled back. "What the bloody hell was that for?"

Justine's fingers touched her neck and came away with blood. "You bit me!"

He rolled his eyes. "I did not bite you. It's a tiny scrape and it was an accident."

She narrowed her eyes. "You're a liar, vampire, and you will never touch me again."

She turned and walked away, fury firing her every step. He caught her in a few strides, spinning her around to face him.

"Justine, let me turn you," he pleaded.

"You're mad," she whispered. "I will not sell my soul to you, not even for the promise of that beautiful body."

"What about for your sister? Will you sell your soul for her?" he asked, softly.

Rage filled her until she was shaking with it. She pushed him back, punctuating each of her words with another shove to his very solid chest. "Do not dare threaten my sister."

Devlin grabbed her wrists with both of his hands. "I am not the threat to her. You are."

She kicked him in the shin and he grunted and released her. "I would never harm Solange," she spat.

"No, but you will be the death of her," he said. "Did you even consider that before you set out on this foolhardy venture?"

"What are you talking about?"

"You are, by all accounts, the most prolific slayer in the history of vampires. They will not let you live, they cannot. If it isn't me who kills you, it will be someone else. You will not have your youth for ever, did you think of that? That one day you will get older, slower? They will kill you eventually, but first they will hurt you. And there is only one thing you care about enough to cause the kind of pain they'll want you to suffer."

"Solange," she whispered. "But she is in a convent and intends to take the vows. They cannot harm her on hallowed ground."

"That is not entirely accurate. It's taboo but it isn't impossible. If a vampire were to harm her on hallowed ground, well, let's just say that God's vengeance would eventually be satisfied. Your sister, however, would still be dead. Is that the sort of death you want for her?"

Justine knew well what kind of death that would be. It was a death that should have been hers. She remembered the tearing teeth and clawing fingernails and in that moment she hated Devlin for making her think of these things. She hated him for making her realize that she hadn't thought beyond her own vengeance. Perhaps she was no better than the silly, selfish creatures who populated the court of the Sun King. There was a time, before tonight, when she had thought that what she did was important, that she made a difference. Perhaps though, what she did was only important to her own vanity. Did she execute these murderers for the greater good, or was it simply to prove to herself and to them that they may have beaten her once but they would not do so again? She was a fighter, a survivor. She didn't know any other way to be.

"I hate you," she whispered, and turned away.

This time, he let her go.

For two weeks Devlin did his best to make her see reason but his pleas fell on deaf ears, and more often than not these conversations led to a physical confrontation. The two of them fought across the length and breadth of Paris and Justine loved every moment of it. Devlin presented her with a fine sabre, even though the sword was not practical for fighting vampires. She lacked the upper-body strength needed to take a head with a sword, preferring her razor-sharp axe for such occasions. Devlin, however, seemed to enjoy watching her fight with a sword. He commented more than once on the beauty of her lithe, graceful movements.

Every night he tested the very limits of her skills and made her a better fighter. She would often goad him into a fight just to see what else he could teach her. It became a game to them and Justine could think no further into the future than where they would meet the next night and for how long she would let him kiss her when they grew weary of sparring.

Until the day the Mother Superior of the Ursulines arrived on her doorstep to tell her that two men in a closed carriage had snatched Solange off the side of the Rue Saint-Jacques in broad daylight.

Darkness could not come soon enough for Justine. Unsure of where the vampires would have taken her sister or what they would do to her, there was nothing she could do but wait until nightfall and her scheduled meeting with Devlin. She penned a note to the stage manager at the opera, explaining that her sister had been abducted and informing him that she would not sing tonight. She hoped that Devlin would be in the audience again and that when he realized someone else was singing the role of Medea he would come quickly to their meeting place.

After sunset, with nothing but a small lantern to light her way, Justine walked purposefully through the Luxembourg Gardens. The trees were like dark skeletons against the sky and the moonless night cast the waters of the Fontaine de Médicis an inky black. Setting her lantern down, she paced and fumed until one sharp turn sent her crashing into Devlin's chest. He reached out to steady her and she grabbed the lapels on his coat.

"They have her, Devlin. They took her right off the street," she cried.

He put his arms around her to steady her. "When?"

"This afternoon."

"In daylight? Darling, are you sure that it is François' men who have done this?"

"Who else would it be?"

"I don't know," he said, absently raking a hand through his short dark hair, "but for vampires to go about in the middle of the day, let alone to abduct a novice off the street, is a sign of insanity or desperation."

"Or both," came a voice from the darkness.

Devlin drew his sword and pushed Justine behind him as a vampire she had never seen before stepped from the shadows. He was a handsome man of average height with honey-brown hair and intelligent, pale-green eyes.

"Antoine," Devlin said, with a nod.

The vampire returned the gesture, spreading his hands out to show that he was unarmed.

"Who are you?" Justine demanded. "And what have you done with my sister?"

"You are correct; François has the girl. She was unharmed when I last saw her but an hour ago."

"What do you want, Antoine?" Devlin demanded.

"I want to tell you a story and I want you to tell me how it ends. But first I have a question to ask of you, my friend."

"All right," Devlin agreed.

"How is it that you came to be here in Paris?"

Justine gritted her teeth, not seeing how such a question was relevant to her sister's abduction.

"I was sent here on the command of the High King himself."

Antoine nodded, seeming pleased. "Were you sent here to kill the woman?" he asked, motioning to Justine.

Devlin shook his head. "I was only told to come to Paris."

"*C'est bon.*"

"Now tell me your story, Antoine."

"The vampires of Paris are divided into two groups. Those who enjoy the kill support François and demand the death of your slayer. But there are those, such as myself, who would be content to follow the laws of the High King and who consider the abduction of an Ursuline novice to be a sin of the greatest magnitude."

"Then why don't you simply overthrow him?" Justine asked.

"A century ago François and I challenged the old Regent for the rule of this city. François won and I lost. The other vampires will not follow me. Now, if a righteous man, or woman," Antoine said with a nod to them both, "were to challenge François and win then I could guarantee the support of those who would follow the High King's laws."

"Your men would follow an English mercenary and a slayer?" Devlin scoffed.

"My men would follow the representative of the High King and the woman who brings justice to those who break his laws. I don't guarantee an easy fight, my friend, but I feel that we would prevail."

"Devlin," Justine said, tugging on the sleeve of his coat, "does your offer still stand?"

He looked down at her, confused.

"The offer to turn me," she explained.

"Do you realize what you're asking?"

"Devlin, I cannot go into a nest of vampires as a human and hope to survive. And I am assuming that is the only way I will get my sister back?" she asked Antoine.

He nodded gravely. "François will use her to draw you out and then he will kill you both."

Her blue eyes pleaded with him. "Devlin, she's lived most of her life in that convent. I have to get her back and if this is the only way to do it, then that is what I must do."

"Are you ready to be Regent of Paris?" he asked.

She gave him a look. "And not have to spend my nights fighting vampires over the bodies of my fellow Parisians?"

He smiled. "Yes, I can think of much better ways to spend our nights. But, Justine, even if I turned you now you would not rise as a vampire for three nights."

She paled, thinking of what François could do to her sister in three days and nights.

"I will guarantee the girl's safety," Antoine volunteered.

Justine narrowed her eyes. "How?"

'François had to hire humans to abduct her. None of our vampires will touch her because of the habit and crucifix she wears. One of my men has the care of her. I will see to it that she is well cared for and unharmed until you come for her but you must come. François is a man of few scruples. If you do not come, eventually he will screw up his courage and kill her. He will have to or risk losing the respect of those loyal to him."

"I will come for her. You tell her that I will come for her."

Antoine nodded. "François has a chateau just outside Paris in Montrouge. You will find her there. My men and I will be waiting."

Antoine turned to go but Justine called after him. "Antoine! I expect you to hold up your end of this bargain. If there is one scratch on my sister's body I will hold you personally responsible."

He turned and, with a flourish of his plumed hat, bowed low to her and then disappeared into the darkness.

"Do you think we can trust him?" Justine asked.

"I am a good judge of men, Justine, and of soldiers in particular. Antoine is an honourable man. He was one of King Henri II's most trusted chevaliers. Let's just hope that he is an equally good judge of the vampires he represents."

She turned and looked up at him. "Devlin, why are you doing this?"

He cupped her face in his large hands. "I have been lost for so long, Justine. You make me feel alive for the first time since . . .

since well before I became a vampire. You make me want to be a
better man. Let me be your knight, my lady. Together we will
take this city and bend it to your will."

She laid her head on his chest so that he wouldn't see the tears
in her eyes. "Then take me home, my knight," she said softly,
"and make me yours."


Naked in her bed, Devlin was everything she'd imagined he
would be and more. She ran her fingers through the crisp hair of
his chest, marvelling at the solid muscle beneath her hands. He
allowed her this liberty only briefly and then he flipped her onto
her back and proceeded to do things with his hands and mouth
that even an experienced courtesan would not admit to in the
light of day.

Justine felt a small pang of regret that the light of day was not
something she would enjoy again after this night. Her regret,
however, was short-lived as Devlin entered her and all thoughts
fled her mind except for the utter triumph she felt in the
knowledge that she would have this spectacular man in her
bed for nights, years, centuries to come. It had been so long, for
both of them, and within minutes they exploded together like
fireworks over the palace at Versailles. At the height of their
pleasure he sank his teeth into her neck and drank from her.
The rush of sensations Justine felt as he bit her hurled her over
the edge once more, leaving her spent and quivering in his arms.

Devlin pulled her on top of him and ran his tongue over the
fresh puncture marks on her neck. "I didn't hurt you, did I?" he
asked.

She sighed. "All I remember about the night I was attacked is
the unimaginable pain."

Worry crossed his face and, as if he were unsure of her
response, he asked, "And tonight?"

She smiled a coquette's smile and began kissing her way
down his hard belly to that part of him that was again flagrantly
demanding her attention. "Tonight there is only unimaginable
pleasure."

Three times during the night he drank from her. When she
was nearly unconscious from the blood loss, he sliced open his

wrist and spilled his blood into her mouth, forcing her to drink. As the sun rose on another glorious spring day, Devlin held her in his arms and watched her die.

Three nights later Justine, the Devil's Justice, rose as a vampire, and Paris was never the same again.

## Castle Tara, Ireland, 1728

Morrigan, Great Phantom Queen, war goddess and harbinger of death, leaned over her sleeping warrior, brushing a lock of his multicoloured hair from his face. His hand came up and caught her wrist as his eyes flew open.

"Why are you here, Morrigan?" he asked, surly even in his sleep.

"Solange Rousseau died in her sleep in the convent of Rue Saint-Jacques last night."

He frowned. "So soon?"

Morrigan shook her head. "The years pass quickly, do they not? She was 68 years old, my love."

He nodded. "So Devlin and Justine will be content to leave Paris now and bend the vampires of the Western Lands to my laws?"

"Yes, they have groomed Antoine to take the Regency of Paris."

"Do you know that already vampires call them 'The Righteous'?"

Morrigan smiled. "We did well."

The High King reached out and ran the backs of his fingers across her cloak of raven feathers. "Yes," he murmured, "we did."

Morrigan dropped the feathered cloak to the floor, revealing the long, pale lines of her naked body. The High King pulled her down into his bed.

"I still hate you," he whispered, as he pressed her soft body against the hard length of him.

The goddess smiled as her lips trailed down the side of his neck. "I know."

# Knowledge of Evil

## Raven Hart

*I* am a scholar. I know more about human history than anyone, yet I am not human. I have learned more about the natural world than anyone alive, yet I am not myself alive and assuredly not natural. I am a vampire.

I have travelled the world in search of knowledge, studied with every important intellectual from da Vinci to Hawking. And still the question that has burned inside me for thousands of years remains unanswered. Wherefore the blood drinker? What is my purpose?

I have entertained the notion that my purpose might be to kill other vampires. I have hunted them almost to extinction on every continent. I have saved the Americas for last.

Why do I destroy other blood drinkers? Because I despise them. A newly minted vampire is subhuman, a barely sentient creature whose bloodlust overwhelms reason. As a man for whom intellect is the most prized of all human attributes, I despise the primal baseness of my own kind. So much so that I cannot suffer them to live.

A young blood drinker is born with the survival instincts to appear and act human, but it is a ruse. It takes decades for the immature vampire to regain the intellect he or she was blessed with as a human being, if they survive that long.

I am a refined, sophisticated creature of the night. I feed on humans, but never to the point of exsanguination. My blood-sucking leaves them weak and my glamour leaves them with no memory of having been preyed upon. Younger vampires tend to seek out the anonymous unfortunates in our culture – the homeless, the addicted, the mentally ill – those who won't be missed. Fledgling blood drinkers are all about the kill.

For my part, I prefer to obtain sustenance from other seekers of knowledge. Thus, I have haunted university campuses all over the world. These venues afford me an abundance of young, sweet-smelling blood upon which to feed, plus the occasional stimulating conversation. And then, of course, there's always the sex.

After I came to the New World, I worked my way down from the universities of the north-east until I found myself in the southern United States, where the mild climate suited me well.

Athens, home of the University of Georgia, calls itself the "Classic City" after the ancient city of my birth. Intrigued, I've settled here for the present. My fake identification papers, in addition to cash, of course, allow me to audit any classes I choose. I drift from night class to night class, absorbing new ideas on everything from philosophy to veterinary medicine.

Fall semester was about to get under way, but the oppressive southern heat still saturated the air with humidity and emboldened the young women to clothe themselves in short, strapless dresses and midriff-bearing tops that exposed their tanned flesh. Their bodies were as ripe for sex as their eager young minds were for higher education.

On this particular night I seated myself on a wrought-iron bench near the library on north campus and engaged in what the moderns call "people watching". Students walked purposefully to and fro, besides the clothing and the mores, not too very different from university students of days gone by.

The breeze rustled the pages of the campus newspaper, *Red and Black*, which someone had left on the bench next to me, and I idly picked it up. It had been turned back upon itself to the features section: "HOLD ONTO YOUR HAEMOGLOBIN: NEW ANTHROPOLOGY PROF. IS EXPERT ON VAMPIRES" read the headline.

Delighted, I read further. Noted cultural anthropologist Professor Victoria Lenox, author of the book *Vampires Through the Ages*, was teaching this semester at UGA as a visiting professor. According to the article, she had devoted her academic career to studying vampire folklore in cultures all around the globe.

A folklorist devoted to vampire myths. How perfectly marvellous. A quick phone call to the college of anthropology indicated I was in luck. The first lecture by Professor Lenox was later that night, and I attained consent to audit the class. I headed off to Baldwin Hall prepared to be highly entertained.

When I arrived a teaching assistant was calling roll. As I entered the hall I attracted the notice of a pair of young women students a few rows in front of me. One elbowed the other in the ribs and inclined her chin in my direction. The one who'd been nudged stared at me wide-eyed for a moment before getting her reaction under control. I smiled at them and they each blushed prettily and turned away.

It has been thousands of years since I saw my reflection, but I have been assured that I am beautiful. In my youth I was adored and was even called upon to model for the *Charioteer of Delphi*, one of the most famous of the great surviving sculptures of ancient Greece. I was made a blood drinker as a man of 35 years, so I will always be in my prime.

Today, young women praise my dark hair, green eyes and flawless skin. I say these things not out of conceit but by way of explanation. I do not need to use coercion to obtain my food. Young women follow me willingly into the shadows – or wherever else I choose to lead them.

I seated myself, and the teaching assistant launched into an awkward introduction of the professor. Her academic credentials and list of publication credits were impressive. I pictured the anthropologist as a middle-aged, bookish and bespectacled scholar along the lines of the late Margaret Mead.

When the young graduate student finished the introduction, he scurried to shake the hand of the professor, who rose gracefully from a seat in the front row. As the tall, willowy academic walked to the lectern in a beige linen blazer over a coral shift dress and matching high-heeled shoes, I noted the regal nature of her carriage, not to mention the shapeliness of her legs.

The scholar who turned to face the lecture hall was not a frumpy, middle-aged matron but a rare beauty. As one, the young men in the hall gathered themselves from their slouching postures and sat up straight. The professor scanned her audience, as if taking their measure, paused only long enough to smooth her long black hair over one shoulder, and began her lecture.

When she began to speak I was as mesmerized by her words as I was by the perfection of her fair skin, the fullness of her lips and the lovely almond shape of her dark eyes.

"The myth of the blood drinker can be found in almost every culture through the ages," she began. "They are powerful, immortal and seductive. Their preternatural strength and beauty make them the stuff of our nightmares and sexual fantasies alike. And yet for all their power, we also feel for them, because they are cut off from the grace of God and cannot walk in the sun."

As she spoke, she stepped out from behind the lectern and walked slowly back and forth, her every movement and gesture elegant and sylph-like. Watching her was such a feast for my eyes it was difficult to concentrate on her words. I let the honeyed tones of her voice flow over me as she lectured about the Mayans and their propensity for filing their teeth into pointed fangs and anointing their nobility with sacrificial human blood.

It seemed in no time at all that the lecture was nearly over. When she'd finished with her prepared remarks, she asked if the students had any questions. Many hands shot upwards, and she called upon a young man a few rows in front of me.

"Do you believe in vampires?" he asked. "Real ones, I mean?"

The audience tittered for a few moments as the professor considered the question. A coquettish smile played over her face and she lowered her voice conspiratorially. "I'll never tell," she said.

The students laughed.

More hands were raised. When she scanned faces in the crowd to pick the student for the next question, her gaze met and held mine for a moment. Without thinking, I raised my hand and she nodded.

"If you did meet a real vampire," I said, "what would you do with him?"

The students laughed again and she smiled. "Why, study him, of course. I yearn for knowledge above all things."

*Be still, my unbeating heart.*

After a few more questions from the students, Professor Lenox dismissed the class. Four or five pupils stayed to ask additional questions while she put some papers into her brief-case, so I took my time walking to the front of the class. By the time I reached her, she was alone.

"Professor Lenox,' I said, extending my hand. "My name is Nick Manos. I can't tell you how much I enjoyed your lecture." If she only knew how much I couldn't tell her.

She put her slender hand in mine. "Mr Manos, how nice to meet you," she said. "Are you a vampire enthusiast?"

"You have no idea. And, please, call me Nick." Reluctantly I released her hand. It was warm and her skin was soft. Her light floral fragrance put me in mind of springtime in the Netherlands.

"Then you must call me Victoria," she said with a smile that made me feel like a warm-blooded creature again.

"Would you care to have coffee with me?" I asked. "I'd love to discuss the subject of vampires further."

Her Cupid's bow lips parted slightly to answer, but she paused. After a moment in which she searched my gaze as if trying to gauge my measure, she said, "That would be nice."

I held the door open for her as we left the building. The coffee shop was a short walk.

"You're not the typical student," she said. Her quick once-over, though subtle, wasn't lost on me. The glance took in my expensive Italian shoes, my 80-dollar haircut and everything in between. And I do mean everything.

"And you're not the typical professor," I countered, remembering my earlier assumptions.

"Tell me about yourself," she said.

I gave her a quick version of my standard cover story, which actually happened to be true as far as it went. I'd inherited and then sold a family shipping business. "With no relatives left in Greece I decided to travel the world," I said. She didn't have to know that my last relative died before Christ was born.

"Travel the world doing what?"

"Why studying, of course. I yearn for knowledge above all things."

"Are you mocking me?" Her gentle laughter was like music.

"I'm perfectly sincere." I laid my hand against my heart, feigning shock at her accusation. "I think we might be kindred spirits, you and I."

"Perhaps we are, at that," she said.

When we reached the coffee shop, I approached the storefront carefully, making sure the light from the street lamps caused no reflections in the glass. Centuries of experience made such cautionary measures second nature.

"Oh, my," Victoria said. "They're closed."

"That's too bad." I looked down the row of restaurants and bars on the opposite side of the street for an alternative.

"Would you like to have coffee at my place?" she asked. "The town house I'm renting is only a couple of blocks off campus."

I thought it unusual that the professor would invite a stranger into her home, but modern women were an unpredictable lot. "That would be fine," I agreed, and we walked on.

"Why vampires?" I asked.

She gave me a sidelong glance that told me she'd heard the question a thousand times. "It's like I said during my lecture. They're fascinating creatures – seductive, powerful—"

"But they're *fictional* creatures," I said disingenuously. "Why devote your academic life to their study when there are so many . . ." I hesitated, searching for just the right word.

"So many *real* things to study?" she supplied.

"Well, yes." I knew I was risking alienating her. She'd no doubt had to explain herself *ad nauseam* to countless persons, including friends and family, for years. But my curiosity was not like theirs. Not at all.

She shrugged. "Nothing else ever interested me as much as the immortal. But what about you? You admitted to being a vampire enthusiast. What appeal does the blood drinker hold for Nick Manos?"

I faked a sheepish grin. "Exactly the same as everyone else. It's the immortality, I guess. I love Stoker, Rice, *Nosferatu*—"

"What about the killing, the violence?" she asked.

"What about it?"

"That's what attracts men to the vampire genre in books and movies, right?"

"Maybe," I said non-committally. If any human were to ever witness death by vampire and live to tell the tale, the horror would render them a raving lunatic for the rest of their miserably short lives. "The attraction for women is different, I'm guessing. I suppose that was the seduction aspect you mentioned before."

"You suppose correctly," she said with a pretty upwards tilt of her elegant chin. "When it gets right down to it, doesn't everything boil down to sex?" She stopped walking. By the light of the street lamp her beauty looked suddenly other-worldly. "Shall we?"

"Excuse me?" I asked.

She treated me to a lilting laugh as she produced her keys from her blazer pocket. We had just reached her door. She unlocked it and went inside. I followed, feeling like an awkward teenager on a first date, something I was entirely unaccustomed to. I feared I was being bewitched.

A quick scan of the rooms through which we passed revealed no mirrors or religious icons. We entered a room with a multi-tude of books and papers strewn about and a desktop computer facing a window. The air held the faint scent of old books – oxidized paper, a bit of mould – and I was immediately comfortable. This was the space of a scholar.

"You're working on a paper," I observed.

"I'm always working on a paper." She placed her briefcase on the floor and shrugged off her jacket. "Make yourself at home."

I took a seat on the sofa and noticed something I'd missed before in the corner of the room. A small table held a number of beakers, a microscope, glass slides and a few amber-coloured bottles of chemicals. I inclined my head towards the assembly and asked, "So, you're a biologist as well?"

"I'm getting into the forensic side of anthropology. There's a great demand for those skills in law enforcement, you know."

I nodded, vaguely aware that several popular television programmes featured crime-solving scientists. I picked up one of the books within arm's reach. She toed off her heels and joined me, drawing up her knees onto the couch.

"*Vrykolakes: Vampires in Greek Folklore.*" As I read the book's title I became aware of an eerie and unaccustomed feeling I couldn't identify making its way down my spine. "I guess I should know about this, shouldn't I?" I joked.

"Definitely. What with you being a Greek vampire enthusiast."

Her teasing manner was playing tricks with my imagination. I could have sworn she had put extra emphasis on the word "enthusiast".

Gently, she took the book from me and laid it aside. Her hand came to rest on my thigh. "You don't really want coffee, do you?"

I must admit that her forwardness startled me. Naturally I was accustomed to the licentiousness of some young women, counted on it, in fact. The Girls-Gone-Wild effect, as I termed it, had secured me countless nights of good blood and better sex. But I hadn't expected such wanton behaviour from her. Not from an intellectual. No sooner had I thought this than I derided myself for the hypocrisy of my double standard. Victoria was her own woman. Who was I to judge her?

"No," I agreed, "I don't really want coffee."

"Then what do you want?" she asked breathily, running her hand higher up my leg and letting her fingers play against the inner part of my thigh.

"I imagine I want the same thing you do." I put my hand over hers and pressed it hard onto my erection.

"Oh good," she cooed. "I'm so glad we're on the same page."

She massaged my cock through the straining fabric of my trousers for a moment more and then turned to straddle my thighs. Running her fingers through my hair, she kissed me deeply. I slid my eager hands underneath her linen dress and caressed her derrière. She broke off the kiss and arched her back against my erection, allowing me to remove her dress in one quick motion.

A quick flick of my fingers and the lacy bra was history. I filled my palms with her full, ripe breasts for a moment before taking her nipples in my mouth and urging them to the hardness of gems. She reached down to free my swollen cock and I ripped away the flimsy slip of fabric between her legs.

She gasped, wide-eyed, as I entered her with one fluid stroke. Then she moaned and wrapped her arms around my neck, riding me – experimentally at first – then harder and faster. Her passion and zeal overwhelmed me, not to mention the perfection of her body. The ardour on her face gave her beauty a savage elegance that I found both wildly exciting and disturbing at the same time.

She thrust herself onto me, her breasts rising and falling in a primitive rhythm that made me fear I would come much sooner than I wished to. I'd honed my sexual control over many centuries until I was a master of my own body and its responses, but with Victoria I felt myself as a schoolboy again.

As I struggled for command over my release, she arched her back again, exposing the tender, pale flesh of her neck. I could not only see the pulse beating rapidly in the delicate vein at the hollow of her throat, but I could see, feel and smell the blood there. I wrapped my arms around her and gathered her towards me, my fangs lengthening involuntarily. When she began to moan and writhe, I bit down on her neck, piercing her fragile flesh and began my own climax.

We wrung every ripple of pleasure from each other as I sucked her blood. When we were through, I concentrated my powers of glamour onto her mind so she would not remember the bite. If the two small puncture marks were even noticed before they healed, they'd be written off as accidental scratches.

With a sigh of satisfaction Victoria asked, "Do you want that cup of coffee now?"

"Not really," I said.

"Me neither."

A wicked smile curved the corners of her luscious mouth as she took me by the hand and led me to the bedroom.

She said she liked to take turns being on top. So the fifth time we had sex she was astride me again. She also said she liked a little light bondage. So my wrists were secured by handcuffs to the thick iron spindles running through the headboard of her antique bed.

When we reached our mutual climax, I closed my eyes and relaxed, savouring the rest. Even with my superhuman endurance, I was still exhausted and dawn was coming. I had to return to my secure resting place for my daylight sleep.

"That was wonderful," I said. "Would you remove the cuffs now, please?"

She kissed me in the middle of my chest and moved up towards the place where my wrists were fixed to the heavy iron. But instead of the clicks of the release mechanisms, I heard slithering sounds. I tried to lower my arms, but my wrists were still held fast. I looked above my head to see that my arms were not only still bound by the metal handcuffs but were now also secured by thick strips of plastic. I tested the bonds, putting my full strength behind the effort.

If the metal cuffs were all that bound me I could have broken them, but the plastic ones that reinforced them were problematic. If I applied enough force to tear them, I would literally sever my wrists. And vampire parts do not regenerate.

"What the hell do you think you're doing?" I demanded.

Victoria pulled on jeans and a T-shirt as she watched my struggle with rapt curiosity. "What's wrong, lover boy? Don't you want to stay and play some more?"

"I have to go. Now."

"What's the rush? We can finally have that cup of coffee on the patio while we watch the sunrise. Wouldn't that be fun?" She went to the east-facing bay windows and threw open the drapes.

Fear was an emotion unknown to me. I had no natural enemies, after all, but now I felt panic rising in my chest. As I tried to calm myself and formulate a light-hearted reply that might inspire her to release me, something about the maniacal gleam in her eye made my blood run even colder than usual. A sudden conviction formed in my mind, one that both terrified and thrilled me.

"How did you know?" I asked.

"Last night on the walk here. You didn't cast a shadow." Her face registered delight, triumph even.

I cursed myself for my carelessness and roared in frustration, not bothering to shield my fangs much less deny the truth. Victoria, by virtue of who she was, would see through any protestations. I strained against my bonds again, but only managed to bend the headboard while the heavy-duty plastic cut into my wrists enough to make them bleed.

Evidently my hostess found my display of strength and ferocity arousing. She leaned against the far wall with an expression of orgasmic ecstasy on her face. "Oh . . . my . . . God! I cannot believe that I have a naked vampire chained to my bed!" She opened a dresser drawer with trembling hands and withdrew a hand mirror. Examining her neck carefully, she cried, "I knew it! You bit me and sucked my blood."

I stared at her, disbelieving. What had become of the learned professor who'd delivered the erudite lecture I'd heard the evening before? Her present aspect put me in mind of the fanatical followers of Elvis or the Beatles in their heyday. Her eyes were dilated, her breathing rapid, her face flushed.

"It started with your complexion," she said. "You're much too pale to be Greek. Your skin looks like flawless white marble. And then there's the way you talk that has nothing to do with being a foreigner. You speak like somebody from a whole different time – an *earlier* time. But the missing shadow clinched it."

For my part, I now realized I should have been more alarmed by her willingness to take me home after having just met me. The seducer had become the seduced. She didn't lack for courage. I'd say that for her.

"Very well," I said. "Your gambit was well played. Now let me go and I won't harm you."

"Let you go? You've got to be kidding. Do you know how many years I've been looking for a real vampire?" she asked breathily.

"Naturally, I'd be happy to answer any questions you may have, if you'll just—"

She didn't seem to hear me.

"For years I've travelled around the world as a guest lecturer or as a visiting professor, teaching only at night. I knew one of you would come to me one day."

"How could you possibly have been sure of that?"

"You came, didn't you? Was it curiosity? Amusement? To have your ego stroked?"

"I might have wanted to kill you, have you ever thought of that? Do you have any idea what I'm capable of?" Since friendliness hadn't moved her, perhaps intimidation would. I issued a snarl to punctuate my words.

"I didn't believe you wanted to kill me. I thought you wanted sex and blood which was just what I wanted to give you." By the look of her, my display of menace only excited her further.

Although the sun was not yet visible, I could feel its approach like an itch underneath my skin. "Would you close the drapes, please?"

She blinked. "How much sunlight would it take to kill you?"

"Not bloody much." Alarm warred with fury in my mind. I had to force myself to stay calm. "What do you plan to do with me? What do you want?"

"I want knowledge."

I remembered her words from earlier in the evening, not to mention the microscope and the collection of slides and beakers. "You're going to study me."

She laughed and there was a hysterical edge to the sound. "I've been fantasizing for years about what I would do if I ever managed to capture a vampire. At first I decided that I would go all Doctor Frankenstein and dissect the blood drinker so I could study it piece by piece under the microscope on a cellular level."

I resisted the urge to squirm. I didn't relish being sliced and diced. Perhaps if I concentrated hard enough I could think of a tactic that would inspire her to free me.

"But then I thought of something else. What better way to find out what it's like to be a blood drinker than to be one? I want you to make me a vampire."

The thought of making this beautiful woman a monster repulsed me. "You don't know what you're asking."

"Oh, yes I do. And it's not just that I want to learn about vampires. I wasn't kidding when I said I thirsted for knowledge – all kinds of knowledge. Think of the possibilities. As an immortal I'll have all the time in the world to absorb all the information and wisdom that's been accumulated in human history."

A frisson of excitement shot through me. Here was a kindred spirit indeed. "I wasn't kidding earlier either. I am a seeker of understanding as well," I said. "You might call me the eternal student."

Coming closer, she sat on the edge of the bed beside me. She looked deeply into my eyes, as if gauging my sincerity. Her gaze was so intense I was sure that, if I'd had a soul, she'd be looking into it. "You're not just humouring me, are you? You really do understand."

"I'm not humouring you. I truly understand your passion for learning."

"What do you like to study most?" she asked breathlessly, her eyes gleaming.

"Earth sciences, art, social science, medicine – everything really. It's why I live near universities." The approaching dawn was starting to smoulder inside me. A faint crimson glow was bleeding over the horizon. "Please. Could you close the curtains now?"

"Will you turn me?" she asked.

"You'll lose your soul," I said. The solar sensation that had started as an itch was burning me in earnest now.

"I don't care. What do I need with a soul when I can live for ever?"

I cursed her and her ancestors as I writhed on the bed, trying in vain to turn my body away from the window. "You will become a monster! A vicious, slathering beast with no conscience. It will take you years to overcome your bloodlust enough to resume your academic pursuits if you even survive that long."

Victoria stared at me evenly, as if waiting for my narrative to worsen until I described a condition she couldn't live with. This was how much she wanted immortality. I began speaking more rapidly, describing a kill in the most gruesome and vivid detail I could imagine. And still she could not be moved.

"What can I do to get through to you?" I demanded. "What do you need to hear to turn you from this path?"

She sprang to her feet and paced the floor alongside the bed. "I need to hear answers! I want to know how the universe was created. I want to know the meaning of life. I want to know if there is a heaven and a hell. I want to know if there is a God!"

"I can assure you there is a God because I know there is a Satan!"

She stopped and tossed her head, causing her raven hair to fall over one shoulder. Her beauty was fierce. "*How* do you know?"

"Because I am one of his demons," I hissed.

My eyes swam red with fury and I unsheathed my razor-like fangs. I felt my face contort into the killing mask that was the last thing my victims saw upon this earth. I'd never seen my own visage at its most monstrous. But I have some idea of its power if the stunned horror on the faces of my fledgling vampire prey were to be taken as a measure. Still, Victoria was unafraid. She was not unaffected, however – far from it. Her face registered an emotion I could not reconcile with present reality. She was aroused.

She was still leering at me as the sun broke over the horizon and I began to scream.

"Will you turn me?" she demanded.

"Yes!" I shouted, burning from the inside out.

"Then let's get started," she said, closing the drapes with a flourish.

Her squeal of triumph was the last thing I heard before I passed out from the shock of my injury.

I awoke in cool darkness after a troubled sleep plagued by nightmares. She'd closed the drapes an instant before I would have gone up in flames. I stretched tentatively to test my injuries, and sensed her warmth. Victoria was curled up beside me, naked.

"I guess you needed some time to rest and recover," she said. "I'm sorry I had to do that to you."

I fought to bring my rage under control before I replied. I had never been as ill used in my long existence as a blood drinker and, by Satan, this minx would pay. "Yes. The rest was very helpful," I said. "Your blood will help to complete my healing."

She became excited again and got to her knees on the bed beside me. "That'll be the first part of the blood exchange that you'll use to turn me, right?"

"That is correct," I said. Little did she know she would never get to the second bit of the process – the part in which she would in turn drink of my blood. She would not survive that long. "Why don't you release my wrists and we'll get started," I suggested as calmly as I could manage and with what I hoped was a winning smile.

From a bureau drawer she withdrew a knife. I had a moment's concern when she approached me with it, but she only cut the plastic fasteners. Then she unlocked the metal handcuffs.

I rubbed my wrists. The marks left by the bindings were already disappearing. Now I smiled in earnest. "Come here, sweetling," I murmured.

There was no need for the kind of violence I abhorred. I would not kill her by ripping and consuming her flesh. Instead I would simply drink her blood – all of it – at my leisure. By the time her draining was past the point of no return, she would be unconscious and helpless to protest.

Beaming, she lay down beside me and swept her hair aside, offering me her throat. "I can hardly believe this is happening. I've waited for this so long. It's what I've always dreamed of."

Dream on, darling, I thought, extending my fangs. I encircled her with my arms and gathered her to me, positioning my mouth to her throat. I bit down without using glamour and she gasped. Her hot blood flowed across my lips and I savoured its sweetness.

"Can you see in the dark?"

"What?" I asked, annoyed that she'd interrupted both my feeding and my fantasies of revenge. "Yes. I can see in the dark."

She sighed and offered her throat again. "I have so much I want to learn from you."

It was not her nakedness or the flavour of her blood that aroused me, but her last simple statement. She wanted to learn from me. "What else do you wish to learn?" I asked, curious.

"Are your other senses as powerful as your vision, like the legends say?"

"Yes."

"And must you be invited into a house before you can cross the threshold? Last night I didn't say the words exactly, but I clearly welcomed you."

"That's all it takes," I said. "You don't have to say the words. You merely have to wish me to come inside." I tried to remember the last time anyone had ever asked me to share my own knowledge. Unsettled, I licked at the wounds in her throat and bit down again.

"How do you feel about literature?"

"What?"

"As my sire, you and I will be together for ever. I mean, maybe I'm being presumptuous, but you are going to be my mentor, right?"

"Uh, right." Because of my aversion to fledglings, I'd never considered the possibility of creating another vampire. Thus, I'd never thought of what it would be like to play Pygmalion – to shape a young blood drinker in my own image no matter how long it took and no matter how much carnage had to take place. "What were you saying about literature?" I asked, distracted.

"Oh sorry. I'm just so excited I'm rambling. You and I can discuss literature. And philosophy. And – everything! Hey, here's a philosophical question – do you think that everything is knowable given enough time, say another thousand years? Do you think cosmologists will have unravelled the mysteries of the universe by then?"

"That is my most fervent wish," I said sincerely.

I bit down again, trying to concentrate on the task at hand even as a fantasy was taking shape in my mind. What would it be like to have a soul mate to share my studies? Someone who shared my ravenous hunger for truth?

Impossible! I could not bear to see this woman reduced to a

ravenous animal. I would rather see her dead, and the sooner the better. To see her as a savage would repulse me. I pressed my fangs deeper into her flesh and drew deeply from her veins.

"How old are you?" she managed to ask, even though her voice was growing weaker.

"What?" I was becoming intoxicated – the point at which I would be unable to stop drinking her blood even if I wanted to; the point at which if I were going to make her a vampire, I would have to feed her my own blood.

"How old are you?" she repeated, her eyelids fluttering.

The thrum of her pulse, so strong at the outset, was becoming thready and weak.

"I was born in Greece hundreds of years before Christ."

"You're from ancient Greece in the classical period? Really?"

This news obviously thrilled her. She rallied just enough to lift her head to stare blindly at me as we were still in the dark.

"Yes. Really."

"What did you do there? For a living, I mean?"

"I was a priest at Delphi."

"Get out!"

"Excuse me?"

"You worked with the Oracle? Is it true the sibyl spoke in riddles?"

"Yes. It was my job to interpret them.'

She swooned in my arms and I was sure it wasn't from the blood loss. "You thirsted for knowledge even then. So much so that you worked your way into the sanctuary at Delphi. That's why you became a vampire, isn't it? You wanted to go on seeking . . . for ever. Just as I do."

"That's right," I said. "That's why I allowed myself to be turned." What a remarkable young woman, I thought, my earlier anger towards her for the pain she caused me was gone. Finally, a woman who understood me, and soon she would be dead at the point of my fangs.

"I have a thousand questions. I can't believe my luck. Not only do I finally find a real, live vampire, but he's an intellectual to boot. I promise I won't interrupt you any more. Is it time for me to drink your blood yet?"

I looked down at her and marvelled at her perfection both in body and in mind. I ran my hand through her silky hair, letting my thumb brush her cheek, which was by now as pale as alabaster. It was such a shame she had to die.

A cold wind sent leaves and litter swirling in a tiny whirlwind that skittered past me while I waited for my next class at Georgia State University. I'd chosen to move on to another institution of higher learning for the winter semester and put behind me the unpleasantness I'd gone through in nearby Athens, Georgia.

For a vampire who always anticipated living for ever, having come so close to death was a sobering experience, so I opted for a change of scene. GSU was an urban university, situated in the heart of downtown Atlanta. The inner city environment with its profusion of drug dealers, pimps and other criminals was a rich hunting ground.

"Come along now, dear. Don't play with your food," I admonished Victoria.

She was dangling her victim off the top level of the multi-storey parking deck on which we stood. She nodded and drew him back on to the concrete surface where she finished draining his blood. The man had made the mistake of attempting to carjack our vehicle as we entered the structure.

Oh, I killed Victoria that night in Athens all right. Killed her mortal body and made her into a blood drinker as she'd asked. For my part, I resolved to set aside my prejudices and tamp down my disgust for fledglings. The experience has proven to be a much-needed exercise in tolerance for me. After all, who am I to question the ways of the vampire?

When she'd drunk her fill, I stuffed the body into a nearby trash can and covered him with refuse. "Shall we?"

She smoothed her hair, straightened her skirt and took my arm. "Of course, dear," she said.

She begged me to let her jump down to street level, but I pointed out that someone would undoubtedly see her. Having to explain herself to a patrolman coming out of Atlanta police headquarters across the street would put a damper on the fun of flying.

"Of course, you're right. Whatever you say, darling," she said sweetly. "What would I do without you to keep me out of trouble? Let's take the elevator."

I removed a linen handkerchief from my pocket and dabbed away the trickle of blood from her chin. In time, she would cease to need the excitement of the kill and we would both feed together discreetly and without the need to hide the bodies of the miscreants she drained of blood.

As we walked to class arm in arm, I reflected on my good fortune. It had taken me some 3,000 years to find the woman meant just for me. I'd enjoyed being a scholar, but until Victoria, I'd never experienced the satisfaction of sharing my knowledge with someone who appreciated it. The student has become the teacher. And, as the youngsters used to say, the teacher digs it. And then, of course, there's the sex. I would never have dreamed that monogamy would be so . . . stimulating.

And what of my most enduring philosophical question – what is my purpose? I am now beginning to believe that my purpose as a blood drinker on this earth was to sire Victoria the vampire. So, at the risk of waxing as romantic as a smitten schoolboy, pardon me and my lady Victoria while we ride off into the proverbial sunset.

# Viper's Bite

## Delilah Devlin

*H*er hips swished beneath her short, flirty skirt, drawing his gaze like a magnet. He suppressed a low, rumbling growl from the beast rising inside him. The splash of large pink flowers on the white skirt stood out like a beacon in the darkness.

He followed her as she left her apartment, sticking to the shadows, ducking into stairwells when she looked behind her as though she sensed someone followed.

Her shoulder-length, flyaway brown hair bobbed across the tops of her slender shoulders. The creamy skin of her exposed arms and legs swung in a rhythm that his heart picked up and matched, beat for stride.

Feeling more like the true predator he was than ever, he suppressed shame that burned like battery acid in his stomach, and continued stalking the woman who walked more briskly now along the darkened sidewalk.

When she turned onto a crowded walkway, her shoulders sank and her steps slowed as she relaxed.

She believed herself safe now.

Little did she know, but her "spontaneous" decision to go out had been at his suggestion – a message telegraphed with tantalizing snippets of fresh salt air, the caress of a soft breeze and a glimpse of sensual pleasure.

She hadn't heeded her own natural inhibition. Hadn't paused to check the clock and note the waning evening hours. Instead, she'd made her decision, wriggled into her sexy little skirt and snug pink T-shirt, slid her feet into strapless sandals and bounded down the stairs, ready to kick off winter's gloom in an unseasonably warm spring night.

He'd made sure she didn't glance even once at the clock or the calendar resting on the bureau in her foyer.

And while he'd provided himself the opportunity to meet her, he'd decided days ago that he wouldn't use his persuasive gifts to bring her straight into his arms.

Tonight, he wanted to savour a natural seduction.

She paused along the gangway that followed the curving street through a long, outdoor mini-mall. At the bottom of one set of stairs leading up into a seafood restaurant, she lifted one foot, planting it on the first paved step.

He drew back the suggestion that had led her here. Her brow furrowed, and she shook her head. Her foot slipped off the step and slowly settled beside the other.

"Did you forget something?" he murmured behind her.

A gasp escaped her, and her head jerked to the side, then tilted up to meet his gaze. Her eyes widened, and then slid over his shoulders before rising again. "You frightened me."

The frown that bisected her brow amused him. She was annoyed and not bothering to hide it. Her eyes narrowed. "I know who you are."

Viper jerked imperceptibly. His heart tripped, and then thudded dully again. She couldn't mean what he thought. "Are you sure you're answering the correct question?" he asked, giving her a slight twist of his lips. More of a smile than most ever saw.

Her head shook, sending her fine, dark hair shivering silkily across her cheeks.

The urge to tuck her hair behind her ears was almost irresistible. He curled his fingers and stuffed his hands into the pockets of his faded jeans. "Who do you think I am?"

She hesitated. "I've seen you before. At one of those Goth clubs. You're the manager."

Viper suppressed a grin. She was talking about Dylan's club. "I'm just filling in for a friend at the Cavern, until he returns home. I have no ambition to run his place permanently."

"The Cavern." She nodded. "That's it. It's a strange place. I did a piece there about young Goths and the rise of Sanguinarian blood rituals.'

"You're a writer then? Or are you a television reporter?" he asked, knowing full well she wrote columns for the social section of the *Seattle Times*.

Her casual shrug belied the fact she was serious about her work. Ambitious even. The social section wouldn't encompass her ambition long.

He'd always loved that about her. She kept her eyes on the prize and rushed headlong wherever her curiosity and drive led her. An excellent quality for a reporter, but one that had spelled disaster for him.

But then, she didn't remember any of it. She hadn't learned her lesson because he'd needed her to remain safe.

"You know, they have a dress code here," she murmured, eyeing his black leather jacket and T-shirt, and then letting her glance slide quickly down his legs before rising again. A faint blush tinged her pale cheeks.

Viper's eyelids dipped. "I'm not planning on going inside. I was waiting . . . for someone."

"Lucky girl," she said softly, then shook her head again. "It's not like I have a reservation or anything, and I'm not dressed for it either. I'm not really sure why I stopped—"

His glance panned the line of people waiting patiently for their numbers to be called by the restaurant hostess who roamed outside, taking names on a clipboard. "Would you like to go somewhere else?" he said quickly, not wanting to let her go just yet, needing to work the moment in order to build her trust.

Time stretched between them. Her gaze flitted down the row of well-lit shops, still open with people walking leisurely along the covered walkway. A soft evening mist muted the glare of the street lamps and the sounds of the people passing them by as they stood at the bottom of the steps leading into the trendy restaurant.

"I promise I don't bite," he said, fighting the urgency building in his body to keep his words light and casual. "We can just take a walk. Find a cup of coffee, if you like."

He wanted her to say yes, without any extra "persuasion" from him. He wanted her to choose him of her own free will.

A long indrawn breath lifted her chest, and she gave him a small, tentative smile. "There's a Starbucks at the end of the mall."

Warmth seeped into his chest. And although he knew tomorrow he'd pay a heavy price, he needed to spend tonight . . . with her.

Viper tugged his hands from his pockets and crooked an elbow, feeling a little foolish for the old-fashioned gesture. His manners felt a little rusty.

Her hand slid around his forearm, her fingers lightly resting atop the leather. Through the barrier he shouldn't have been able to note the heat of her hands, but he did.

"Shall we?" he asked, and then stepped out, shortening his natural stride to allow her to walk comfortably beside him.

"You haven't even asked my name."

*It's Mariah.* "You haven't asked mine."

Soft, rueful laughter floated around him. "I'm not like this. I don't let strangers lead me around." She ducked her head, perhaps to hide the new blush staining her cheeks. "I'm Mariah Cohen."

He pressed his lips to halt the automatic response. Tonight he wasn't Viper. "I'm Daniel Vacarro," he said softly and held his breath. Would the name niggle at her memory?

"Daniel. Not Danny?"

He shuddered.

She laughed again. "Not manly enough?"

He gave her a narrowed glance.

"See?" she said, a smile curving her lush lips. "We're already getting to know each other."

"Are you always a smart ass with complete strangers?"

"We aren't strangers, *Daniel.* I admit, tonight I feel just a little reckless, but I recognized you right off. We're just taking a short walk in the middle of a crowd of people. What's the worst that can happen?"

Viper shook his head. The woman was crazy. But she was right. The only danger he posed was to her sweet, curvy body.

His fingers curled over hers, pressing them against his forearm. "This is the place." He swept her into Starbucks and stood in the long line.

As the people waiting in front of them peeled away, one at a time, some patting pockets for "missing wallets", some squinting at the menu board as though they suddenly couldn't read it, Mariah stood quietly beside him, bewilderment rounding her eyes as the line melted completely away. "This never happens."

"What would you like?" he deferred to her, hiding a smug smile. So, he'd worked a little of his magic on the other customers. *Bite me.*

She placed her order, and then lifted a brow.

"Nothing for me."

"You didn't come for the coffee?"

"I'm not an addict."

"Afraid you won't be able to sleep tonight?"

"Who's gonna sleep?" he murmured under his breath.

Her tongue swept out to wet her lower lip, but she let him pull her aside to wait at the end of the barista's counter. "But you didn't pay."

Viper shrugged. "I know them."

"Right," she said, her tone indicating she didn't quite believe him. "Did you wink at the girl or something?"

"Why? Do you think I'm irresistible?"

Her soft feminine snort was followed by a slow, dazed shake of her head. "I'm here, aren't I? And we just met ten minutes ago."

Viper closed his eyes for a bit, trying to keep his memories at bay and just enjoy the moment. She had no way of knowing how much her innocent comment ate his resolve. They'd met a long time before this night.

Her order was called, and he opened his eyes, watching as she gave him a concerned look, and then stepped forwards to claim her cup. "Do you want to stay here?" she asked.

The press of warm-blooded bodies around him felt suffocating and far too tempting. "Let's walk."

Outside again, he raised his face to the warm breeze and drank in the cleansing air. "Sorry about that. I don't like crowds much."

"I got that. There are tables just down the way. Want to sit down?"

He nodded, hoping his sudden melancholy would vanish. He had only a few hours to spend with her, if she let him, before he had to return to his world.

As she walked, she played with the plastic lid, then took a quick sip. Her eyes drifted closed. "Mmmm . . . this was just what I needed."

They reached the tables outside a cafe. Viper chose one at the outer edges of the extended courtyard and pulled out a chair, waiting as she settled before taking his own beside hers, rather than across the table.

She didn't seem to mind, just sipped her coffee quietly while eyeing him above the rim of her cup.

He wondered what she saw.

He'd been careful with his appearance. Sure he wore the same weathered jacket, a plain T-shirt and jeans, but he'd polished his boots and used a brush on his long black hair instead of his fingers. He knew women found him attractive, but Mariah wasn't into dark, dangerous men with sharp-edged features and hungry eyes. Or at least she hadn't been.

"Are you always this talkative?"

Right. He should at least pretend to be polite, however out of practice it felt. "Does it bother you? My not talking."

"It's a little unnerving." Her glance met his then slid away quickly, but her shoulders tilted towards him. "I expected you'd be hitting on me by now.'

The subtle body language, crossed messages of shy interest, set his blood simmering. "Are you disappointed I'm not?"

"Just a little uncomfortable," she said, placing her cup on the table and then wrapping her hands around it.

"Why?"

"Because I'm tempted to hit on you." She wrinkled her nose. "I did just say that, didn't I?"

His lips stretched. "Yeah, you did."

Her head canted as she eyed his mouth. "Are you gay?"

"Do I give off that vibe?"

"Not at all. But in my experience, a man doesn't need more than a smile as encouragement to bust a move."

"And you think I might be gay because I'm trying to be a gentleman?"

"You have to try?"

He nodded slowly.

She blew out a breath between pursed lips. "That's a relief. Although I'd already guessed you're a predator."

He lifted both eyebrows. "Do I seem that sinister?"

"Not like a serial killer, but you could probably have any woman you want without even trying, so why haven't you tried . . . with me . . . seeing as you're not gay?"

"I wasn't sure you were interested. You seemed to hesitate back there at the restaurant. I didn't want to spook you."

"So you do—" She sucked her lower lip between her teeth.

"I do what?"

"Want me?" Her gaze rose slowly to his again, her breath hitched, lifting her small breasts.

He swallowed, wondering if he'd subconsciously sent out the idea, making it impossible for her to choose.

Her eyes blinked rapidly. "Don't feel like you have to," she said quickly. "I didn't mean to put you on the spot. I guess I'm just in a funny kind of mood. I don't want to say goodbye to you. Not yet."

Viper settled back in his chair. "You don't have to invite me to your bed if all you want is company," he said gruffly.

Her glance slid away as she pretended to study the string of lights surrounding a toy shop across the courtyard. "But what if I want more?" she whispered.

Because he wanted to read her expression, he gave in to the urge to touch her hair and tucked a softly curling lock behind her ear.

Her gaze swung back to him. Her lips parted as she drew in a soft, shaky breath.

He cleared his throat and leaned closer to whisper for her ears only. "I'd ask, why me? Why tonight?"

Again, her plump lips pressed together, then parted. "Well, it's not because you were the first man to say hello to me tonight, if that's what you think. I wasn't really prowling for sex."

"Then what was it?"

"Fishing for compliments?" When he didn't respond, she lifted her shoulders. "Guess you don't need them."

Viper held himself still, determined to wait her out.

Her finely arched brows drew together and her jaw tightened for just a moment. "All right. I just feel – I don't know – a little lonely tonight. I thought maybe you felt the same way."

Viper felt a burning at the back of his eyes and looked away. Because he couldn't speak past the lump lodged at the back of his throat, he nodded his head.

Her hand reached out and smoothed over the top of his. Her large brown eyes looked at him with sadness that mirrored his own. "Maybe we just need each other tonight. That's all it has to be."

She was reassuring him that there wouldn't be any strings? "You should expect more," he rasped.

"Maybe tomorrow I will. But tonight, I'd just be satisfied to know you don't want anyone but me."

Viper forced a small smile. "Want to fall in love with me tonight?"

"Does that sound so silly?"

His hand lifted and cupped the side of her face. "It sounds just about perfect."

Mariah tilted her head to deepen his caress. "I don't live very far from here."

He couldn't believe how quickly things had progressed. How *naturally*. "Sure you want to bring me back to your place?"

"I'm inviting you, aren't I?"

"You'll be safe with me. Tonight."

Her eyes widened. "I just shivered."

"Call a friend. Knock on a neighbour's door. Let them see my face; I'll give them my ID. I don't want you to worry about me."

Her gaze locked with his for a long breathless moment, then the corners of her lips lifted in a whimsical smile. "I'm not worried you'll murder me or anything. And since I've already offered you my body – that pretty much rules out any molesting, unless it's me doing it to you."

Viper drew in a deep breath and began to relax, determined to enjoy her gentle aggression. "We haven't even kissed. How do you know you'll like being with me?"

One brow arched. "Are you kidding me? Have you looked in a mirror lately? Maybe you don't find me all that attractive."

"Who hit on whom?"

Her smile deepened. "Ooh! A man who knows his grammar. I'm completely turned on now. Not the most elegant sentence, but there's something to be said for brevity."

"Are you nervous?"

"Why do you ask?"

"You're beginning to ramble," he murmured. His fingers tugged at the lock of hair that kept slipping from behind her ear. "Come closer."

Her glance dropped to his lips. "You're thinking about that kiss we haven't shared?"

"I want a taste of that coffee you sighed over."

She leaned closer. "Did I sound too orgasmic?"

"Is that even possible?" he said, his lips curving again.

"Why do I get the feeling you don't smile very much?"

"Because I don't."

"You don't have to be lonely, so why are you?"

Deflecting the question, he drew back a fraction of an inch. "You're attractive enough that a thousand men would want you. Why are you lonely?"

"I guess I just haven't felt a connection. Do you know what I mean?"

Viper knew exactly what she meant. He sat across from the only woman he'd ever felt he belonged with. "I never gave it much thought," he lied.

Her eyes narrowed. "That is such a *man* thing to say."

Because he didn't want to lie again, he raised his other hand slowly and slipped it behind her neck. Her eyelids fluttered closed, and her head fell back, supported by the palm cupping her now. He shifted towards the edge of his seat and leaned into her, staring at her parted lips.

The first tentative touch almost made him come unglued. His body tightened against the urge to take her to the ground and cover her. Instead, he breathed softly through his nose, pressed his lips against hers and canted his head to deepen the pressure. A low, breathy moan seeped into his mouth. He circled his head slowly, dragging his lips over hers, suctioning softly until she gasped, and he gently thrust his tongue inside. The taste of her – coffee, a lingering hint of mint from her toothpaste, her own sweet flavour – sent a fine tremor racing down his spine.

Her head drew back and her tongue traced her bottom lip. "Are you reassured now we got that out of the way?" she asked, the glibness of her words betrayed by the breathless delivery.

Viper settled his forehead against hers. "How far did you say your place is?"

"We can be there in five."

"Make it four," he muttered, and then stood, holding out his hand to pull her up.


They arrived hand in hand and winded at her front door.

Viper cut a quick glance around them, straining for the crunch of footsteps and the beat of telltale heart, but none lingered in the shadows around them.

They hadn't been followed.

Earlier, before he'd stalked her, he'd been careful not to lead anyone to her door. He'd scrubbed the scent of blood, booze and cigarettes from his skin and hair, and dressed in freshly laundered clothing. He'd laid down a trail in the opposite direction from her house and backtracked. No one would ever connect her to him. No one could ever know how precious she was. The seamy underbelly of the dark world he moved inside would never touch her.

He'd sacrificed everything to make sure of that.

Her keys jangled as she clumsily fit one into the lock. "Don't be expecting too much. I didn't know I'd bring company back with me tonight."

The door swung open, and she stepped inside.

Viper followed on her heels, not letting her put space between them. His hands gripped the sides of her hips, and he pushed her deeper inside before kicking the door closed behind them.

Then he pulled her backwards, wrapping his arms around her waist and gliding his lips along the top of her shoulder and up her neck, finding the pulse thrumming just beneath the skin.

Her head fell back, and his teeth began the slow slide downwards. He jerked back his head, trying to get control of himself.

She drew deep, rasping breaths into her lungs. "What's wrong? Why did you stop?"

Knowing he'd lisp around his elongated teeth, he shook his head against hers and smoothed his hands over her firm belly, then upwards to cup her breasts through her clothing.

She kicked off her sandals and slid downwards. Her clothing rustled. When her skirt dragged against his jeans on its downward journey, he rucked up her shirt and pulled it over her head.

She opened the front clasp of her bra and his palms enclosed her breasts, squeezing lightly.

"I like that," she whispered, rubbing her back and shoulders against him. "But you have too many clothes on."

He turned her in his arms, reached down to cup her bottom and lifted her.

Her legs wrapped around his waist and her mouth landed on his cheek, his chin . . .

He turned his face to avoid her mouth. "Your bedroom?" he bit out, although he already knew.

Mariah lifted her arm to point and snuggled her cheek alongside his as he moved through her darkened living room and down the short corridor to her bedroom.

A single lamp beside the bed lit the room. He stepped towards the bed and climbed onto the mattress, taking her to the centre before lowering his body to blanket her.

"This isn't going to work," she murmured.

He ignored her complaint and trailed his mouth down her neck, shielding his teeth behind his lips until he reached her breasts.

A soft cry filled the air above him as he stroked her with his tongue, chancing nibbles with his front teeth.

Her fingers thrust through his long hair, combing it, pulling it as he deepened the suctioning that drew her nipples into taut beads.

"Danny . . ."

Not Daniel, as he'd insisted. Did some small corner of her mind remember him after all? He pulled away and sat up to strip off his jacket and his T-shirt, then tossed them to the floor behind him.

Her hands reached for his belt and opened it. She thumbed open the waist of his pants, then groaned when he backed off the bed to remove his boots and jeans.

When he climbed back on, her greedy gaze raked his body. Viper noted her heightened arousal in the flare of her nostrils and quickening breaths.

Her legs parted at his first gentle nudge. He reached down to lift her knees and arrange them on either side of his hips. Then he lowered himself, closing his eyes as his skin met hers. *Pure heaven*.

He was gonna roast in hell.

"This too fast for you?" he gritted out.

"I need you moving inside me. Now, please."

Her tight, urgent words were exactly what he wanted to hear. He lifted his hips and slid a hand between their bodies. His fingers closed around himself, and he fitted the tip to her entrance and slowly thrust inside.

Her eyes closed tightly and her thighs clasped him, her hips tilting to receive him.

He settled his cheek beside hers and stroked deep into her liquid heat. Surrounded by her creamy walls, he began to move, his body shuddering, already in the grip of his growing arousal.

Planting his knees in the mattress, he slipped his arms beneath her thighs and lifted her hips off the bed, churning, thrusting and circling his hips to tunnel deeper inside her sweet body.

Her arms wrapped around his back. Her fingertips scraped up and down, digging into his skin to urge him deeper, faster.

His motions increased in strength and intensity. He jerked against her, beginning a sweet pummelling that moved her up the slippery silk comforter. He followed, not letting her escape, not giving her a moment to deepen the quivering breaths that gusted against his cheek.

Wrapped inside her arms, sliding into her deliciously wet channel, he fought the tension growing inside him, not wanting to surrender, not willing to allow the beast inside him to crawl out and take his pleasure and her blood.

The internal battle he fought made him sweat and tremble.

When her first shivers rippled along his shaft and her internal muscles clamped hard around him, he groaned and opened his mouth to suckle the salt and perfume from her neck, testing with his tongue until he felt the surge of blood beneath her skin, and he gave into the urge to taste.

His razor-sharp teeth slid into flesh, nicking the artery.

A sharp hiss sounded in his ear and her hands came between them, shoving at his chest. Her body bucked, writhing under him.

But he didn't let go, even knowing he'd hurt her. *Wait, let it happen.*

The next frightened roll of her hips brought him deeper and she groaned, her fingers now sinking in the hair on his chest to clutch him closer.

Her body spasmed, her back arched hard and a low agonized moan squeezed from her tight throat.

Still he held back his own release, letting hers sweep through her, knowing the exact moment it happened because a keening cry rose around them.

When the quivering beneath him lessened, he withdrew his teeth, lapped at the tiny wounds to close them and drew back his head to stare down into her pale, shocked face.

"I know who you are," she said, her voice rasping painfully. Tears welled in her eyes, but didn't spill over. Her lips trembled.

"Who do you think I am?" he asked, afraid she might have gleaned the truth.

"Husband," she whispered, moisture finally leaking from her eyes to track down the sides of her cheeks and slip into her sweat-dampened hair.

Viper dived down to cover her mouth, stroking his tongue inside, greeting hers, claiming the taste of her as he continued to plow deep inside her body.

"Let me see," she said, tears thickening her voice.

Viper closed his eyes and let the beast surface, welcoming the primal force that scratched its way through his conscience to reveal itself.

His body stiffened, muscles hardened. Every part of him strained outwards. Even his sex, lengthening, thickening, pressing relentlessly against her inner walls until her hips undulated beneath him.

Another wash of quivering release shook her body, shuddering through him, as she cried out, her nails scraping harder, drawing blood from his back.

A deep, rasping growl built at the back of his throat, and he drew back his hips and lunged forwards, powering into her now, sliding through her tightening channel, churning in the cream that slid around him, until, at last, he threw back his head and roared.

Viper didn't know how long he lay atop her, his body racked by fine tremors as the beast eased away, sliding back into his cavern. But he came to awareness with her hands gliding over his skin, cupping his shoulders, petting his hair, sliding along his slick back as she hiccuped beneath him.

She was crying.

Slipping his hands beneath her, he rolled onto his back, bringing her over him. He cupped the back of her head and urged her face into the crook of his neck. His lips brushed her crown once, then he settled beneath her, waiting for her tears to dry while he held her close.

"I remember everything," she whispered.

"I wish you didn't," he said tonelessly.

"How cruel is that?" she bit out, lifting her head to glare into his face. "You took everything from me."

"I wanted you safe."

The corners of her lips turned downwards. "I understand why you did it, but how do you bear it? Knowing what we had."

Viper swallowed and slipped his hands around her back to

hug her closer. "I get through every single day," he said, his voice roughening, 'because I know you're nearby. I know you live. And that's enough."

Her head shook slowly. "Will you leave me again without even a glimpse of our past?"

The rasp in her voice scraped him raw. "I . . . have to."

She snorted, her mouth stretching into a sad jeer. "This is why I can't move on, you know. Something inside me knows about you."

Move on? He closed his eyes, praying for the strength. "I can take that as well." He opened his eyes to meet her steady gaze. "I can free you."

"You'd let me take another lover? Another husband?"

While inside he wailed and thrashed, he schooled his face into a mask. "I want you happy. Safe."

She laid her head on his shoulder and rubbed her cheek against him. "It's our anniversary today, isn't it?"

Hoping she'd given up and had decided not to rant as she had the last time he'd sought her out, he exhaled slowly. "I'm sorry. I didn't get you anything."

Her fingers plucked his chest hair hard. "There are other choices you know," she said, her voice hardening. "Ones I should have the free will to make."

"You can't come with me."

"Because it's too dangerous? I remember that. You shoved me out the door of that warehouse, out into the street, while you stayed inside."

"I saved your life."

"You sacrificed ours. You didn't have the right to make that decision alone."

"Well, it's done now. No going back."

"Except you do – keep coming back, that is."

"So I'm weak."

Her fingers relaxed, and she lifted her head. "You could let me come with you."

The plea in her brown eyes nearly had him relenting. "You can't come with me," he repeated dully. "I don't want you to see what I've become, how I live."

"You're a vampire." She pressed her face into his chest. "God, they really do exist. I kept thinking there was something more . . ."

"That Goth club isn't just a place for the wannabes. Vamps feed there. Not all of them are nice. You shouldn't have gone there."

"Why can't you just make me one, too? Let me stay with you."

"Turning is too dangerous. As many die as make the change. I won't risk you."

"Don't I even get a say?"

"Mariah . . ." He lifted her head, forcing her to meet his gaze. How could he make her understand? "Dying isn't the worst thing that can happen."

Her eyes and nose were red now, her face wet with smeared tears. "Then explain it. Make me understand how you could just abandon me."

His thumbs wiped away the tears, then he slipped his hands beneath her arms and pulled her higher until her face hovered just above his. "Your soul could slip away, not make the journey. If that happened, I'd have to kill you." He forced himself to finish it, despite the jagged edge entering his voice, despite the burning at the back of his throat. "I just . . . can't." Tears landed on his cheeks.

"I remember the day you disappeared. I thought I saw you outside. On the sidewalk."

"I had been attacked, turned. Bloodlust overcame me. I had just enough sense left to know I couldn't come to you. I would have devoured you."

"Where did you go?"

"To a den. An orgy. Blood in buckets. I sated myself, then got sicker than a dog."

"What about women? Has there been anyone else?"

Although he knew the answer would hurt her, he wouldn't lie. "No one that mattered."

Her eyes closed.

"Bloodlust, sexual lust. They're both primal hungers and have to be fed or we get crazy. Even the most devoted lovers have to feed outside their relationship."

She sniffed and wiped a hand across her face. "I don't know if I could do that. Let you be with someone else."

"Do you see why I left? Why I didn't seek you out?"

"You couldn't have just broken it off? Left me something, if only my memories?"

"I was afraid you would try to find me. That you wouldn't be able to resist.'

Her eyes narrowed. Then a small, tight smile curved her lips. "Again, you think you're so irresistible?"

He lifted one brow. "Aren't I? To you?"

Wry humour gleamed in her eyes. "You had me here in this bed inside a half an hour. I guess you're right." She released a deep sigh. "Danny, what happens now?"

"We have a little time left before I have to get back."

"How will you do it? Make me forget?"

"I'll kiss you. When I leave you won't remember me at all."

"Danny . . ."

"Yes?"

"You've come to me before, haven't you? Like this. I don't want you to free me. If this is all we have, just these few hours of . . . connection. I accept it."

"It's not fair to you."

"How would you feel, knowing I'm in this world, but not waiting for you?"

She wasn't thinking about herself. The thought nearly made him weep. "I'd be in hell," he muttered. "But I'm willing to let you go. I want you happy."

"I'm not unhappy. Just . . . asexual. And I don't miss it. I don't even know I shouldn't feel that way. I want this again. With you. Please."

"All right," he said gruffly, his throat tightening.

Her head canted. "Have you offered me this choice before?"

"Yes."

Her eyebrows rose and small grin stretched her lips. "It's good to know I'm consistent. Are you still a cop?"

"I work undercover," he hedged. How could he explain he ran one of those vampire dens now, rolled around in bed most nights with willing blood hosts and pretended to befriend the most vicious of the undead? Even if it was for a just cause? "You done crying?"

"I don't want to waste our time together crying, but I do have one more question. Where's my wedding ring?"

Viper sighed and untangled himself from her body. He rolled off the bed and reached for his jeans. He drew out his wallet, slipped his fingers into a narrow pocket and pulled out the gleaming circle of gold.

When he turned, she lifted her hand and waited while he slid it onto her finger. He curled her fingers and raised her hand to his lips, giving it a kiss. Tears gleamed in her eyes, but she smiled and opened her arms. He climbed over her, stretching his body to cover every part of her.

"Was it the bite? Is that how I remembered you?"

He nodded as he tenderly brushed the hair from her cheeks. "I can't seem to resist that part."

"Don't ever come to me without letting me see."

"I promise."

"Make love to me again?"

"I can't think of anything I'd rather do. But if you want, I can just hold you."

Her nose wrinkled. "You were never a snuggler."

"I've matured," he scoffed, feigning a lightness of heart he just couldn't feel. "I'm content just touching you."

"Well, I'm not." She pulled him closer and opened her legs. "Leave me aching. I'll wonder about it in the morning. I'll think I dreamed it all."

He bent down and kissed her, not wanting to think about leaving her again.

This time, urgency didn't drive him. He took his time, entering her so slowly she complained, lifting her hips to force him deeper.

Their loving was slow, savoured, poignant, because this time they both remembered the many times they'd been here, holding each other tightly. Their kisses were all the sweeter because they knew they'd have to make them matter.

He held back, thrusting faster, harder. Sliding a hand between their bodies, he caressed the tiny knot of nerves that shot her ahead of him, so that he could watch her come.

As her mouth opened around a quiet scream, he let go, joining her, groaning deeply as his body and heart emptied into her.

Viper waited until her eyes fluttered open, and her gaze met his for the last time. Her smile said she forgave him, and she touched his cheek.

The kiss wasn't needed, but he wanted her to close her eyes. He closed his as he stole one memory after another, letting them flicker through his mind.

Their first meeting at the station house where she tried to prise information about a drug arrest. She'd spotted him and become distracted enough that the exasperated PR officer slipped away. The first time they'd made love. A frenzied, delirious coupling in the front seat of his car when he'd tried to play the gentleman and drop her at her door after their first date. Fishing on a borrowed boat. Only they hadn't caught a single thing, except raging sunburn in intimate places.

Their wedding. Mariah dressed in white and beaming as she'd stood in front of the Justice of the Peace and repeated her vows in an excited rush, eager for the pronouncement that would make her his for ever.

When at last he'd finished, he sobbed once, kissed her closed eyes and slipped from the bed.

Lieutenant Moses Brown waited outside, his large frame leaning against his unmarked car. When he saw Viper, he straightened and flicked away his cigarette. "Thought I might find you here. Need a ride back?"

Viper slid into the passenger seat, keeping his face turned straight ahead. Not looking back.

"Did you let her go this time, buddy?"

Viper nodded.

"It's for the best. The girl can get on with her life."

"I know."

"We have work to do. With Navarro gone, the natives are getting restless. They think the territory's up for grabs."

"Guess I'll have to make a play for it, won't I?"

"Damn shame about the missus."

"I don't want to talk about it."

"I understand. You sure you didn't leave any clues? Nothing she might use to connect the dots this time?"

"I wiped her mind of everything. I'm sure." Feeling drained, he leaned his head against the headrest and closed his eyes.

Then he remembered. *The ring*. He hadn't removed it from her finger.

He jerked upright.

"You OK? You forget something?"

It was on the tip of his tongue to tell his friend to turn around. Instead, he relaxed. Maybe she'd wake up, find the ring and wonder, but without the memories to accompany it, could she really find him?

The tantalizing thought was just enough to ease him past the sadness he thought he couldn't bear. Maybe, this time, she'd find him.

It was enough. A wisp of hope to hold on to. Feeling lighter, he rolled down the window and let the soft, salt breeze whisk away his dour mood. "So, about these natives, Moses. We talking fangs?"

# Dreams

## Keri Arthur

In the dreams they shared, there was always desire.

It was the slip of a hand across silky, golden skin. The sigh of quick breath past the lips he always longed to kiss, both in these dreams and in life.

The way she thrust back her head and moaned as he caressed her breasts, the gleam of her red hair under the candlelit warmth that always seemed to encase these moments between wakefulness. Whether that light was by her design or his didn't really matter because all that *did* matter was the two of them.

And these precious moments of intimacy.

The dream went on. He watched the rapid beat of the pulse at her neck. Could almost smell the thick sweetness of the blood that ran underneath her skin. Blood he ached to roll across his taste buds yet again.

She moaned his name, a sound sweeter than life itself. He reached for her, pulling her spirit towards him, wrapping his own around her. Claiming her with a completeness that she would never allow in wakefulness.

But she was his in a way she would probably never understand. He might one day be forced to walk away, but he could never let her go completely. She was a part of him. He'd shared his blood with her and tasted her soul, and there was no turning away from the consequences of that. Not for one such as him – a creature who was more myth and magic than darkness.

He was something that should not be, even in this age of vampire rights and human acknowledgment – if not complete acceptance – that the things that went bump in the night were very real indeed.

But for now, there were just the two of them and this dream. It was everything and nothing, and it would do until they met again in the flesh.

Which would be soon. They'd been apart for too long now.

So he kissed her, caressed her, loved her, until the heat that rose between them would not be denied. And then he took her, their dream bodies merging, hot phantom flesh against hot phantom flesh – desperate, hungry and demanding.

The intensity, the desire, rose to even greater heights, until they were shaking with the need of completion. And as she came, he bit her, sinking his teeth into her imaginary flesh, into her vein, until both her blood and her being rushed into his mouth. And it was so sweet, so rapturous a sensation, that he came, his body thrusting against hers urgently, as needful as she.

But however sweet the dreams, their aftermath was always sour. Because there was no lying in the sweaty heat of each other's arms. No holding her sated body until sleep claimed them both. No savouring the delicious rush of warmth through his body that her blood always provided.

There was nothing more than a fading into blackness, until the feeling of utter loneliness once again filled the void of his world.

He sighed and opened his eyes. The pleasure he'd shared in the dream still assuaged his body, and his heart beat with more vigour than usual, though it was nowhere near that of a human in normal circumstances, let alone after lovemaking. And yet he felt incomplete. The dreams were good, but he wanted more. Wanted her, for real. In the flesh.

Up ahead, the lights of Melbourne twinkled, neon bright against the clear darkness of the night. He hadn't actually come down here to see Riley Jenson. Indeed, given how angry she'd been after his ultimatum that she either include him in her life willingly or he'd force her compliance, he'd pretty much figured he'd better let sleeping dogs lie for a while. And given she was a werewolf that was no mere figure of speech. As bitches went, she could be pretty damn ornery when she wanted to be.

And yet the very thing that annoyed him the most was the same thing that pulled him towards her – her vitality, her strength, her independence.

He wanted that tonight. Wanted her.

He leaned forwards and pressed the button that lowered the screen between him and the limo's driver. "Henry, there's been a change of plans. Head for Ms Jenson's address first."

"Yes, sir." The driver's voice was polite and unfazed. But then Henry had been working for him for several hundred years now. The unexpected had become somewhat commonplace.

The streets slid by smoothly and his anticipation grew. Odd that after all these years a mere pup could have him feeling so alive again – even if she did also frustrate the hell out of him with her werewolf morals and free-and-easy ways.

But he had every intention of changing that. Eventually. He was not fool enough to think such things would happen overnight, however much he might wish otherwise.

The limo came to a halt outside the dour brick building that was her home. He looked up, seeing no lights shining from the top-floor windows. She was still asleep, then.

He fought the images of sliding naked into bed beside her, of caressing her flesh for real and not just in dreams, and climbed out as Henry opened the door. "Go to the hotel and get some rest," he said, breathing in the cool night air, letting the heat and life of those within the building flow through him. "I'll call when I need you."

"Thank you, sir."

He smiled at Henry's formality, then walked up the grimy concrete steps and went through the door. This building was rarely locked, the inhabitants apparently unconcerned about the drug-related crimes that abounded in this area. Odd considering the only ones truly capable of protecting themselves in this building were Riley and her brother.

He climbed the stairs rapidly, making little sound. The thick heat of life swam all around him, the melodious beat of blood through human flesh, such a wonderfully haunting sound.

He reached the top floor and opened the stairwell door. A solitary globe gleamed forlornly down the far end, leaving the rest of the hall to shadows and darkness. His friend, this darkness, and Riley's. Perhaps that was why she never insisted that maintenance replace all the broken lights. As a part vampire, she could hide in the shadows as well as he.

He walked to her door, letting his senses expand, feeling for her. She slumbered, waiting for him, as insatiable in her dreams as she was in life.

She wasn't alone in the apartment, though. The beat of another heart echoed through the silence. Rhoan, her brother, undoubtedly.

He smiled and entered her apartment. She'd invited him over her threshold long ago, and there was nothing now that she could do to keep him out. It was one of the few vampire laws literature actually got right.

The apartment was in its usual mess, clothes and newspapers strewn everywhere. Neither she nor her brother enjoyed housekeeping, though Rhoan tended to be a little more domestic than Riley.

His smile grew as he headed for her bedroom. Only to stop short in the bedroom doorway.

The other life he'd sensed wasn't Rhoan. She might be asleep and dreaming of him, but she was sharing her bed with another wolf. His nemesis, and rival for her affections, Kellen Sinclair.

Rage rose in him, thick and fast, and, for several seconds, it was all he could do not to rip the other man from the bed and throw him out of the apartment. Not out through the door, but through a window, so that he could smash down onto the pavement below and be gone from her life for ever.

Damn it, she was *his*. His being had claimed her, and he would not willingly share her, no matter what she thought or desired.

She must have sensed his anger, because she stirred under the sheets, murmuring something he couldn't quite catch. She turned, the sheet slipping down her body, revealing the golden skin and full breasts he'd been caressing in his dreams.

Desire stirred beneath the anger. He wanted her for real. Right here, right now. And he'd be damned if he'd walk away and leave her in the arms of his rival. Not tonight, when loneliness was high and his body and soul ached with need for her.

His gaze switched to Kellen. Slipping into the other man's slumbering thoughts was easy enough, as the fool wore no shields against psychic intrusion. His dreaming state was filled with sated thoughts and happiness, and again the anger stirred through Quinn. It would be easy enough to slip deep into unconscious thought, to command Kellen to walk away and never come back. To never touch or contact Riley again.

So easy.

So, *so* tempting.

But Riley would wonder why he'd walked so abruptly, and she'd go after him for a reason. Given her considerable psychic talents, it wouldn't take her long to uncover his interference.

And that would only make her angry. Possibly angry enough to end their somewhat tenuous relationship. The risk wasn't worth it, not until he was sure of her feelings.

Though nothing could stop him from ordering the man away from her side now.

He connected lightly to her sleeping mind, keeping her unaware. Then he forced the young wolf up, ordered him to dress and marched him out of the apartment. He stopped at the door, but kept the mental leash on the young wolf until he'd driven away. He'd wake in his own bed and wonder how in the hell he'd gotten there.

Amusement ran through him. No one had ever said love was fair, and he had every intention of playing as dirty as he could to win Riley's affections.

He blew out a breath, and turned to re-enter the apartment.

And in that moment, he sensed the wrongness.

He froze, reaching out with both his telepathic and empathic senses, searching for anything – or anyone – out of place. Riley's apartment was peaceful, the beat of her life force strong and rich in the silence. There was no hint of anything wrong.

No, whatever it was, it was coming from below.

He frowned, letting his senses flow downwards, sifting quickly through the various floors, searching for the source of that oddness. Humans dozed, some dreaming, some not, the beat of their lifeblood thick and strong in the darkness. Hunger stirred, but it was a slumberous thing, easily controlled.

There were no humans, no non-humans, not even rodents, in the building's basement. But the sense of wrongness seemed to be coming from there.

Only what might be causing it, he couldn't exactly say. There was an odd sort of deadness to the feel of the thing, as if whatever it was had no heat or breath of life. It wasn't moving, wasn't even doing anything untowards, but yet its mere presence made him uneasy.

It wasn't something that should be in this building.

He turned to investigate, but at that moment, Riley appeared.

"And the dream man appears in the flesh." Though a smile touched her lush lips, annoyance sparkled in her cool grey eyes. "Which undoubtedly means you're the reason Kellen's no longer asleep in my bed."

"I'm afraid so." Surprisingly, she'd dressed – if you could call a thigh-length T-shirt and little else dressing – and in the cool night air, the heat of her golden skin flowed across his senses as sweetly as a caress. It made him hunger to touch her, taste her, and he curled his fingers into a fist to stop the impulse to reach for her. "He'll wake safe and secure in his own bed, although he may be a little confused as to how he got there."

"You'd better hope he comes to no harm as he sleepwalks his way home." Her annoyance momentarily caressed the air, a rumble of distant thunder that held the promise to be a whole lot more. "It would have been easier if you'd just phoned ahead and let me know you were coming."

"I would have, but it was a last-minute decision."

"And as usual, you simply expect me to be sitting around in my apartment waiting for you." She shook her head, then added, "Is there any particular reason you're haunting the hallway rather than coming inside?"

"I've just sensed something out of place in the basement."

She frowned, and power shimmered across his skin as she flung out her psychic senses. In very many ways, her psi powers were as powerful as his. Only hers were still growing.

"It feels very odd." Her gaze met his again, and this time those silver depths were alive with excitement – and not just the excitement of the chase. Danger was an aphrodisiac to a wolf, and her hunger had his own blood racing. Such a reaction was a pleasant sensation for one as old as he, and it was something she'd brought back into his life. "Shall we go see just what might be down there?"

His gaze slid down her luscious body. "Dressed like that?"

Amusement teased her juicy lips. "You're right. Wait until I get some shoes on." She turned and ran for the bedroom.

He shook his head and smiled. Only a werewolf would consider shoes the only thing that outfit needed to be decent.

She came back with sturdy-looking sneakers on her feet and a laser in her hand. Once upon a time, carrying a gun would have been unthinkable to her. He wished it still was, simply because the more she carried, the more it meant she was sinking deeper into the world of the guardians. And he had no doubt that it would take her life one day. Not even a werewolf with vampire blood and extraordinary powers could keep flirting with death and not have it eventually take control. Although, if carrying a gun kept her safe for that little bit longer, he wasn't about to argue against it.

Because above everything else, he wanted her safe.

They walked back to the stairs. Though they moved as quietly as possible, their footsteps still echoed down the stairwell. In the cellar, the darkness stirred, and a sense of anticipation seemed to flow across the blackness.

"Whatever it is, it waits for us."

He glanced back at her as he spoke, and she raised an eyebrow. "Us specifically?"

"It would seem so."

She grunted, and her fingers tightened around the laser. The weapon whined as it powered up. "So why the two of us in a building filled with people?"

"I don't know." He opened the stairwell door. The basement was dark – no surprise given the lack of lights in the rest of the building. Not that it was a problem for either of them – their infrared vision made the most out of darkness.

"You can't read it empathically?" she asked.

"Not at the moment." He caught the door with his fingertips once she'd stepped through, easing it closed as quietly as possible.

Energy burned across his skin as she probed the darkness telepathically. "There's a deadness ahead that feels oddly familiar."

Though little more than a whisper, her words seemed to jar the stale air. Deep in the basement's darkness, something stirred, and the sense of deadness seemed to retreat.

"It's moving," he said, rather unnecessarily.

"Yes."

Her heart was racing, the beat as sharp and as delicious as the excitement that teased his senses. His hunger stirred again, but this time, it was accompanied by desire. Although the desire had never really left him – she was simply fuelling the embers of it.

He led the way forwards through the wasteland of old machinery, boxes and rubbish. They quickly reached the far side of the room, but, even so, they were too late. The creature had left – and the only way out was via a fissure in the old brick wall.

"I've never noticed that before." Riley squatted and picked up a chunk of broken brick. She studied it for a moment, then held it up for him to see. "It looks clawed."

"And newly broken. Whatever that thing is, it's created itself a tunnel to get into here."

She tossed the brick back down and rose. "It's big enough for us to get into."

"Not by chance, I'd imagine."

She looked at him. "A trap?"

"Could be." Why else would it attract their attention then retreat?

Her sudden grin was as sexy as hell, and he found himself cursing the thing even as his fingers twitched with the urge to reach for her.

"So let's go spring it," she said, her voice low but as sexy as the smile.

"How about I go spring it, and you go upstairs and wait?" Even as he said the words, he knew it was useless, but he had to try. Women's liberation might be standard fare in this day and age, but he still couldn't see the sense in allowing any woman to put her life on the line unnecessarily. But then, he was a very old vampire who was somewhat set in his ways, despite the fact he'd seen eras go by and conventions change many, many times.

"You already know the answer to that, so why bother asking?" Her voice was wry, but her eyes danced with amusement and again the hunger rose in him.

He pushed it down again, even as he wished he didn't have to. "Because one of these days, you're going to do the sensible thing and shock the hell out of me."

She smiled again. "Me and sensible? I don't think so." She paused and looked in the hole. "But I will allow you to go first."

"I'd really rather be upstairs, with you, in bed." He wrapped his fingers around hers. The warmth of her grip flooded through him, spinning desire to greater heights.

"You should have thought of that before you began this chase," she murmured, the amusement so evident in her eyes finally lacing her tones.

"True."

He tugged her forwards. The tunnel's entrance was jagged, the brick cut unevenly with claws. The creature, whatever it was, had a lot of strength behind it. But brick quickly gave way to clay as the tunnel headed downwards, although the earthy smell of soil was quickly overrun by a more odorous scent – human waste.

"Oh Christ," Riley said, dread in her voice. "We're heading into the sewage system. I think I'm going to puke."

"Breathe through your mouth."

"It's not helping."

The tunnel broke into a pipe large enough to drive a car into. He jumped into the muck flowing gently downwards then turned to help her down. "At least it's late at night. Not as many people will be flushing their business."

"Thanks for that cheery thought." She grimaced as her feet disappeared into the flow. "Wrong shoes for this sort of walk."

"You can always go back."

"And you can always shut up and get moving."

He smiled and led the way forwards again, following the flow of the water. The creature was somewhere ahead – a blot of "wrongness" his senses could get no real fix on.

But the closer they got to it, the more its anticipation grew, and the uneasier he grew.

Riley suddenly stopped. "I *have* felt this thing before. It's a chameleon."

Chameleons were a rare breed of nonhumans, who could take on any background and literally become part of it. They were also ferocious flesh-eaters and extremely hard to kill.

He frowned. "Chameleons aren't usually city dwellers. They prefer the wild areas."

But even as he said it, he flared his senses outwards, taking a stronger, closer look at the creature ahead. It *did* feel like a chameleon.

"Maybe so, but this one is old. And it rots, just like the ones we encountered in that underground lab." She hesitated. "You don't think it could be the same ones, do you?"

"I doubt it. The Directorate cleaned that whole place out, didn't they?"

"Yeah, but who's to say one didn't escape?"

"It still makes no sense for it to come here."

"It does if it wants revenge for its kits and partner being killed. It might well hold us responsible because we discovered them."

It was possible. While chameleons were often considered little more than basic animals, that wasn't based on any actual scientific evidence, as the creatures were elusive and difficult to study. And this creature *had* led them here. That in itself suggested a high degree of intelligence.

"In which case, this trap will be a well-prepared one. Perhaps you should retreat and call in the Directorate," he said.

"Leaving you to face this thing alone." It was flatly said, and the air fairly burned with her disapproval.

"Riley, I have an advantage over these—"

"Quinn, I'm not going to walk away and leave you to face this thing alone."

Annoyance rolled through him, and he was tempted, *so* tempted, to roll her with power – forcing her to leave, and therefore keeping her safe. But she would never appreciate the concern behind such an action. Indeed, even if he succeeded in forcing her away from danger, in the end it would probably damage his long-term aim of making her his.

So he shook his head and continued walking. The chill in the air seemed to sharpen, as did that sense of anticipation. The rank aroma of sewage swirled around them, but underneath it ran the fresh aroma of earth. His gaze swept the dank walls ahead, but he couldn't see anything that indicated another break in the walls.

He glanced at Riley. "Can you smell that?"

"Define *that*." Her voice was clipped. "Because this place has a lot of different smells, most of them vile."

"Earth. Freshly dug earth."

"It's ahead, another ten yards or so."

He couldn't see it, but then she was relying on senses other than sight.

"The sense of anticipation is growing," she added. "I'm not liking the feel of what we're walking towards."

Neither was he. He slowed his pace, forcing Riley to do the same. Another fissure came into view, this one larger than the other. Dirt, rocks and concrete had tumbled out, half blocking the meagre flow and redirecting it into the crack.

"There's something odd—"

Her words were abruptly cut off, and her hand ripped from his. He swung around but there was no sense of her in the darkness, no spark of her life force. It was as if she'd completely disappeared.

The fury that swept through him was as cold and as angry as anything he'd ever experienced in his 1,200 years of life. But as quickly as it rose, it went, replaced by a hard emptiness.

An emptiness that was filled with the certainly that he would get back what was his.

He turned around, using his psychic senses to search for any hint of her. The darkness held its secrets well – there was no sign of her life force, no melodious beat of life.

She had to be unconscious, and in the grip of the chameleons, hidden by their ability to merge with the background.

She wasn't dead. Not yet.

He reached down, deep down into that place in his soul that had never been human, had never been vampire, using powers long since gone from this world to disappear into the darkness. It was more than just wrapping the shadows around him, more than just merging with the background, as the chameleons did. He became the darkness, became the air, became a shadow that held no substance – one that would not be seen or heard or felt.

He floated towards the fissure. There was nothing else he could do. The chameleons had sprung their trap; all he could do now was track them down and make them pay.

The water that trickled underneath his feet began to swirl as he reached the obstruction he'd noticed earlier. He swung left, into the fissure created by the creatures. The walls were raw, bleeding moisture, the air thick and rank. Though the sense of anticipation had gone, and there was now no sign of either the creatures or Riley, he knew they were up ahead.

The part of him that had shared her blood could feel her nearness, even if he could not see her life force or hear her thoughts.

The tunnel continued on through the earth, winding slowly downwards. Gradually, the way began to widen, until he was in a huge old cavern.

They were here.

He stopped, taking it all in. He saw the dark-red blurs of life that were the chameleons; saw Riley, a blaze of heat and life lying on the ground. He regained form and attacked.

There were four of them – one larger, three smaller – and they hadn't yet sensed his presence. They were too intent on their prey.

He swept in, grabbing two of the youngsters and tossing them across the cavern. He grabbed the third one just as the mother lashed out, her claws raking his side and drawing blood. The scent of it stung the air and hunger stirred through the darkness. But the flesh eaters wanted more than just his blood.

He crushed his hand around the neck of the third one, and flung it with all his might at the mother. She screamed, a high-pitched sound of fury, as she tried to catch and save her child.

With the chameleons distracted, he grabbed Riley and dragged her out from under their feet, hauling her across to the other side of the cavern, near the fissure but not actually going into it. Fighting in close quarters was never a good choice.

With one eye on the creatures, he slapped Riley's face. Hard. There was no time for niceties in moments like this. She muttered something unintelligible, then her eyes opened. "That hurt."

"So will the chameleons if you don't get moving."

The mother's roar just about drowned out his words. He turned, standing in front of the still-groggy Riley.

The creatures merged with the darkness. He switched to infra, following the muted flame of the mother's life force, waiting until she was almost upon him before he launched at her, hitting her hard in the gut, thrusting her backwards, into her milling kits. One caught the full force of her weight, driving it into the ground, its short scream suddenly cut off.

He wrapped his hands around the creature's neck and squeezed as hard as he could, but the skin was thick and leathery under his fingers, its neck thickly corded with muscles.

Claws tore at his back, shredding skin and drawing blood. He hissed in pain but refused to release his grip, tightening instead.

"Hey, bitch," Riley said from behind them. "Let him go or I'll kill your munchkin."

The chameleon froze.

"Quinn," Riley added, almost casually, "I don't think strangling it is the way to go."

"You might be right there."

He may have killed chameleons before, but never with bare hands. Weapons were best – the only trouble was, they didn't have any. Heaven only knew where her laser was.

He rolled off the creature, felt its hatred sweep across him, frying his senses. But as he backed away the wrongness in the air increased suddenly.

"Riley, watch out—"

The words were cut off as a huge paw swept him up into the air and tossed him like rubbish against the cavern wall. He hit it hard and fell to the ground on all fours, the cavern spinning around him and anger rising like a thick and bitter wind within him.

He got to his feet. Riley had been backed against the wall, a blob of darkness towering above her, slashing with sharp claws. Though she managed to avoid most of the blows and land a few of her own, bloody rents marred her golden skin and a darkening bruise decorated her forehead.

*No one hurts what is mine.*

He ran forwards and leaped upwards, landing on the back of the creature, wrapping his arms and legs around its body. But instead of trying to choke it, he reached again for that ancient part of his soul, becoming one with the darkness and the air. Only this time, he rolled it outwards, moving it from him to the chameleon, letting it flow across every part of the creature's body, until they were both encased.

It didn't sense the danger. Didn't know it was about to die.

He drew the net of air and darkness tighter, letting it invade skin and muscle, blood and bone, until the creature was one with the air just like him.

It sensed the danger then, sensed the wrongness.

It began to writhe and twist in an effort to get him off its back, but it was too late. Far too late.

He drew in all the threads of energy, then took a deep breath and exploded outwards, thrusting the particles of air and darkness that were both him and the creature into 1,000 different directions. Scattering their molecules and forever destroying the chameleon.

His own molecules reformed, until what stood on the earth of the cavern was once again vampire.

A vampire whose veins pounded with the need to take blood and regain the strength he'd just expended.

Riley was staring at him, eyes wide and perhaps a touch of fear in those silver depths.

"What the fuck did you just do?"

"Destroyed it." He turned to the muted flame that was the mother chameleon. "Your partner is dead, as is one of your kits. Two remain. If you leave now, and forget this madness, they just might stay that way. Stay, and I will destroy you all."

The chameleon screamed, a sound filled with fury and pain. He felt nothing for her – certainly no pity – and he would kill her if he had to. But the truth was, his strength was down and one chameleon might still be more than he and Riley could handle.

The creature screamed again, but this time her remaining kits gathered around her.

"Go," he said softly. "And live. But return here, go after either of us again, and I will hunt you down and destroy you all, if it is the last thing I ever do on this earth."

The creature left, which only proved that they were far more intelligent than anyone had presumed.

With the danger gone, weakness returned. His knees buckled, and, if not for the fact that Riley was suddenly there, offering him a shoulder, he would have fallen.

"You need blood," she said, and underneath the concern he could taste her alarm. She feared what he'd done – feared it enough to perhaps walk away.

He couldn't allow that. Wouldn't allow it.

"Yes," he said softly. "It took more strength than I remembered to destroy that creature."

She hesitated just a little, then shifted and offered her neck. The sweet pulse of life called to him, and his canines lengthened.

She gasped as his teeth broke her skin, but the sound became one of pleasure as he began to drink. The richness of her blood flushed the weakness from his body and, as she became lost in the experience of a vampire's feast, he let his mind merge with hers, becoming one with her, keeping her unaware and unknowing as he drove down into those parts of her mind that held her memories, altering what she remembered. No one knew what he could do and he intended to keep it that way – for now.

As he began his retreat, he did one other thing – left her with the gentle desire to take fewer lovers and not visit the wolf clubs as much.

Unfair, perhaps, but he'd learned long ago that those who played by the rules lost.

This time, he had no intention of losing.

He withdrew his teeth, then kissed her neck to take the remaining sting away.

She smiled at him, bright eyes still filled with lust, the desire he'd raised by feeding from her unquenched by his own design. The dreams that had begun this night had yet to be fulfilled in the flesh.

"I think," she said softly, her fingers twining through his, spreading the warmth of life across his flesh. "That we both need to go upstairs and take a bath."

"As long as the bathing involves sex, I don't really care."

She laughed, a rich, throaty sound that rolled across his senses and raised a hunger of a different kind. "You, vampire, are insatiable."

"I think it's the company I keep."

She grinned and tugged him into the tunnel. They moved quickly back through the sewers and into her apartment. It didn't take long to run the bath, and in the aromatic water they washed the grime and blood from each other.

As she leaned back against the bath, he captured her foot and gently kneaded her arch.

"So," she said eventually. "You came all the way from Sydney just to shag me in person?"

"The dreams were not enough tonight."

"You know all the right words to say, even if they are lies."

She shifted, pulling her foot from his grasp and running her hands up his stomach, making warmth and life flood across his body. There were many vampires who couldn't stand the touch of another, who took the blood they needed with as little contact as possible. He had never been one of those, which is why he always tried to take what he needed while making love. Blood might sustain his life, but it was physical contact, the warmth of another, that nourished his soul. That made the effort of going on through the darkness and the loneliness that much less of a fight. Even emotionless contact was better than nothing.

But he and Riley had never been emotionless.

Her body followed the journey of her hands up his body, until she was lying on top of him, her full breasts squashed against his chest and her heart beating like a trapped thing. Her desire swirled around him, as tasty and warm as the cadence of her blood.

She raised a wet hand and lightly ran a finger around his lips. It was so soft, that touch, and yet so arousing. The blood need rose in him, as thick and as strong as desire.

"And just what were your original intentions?" she said softly. Teasingly. "Before we were so rudely interrupted by the chameleons, that is."

He wrapped a hand around the back of her neck, holding her still as his lips met hers. But this kiss was no gentle thing, but rather fierce, filled with all the hunger and desire that was in him.

"Good intentions," she gasped, when he finally let her go.

"That is only just the beginning." He kissed her chin, nuzzled the pulse point at the base of her neck, drawing in the scent of her, the wild muskiness of woman and wolf combined with the sweet freshness of rain on a summer's day. A scent that was uniquely her own, a scent he would never forget, no matter what happened between them.

He slid his fingers down her flesh, then wrapped his arms around her, sending a wave of water crashing over the rim and onto the tiles as he spun them around, until she was on the bottom and he was on top.

"Ah, the control freak strikes again," she murmured, eyes bright with amusement. "Can't stand having a woman in charge and all that."

"As if there is any way to control you," he murmured, releasing her arms and sliding down her body again.

When he took one nipple into his mouth and sucked on it lightly, she gasped softly, her body arching into his, urging him on silently.

He teased her, touched her, aroused her, until her blood was humming and her body shuddering, and all he wanted to do was bury himself deep inside her, release himself as he filled his soul with her blood and her life.

But not yet. Not quite just yet.

He rose and claimed her lips yet again, his kiss as urgent as before, filled with the unleashed desire that burned between them.

"You know," she gasped, "for a so-called control freak, you're doing a very tardy job of taking what you want."

He smiled at her, his gaze roaming over her features, features that could be as sharp and as pretty as she was. "I didn't think you'd appreciate such assertiveness if it meant cutting short your own pleasure."

"Trust me, you wouldn't be cutting short anything."

He shifted position, so that he was between her legs, his cock pressing against her, teasing, but not entering. "So you're saying that you would like me to take you?"

She grinned. "Unless you've got something better to do."

He paused a heartbeat, pretending to consider. "Nope," he said, "I don't believe I do."

And with that, he rammed himself deep inside her. And it was glorious, so *glorious*. The way her body enveloped him, the heat of her surrounding him, claiming him, with the same sort of need and urgency that raged through him. There was a completion in this moment, a wholeness that went beyond mere pleasure. It might create life in others, but for him, it was all about sustaining it.

He began to move, and she moved with him, her supple body shuddering with the force of the pleasure building within her. He could taste her desire, taste her need, as surely as he would soon taste her blood, and it only fuelled his own lust to greater heights. He began to move fiercely, urgently, and she was right there with him, wanting everything he could give her.

She gasped, grabbing the bath top for support, as his movements grew faster, more urgent. Everything broke, and she was unravelling, groaning with the intensity of her orgasm. Then his own hit, and thought and time stopped as he came, thrusting deep and hard, losing himself inside her as his teeth entered her neck and he took the lifeblood he needed.

She came again, her shuddering rolling across his body, her mind filling his, completing him. Making them one.

She was his – in dreams and in life – and one day soon she would know it.

He'd make sure of it.

# Love Bites

## Kimberly Raye

I t was the perfect place to meet a vampire.

A fast, retro dance song pounded over the state-of-the-art sound system and vibrated the walls of the trendy club located in Manhattan's Meatpacking District. Cigarette smoke thickened the air. Liquor flowed from the wall-to-wall bar. There were mirrors everywhere – the massive walls, the floor, the ceiling. Red velvet couches and small glass and chrome tables edged the room. Strobe lights twirled and sliced through the darkness, casting flickering shafts of lights on the sea of bodies that gyrated on the dance floor.

The place oozed decadence and sexual tension.

It also oozed bullshit.

I stood off to the side near the far edge of the bar and watched a man, mid forties, dressed in slacks and a plain white button-down shirt, approach two young women sipping Cosmos. They ignored him at first, sucking down their drinks and rolling their eyes, but the more he smiled and talked, the more they seemed to relax.

The man definitely had game.

In everyday life, he was James Blumfield, Manhattan's representative for the Snipers of Otherworldly Beings – SOBs for short. By night, he was Jimmy Blue, a music-video producer. At least that was the cover he used in places like this.

James spent his days pushing pencils and mapping every vampire – made or born – and every Were (from wolf to chihuahua) between Chinatown and Harlem. Jimmy took over at night, tossing around the bullshit so that he could locate his designated target and make the actual kill.

He was one of the best SOBs in the business.

He was also my boss, mentor and uncle.

My name is Danielle Blue and I come from a long line of SOBs. My great-great-great-great-great-great-great (I think that's enough greats) grandfather made the first ever vampire kill back during the twelfth century. We Blues have been killing Others ever since.

Life for a Blue went something like this – birth, dysfunctional childhood (*you* try being raised by a pair of supernatural assassins), emotionally traumatic teen years (on account of this is usually when a Blue realizes that Mom isn't the PTA president and Dad's not using that wooden stake to put up a tent), high-school graduation and then the family business. My entrance had been a little delayed because I'd been determined to buck tradition and do something different. I'd spent a year fantasizing about being a famous artist (I'd painted dozens of pictures and had sold a whopping zero). I'd wound up broke and living at home, which had ended with me finally giving up my brushes and enrolling in SOB Special Weapons 101.

I know what you're thinking. Having "Dani Blue, SOB" imprinted on my business cards is sure to kill my dating chances.

Well, you're right. But some things, like an 800-year-old legacy, are just more important than getting laid.

Especially if you're like me and getting laid hasn't been all fairy dust and rose petals like in the movies.

Where's the back hair and the farting and the "Hop on, honey, and take a little ride on the love pony"?

I kid you not. That was my last boyfriend's favourite pick-up line. It worked the very first time, after I stopped laughing and realized that he was, you know, sort of cute. But cute can only last so long (two years in my case, on account of I'm somewhat of a slow learner when it comes to guys). I've had a total of three boyfriends.

My first crush back in the seventh grade (which I'd repeated twice because I just hadn't been able to nail the maths) had lasted all the way until sophomore year because no matter how many loogies he spit at me, I just couldn't stop thinking that maybe, just maybe, he had some sort of excessive spit disorder. I had a severe algebra block, so who was I to point fingers?

And then there was my high-school boyfriend, Todd, who had a bad habit of boinking cheerleaders behind my back, yet I kept giving him a second chance because – hey – we're talking an obvious addiction. I'd had it bad for Twinkies and Oreos back then, so I knew the feeling.

And then there was Ryan (see pony reference above).

Anyhow, I'm 22 now and ready to take a nice long hiatus from men and relationships and bodily noises. It's time to put the last four years of SOB training to the test.

My thoughts slammed to a halt as someone bumped into me from behind and I pitched forwards into a young woman holding an Appletini.

"Bitch," she muttered before I could give her so much as an apologetic smile.

"Sorry," came a slurred voice behind me, followed by a slosh of beer on the back of my faded-blue-jean jacket.

Just for the record, I'm not much of a clothes hound. I never could master the art of shopping and so I've been buying the same brand of button-fly Levis for the past ten years. The only thing remotely stylish about me was the pair of regulation Ray-Bans I wore to protect myself. See, vampires can read minds and influence humans, but only if they stare directly into the eyes.

Other than the ultra-cool glasses, I was dressed not-so-ultra-cool in my usual: jeans, a worn, paint-splattered T-shirt leftover from my starving artist days, tennis shoes and my favourite hand-me-down jacket.

One that now smelled like Heineken.

No sooner had I recovered than someone else bumped into me. I shook some bourbon off my shoe and shifted my gaze back to my Uncle Jimmy. But there were too many people and I could no longer see him.

Yep, it was the perfect place to meet a vampire, all right.

Unfortunately, it wasn't the perfect place to kill one.

While I'd been extremely lucky on the written part of my finals, I hadn't done so well in the actual field test. Not that I didn't know my way around with a stake, or a .350 Magnum loaded with silver bullets. It's just that my aim sort of, well, sucked.

During the field test I'd been placed in a back alley with a pseudo-vampire and three stuffed mannequins a.k.a. humans. I'd bumped into human number one, decapitated number two and staked number three in a place I'd rather not mention (let's just say he won't be fathering any stuffed babies any time soon). Since the primary mission of an SOB was to rid the population of Others to preserve the safety and well-being for all human-kind, I'd gotten a great big F.

Luckily my graduation wasn't just based on the field test, but a combination of the written portion, the field demonstration, and a lot of begging and pleading on my Uncle Jimmy's part. He'd put his reputation on the line and convinced upper SOB management to give me a chance.

Hence the SOB ID card in my pocket. It was official and I was about to make my first kill.

*The* kill.

While I had my card and I'd already filled out the paperwork for health and dental and even the 401(k), I was still on proba-tion. My future as an SOB depended solely on tonight. Now.

Shit.

I inched my way through the mass of people until I reached the spot where I'd last seen Uncle Jimmy. He was gone and so were the two women he'd been chatting up.

Two *human* women, to be more exact, with strong ties to the vampire community, or so we suspected. One of them was rumoured to be a blood slave to an entourage of made vampires based in SoHo. Jimmy's objective was to confirm the information and find out if any of the vampires she serviced were here tonight.

With a specific target identified, I would step in, do my thing and prove myself.

*If* I could find Uncle Jimmy.

After 20 minutes of looking, I finally spotted him near the far edge of the dance floor. Uncle Jimmy was talking to a different trio of women. One of the women whispered something, he smiled and my stomach somersaulted.

Bingo.

"Right behind you," he murmured as he came up to me. "The couple near the rear exit door." I started to whip around and he warned, "Slowly. We don't want to alert him that we're on to him."

I drew a deep breath to slow my frantic heartbeat and did a casual turn and look-see. My gaze swept past several clusters of people until I reached a man and woman. I stalled for a few extra heartbeats, drinking in the scene as quickly and as thoroughly as possible.

His hair was dark and spiky. He wore black slacks, a fitted black silk button-up and a hungry look. I could see the predatory light in his gaze as he stared down at the lush blonde on his arm.

She stared up at him, transfixed.

"Him," Jimmy confirmed my thoughts. "Get in, stake him right in the heart and walk away. Easy."

For a man with bullseye aim.

"You can do this," he added, clapping a strong hand on my shoulder and giving me a reassuring squeeze. "You're a Blue."

Lucky me.

I squelched the traitorous thought.

I *was* lucky. I had the prestigious job of saving the human race, for Pete's sake. Unfortunately, I also had the prestigious job of family wuss. I was the kid who'd brought home every stray animal and cried when my first-grade teacher read *Old Yeller*. I got freaked when I saw a spider, and I *always* closed my eyes during scary movies. And while I knew my intended target had probably bitten thousands of people the world over and left plenty of them to bleed out and die, I hadn't seen him do any of it first-hand.

Other than staring lustfully at the woman next to him, he wasn't even doing anything now. No murder or mayhem.

Yet I was supposed to kill him anyway.

"Go," Uncle Jimmy told me, shoving me forwards before I could blurt out any of the objections that rushed through my head.

But none of them mattered. I *had* to do this. I'd sucked at everything in my life – from school to relationships to painting.

But not this.

*This* was my calling, just like every other Blue before me. The one thing I was going to be good at.

If I ever managed to perfect my aim, that is.

I forced the doubts aside and tried to concentrate on the positive aspects of the situation. Sure, it was crowded, but at least my target was a vampire and not a Were. I didn't have to fire off a round of bullets. All I had to do was walk over to Hot and Hungry and stab him directly in the heart and – this was the biggie – not toss my cookies while I was doing it.

*Done.*

I put one foot in front of the other and started to move. A few steps shy, I eased my hand beneath my jacket. My fingers closed around the stake. I inched the sharp wood from my waistband slowly. Almost there. Almost there. Almost –

His gaze shifted, pinning me in place when I was just two steps away from reaching him.

Crazy, right? I had my Ray-Bans firmly in place. He couldn't read my mind or seduce me or influence me in any way. I was totally immune to the lust in his dark-brown eyes with their whisky-gold flecks, as well as to the whole sex vibe that he was giving off.

Mostly.

It's just that while I'd sworn off relationships, I hadn't meant to say adios to sex as well. I missed it. I liked it. I wanted it.

"Do you want something?" His deep voice slid into my ears and echoed my thoughts.

Uh-oh.

'I . . .' OK, where was my voice when I really needed it? Wait a second. I didn't need my voice. I just needed my stake. Yeah, the stake.

*Don't talk. Don't lust. Just do it.*

My fingers closed around the wood again and my heart stalled.

He let go of the blonde on his arm and she faded into the shadows, dazed and confused thanks to his vampiric charm. It was just the two of us in that darkened corner now.

Just the two of us. The loud, pulsing music. The lust.

I ignored the crazy thought and slid the stake free. The hair on the back of my neck prickled and I felt Uncle Jimmy's eyes on me. He was watching. Waiting. Ready to report back so that my future could be decided by the higher-ups. Would I succeed this time or fail like all the other times?

Everything shifted into fast-forwards then. One minute I was aiming at his heart and the next I was pinned up against the wall, his hard body pressed into mine.

"I'm too old for a first-timer," he told me.

"This isn't my first time," I heard myself blurt. Wait a second – SOB rule number one – no talking to the target.

*Aim and fire.*

Impossible with my arms pinned on either side of my head, the stake dangling in one hand.

I tried to glance around for help. Surely someone could see? Uncle Jimmy? One of the monster bouncers I'd passed on my way in? At the same time, the place was much too crowded. If I couldn't see them, then they probably couldn't see me. And with this vamp blocking my view, pressing against me and pinning me to the wall, we looked like any number of couples making out in the far corners of the club.

He tightened his grip on my wrist and my fingers went limp. The stake fell to the floor and he leaned into me even more. "You're a virgin, all right." He grinned, his teeth a dazzling white in the dim lighting. "The SOBs must be getting pretty hard up to send a virgin after me. Do you know who I am?"

"Do I care?"

"Maximillian Marchette. My friends call me Max."

"Is that supposed to mean something to me?"

"The Marchettes are one of the oldest-born vamp families in existence. Do you know why that is?"

"Again, do I care?"

"Because we know how to handle an SOB." His dark gaze burned into mine and if I hadn't known that he was talking about death and destruction, I would have sworn he wanted to take me to bed.

Not that I was falling for it. No matter how much I missed sex, this vamp was going down.

"Do you know how many times someone's tried to stake me?" he went on.

"What's with the twenty questions? I don't know and I don't care, so just get to the point."

"It's not going to happen. Certainly not with a virgin behind the stake. The SOBs must be getting sloppy."

"Maybe they're just getting smart."

He eyed me for a long moment. "What's that supposed to mean?"

"This." And then I did what I'd been wanting to do since the first moment our eyes had locked.

I kissed him.

Not because I was desperate and horny or because he practically oozed sex appeal, of course. It was a purely calculated move to get his mind off the fact that I was trying to kill him and on to the fact that maybe, just maybe, I might be an easy lay.

Or at least a quick bite.

Either one would distract him enough so that I could retrieve the second stake from my back pocket.

If he loosened my arms.

Sure enough, once he recovered from the initial shock of me laying one on him, his mouth grew stronger and more purposeful. He slid his tongue past my lips, stroking and delving. His grip on my wrists loosened and his hands dropped to my waist.

I played along.

OK, so I sort of got pulled along for the next few moments. I kissed him back, tasting and feeling and enjoying the hardness of his body pressed to mine until I felt the sharpness of his teeth against my bottom lip. A bolt of excitement rushed through me, twisting my priorities for several frantic heartbeats before zapping me back to reality. Back to the fact that he was a vampire and I was here to kill him and I could kiss my 401 – and my future – goodbye if I failed here.

My hands trembled, but I managed to get my arm behind me. My fingers closed around the stake and a split second later, I was pushing it deep into his ribcage.

"We have to get rid of the body," Uncle Jimmy said a half-hour later.

We stood in the back alley of the club near a large orange dumpster. The vampire lay in a heap against the side of the building. Blood bubbled up around the stake lodged in his chest and drenched the front of his shirt, and he was even paler than usual.

"I'm sorry," I whispered. Not that he heard me. He was so still, his eyes closed. My chest tightened.

"Forget about it," Uncle Jimmy said. "I don't expect you to do disposal duty, too. It's your first night. Go home and savour the moment and I'll take care of the rest."

But I wouldn't be savouring anything. Already I felt sick to my stomach. And scared.

Because any second Uncle Jimmy would lean down and take a closer look. He would realize that my aim had been off and that the vampire was still alive.

I could still feel the pulse of his heart against the palm of my hand. And the blood.

I swallowed the sudden lump in my throat.

"I'll do it," I blurted when Jimmy started to lean down. "It's my kill. I should get rid of it."

He looked uncertain. "You remember the rules, right?"

"Remove the stake, cut off the head and dump the rest at the nearest SOB warehouse." I nodded frantically. "I've got it." When he didn't look convinced, I added: "Please. I really want to do this. All of it. It's my responsibility. Just grab his feet and help me get him into the van. I'll take it from there."

"He's really heavy."

"I haven't been working out every day for nothing." I flexed a muscle. "Besides, I need to learn how to do this myself. Once I'm out in the field, I'll be on my own. I'll have to do it. I might as well start learning now."

He finally nodded and reached for the vampire's feet.

I inched my way behind, slid my hands under the vampire's arms and prayed that he'd lost enough blood to keep him unconscious a little while longer. Otherwise, Uncle Jimmy would realize the truth, re-stake him and the bloodsucker would be dead for sure.

And for some insane reason – my overly sensitive conscience or his vampiric charm, or maybe a little of both – I didn't want that to happen.

No, what I really wanted was for Max Marchette to wake up in my arms.

And I *really* wanted another one of those kisses.


The SOBs had a disposal warehouse on the upper east side of Manhattan. It was the perfect place to slice and dice and rid the world of fanged vermin. Uncle Jimmy phoned them that I was coming and waved me off.

Once I was out of sight of the club, I hung a left and headed for Brooklyn. I had a two-bedroom condo with a postage stamp for a yard. It wasn't big, but it was home.

Even better, it was safe.

I pulled up out front and spent a good fifteen minutes pulling and tugging Max out of the back of the van. I had him cocooned in canvas and, luckily, the blood had stopped so he wasn't bleeding through the fabric.

"New rug," I told my insomnia-suffering next-door neighbour when he poked a head out and asked me if I could use a hand. I nodded and the old man came down to help.

"I could help you unroll it," old Mr Wimble offered once we had the bundle inside my condo. "No trouble."

"I haven't decided where to put it, but thanks." I watched the old man leave and then turned to Max.

After several pulls and tugs, I managed to unwrap him and drag him into the bedroom. Getting him on the bed wasn't as easy, but I finally managed. Once he was sprawled on top, I went about the sticky business of extracting the stake. I tugged and pulled and, finally, it slid free. He bucked off the bed with a loud gasp. Blood bubbled from the open wound for a few seconds and then, just like that, it stopped.

I unbuttoned his bloody shirt and did my best to bandage him up. I secured the blinds and drapes, covered Max with a blanket and then collapsed in a nearby chair to wait.

*Not* to sleep, I reminded myself. I had to be awake when he opened his eyes, otherwise I would find myself bitten and bleeding . . .

With heavy eyes I took in his sleeping form. It was daylight. He had to sleep, right? At least that's what the books had said. Which meant I had a few hours. I could close my eyes just a little and take a catnap. Maybe fifteen minutes. Maybe . . .

Zzzzzzzzz.

And just like that, I was out.

I opened my eyes later that afternoon to find him propped up against the wall, watching me. He still looked pale and weak, but I could tell he was feeling better. He'd removed the bandage and I saw that the gaping hole was starting to come together and heal.

"Why'd you do it?" he asked me after a few silent moments.

Guilt tugged at me, but I tried to force it aside. "Let's see. Oh, yeah. You're a bloodsucker and a murderer."

"Not the stake." His gaze pushed into mine and I realized all too late that I'd left my Ray-Bans sitting on the nightstand. "Why did you save me?"

"You're a vampire. You tell me."

His eyes fired a bright, brilliant gold colour for a split second before a strange expression lit his face. His eyes fired again, as if he were determined to push into my thoughts and see everything for himself.

He couldn't.

I saw it in the frustration that etched his forehead and the surprise that blazed in his eyes.

"Tell me," he demanded.

I shrugged. "My aim's off."

He shook his head. "Bullshit. You haven't got the balls for this job and you know it."

I did know it. It was a truth that had been nagging me ever since I'd failed the field test and I'd just been too scared to admit it.

To my family.

To myself.

"So tell me the truth. Tell me why you saved me."

"You didn't deserve to die." I wasn't sure why I said it, but I did. "At least not that I know of. You didn't try to suck my blood or hurt me in any way."

"Maybe I will now."

"Maybe." I gathered my courage and stared him down. "And then I will have to kill you."

He kept staring at me, as if trying to figure me out, before he finally shook his head and slumped back down on the pillows. He hissed against the sudden movement.

"Does it hurt?"

"Our senses are magnified," he growled. "What do you think?"

"Can you take ibuprofen?"

He nodded and I hurried into the kitchen.

A few seconds later, I returned with a glass of water and two tiny pills. "Here." I sank down gently onto the side of the bed and helped him lift his head. He opened his mouth and I plopped the pills on his tongue. His lips grazed my fingers and awareness bolted through me.

It was the same feeling I'd had back at the club those few moments he'd had me pinned to the wall.

The feeling of being alive. And tingling. And desperate.

As if I needed him right there. Right now.

He caught my hand with one of his and placed a kiss on my fingertips. "Not all vampires are bad. Yes, we drink blood." He pulled his lips back and his sharp fangs grazed the tender inside of my wrist. I stiffened and he let me pull away. His eyes gleamed even brighter and I could see the hunger in his expression. "We drink for survival." He blinked, seeming to get control of himself and the fierceness in his eyes eased. "We don't all mutilate and slaughter."

Maybe not, but I was still trembling. From fear? Or from the fact that my fingers were tingling where his mouth had touched them?

I gathered my courage and touched the glass to his lips. Something flickered in his dark gaze as he stared up at me. I knew he couldn't read my thoughts, but I had the strangest feeling that he could sense my body's reaction to him. My pounding heart and my trembling knees and –

"You should get some rest," I blurted, setting the glass of water on the nightstand. The bed dipped and I moved back to the chair.

*Fear*, a tiny voice whispered. *You should be afraid of this vampire*.

But I wasn't afraid, I realized, as I folded my legs beneath me. While I knew all of the awful things that he was capable of, the only threat he'd posed so far had been to my hormones.

He stared at me a long moment before he finally nodded. He settled back down on the bed and closed his eyes.

And then he went to sleep.

He slept for the next four days while I dodged phone calls from Uncle Jimmy who wanted to know where I'd dumped the body because none of the disposal sites had reported any new arrivals. While Max could heal as well as the next vampire, without blood – and despite the lust that raged between us, I wasn't up to volunteering mine – the process took longer. He would wake for a few hours here and there. I would hand him more painkillers and water and he would nod back off.

But first we would talk.

In the beginning, it was mostly small stuff, like where he lived and where I was from. Favourite movies and songs. But eventually the conversations grew deeper until I was asking him questions about being a vampire and he was asking me about the SOBs. He told me about his own family and how he had two brothers and a sister who owned and ran a successful dating service in Manhattan. I learned that even more than sucking blood, born vampires liked to procreate and make money. In turn, I told him about my mom and dad and my Uncle Jimmy, and, how even more than making money, I wanted to actually be happy. I wanted to find something I was good at – to be myself. Whether that was as an SOB or the fry girl down at the local hamburger joint. I even mentioned that I used to paint and showed him some of the pictures I'd done.

"You're good," he said, his gaze fixed on the large abstract hanging on the far wall.

"You're just saying that because I saved your afterlife."

He grinned and then a serious expression lit up his face. "I mean it. You're *really* good. You ought to take these to a gallery."

"So sayeth the painkillers," I said, but I couldn't suppress the tiny thrill that went through me. A gallery? Me? Did he really think . . .

Maybe.

We talked so much that by the time his wound actually healed, I felt a little sad. Max Marchette had stopped being a vampire and started being real, and I actually liked him.

He was leaving tonight and, oddly enough, I didn't want him to go.

I spent the last few hours before sunset watching him sleep. I couldn't help myself. He wasn't working his vamp mojo on me, yet I still thought he was the hottest-looking guy I'd ever seen. He had a broad chest sprinkled with dark hair that whorled into a tiny funnel that bisected his six-pack and dipped below the edge of the sheet. He smelled like excitement and danger and something I couldn't quite identify.

Something rich and sweet and decadent.

My stomach grumbled and I found myself thinking about how long it had been since I'd actually had sex.

I hadn't even masturbated lately and so when Max Marchette finally opened his eyes just as the sun dipped below the horizon, it was no wonder that I couldn't resist the sudden lust that flared in the dark depths.

He didn't say anything and I didn't say anything. We just stared at each other. And then it happened.

He reached for me, pulling me onto the bed, pressing me down into the mattress. He kissed me, plunging his tongue inside to explore and savour until I gasped for breath. I felt his erection, hard and eager against my stomach, and I knew this was *it*. The moment I'd been waiting for since that very first kiss.

He nibbled a path down my neck and I tilted my head back.

Pleasure rushed to my brain and the anticipation built. He licked his way down the slope of my breast and found my nipple. I gasped, burying my hands in his hair, holding him close. My legs parted and I felt him hard and hot, pushing into me—

"Wait—" I gasped, but he silenced me with a quick, desperate kiss.

"You won't catch anything from me," he murmured against my lips. It was the oldest line when it came to sex, yet a valid one in this particular situation.

Because Max wasn't a typical guy. He was a *vampire*.

The thought stirred even more than it spooked and I opened my legs wider. In one swift thrust, he plunged into me. Pleasure burst through me and the air lodged in my chest.

I stared up at him and his eyes blazed back at me. Hot. Bright. The tendons in his neck tightened. His jaw clenched. His mouth fell open and his fangs gleamed.

But I wasn't afraid. I knew he wouldn't bite me. Not without my consent. If he had wanted to, he would have done it long before now to speed up his healing.

No, this wasn't about blood. It was about sex.

I wrapped my legs around him as he buried himself deep. And then he started to move. In and out. In. Out. Until my body tightened and I came with a loud moan. He followed, bucking and groaning, his muscles strung tight.

He collapsed beside me, pulling me up next to him, his arm around me. I nuzzled his neck and tried to catch my breath. My hand crept across his chest.

I lay there for several long moments. Finally, once my heartbeat had slowed and I could actually think, I opened my eyes. My gaze caught the ID card sitting on the nightstand and the enormity of what I'd done crashed down around me. I'd not only violated the SOB creed and saved a vampire, I'd slept with him, fallen for him.

I had. I realized this as I lay there my head in the crook of his shoulder, his heart beating a steady rhythm against my palm.

I was a failure. A traitor.

Oddly enough, this didn't make me feel all that bad. Because Max Marchette, vampire or not, felt so right.

I wasn't sure how I was going to tell my family or pay my bills or anything, and yet I knew deep inside it would all work out somehow. Maybe with my painting. Maybe not. Either way, everything would be OK. I felt peaceful, calm, confident.

*Mesmerized.*

It's that old vamp magic. That's what I told myself, but I didn't believe it. I'd seen the surprise in his eyes when he hadn't been able to read my thoughts. I was different. He was different.

His hand stroked down my spine and a shiver went through me. My body started crying for more.

"This is definitely the end of my career as an SOB," I murmured.

He rolled me over to tower above me and stare deep into my eyes. My heart gave a little kick. "One ending is just another beginning."

I eyed him, a smile playing at my lips. "And this is the beginning of what?"

He grinned. "Us." And then he kissed me again.

# What's at Stake?

## Alexis Morgan

"Has the accused been brought in yet?"

Josalyn Sloan prided herself on her stoic control. Her escort shook his head, but gave no indication that he thought her question was anything but professional curiosity. After all, why would he? As far as anyone knew, this was just one more case, one more judgment to confirm, one more execution to carry out.

She'd originally thought the assignment was someone's poor idea of a joke. But no, the request for her services had come straight from the prisoner himself. Standing at parade rest, she kept her hands firmly clasped behind her back. It was imperative that she maintain a calm façade when she walked into the interrogation room to face the most powerful vampire of his generation – Rafferty O'Day, her former friend and almost lover.

The door on the far side of the room opened as a uniformed guard stepped through and motioned her forwards. "The prisoner is ready for you, Chancellor. Please leave any weapons out here."

Josalyn curled her lip in disdain. "You dare tell me how to do my job? Did you think I would stake him this quickly? Where's the fun in that?"

Shoving her way past the startled guard, she held up her scanner. The dials immediately lit up and shrieked, setting off an ear-piercing alarm.

She spun back towards the guard. "Turn off whatever monitors you have running in there. If they come on again while I'm interviewing the prisoner, I will report the infraction

150 Alexis Morgan

to my superiors. I'm sure they will be only too glad to let me express my displeasure any way I choose." Stepping closer to the guard, she used her superior height to her advantage and glared down into his frightened eyes. "The prisoner may be as guilty as hell, but he's not without his rights unless I say so. Interfere with my investigation again and there will be a price paid in blood. Your blood. I'm sure the prisoner would like something fresher than that bagged stuff you've been feeding him."

This time she included her escort in her promise. "And if he walks because of a miscarriage of justice, you two will be sitting in that cell."

Then she smiled, showing her own fangs to emphasize her point, reminding the two human males that while she was not actually a vampire herself, she certainly wasn't human either. Like all Chancellors, she was something in between the two other species, and stronger than she looked.

The guard punched a code into the keypad by the door. Evidently he forgot that along with her superior strength, she could also hear far better than he allowed for. His mumbled, "Pushy bitch!" came through loud and clear, despite the continued shrieking of her scanner.

She leaned in close again, dropping her voice to an angry whisper. "Oh, sweetie, you have no idea how pushy I can be. Better hope you never find out." Then she walked through the door and slammed it behind her.

She took one last deep breath to ease the knot of nerves in her chest. Nothing was going to make this any easier, so she pushed the door open. She kept her eyes firmly on the door itself, not wanting to face Rafferty one second before she had to. Reminding herself that she was no coward and delaying any further wouldn't help, she entered the holding cell.

After checking her scanner one last time, she stepped towards the table. Rafferty didn't look up, giving her eyes a few precious seconds to drink their fill. His hair was shaggier than she remembered, and the usual shine of his unique blend of chestnut and blond was missing. Obviously, the North American Coalition didn't waste money on prisoner hygiene.

But she wasn't here to judge Rafferty's appearance, only his guilt or innocence. Once she was convinced that he'd been fairly tried and convicted, then she would decide how he would die. Some of her kindred loved to draw out the process, soaking up the fear and pain to savour long after their prisoner had breathed his last. She didn't approve of either their attitudes or their techniques.

She was paid to execute, not torture, and then only after she completed her own investigation. If she disagreed with the court's findings, she could overturn their decision. It was the only thing that made her job bearable.

Rafferty stirred, the chains that bound him to his chair rattling slightly as he straightened up and at long last met her gaze.

"Josalyn."

"Rafferty." She sat down across from him and pulled out her notes on the case.

"I apologize for not standing."

His smile looked a bit strained as he tugged on his chains with no real show of strength. His wrists were already raw and bloody from previous attempts. She considered ordering the restraints removed. The Rafferty she had worked with wouldn't hurt her, but judging by the fury burning in those ice-blue eyes, maybe he'd changed. His face was thinner, too, as if all the charm and easy smiles had been burned away.

She leaned back in her chair and crossed her legs at the ankles. "I've reviewed your case. Anything you want to tell me?"

He shrugged. "If I said I was innocent, would you believe me?"

She'd wanted to, but the evidence had been pretty damning. "I'll listen to your version of the facts. It's as much as I can promise."

"Then I won't waste my breath, Joss. Send me back to my cell. I'm missing my evening nap."

She ignored his use of his pet name for her. "If you didn't want to talk to me, why request my services? A hundred other Chancellors would've jumped at the chance to handle your case."

Josalyn sat in stony silence while she waited for him to respond. The truth was he'd been offered a list of Chancellors to choose from, but hers was the only name he'd considered. If he were to die the final time, ending his long life, he wanted her face to be the last thing he saw.

She'd hate knowing that, especially when it was too late for either of them to do anything about it. Rather than tell her the simple truth, he settled for the easy lie.

"I knew you'd at least try to make it painless for me."

Josalyn slammed the file down on the table as she leaned forwards to glare at him. "This is no game, Rafferty. I may not always like my job, but I am damn good at it. Painless or not, you'll still be dead."

He hoped not. He really did, but it was too early to predict how this was going to play out. His gut feeling was that his chances for survival had improved dramatically when Josalyn had sauntered through that door.

"Talk to me, Rafferty." Her voice dropped to a whisper. "I don't want . . ."

When she didn't go on, he prodded her a bit. ". . . to be the one to shove a stake through my heart? Or to think me capable of murder? We both know I'm only here because the dead guy was human and not a vampire." He was baiting her and they both knew it.

"Stop it, Rafferty. You know as well as I do that I'm not paid to make moral judgments. My job as Chancellor is to review the testimony, verify the facts and then decide whether you received a fair trial."

"All right, fine. Where do you want me to start?"

"At the beginning works for me." She sounded as tired as he felt.

Where it really all started for him might not be what she had in mind, but it was his story.

"Remember the first time you sat down across a table from me?" He didn't wait for her to answer. "Well, I do. You were nervous. It was your first negotiation as an Arbitrator facing a room full of angry humans and vampires. I don't even remember what we were feuding over."

Josalyn shook her head in disgust. "The humans said your younglings were preying on theirs. The truth was that the humans ventured into vamp territory on a dare and some paid the price."

Rafferty fought to urge to smile. The meeting had been as memorable for her as it had been for him. "As I said, the details escape me, but the image of you is sharp and clear. Despite being outnumbered, you took charge and didn't stop until both sides conceded defeat." She'd been so vibrant, so beautiful, but she wouldn't want to hear that from him. Not yet.

"This stroll through the past is entertaining, but it's not getting us anywhere."

OK, so maybe he would tell her. "That meeting changed everything. I'd never met anyone quite like you. Before that, I hated my mandatory time on the Coalition Council: being shut up for days and days with the stench of humans, arguing over the stupidest details. The day you came in as the new Arbitrator was the real beginning of this mess."

Josalyn surged to her feet, her eyes blazing. "So the fact that you've been convicted of murder is now my fault? That's your defence?"

"No, but meeting you was the catalyst." He waited for her to sink back down into her seat. "I was the chief negotiator that first time only because they forced me. After that, I volunteered as often as I could without raising suspicions, but I wasn't cautious enough. My interest in you must have become too obvious."

Josalyn was always quick to understand the subtext of any conversation. "So that's why your mate-to-be hated me."

"Yeah, well, Petra hated me more." She hated him enough to arrange to have him executed, at least.

"Did she have reason to?"

He answered her real question. "I have to feed, Joss, even when she's not around. That's part of what we are and has no significance other than simple sustenance. Besides, Petra chose me because of my status, not out of any emotional attachment. When she grew increasingly unhappy about my prolonged absences on Coalition business, I happily offered to end our connection. After all, there are others among our kind who would meet her requirements in a mate just as well. She didn't hesitate to accept my offer."

Josalyn arched an eyebrow, clearly questioning the truth of that statement.

"What are you thinking, Joss?"

"I think you badly underestimated Petra's feelings for you. If she hates you enough to destroy you, she must have loved you."

Rafferty had considered that option and rejected it. "I doubt Petra is capable of loving anyone other than herself. No, I think she figured out that the real reason I set her free was to be with you. If I had formed an alliance with another female of our kind, she would've accepted my decision. After all, she'd dissolved a previous connection of her own to pursue one with me. I'm convinced she viewed my interest in you as an insult to her standing among our kind."

He leaned back in his chair and waited for the explosion. It wasn't long in coming.

"Rafferty, we never crossed the line, no matter what she thought. Not once. Not ever." Josalyn lurched to her feet to pace the short distance across the room and back.

"That's not quite true, Joss."

She froze mid-step and slowly turned to face him. "You mean the night you fed from me."

The heat in his gaze reminded her of the truth, not that she'd really forgotten. Her hand itched to touch the twin scars he'd left, but she managed to control the urge. He knew where they were, even if no one else did. How could they? The small marks weren't where anyone could see them except during a medical exam.

Her mind shifted back to that night. The vampires had been feuding amongst themselves, with allegiances changing from day to day, even hour to hour. As Rafferty had reminded her, feeding from each other was normal, even expected. But vampire politics were complicated, and someone in Rafferty's position had to be careful whom he picked even as a temporary partner. Rather than risk his neutrality, he'd gone too long between feedings.

From the beginning, they had often taken long walks together, keeping to the public pathways. On much rarer occasions, Rafferty had walked her home after the night-long meetings, but always stopping at the end of the street to maintain the illusion their friendship was casual at best.

But that one night, it all changed. He'd been on the verge of collapse after the meeting. Her home was the closest, so she'd dragged him there and offered him her wrist or her neck. He'd refused because the evidence would be impossible to hide. With dawn but a short time away, she'd offered him another, much more intimate choice. She could still feel the sweet brush of his lips on her skin as he'd slowly lowered his mouth to the pulse point at the top of her thigh. One touch was all it had taken to have her craving his body on hers, in hers. They'd been strong enough to resist the overwhelming temptation, a fact she'd regretted more with each passing day.

"You were dying."

"That was only an excuse, however true." He started to stand up, obviously forgetting the chains. "I was out of my mind with the need to simply touch you. I'd already decided to break off my betrothal."

"You never told me that." Not that it would have mattered. She'd resigned her position, knowing she could no longer be neutral in any dispute that involved Rafferty.

"Damn it, Joss, you didn't give me the chance. My time on the Council was almost over. Once it ended, we could have had a future together. But if what I had planned had gotten out, it would've jeopardized the Council's work for that entire session. Even if I'd been willing to risk it, you wouldn't have."

Regrets and memories wouldn't change the present circumstances. It was time to deal with reality, not dreams.

She resumed her seat, doing her best to sound professional and calm. "So you suspect that your former betrothed has set you up?"

"Yes, I do. It's the only explanation that makes any sense. The dead human and I had a history of conflict. Petra had to know I'd be charged, and that I'd ask for you. She couldn't risk killing both of us, but . . ."

"If I execute you, it allows her to strike back at both of us from a safe distance."

She'd only met Petra a handful of times, but there was no denying the instant dislike they had had for each other. Josalyn was honest enough to admit that a healthy dose of jealousy coloured her reaction to Rafferty's betrothed, but that wasn't all there was to it.

The female had treated anyone other than the upper-echelon vampires with disdain. She caused so much animosity that it had jeopardized the Council's work whenever she attended the sessions. If Petra was behind the charges against Rafferty, Josalyn wouldn't hesitate to take the bitch down.

He must have sensed her decision. "So what do we do next?"

"We? You seem to be rather tied up at the moment." She gave a pointed look at his chains.

"You can change that."

It was true that Chancellors could take prisoners with them to investigate the case. However, if the prisoner escaped, the Chancellor paid an awful price. They would wear matching ankle bracelets that released a warning shock if they became separated by more than 50 feet. The power of the jolt increased greatly with distance, until the charge would immobilize the strongest vampire or Chancellor until law enforcement officers arrived to collect them. The felon was summarily executed, and the Chancellor was sent to prison to serve out the rest of the felon's original sentence.

Considering the usual calibre of clientele Chancellors dealt with, it was no wonder the practice was rare. Did Josalyn trust Rafferty that much? Apparently she did. She was on her feet and yelling for the guard before she was even aware of having made her decision.

One thing he'd always liked about Joss was that once she made up her mind to do something, it got done and the gods help anyone who tried to stop her. Right now his body was rapidly repairing itself thanks to the donation of fresh blood singing through his veins. The guard who'd argued with Joss over taking Rafferty with her had learned the hard way not to cross her. The fool's sore neck would reinforce that lesson.

"Thanks for the meal, Joss. Prison guard isn't my favourite vintage, but it's a vast improvement over my recent diet. Rat blood is too weak."

She came to an abrupt stop. "They were feeding you rats?" The dead calm didn't disguise her anger.

"No, they fed me the legal minimum of expired blood from the blood bank. I supplemented that with rats or they would have had to carry me into that holding cell to talk to you."

"Bastards." Her dark eyes promised there would be a reckoning the first chance she got.

"So where are we going?" he asked as they headed for her transport. He liked that he didn't have to shorten his strides to match hers. Those long legs of hers had featured in his favourite fantasies.

"To my hotel." She checked the clock on her scanner. "We don't have much time left before sunrise. I was going to set up interviews with some of the witnesses this morning, but that won't work now with you tagging along."

Yeah, vampires and sunshine didn't mix well. If he had to follow her on daytime interviews, she might as well stake him now. "How many are you going to talk to?"

"All four of them. Normally I wouldn't want them all in one place – too much chance of contaminating their testimony – but the Council will only let me have you for three days. And today counts as one of those days."

She'd have him for a lot longer than that if things worked out. If they didn't, at least he would have spent his remaining hours with her. He looked down at his clothing and grimaced.

"I'm not exactly dressed for the occasion."

She straightened his collar. "Yeah, this does lack your usual style, but I have to interview them alone anyway. Talking to a Chancellor is scary enough without having to face the vampire they helped condemn. We can't risk anyone recanting their testimony and then later claiming they were coerced."

He nodded. "OK, I'll be a good little vampire and cower in the next room."

Joss laughed. "Oh, yeah, I can see that. I don't think 'cower' is in your vocabulary. Even if I'd come ready to stake you, you wouldn't even have flinched. Your pride wouldn't let you."

They climbed into her transport. Joss rarely did things by half measures. As soon as the engine engaged, she ripped off down the road.

Gods above, he was tired. Eventually the daylight would force him to sleep. When he was at full strength, he could get by with only a few hours of rest. However, the strain of the past few weeks and the substandard prison fare had taken a toll.

"You can listen to the recordings of their testimony later. Most of their evidence is circumstantial, confirming the fact that you and the victim had a past." Joss braked for a pedestrian.

"That was no secret."

"And if that's all the evidence the Council had, it wouldn't have been enough to convict you. No, the damning evidence was your knife sticking in the bastard's heart, which will be our next point of focus." Joss tried to sound optimistic, but they both knew it wasn't looking good.

She mustered up a half-hearted smile. "Look, I don't know about you, but I need a shower and sleep before I can think straight. It will be dawn soon, so let's just get to the hotel."

He wrapped an arm around her shoulder as she drove. "All you can do is try, Joss. We both know clearing my name is a long shot."

She didn't argue.

Twenty minutes later he sat in the hotel room while Joss showered. He eyed the bathroom door, wondering if she was willing to share her shower with him and, if so, what was were the chances she'd share her bed. A vampire could always hope.

He fought the temptation to test the effectiveness of the ankle bracelet. Maybe if it was just *his* life at risk, but he wouldn't hurt Joss. So for the moment, he contented himself with enjoying the relative freedom of the hotel room. The decor might be bland, but it beat his prison cell all to hell.

The sound of a heartbeat in the hallway preceded a sharp knock at the door. Rafferty yanked the door open to see a uniformed hotel employee holding out a shopping bag.

"Uh, the clothes you ordered, sir."

The young man looked understandably nervous to be addressing a vampire, which improved Rafferty's mood considerably. "Where do I sign?"

The bellhop held out the bill. After Rafferty scrawled his name on the paper, the boy shoved the bag at him and bolted away. Rafferty could have told him that the worst thing he could do in front of a known predator was run. But rather than give chase, Rafferty focused on the prey he was really interested in, the one who had just finished her shower. A naked and wet Joss was much more to his taste.

Only the fact that he still reeked of prison kept him from cornering her in the bathroom. No, he'd scrub himself clean before making his move. They had only a limited time to track down Petra and clear his name. There was a good chance they'd fail, and he wasn't going to miss out on his one opportunity to bed Josalyn. She might knock him on his ass for trying, but even that had its own appeal.

The bathroom door opened in a cloud of steam. Joss stepped out, still towelling her hair dry, her skin rosy. Her pulse was racing far faster than her calm expression could account for. She smiled at him. "Your turn. I even left enough hot water for you."

Hot, cold, he didn't care. He stripped off his prison attire and tossed it at the trash can. Cranking the water up to full force, he scrubbed his skin clean. He could have spent hours luxuriating in the stinging spray, but he didn't want to give Joss time to build up her defences.

As he dried off, he eyed the new clothes and decided it would be easier to crowd Joss if he wore nothing more than a towel and a hungry smile. As a vampire, he couldn't check his appearance in the mirror without forcing his image to appear. He had a better use for his remaining energy.

Besides, Joss had already seen him at his worst and had not run screaming the other way. That didn't mean she was going to fall into his arms. She wanted him as much as he wanted her, but her overdeveloped sense of duty could get in the way. She might try to resist his charm, but she'd be fighting the battle on two fronts – his desire for her and her own for him.

She was a warrior woman and would no doubt bring all that strength and intensity to the confrontation. Should be fun to see which one of them ended up on top when he finally did get her into that bed. Not that he cared. He reached for the doorknob and prepared to do battle.

Rafferty would be coming out soon. Josalyn hadn't missed the predatory gleam in his eyes. Staring at the door, she was torn between drawing her weapon to keep him at arm's length and stripping off naked to save both of them time. As reckless as that would be, it would be worth it to see his reaction. She'd lose her job if she gave into temptation, but her career was over with anyway. It would destroy her to execute him. If she didn't have to, she planned on never letting him out of her sight again.

If she couldn't make the Council happy, she might as well please herself.

She peeled her shirt off over her head. Her pants quickly followed, leaving only her pragmatic, government-issue underwear. She wasn't much for lace and satin, but still felt a momentary regret. Knowing Rafferty, though, she wouldn't keep it on long enough to matter anyway.

Should she stretch out on the bed or wait across the room? Definitely the latter. As the door opened, her breath caught in her throat as she waited for Rafferty to spot her. It didn't take long.

The towel around his waist did little to hide the fact that their minds had been running along the same track. He stalked towards her, his fangs peeking out. Oh, yeah, this was going to be good.

He stopped just short of where she stood waiting. "I thought I'd have to convince you."

The slight hint of indecision in his gaze vanquished the last of her own doubts. "This might be . . ."

He shushed her by putting his fingers on her lips. "Tonight is just for us."

It had been months since he'd last touched her, but she remembered so clearly how it had felt to have his strong body pressed against hers as he'd fed. They hadn't gone beyond that intimacy, but she'd wanted so much more. This time she wasn't going to settle for almost. This time they were going to have it all.

She took the last step, leaving only a breath of space between them, to slide her hands across the smooth muscles of his chest. In response, his arms locked around her waist, pulling her tight against his erection. Both of them moaned at the sensation.

"Kiss me."

She did as he ordered, brushing her lips across his and then tracing the length of his fangs with the tip of her tongue. Finally, their mouths fused together, giving into the need for that first taste.

He growled his approval deep in his chest, the vibration making her breasts ache and her nipples harden. His fingers traced the small scars he'd left on her skin, before moving on. He murmured his pleasure as she rained a trail of kisses down his jaw to the pulse point at the base of his neck.

In a sudden move, he ripped the back of her bra apart. She giggled and shrugged it the rest of the way off, before tugging his towel loose. Then her panties went the way of her bra. The differences in their heights was negligible, but he swung her up in his arms as if she shared the petite build of his ex. Shoving the thought of Petra to the back of her mind, Josalyn basked in the strength of her vampire lover. Once they were horizontal on the bed, he kissed her until she wasn't sure where she stopped and he started.

"I want this to be perfect, Joss, but it's been building for too long for me to wait much longer." He made room for himself between her legs.

"We've waited too long already. Make me yours, Rafferty."

She wrapped her arms around his shoulders and held on as he thrust deep inside of her. When he tried to slow down, she urged him on, chanting his name and digging into his skin with her nails.

He drove them both hard, staking his claim to her with his powerful strokes. When the first ripples of her climax began to build, he stared down at the pulsing blood vessels in her throat. "Joss?"

That he'd ask rather than assume made her smile. "When I said make me yours, I meant it."

"I'll try to be gentle." His fangs had run out far enough to make it hard to talk.

"I'm not fragile, Rafferty." She turned her head to the side, granting him easier access.

He drew a shuddering breath and then struck. The sharp pain was lost in a flare of soothing heat. She was no innocent, but she'd never before experienced such intimacy as having Rafferty plunging into her throat and her body at the same time. The sensations burned through her from head to toe, immediately shoving her screaming over the precipice.

When the world righted itself, Rafferty lifted his head, gently withdrawing his fangs from his lover's neck. He carefully licked the wounds closed, not wanting to leave a scar this time. The last time she'd allowed him to feed, he'd given in to the primitive urge to leave his mark on her. The small scars he'd left made sure she'd never forget that moment when he'd taught her what it meant to give herself over to a vampire lover.

She stirred restlessly beneath him. He moved to the side, knowing she'd need her rest if they were going to bring Petra to bay. He'd only taken a little of Josalyn's blood, enough to whet his appetite for more. But he couldn't risk weakening her, not with his murderous ex out there plotting their downfall.

"Rafferty? You're frowning pretty hard for a man who just indulged in life-altering sex." Josalyn's smile was tired, but extremely satisfied.

He couldn't help but grin, delighted with his lover's opinion of him. "Sorry. I was just trying to decide if I could survive a second helping."

"Give me a few minutes to catch my breath and we can find out. If we don't live through it, at least we'll die happy."

When she yawned loudly, he chuckled and tucked her in close as she tumbled over the edge into slumber. While she rested, he'd savour these moments of holding her in his arms.

Rafferty didn't want to wake up, not if it was in his prison cell. Rather than open his eyes, he used his other senses to learn if he'd only been dreaming about Joss in his arms. He smiled. He could definitely hear a heartbeat and the sound of breathing. His skin soaked in the warmth of a feminine leg sprawled over his and a hand carelessly flung across his chest. Breathing in slowly, he drew Joss' sweet scent deep into his lungs.

It was no dream.

Joss stirred. "Something wrong?"

He tightened his arm around her and finally allowed his eyes to open. "No, we're fine."

She lifted her head up to blink at him sleepily. "What time is it?"

He didn't need a clock to tell him. "The sun's going down."

"So, we need to get moving."

"Not yet. A few minutes more." Not enough time to do more than kiss her and hold her close, but he wasn't going to give up even that much. But maybe if he hurried . . .

He scooted down, intent on revisiting a few of his favourite spots on Joss' body along the way. She had to be a bit sore from this afternoon, but there were other ways to please his woman. She grabbed his hair, stopping him just short of reaching his intended target.

"As much as I appreciate the thought, Rafferty, we have work to do. We don't have time for this."

The stubborn set to her chin said she meant it. "Fine. Be that way. Do you want the shower first?"

Her mouth softened into a wicked smile. "Why don't we share and save both time and water?"

When she released him, he rolled out of bed and held out a hand to her. "Let's."

The shower lasted longer than it should have, but Rafferty had used his considerable charm to coax her into a few intense moments that had nothing to do with getting clean. It was amazing what he managed to accomplish in a shower stall never meant to hold two people, much less two people engaged in mind-numbing sex. If his lovemaking had a desperate edge to it, she pretended not to notice.

Under the circumstances, she'd be a fool to get used to having Rafferty in her life, much less her bed. But the past 24 hours had only cemented her determination to clear his name. Rafferty wasn't perfect, not by any standard. He was cocky, egotistical and all too full of himself. The one thing he wasn't was stupid. And killing a known enemy with his own knife and leaving it stuck in the corpse was stupid beyond all belief. She didn't doubt for a moment that Rafferty was capable of killing, but this crime made no sense – unless it was a set-up.

She pulled out his file and began flipping through the pages. Up to this point she'd been focusing on the trial and the testimony of the witnesses, but hadn't there been a mention of a lien against the estate? Running her finger down the pages, it took her a while to find the reference buried in a paragraph of legal jargon.

"Rafferty, who stands to profit if you die? The Coalition will deduct the cost of your case from your estate if you're executed. But who gets what's left over?"

He finished tugging on his shirt before turning to face her. "I don't have any family left. After any outstanding bills are paid, the rest will go to my heir." His eyes shifted away, focusing on a point on the far side of the room.

"So who's your heir? Could he be behind this?"

If she didn't know better, she would have thought he was blushing. "It's not a he; it's a she."

"Your ex?"

"There's no way I'd give that greedy bitch a dime." He turned back to face her. "I named you as my heir. So unless *you* set me up . . ."

She was stunned. "You named me as your heir? Why would you do that?"

His temper, never far away, blazed hot. "Damn it, Joss, after the day we just spent in that bed, all but killing each other with the heat between us, you have to ask a stupid question like that? How many ways do I have to show you that I love you? Until this mess blew up in my face, I was on my way to claim you."

Shock shorted out her ability to think. "You love me?"

He stared at her, the same intensity in his eyes, but his voice was gentle. "Yes, Josalyn, I love you. What's more, you love me."

He didn't sound convinced of that last part, so maybe it was more of a question. Well, if he could confess all, so could she. She dropped the pile of papers on the bed to step into his arms. "Oh, yeah, I love you." Then she kissed him for a long, long time.

Finally, breaking away, he rested his forehead against hers, bringing them both back to the matter at hand. "As much as I'd like to continue this particular discussion, you sounded as if you were on the trail of something important."

"What? Oh, yes, the papers." She fumbled through them to the right page. "Someone has a lien against your estate. We need to know who and why."

She booted up her computer and typed in a request for the information. Marking it as high priority, she sat back and waited for someone at the other end to scramble into action. The answer wasn't long in coming.

She scanned the page. "I think they're claiming a breach of contract."

Rafferty crouched down to look over her shoulder. He ran his finger down the screen to settle by the name of the company and started cursing. "The damn bitch didn't even bother to cover her tracks. She probably figured the Coalition wouldn't pick up on the company name 'Part-E Inc.', but that I would. Unscramble the letters and you have her name. Petra still wants her pound of flesh. It's not enough to kill me, but she wants my money, too."

Josalyn looked disgusted. "The court wouldn't look any further than to make sure the claim came from a legitimate company. If her name isn't on the paperwork, they would have no reason to suspect anything. Well, Petra doesn't know who she's messing with." The female would be lucky if she didn't end up spending the rest of her centuries locked in the cell Rafferty had vacated.

Josalyn's fangs came out, a predator ready for the hunt. "Now I can call her in for a talk."

Rafferty leaned in to slide his fingertip over the sharp points of her canines before kissing her. "This should be good. Can I watch?"

Common sense reared its ugly head. "No, and I'm going to call in a second Chancellor because we need to tread carefully. It's not enough to prove that the lien is false. We need to get her on the murder charge or the two of you could end up in adjoining cells."

His expression sobered. "Until my execution."

She nodded. "Like I said, we need her confession. But if she's being this reckless, it shouldn't be hard."

It took Josalyn more time than they could really afford to track down Ambrose, her boss, and convince him that she needed his assistance. Chancellors were supposed to be able to handle any situation. Short of telling him that she was sleeping with her prisoner, she had to rely on convincing him that Petra's family connections merited special care.

Once she had him convinced, she issued the order under his name to have Petra brought in for questioning regarding the prisoner contesting the lien. Then there was nothing left to do but wait.

Petra swept into the meeting room an hour late for her appointment and with a handful of lackeys trailing in behind her. Ambrose gave Josalyn a brief look, arching an eyebrow at the parade. He wouldn't have questioned Petra's decision to bring legal representation, but this group looked more like she'd been called away from a social event and had brought the party with her.

If Ambrose had doubts about Josalyn's assessment of the case, they were gone now. The smug look Petra gave the two Chancellors sealed her fate. Even if Ambrose thought Rafferty was guilty, he wouldn't take the woman's casual disregard of protocol lightly.

In chilling tones, he expressed his displeasure. "Unless one of these people is your attorney, they can wait outside. They will also pay the same fine as you for keeping us waiting. The amount will increase geometrically for each additional second they remain in my presence."

The crowd hissed in shock and scurried for the door, leaving Petra sputtering in indignation. She shot a venomous look at Josalyn. "What is she doing here?"

"You know very well why I'm here, Petra. I'm in charge of Rafferty's case."

"What? He hasn't been executed yet?" Her smile turned nasty. "Do they know you two were lovers when you were on the Council?"

Ambrose slammed his hand down on the table. "Madam, you *will* treat this hearing with the respect it deserves. Chancellor Sloan's prior relationship with her prisoner is none of your concern. However, this bogus lien against his estate is."

"The lien is legitimate. There was a breach of contract." Petra shot a nasty look in Josalyn's direction. "The accused ended our betrothal. His action cost me a great deal of money and emotional pain."

Ambrose clearly wasn't buying it. "Broken betrothals are hardly a rarity among the vampires. And considering you've broken at least one betrothal yourself, I have a difficult time believing that this was little more than an inconvenience."

Josalyn decided it was time to toss more fuel on the fire. "I'm sure it can't have anything to do with the fact that you believe Rafferty ended your betrothal because of his friendship with me."

"Friendship! We both know it was more than that." Petra's pretty face wasn't quite so lovely when contorted with rage. "You Chancellors think you're above the rest of us, but you're half-breeds at best. With Rafferty's lineage, he should be executed for consorting with the likes of you."

Rafferty was supposed to wait in the next room until he heard himself summoned, but he wasn't going to sit around and listen to Josalyn be insulted. He strolled into the conference room. Ignoring his ex-fiancée, he moved to stand between the two women.

Just as he expected, Petra immediately turned on him. "What are you doing walking around free? I thought you'd be dead by now."

"You mean you hoped I'd be dead by now." He nodded in Ambrose's direction. "I apologize for barging in uninvited, Chancellors. I'd also apologize for Petra's manners, if she had any." He glanced in her direction. It wouldn't take much more prodding to make her lose all control of her tongue. "I hope I didn't interrupt anything important."

Josalyn smiled. "Not at all. I believe we were about to deny the lien on your estate as being without merit. Any monies, after *legitimate* costs are deducted, will go to your heir."

"Good. I'm relieved to hear that. I wouldn't want the woman who framed me for murder to profit from my death. I hope you'll think of me when you spend my money, Josalyn." He held his breath, waiting for the explosion.

It didn't take long. Petra screamed and charged towards him, her fangs running out. "I should have simply killed you myself, you bastard! It's not too late!"

It took both Ambrose and Josalyn to pull the enraged vampire off of him. No matter how much he hated her, Rafferty didn't want to be the one to kill her.

Once Petra had been subdued, Ambrose called for the guards. "You will be charged with both the murder of the human and the attempted murder of Mr O'Day. Your assets are hereby frozen to cover the cost of your trial and to compensate Mr O'Day for any inconvenience he's suffered at your hands."

Petra was still cursing them as the guards dragged her away. Once she was gone, Ambrose turned his attention to Josalyn and Rafferty. "You two played a very dangerous game. If she'd controlled her mouth, you would've been on your way back for immediate execution."

"It was a chance we had to take." Josalyn looked pale. Clearly the strain of the past few days had been hard for her.

"I'll need your resignation by the end of the week, Chancellor Sloan."

Rafferty snarled, "But she—"

"Enough!" Ambrose included both of them in his glance. "Chancellors have to be neutral. You both know that. Looking back, I realize her feelings for you are the real reason she left her position as Arbitrator. And the way you leaped to her defence only confirms my opinion. Your last duty as Chancellor will be to write up the paperwork exonerating Mr O'Day here of any wrongdoing. I would do it, but I'll be busy with the charges against his ex-betrothed."

Rafferty tried to feel some sympathy for Petra, but couldn't. "If you need my testimony . . ."

"I'll let you know when I've had time to review the case in its entirety."

Josalyn took Rafferty's hand and faced her superior. "Thank you for your assistance, Chancellor. For the record, I'm sorry. Petra is guilty of a lot of things, but she did have some cause to resent my feelings for Rafferty."

"I'll take that into consideration." Ambrose gathered up the papers. "Now I must be going. I imagine the two of you have plans to make."

Rafferty held his hand out to the older man. "That we do, sir. Would you like an invitation to the wedding?"

Ambrose smiled for the first time as he shook Rafferty's hand. "Most certainly."

When he was gone, Josalyn pursed her lips and narrowed her eyes. Rafferty realized he'd been a bit high-handed announcing their intent to get married before discussing it with her.

"About this wedding . . ."

"I should have asked you first."

"Yes, you should have, but for the record, I accept. But there's one thing you should know."

The twinkle in her eyes told him it was going to be all right. "And what's that?"

She grabbed his collar and pulled his face down close to hers. "I don't believe in long engagements."

Then she kissed him.

# Coming Home

## Lilith Saintcrow

*E*ven a magus raised by a demon might have a little trouble with *this*. Liana Spocarelli's hand locked around the doorknob, her other hand cramped tight around the katana's scabbard. "What the hell do *you* want?"

The Nichtvren on her porch – a tall, deceptively slight male with a shock of dirty blond hair and the face of a celluloid angel – tilted his head slowly, his hands in the pockets of his linen trousers. His aura was the deep, deliciously wicked fume of colourless Power that meant *not-so-human*, without the pleasant edge of spice attached to so many of her childhood memories.

"It is a pleasure to see you again, *chérie*," Tiens said quietly. His suit, as always, was wrinkled, rumpled and pristinely white. "May I come in?"

"No. You may not." Liana let go of the doorknob. "Go suck on some virgins or something. Leave me alone."

Behind him, the night breathed, redolent with rain and cold metal, the edge of radioactive damp that meant Saint City.

Home. And here she was, all the way across the city from any house that was hers. Specks of hovercraft glow danced overhead, a river of fireflies.

"*La Belle Morte, ta mere,* said I should not come."

*Well, now, isn't that special. Since she can't leave me alone, she tells* you *to.* Her cheek burned, the clawed triple-circle tattoo moving and tingling in response to the weight of Power covering him. Nichtvren night-hunting masters: the top of the paranormal food chain – except for demons.

Always except for demons. Liana's arm loosened, dangling her sword. "How's Jaf?" The irony of inquiring about the well-being of a Fallen demon didn't escape her.

"*M'sieu* is well. He also said I should not come. He said my welcome would be uncertain at best." Tiens' thin lips curved into a smile, his eyes gas-flame blue holes in the dimness. The single bulb on her porch was deliberately weak; a bright light would disturb her night vision.

Besides, she hadn't got round to changing it.

"I wouldn't call it *uncertain*, Tiens. I'd call it *nonexistent*. I repeat, what the ever-loving hell do you want?"

"Your help, *petite sorcière*." The smile dropped as quickly as it had bloomed, and he was once again the familiar Tiens of her childhood, ageless and accessible at once, the object of her painful schoolgirl crush and the last broken heart she'd ever allowed herself. "I have a death I must achieve."

Her entire body went cold. "I'm no contract killer, Tiens. Go ask Dante, I'm sure she'll be more than helpful. Goodnight." She stepped back, sweeping the door closed, and wasn't surprised when he put up one elegant hand. The heavy iron door stopped cold, as if it had met a brick wall.

"She cannot interfere, and neither can *M'sieu*. I need you, Liana."

"Go away." She retreated two steps, realized her mistake, but by then he was already in the hall. "I didn't invite you in."

"When have you ever left me on the cold doorstep?" If he meant it whimsically, he must have realized it was a mistake. The air stilled, and she realized any other psion in her place would be utterly nervous to have a Nichtvren in her hallway.

"I thought you bloodsucking maniacs couldn't cross a threshold without an invitation," she returned, as coldly as her hammering heart would allow. She turned on her bare heel and headed for the kitchen. Her right hand itched for the hilt, but there was a plasgun under the counter that would serve better. Habit and instinct sent her hand to the sword most times, probably the result of growing up in a house where the katana was a metaphor for any combat, any honour, any guilt. Dante's standard response for any problem was to slice it in half.

Not that there was anything wrong with that, as far as Liana could see.

"Liana." He tried again. "I am . . . sorry. I did not mean to wound you."

*But you did.* That was uncharitable, however, and worse, untrue. He had simply, kindly, refused her, because she was too young and human besides. Only human. Even if she was a combat-trained magi.

*God, how I wish I was something else. Even a sex witch would be better than this.* "Shut the door, Tiens. And make sure you're on the other side of it."

"I have asked for your help, *petite.* I am desperate." He even sounded the part, his usually melodious voice suddenly ragged. "I will beg, if it pleases you."

Liana shut her eyes, put out her right hand, and touched the wall. It thrummed under her fingers, the house's defences humming along as if a Nichtvren hadn't stepped right through them. Of course, he knew her work and, if she had to be honest, she hadn't really wanted to keep him out, had she?

"It's not even me you want." Her throat was dry, the words a harsh croak. "It's the glove."

He drew in breath to speak – and wasn't *that* a joke, because Nichtvren didn't need to breathe. They only did it when they needed to seduce someone into something. Liana shook her head. The sword in her left hand made a faint noise through its scabbard, a high, thin note as her distress communicated itself through the metal.

*This is your honour, Liana. It must never touch the ground.*

"Don't bother lying to me again, Tiens." Even to herself she sounded strange. "Just shut the goddamn door. I'm going make some tea." She took an experimental step. All her appendages seemed to be working just fine. "When you're ready, come into the kitchen and tell me who you want me to kill."

"She arrives on a private transport, midnight tomorrow. Nikolai cannot interfere, as I am not his vassal." Tiens stared into the blue mug full of hibiscus tea – astringent enough that a Nichtvren could drink it without severe stomach cramps, red enough that it could be pale blood. Still, he merely inhaled its fragrance and watched her with those blue, blue eyes.

"What about Jaf? Can't he make her go away?"

"He has . . . other worries."

*Story of my life. Worries other than us petty mortals. He's busy keeping Dante from chewing at her cage or her own wrists, busy keeping the Tithe back from Saint City, busy dealing with the Hegemony's demands. Busy, busy, busy.* "Which don't include taking care of you right now?"

"I have not asked, Liana. *M'sieu* has enough problems." He frowned, every line on his face drawn for aesthetic effect.

"So why do you want to kill this Amelie, anyway?" Liana tapped her bitten fingernails against the counter. This city was too cold. She'd fled south as soon as she'd finished her Academy schooling, and never looked back.

*Right. Never looked back. That's why I'm here now.*

His blue, blue eyes tilted up, and there was a shadow in them she didn't care to name. "She is my Maker. And she has come to reclaim me, or to make trouble for *M'sieu*. Either way, she must be dealt with. And where else can I turn if not to you?"

*Not fair. So not fair.* But Liana's fingers tightened and a flush rose on her throat. "She's your Maker, so you can't attack her. How in the hell am *I* supposed to—"

"I can distract her by fighting her command. I am old and a Master in my own right, *petite*. I will keep her occupied, you take her head and free me. Easy, no?"

"Nothing's ever easy," Liana muttered. *I sound like Dante. Well, I should, she raised me.* "How the hell am I supposed to kill a Nichtvren? I'm *mortal*, Tiens. As you reminded me until you were blue in the face."

"Separate her head from her body. It will not be so hard." He paused, as if there was more to say.

Liana sighed, rolled her head back on her shoulders, easing the tension creeping up her neck. "You want me to risk my neck decapitating your Master. Why should I?"

"There is no other I would trust." He didn't give her a wide-eyed, dewy, innocent stare, but the way he dropped his gaze into his tea was almost as bad. Liana half expected to hear a splash.

"You would grind my heart to powder if you could, and I do not blame you. Betrayal, however, is not in your nature."

*I wouldn't be so sure about that if I were you.* "You can go away now, Tiens. Come back tomorrow at dusk and I'll let you know."

"Not now?"

"You told me to wait once. I'm returning the favour." She stared at her sunny yellow mug against the scratched and gouged countertop. "One question, though. How did you find me?"

"If I must wait for your answer, you may wait for mine on that score." Tiens eased off the stool, soundlessly touching the scarred linoleum. This place was a wreck, and Liana was briefly, hotly ashamed. But it was cheap, and she'd thought nobody would notice she was home, back in the bad old cradle.

*Guess I was wrong about that, wasn't I?* "Fine. Close the door on your way out."

She listened as he paced down the hall, his feet deliberately making noise for her benefit. With her eyes closed, she could *see* his aura as well, the disciplined, deliciously wicked-smelling glow of a night-hunting predator. They were machines built for seduction and power, the suckheads. For a moment a roaring rose in her ears, the body's instinctive response to something inimical to its survival.

Like a sheep trembling at the smell of a wolf.

The front door opened, closed and the shields over the house – carefully laid, but not strong enough to put out a huge neon sign screaming HERE I AM, COME TAKE A LOOK! – resonated as his aura stroked them, once: an intimate caress. Then he was gone, vanished into the pall of night covering Saint City, perhaps a little shimmer hanging in the air as he performed the "don't look here" trick Nichtvren were famous for.

Liana opened her eyes, stared down. Her left hand curled around the katana's scabbard, the metal inside quiescent. Her right hand had knotted into a fist, bitten fingernails driving into her palm. The ring, three braided loops of silvery metal, its clawed setting grasping a dead-dark gem, glinted in the light from the overhead fixture. A single pinprick of green struggled up from the depths of the stone, winked out as she breathed in, slowly, blowing out tension the way Danny had taught her. *That's your best friend right there,* her foster-mother had said in her melodious, queerly husky voice. *Use your breath; it's completely under your control. Not like other things.*

Not like a heart, or a dreaming mind, or the hint of spice in an aura that made you a magus instead of a necromance or even a shaman. Not like an accident of genetics that made you liable to snap Hegemony Enforcement inspections or the hatred of normals.

Her right hand crept towards the blue mug, curled around its heat, almost scorching her fingers. She lifted it to her lips, rested them for a moment where his would have rested if he'd bothered to drink even a single sip.

*I could toss this on the floor. Throw it through the window. But then I'd have to clean it up.*

She settled for sliding off her stool, stalking to the sink and pouring the liquid away. The tea bag landed, red as a blood clot, with a plop. She opened her fingers, let the mug drop and wished immediately that she'd thrown it.

An old-fashioned, chunky plastic vidphone hung on the wall, and she picked up the handset. She dialled a number burned into her memory, hoping he would answer.

There were two rings, a click and silence. Whether it was him listening or a machine taking messages was anyone's guess.

"It's me," she said into the black mouthpiece, staring at the "Video Disabled" flashing across the flat screen. "I'm home. I need you."

And before he could reply – if he was there – she disconnected.

The tower, downtown on Seventh, had a shielding so powerful it was almost in the visible spectrum, moving in lazy swirls, the black-diamond fire of a demon's Power resonating with the flux of ambient energy. There was a keypad, a slot for a credit disc and a retinal scan, but even before she pressed her ring finger onto the keypad the shielding had changed, tautened with attention and expanded a few feet to tingle on her shoulders and the roots of her hair. The door slid aside before she even finished keying in her personal code.

She stepped through and into a lift, felt claustrophobia touch her throat briefly. She dispelled it. Her scalp itched. *I'll be damned if I clean up or dress up to visit her.* She hadn't changed since arriving by freight hover two days ago.

*Sackcloth and ashes, anyone?*

The lift was high-speed, and even though it was pressurized her ears popped a few times as it ascended. The building looked so slim and graceful from the outside, it was easy to forget just how big it was, and how much was said by its construction. Saint City was one of a handful of places that hadn't been affected by the first Tithe, when the mouths of Hell opened and madness poured out. A twentieth of the Hegemony population had died, either that night or in the week following, when the citizens of Hell hunted at their leisure or simply, merely, drove the normals to suicide or insanity. Magi had died in droves trying to drive them off, other psions had died trying to protect Hegemony troops or just by being in the wrong place at the wrong time. It had been even worse in the Putchkin Alliance, the chaos reaching global proportions before suddenly, inexplicably, waning. All was well for seven years . . . and then the mouths of Hell gaped again.

Liana had been nineteen that second time, and she remembered the Hegemony ambassadors coming to her mother. *This city hasn't been affected by the Tithe. Why?*

And Dante's reply. *You know better than I do, you supercilious jackasses. Come in and ask him what you've come to ask.*

The lift chimed and halted, chimed again, and the doors slid open. The familiar entry hall – white floor, white walls, a restrained Berscardi print hanging over a neo-Deco table of white enamel – swallowed her whole. Her whole head itched, long dark hair matted and hanging lank, and she was sure her clothes were none-too fresh, despite the antibacterium impregnating the microfibre explorer's shirt and the leather-patched jeans. The non-slip soles of her boots squeaked slightly, echoed by the faint sound as the double doors at the end of the hall swung wide.

Grey, rainy, winter light poured through, glowed mellow on a wooden floor. The sparring-space was huge, cavernous and walled with mirrors on one side and bulletproof tinted plasglass on the other. A ballet barre was bolted to the mirrored side, varnished with use and wax, and a slim shape in loose black silk with long, slightly curling dark hair stood precisely placed, her back to the door, the golden tint to her hands clearly visible.

Dante Valentine turned and regarded her foster-child. The same sharp, hurtful, intelligent wariness in dark liquid eyes, the same high cheekbones and sweet, sinful mouth pulled tight in an iron half-smile, the same tensile grace to her shoulders and her left hand holding a long, curved shape. The emerald set in Dante's cheek spat a single welcoming green spark over her tat, a winged caduceus that ran under her skin. Liana's own tattoo betrayed her, ink prickling with diamond feet in her flesh, answering. The ring tightened, green swirling in its depths before it relaxed into dead darkness again.

They regarded each other, and Liana felt herself bulge shapelessly like a blob of reactive paint in zero gravity. *You're the very image of your mother,* Dante had said over and over again. *She was so beautiful.* And each time, Liana flinched. She hated being the image of a dead woman she couldn't remember even with the holostills of her precise little smile and dark hair. She wanted to be as pretty as her *foster-mother*, the most famous necromance in the world. The woman who had raised her, the woman whose demon had played with her for hours in the long dim time of Liana's childhood.

As usual, Liana's nerve broke first. "The prodigal returns." Her tone was a challenge, and she winced inwardly as Dante's shoulders hitched slightly, as if bracing herself for a blow.

"I've never known you to waste much, Lia. I didn't know you were in town."

"A thief in the night." *Ask me what I'm doing here. Get angry, for fuck's sake. Say something.*

"Are you . . ." Dante caught herself. *Are you all right? Are you well?* She would never ask. "Are you staying long? I—"

"Not long." *Now that Tiens found me.* "I just came by to say hi. And to see Jaf."

Again, that slight movement, as if her words were a blade slid into flesh. "Nothing else?" Other questions crowded under the two words – questions such as: *Do you forgive me? How long will you hate me if you don't?*

Questions with no real answer.

"Not really. I suppose he's at the office?" *I knew he would be. Coordinating defence and taking care of the business of keeping this city afloat. Probably organizing refugee camps, too.*

"Yes." Dante tilted her exquisite head slightly, silk fluttering as she took a single step forwards. Loose pants and a Chinese-collared shirt, reinforced in patches, not the jeans and explorer's shirt she would wear if she intended on stepping outside the tower. "I worried about you, Lia."

More unspoken words crowded the still, grey air. *It's my job to protect you. I promised your mother.*

And Liana's response, flung at her in the middle of screaming matches during the storms of adolescence. *I don't care what you promised her! I'm not her!*

"Tiens visited me," she said. She heard the catch in her voice and hated herself. "Don't tell Jaf, but I'm doing dirty laundry for him. Like mother, like daughter, huh?"

Dante sighed. "If you wanted a fight, you could have come a little later in the day. You know I'm not ready for homicide before noon."

Liana's heart squeezed down on itself. "Sorry to disappoint."

"*Sekhmet sa'es.*" But the curse didn't have its usual snap. "What can I do, Lia? What do you want? Blood?"

*Not like you could bleed over me anyway. The instant you cut yourself Jaf would show up, and I'd have to deal with the disappointment on* his *face too. Isis preserve me.* "I just wanted to say hello. I'm allowed that, aren't I?"

"You're the one who keeps away." The necromance made a swift, abortive movement, too quick to be a flinch. "Can I take you to dinner? That noodle shop on Pole Street is still open. Or we could go for a walk. Even . . ."

"Even sparring? You'd do that just to keep me in the room a little bit longer, wouldn't you?" *Listen to me whine. I promised myself I wouldn't do this.* "I'm a lot better than I used to be."

"So I've heard." Dante's shoulders relaxed. "What are you really here for, Lia?"

*I wish I knew.* "Just to say hello, *Mother*." Deliberate emphasis on the word, watching as Dante turned into a statue carved of fluid golden stone, every inch of her braced and ready, giving nothing away. Except her eyes. The pain there was half balm, half poison. "I'll be on my way. Give my regards to Jaf."

"Come back soon," Dante whispered. Her aura, full of the trademark glittering sparkles of a necromance, embedded in black-diamond demon fire, turned dark and soft with hurt. "Please. Lia—"

"Maybe. Hold your breath." And Liana stalked away. *There. Mission accomplished. Now I can go.*

As usual, though, Dante got the last word. "I love you." The words were soft, scarred with deadly anger, and so husky they almost refused to stir the air. "I always will."

Liana made it down the hall and into the lift before she started digging in her pockets with her free hand. *Well, that went well. I saw her. Now I can go away again. I can catch a transport in an hour and be back in Angeles Tijuan by nightfall.*

But the tears, sliding hot and thick down her cheeks, said otherwise.

Taking a cheap hotel room on the fringes of the Tank was merely a gesture. She wasn't even really surprised when she exited the shower, dripping, every hint of grime washed away and her scalp thankfully not itching, and found him sitting on the bed, hands loose on his knees. Darkness had fallen, pressing against the curtain-shrouded window with the pock-pock of projectile fire and a scream down on the corner. They might have found a cure for the worst drug of the century, but people still got addicted to Clormen-13 and shot each other, or innocent bystanders. The blight of inner-city rot fuelled by addiction still crept outwards, though not as quickly as twenty years ago.

Tiens' eyes glowed in the dim yellow light from the bedside lamp. "Charming."

*Fuck you.* Liana dropped the towel on her pile of dirty clothes, picked up her clean shirt and shrugged into it. Her skin tingled with chill, the room was barely heated. The long thin scars on her buttocks and side twitched; Tiens drew in a sharp breath. *Goody for me. I've surprised him.*

"What is that?"

Liana sighed, buttoned up her shirt, pulled on her panties and stepped into her jeans. The leather patches were dark from chemwashing. She dropped into a rickety chair and pulled her socks on, laced up her boots and double-knotted them. "Just a demon." *And a very, very close call. Closer than you would ever believe.*

The walls between Hell and the world were so thin now, and it took so little for a demon-trained magus to break them. The only trouble was, she had little control over what came through – and the name she used to make the walls thin down to transparency was the name of a demon the new Prince of Hell either feared . . . or wanted to punish.

"*M'sieu* –" Tiens began.

"Don't you *dare* tell Jaf. If I'm going to be helping you, you don't get to go carrying tales to him. He's got enough to worry about and it's not his fucking business anyway. Clear?"

"I cannot—" His throat moved as he swallowed, and a nasty gleam of satisfaction lit in Liana's chest.

"If you can keep what almost happened between us a secret, you can also keep a little bit of lost skin to yourself." She finger-combed her dark hair, then began braiding it back with quick motions. "Now, if we can get down to business. What does this Nichtvren look like? I don't want to kill the wrong one."

"Female. Dark. Very young." He made a restless movement as she tied off her braid. "I will be there to meet her, and her thralls—"

"How many?" *You didn't say anything about thralls before, dammit.*

"I do not know. All I know is that she will arrive, and God help me afterwards."

*This just keeps getting better.* "Anything else you want to tell me, Tiens?" *If I was my mother right now I'd be kicking your ass. But I'm just me, and I don't even know why I'm doing this.*

Her heart turned into a heated bubble inside her chest. *I'm lying. I know why. Because once I do this, we're even and I can leave again.*

He rose slowly, and Liana dropped her eyes. Her left hand shot out and closed around her katana, which was leaning against a spindle-legged table that passed for furniture only in the most charitable of senses. She dragged it closer to her like a lifeline.

The air turned hard, tensing, and Tiens halted a bare two feet from her.

*This is your honour, Lia. It must never touch the ground.* Dante's voice, from the very first time a ten-year-old Liana had touched a sword.

The first time she had known what made her different, and only human.

"I could say I am sorry, and that I wish I had chosen otherwise. But you would not believe me, since I need your help." A slight sound of moving fabric, and he leaned down, his warmth – he must have fed, blood or sex providing the metabolic kick to fuel his preternatural muscles – brushing her cheek. "And have committed the sin of *asking* for it, as well. Tell me, if I asked for that offer again, if I begged and said you were right, would you bare your throat to me?"

His lips almost touched her cheek, his breath a warm dampness, flavoured with night and, oddly enough, a little bit of mint. *He must have brushed his fangs.* She pushed down hysterical laughter at the thought, her body stiffening, remembering soft kisses and murmurs, the feel of his fingers in her hair, the slow unhurried skimming of his fingers over her damp, young, mortal flesh. Air caught in her throat, let out in a sipped gasp, and her right hand twitched towards the katana's hilt.

Tiens retreated, blinking out of existence and reappearing across the room. Two inches of steel gleamed, glowing blue with spidery runes, the dappled reflection against cheap wallpaper giving the entire room an aqueous cast.

"And she reaches for a knife, to make her lover disappear." Tiens let out a sound that might have been a laugh. The walls groaned sharply under the lash of his voice, a sound she remembered from childhood, the physical world responding to a more-than-human creature's temper.

"You aren't my lover, Tiens. You made that very clear—" the sword slid back home with a click and an effort that left her sweating "—five years ago." *Five years, two months, fourteen days. Should I count up the hours too? But I've changed. Living down south where life is cheaper than a bottle of soymalt-40 will do that to you.*

"Does this mean you will not aid me against my enemy?" He stuffed his hands in his pockets, for all the world like a juvenile delinquent on a holovid show.

*Isis, save me.* Liana shrugged. "I'm here, and I already bought more ammo. It would be a shame not to use it."

Private transport docks radiated out from the main transport well servicing the west half of Saint City, and this one was a long, sleek, black metal tongue extending out into infinity. Liana hugged the shadows at the end of the bay, wishing she could use a plasgun. If she could outrun the blast when a plas field interacted with reactive paint on the underside of a hover, she could just blow this Amelie bitch up and not stop running until Saint City was a smudge on the horizon behind her.

*And if wishes were noodles, nobody would starve.*

Tiens stood at the end of the dock, the orange glow of city light and freeplas tinting his pale hair and now-wrinkled suit. Liana's left hand hovered, touched the butt of a plasgun, then returned to the 9 mm Smithwesson projectile gun. Hollowpoint armour-piercing ammo; hopefully she could bleed the Nichtvren out in short order – if she could *hit* her, that is. She wasn't a preternatural crack shot like Dante, didn't have Dante's grace or unthinking berserker speed. Seeing her foster-mother fight was like seeing fire eat petroleum fumes. Human reflexes could only do so much, and Nichtvren were dangerous.

*How many thralls is she going to have?* Miserable acid boiled in Liana's stomach. *I have a really bad feeling about this.*

*So why am I doing it? Because I have to (the oldest reason in the world). What am I trying to prove? Only that I can.*

A sleek, silver hover detached itself from the traffic-holding pattern overhead and dived gracefully, gyros making a faint whining as its underside swelled with frictionless reactive paint. The whine of antigrav rattled Liana's back teeth, crawled inside her skull and stayed there. *I wonder if he got my message. I wonder if he's even in town. I wonder if he'll show up. He could always find me, he said.* Her heart decided to complete the fun and games by hammering up into her throat, bringing the taste of sour copper with it. *I wonder if now's the time we're going to test that statement.*

The hover was combat- and mag-shielded. It nosed up to the dock as Tiens stepped back a single pace, his shoulders slumping. Liana didn't scan it – whoever was in there would be able to feel her attention, and that would go badly all the way around.

The hover's main passenger hatch dilated, antigrav reaching a whining peak and receding as systems shut down. Liana's fingers touched the plasgun's hilt again. If she squeezed off a shot . . . but Tiens was right there, too.

*Do I care?*

She drew the projectile gun, smoothly, slowly. There would be no glint off the barrel, this catwalk was too deep in industrial gloom. Four escape routes, one of them straight down and onto another slim grating hanging out over space.

*This isn't good.* She watched Tiens, his shoulders bowing under an invisible force, as two small lights gleamed, down low, in the shadowed hatch. *What the hell?*

It couldn't be a Nichtvren. If it was, it was a joke and not a good one. It was the kind of joke immortal beings play on humans without thinking of horrific consequences, just because they can.

The little girl wore a blue gingham frock and shiny red patent-leather shoes. Her hair hung in carefully coiffed ringlets and her feral little face caught a random reflection of light, filling with the stray gleam like a dish with milk. She had a sharp little nose, plump cheeks, dark eyes like coals with the dust of centuries over them. Her aura swirled once, counterclockwise, and ate the deep bruising that was Tiens on the landscape of Power whole, enfolding him.

*You didn't tell me she was a goddamn nine-year-old, Tiens.* Her mouth was dry and as slick as glass. Liana sighted as the blond Nichtvren went to his knees. There was no way even such a creature as old and powerful as him could fight whatever was in that little-girl body. *Isis save me. She's got to be ancient. At least a Master, maybe as strong as the Prime – though I just saw the Prime that once. Scary fucker he was, too.*

Her hand tightened, the hammer clicking up as the trigger eased down. Their voices drifted up to her, some archaic language – maybe Old Franje, mellifluous and accented: Tiens, with a ragged, breathless edge to these words Liana had never heard before; the other Nichtvren in a sweet bell-like tone over a sucking whirlpool of something candy-sweet and rotten.

The little girl stepped forwards, her shoes glittering like polished rubies in the backwash of landing lights. Tiens crumpled and a low sound of agony scarred the night. He sounded like something red-hot had just been rammed into his belly, his body curving over to protect violated flesh.

*Let him suffer. Gods know I suffered enough.*

And yet, she'd taken the job. *This is your honour, Lia. It must never touch the ground.*

The thing was, the ground kept moving. Liana squeezed the trigger.

The bullet flew true, and half of the little girl's head evaporated. She toppled backwards, and Liana was already moving, her hand slapping the guard rail as she vaulted, a moment of weightlessness before her boots thudded onto the catwalk below. *Move, move, move!*

The world exploded, turning over, metal screeching as it tore under a lash of razor-toothed Power. She fell, cartwheeling through space, the catwalk peeled back like so much spun sugar, and she landed *hard*, the gun skittering from her grasp as something snapped like greenwood and a wave of sick agony spilled down her left ribs.

A molasses-slow eternity of rolling to bleed momentum left Liana, hyperventilating, on the cold metal of the dock, her arms and legs twisted oddly and something wet and sticky dripping in her eyes. Firefly points of light streamed through the dark sky, the traffic patterns of both freight and passenger hovers trembling on the edge of coherence for a moment before darkening as something bent over her. Left arm useless, a bar of lead, right arm still working, fingers against a leather-wrapped hilt and the sword rising as every muscle in Liana's body screamed. It was an arc of silver, a solid sweep of metal, and it sank into the side of the little-girl Nichtvren's scrawny neck with a sound like an axe hitting hardwood.

*Isis save me, this is going to hurt in a moment.* The pain turned red and rolled over her as blood sprayed, impossibly red, a tide of stinking copper death.

And the little-girl Nichtvren screamed something no doubt filthy in her mother tongue, claws springing free of her delicate childish fingers, half her dress soaked with bright claret from the swiftly rebuilding ruin of her skull. Other noises intruded under her screeching – a tide of roars and screams, the sound of a projectile rifle stuttering on automatic, howls of pain and at least one spiralling death scream.

Then it happened, the way it always did.

Time stopped.

Liana's bloody hand gleamed, slick and wet, the ring's shine lost under liquid. A pinprick of green flared in the gem's depths, opened like a hover's fisheye hatch, spat a single spark that turned black as it imploded. Emerald light crawled through the widening aperture, sending vein-like traceries through the coating of blood, and flared to cover Liana's right hand in a supple, metallic glove of green light.

Strength like wine jolted up her right arm, spilled down into her chest, burned fiercely in her broken left humerus, pulled Liana to her feet as if she were a puppet, the strings tied to flexible fingers that bent in ways no human's should. Green flame crawled like liquid oil down her fingers, mixing uneasily with the blue glow of runes in the depths of blessed steel, and threaded through the small female body that was even now screeching, thrashing with flesh and Power both, metal crumpling and thin trickles of hot blood tracing down from Liana's ears.

*I knew this was going to happen*, she thought, and felt only a drowsy sense of panic.

The repeating projectile rifle spoke again. The rest of the little-girl Nichtvren's head exploded, gobbets of steaming preternatural flesh smoking and splatting against shredded metal and cracked concrete. The rifle went back to speaking in stutters. Liana tore her sword free and raised her head as the body thumped to the ground, runnels of self-cannibalizing tissue fuelled by an extra-human metabolism turning into rot.

*Damn, they go quickly.*

Her legs folded again as the green light spilled away, back into the depths of the ring. A low, keening hum drilled through her head and receded; Liana found herself sprawled on the dock as the noise drained down through whimpers and yelps into silence. There was one last spatter of projectile fire, then the whine of antigrav that might as well be silence swept over the dock.

Liana decided to stay right where she was. She blinked, and another shadow fell over her.

"*Chérie?*" Tiens, his angelic face twisted with worry, came into view. His hair was full of blood, and it striped and spattered his shredded suit. He looked like he'd gone a few rounds with a vegaprocessor. "Liana?"

*Go away.* Her mouth wouldn't work to frame the words.

Then, wonder of wonders, the best thing in the world happened. Another shadow mated with Tiens' over her and a pair of yellow eyes under strings of lank dark hair met hers.

"You look like shit, *chica*," Lucas Villalobos said hoarsely, in his throat-cut voice.

But Liana had already passed out.

Lucas set the bonescrubber, his fingers deft and as painless as possible. A sharp jab of heat, the numbing of analgesic, and the silvery cuff around her left upper arm began to fill with red light. When it faded to green the break would be mostly healed and she would just have to be careful for a few days while the fresh tissue settled. Two hot tears trickled down Liana's cheek and she couldn't wipe them away because her right hand was locked around the scabbard.

Tiens stood, his hands in his pockets and his head down. "I did not know," he repeated, and Liana felt only weary amazement that he would repeat the obvious.

"Of course you didn't know." The analgesic made her tongue feel too thick for the words. "Isis save me, Tiens, you think I'd come back here for *you*? You tore my heart out, threw it on the floor and stamped on it a few times."

"Why didn't you use the rifle?" Villalobos said for the third time – a sure sign of his irritation. The thick-ridged scar running down the side of his face twitched, its seams and puckers moving independently to his mood. They called him the Deathless, and even Jaf respected his ability.

Of course, any demon might be wary of an assassin who couldn't die.

"Decapitation's surest." Liana squeezed her eyes shut, wishing she could rest. *And I had to prove I could do it.* "I presume the money's safe?"

"You bet." Lucas shrugged, then peeled the latex gloves off with small snapping sounds.

"Money?" Tiens sagged even further.

"You weren't the only one wanting that bitch dead." Liana let out a small, painful hitching laugh. "Come off it, Tiens. A Master of that calibre wouldn't be coming back just for you. She'd made a lot of enemies with the games she liked to play; you were just an afterthought. Our client paid double for her to be killed in transit to New Bangkok. Just be glad I'm not charging you for the dust-up, too."

"For *money*?" Tiens was having a hard time with this. "You were raised better, *petite*."

*This is your honour*. It stung just for a moment through the painkillers. Liana opened her eyes and stared at him. "You can go away now." *Now that I've proved to myself that I can stay away from you. Like mother, like daughter, huh?*

"Lia—"

"I'd take that offer if I was you, suckhead." Lucas' whisper was as soft as ever. The shiver that usually traced down Liana's spine at that tone was muted, but still there through the chemical numbness.

The bonescrubber cuff clicked and hummed to itself. A sharp twinge of pain buried itself under the analgesic, shooting through her arm, and Liana sucked in a breath.

"Liana—" Tiens tried again.

"Get the hell out of here," she said tonelessly. "Hold your breath until I call."

It wasn't as good as it could have been, because he'd be able to hold his breath anyway, at least until he wanted to seduce someone new. But he left, thank the gods, walking heavily one step at a time like a mortal human to the door of the room Lucas had rented deep in the Tank's seething mess of crowded tenements. The hinges squeaked, the door opened and closed, and Liana waited until the disturbance of his aura vanished into the psychic noise of so many poor people crowded all together.

"You OK?" Did Lucas actually sound, of all things, *tentative*?

*Wonders never cease*. "Just fine," Liana murmured. She glanced down at her right hand. The gem was dead-dark and quiescent, and she suppressed a shiver at what she might have to do on the next job. "Where are we headed next?"

"Fuck, girl, don't you want to take a rest?" But there was no heat to it. He, of all people, understood how she felt about this city, this place, the obligations and duties lying just under the streets to trip her up, rising like invisible wires. A net that would catch her if she stayed here much longer.

"Goddammit, Lucas," she said wearily, "just tell me what the next job is. I've got to get out of here."

"What about . . ." The question failed on his lips, and Liana looked up at him. The Deathless looked tired, grey riding under the sallow of his skin.

"Tiens and I were over a long time ago, Lucas. I told you, I'm with you now. I'll let you know if that changes."

He nodded, but he didn't look relieved. "Did you see your *madre*?"

She almost shrugged before she remembered the bonescrubber, forced herself to hold still. "I got that out of the way. She won't expect me for another couple of years now. Wish I'd gotten to see Jaf, though."

"I dunno." Lucas settled on the bed. "Thought you were a goner, *chica*. You got some balls."

*And a broken heart. And a serious need to get out of this town before it eats me alive.* "That's one way of putting it," she agreed, and dropped her gaze to the bonescrubber sleeve, waiting for it to turn green so she could peel it off.

And get the hell out of Saint City.

On to the next job.

# To Ease the Rage

## C. T. Adams and Cathy Clamp

E ven cops get scared sometimes. Oh, we're taught to ignore it – to fight even when our instincts scream for flight. But the fact is that, occasionally, underneath all that adrenaline and razor-honed training is a thread of fear. This was one of those times.

"My God, Sylvia. I can't believe you're just telling me about this now. How long's it been going on?" Linda Montez was one of my best friends on the force. She shook her head incredulously before pouring herself another glass of beer from the half-full pitcher on the table. Normally, I'd be chugging one down with her – but I couldn't afford to be at less than my best right now.

"About two weeks, although it might be longer. But it was a week ago Wednesday when the first call came." The vinyl covering of the booth squeaked in protest as I leaned back and I reached down to shift one of the springs that was trying to come out of a hole in the fabric. I scanned the crowd of the bar, looking for anything out of place. But I knew every person I saw – other cops, neighbours, people I'd grown up with. If my stalker was among them, it was that much more frightening.

"So, just 'I remember' and then he hangs up? But . . . I mean, you've turned this in, right?" Her tongue flicked out to wipe off the moustache of foam on her upper lip. But her eyes were concerned.

I nodded. "Of course. The department's being great about it, what with those cops over in Martinville having gone missing. They traced the calls . . . but they're being made from those throwaway prepaid cell phones. So, it's someone smart. No decent fingerprints or footprints around my place, even though I *swear* I saw someone running into the shadows away from the window. Nothing on the security cams or even the traffic cams. Nobody I've busted has gotten out recently, and older parolees have alibis. They're taking it seriously. They just don't have any leads."

"Could you change your number? Move? Request drive-bys for a while?"

I knew Linda was trying to be helpful, but she didn't raise any ideas I hadn't already thought of.

"I've changed my number twice now, and it's unlisted. I don't *want* to move. I just barely signed the contract with my landlord to buy the place . . . and I *refuse* to be chased into hiding. And yeah, Jenkins and Arellano already offered to add my street to their beat. It's just so damned frustrating."

Linda didn't have anything more to add other than a kind offer to let me stay at her place until they caught the guy. But staying out of harm's way wasn't an option. I wasn't willing to run or hide . . . probably a failing on my part. "Can't. No, I just want to catch the guy."

Linda paused and then looked around before lowering her voice and leaning forwards. "You don't suppose . . . it could be one of *us*, do you? I mean, the timing . . ."

I let out a deep, slow breath. I didn't want to think about that either, but the fact was that nobody in the department had expected me to get this last grade promotion. I beat out several guys who'd been on the force longer. "I hope not. I'm trying not to believe one of them is capable of it. And I don't know what it would solve for one of the guys to have done it. It wouldn't change the promotion and I can't imagine a couple more bucks a month is worth killing me over. It's just not logical."

Linda patted my hand and lifted her purse strap to her shoulder. "Not everything in life is logical, Sylvia. You know that. Emotions are at the root of more than half the crimes in the city."

I snorted derisively. "Try closer to 90 per cent. So, yeah, I know. I need to keep my options open . . . look at everyone with a critical eye." I lowered my brows and gave her my best "hard cop" look. "It's not *you*, is it?"

She laughed, a bright happy sound that at least eliminated one suspect. "Yeah, right. Like I'd take *you* on. I might have failed my academy finals, but even *I'm* not that stupid." With a shake of her head and a chuckle she slid out of the booth. "Look, I've got to get home. The kids are probably home from choir practice by now and I have to put dinner on the table." She reached out and touched my arm. "If you won't stay on our couch, will you at least be really careful? Don't go chasing people into dark alleys without calling for back-up. OK?"

She knew me far too well. That tendency of mine was probably responsible for my promotion, but had cost me several partners. Only Tim had really understood the need to *act*, and it had cost him his life when he chased a fugitive down a dark alley.

I shrugged and nodded. It made her roll her eyes and sigh, but she knew it was the best she was going to get. She left me to be swallowed by the thick haze of fragrant anise and tobacco. The bar was a smoky island refuge in a city of clean air, a throwback enclave township that wouldn't bow to pressure.

My soda was flat and watery by the time I heard last call being announced. The loud, old-fashioned bulb horn the bartender used cut through the cacophony of televisions, music and conversation and pulled me out of my musing. It was no good. I just couldn't add up the pieces in my head. At least I was off shift tomorrow, so I could sleep in.

The scattering of coins I left on the table wasn't much of a tip, but she hadn't been much of a waitress. Then it was out into the sultry night air. By the time I'd walked three blocks, silence had settled around me. Only the thumping of timed sprinklers and an occasional dog bark interrupted the soft padding of my sneakers on the concrete. The quiet, tidy neighbourhood of retirees was the reason I moved here. Like the bar, it was a haven – a place to escape the madness of sirens and screaming.

I began to jangle my keys lightly as my house came into view. Like the others, it was perfect – fresh white paint, every grass blade an identical length, hedges shaped just so, windows . . . *broken*?

I stopped as my brain zeroed in on the black hole where a pane used to be. My gaze flicked to the shining shards scattered over the ground. Then a shadow moved across the window and adrenaline raced through me, bringing the hyper-clarity that years of training have instilled. I started to move forwards, my legs tensed and ready. He'd gone too far this time. The stalker had taken that last step. But I remembered Linda's words just before my foot pushed off and I reached into my pocket for my phone.

Three buttons plus the send command later and I heard ringing in my ear. "Nine one one. Please state the nature of your emergency." The voice was sleepy but polite.

I stared at the window then scanned the surrounding area, searching for movement – a partner in crime, a running vehicle. But not even the breeze rustled the leaves. My voice came out equally soft. No reason to tip him off. "This is Officer Sylvia Beck with Precinct 4, badge 51476. I've got a 10-31, burglary in progress on my personal residence, 2942 Fox Court. I need a car here pronto. If they come in silent, we might catch him in the act." Frankly, I was a little surprised that there wasn't a car here already. I have a security system that should have tripped with the sound of breaking glass.

I heard the clicking of keys over the line as she verified my badge, and possibly the flag on my address from my reports. The operator came back sounding alert. "Address 2942 Fox Court. We've got it. We'll have a car there right away, Officer Beck. Can you give us any information about the intruder? Race, build? Is he armed?"

I shook my head, even though she couldn't see. "I've just arrived and have a broken window and movement inside. I'll know more once I'm inside. I'll try to keep the line open." I took a step towards the house, my muscles twitching, eager to start the chase.

Another pause and then a reply. "Negative, Officer. Dispatch requests that you maintain surveillance and wait for back-up. A car's on the way."

My shoulders slumped at the same time a snarl erupted from my lips. Yes, it made sense. I wasn't armed, didn't have a clue who might be in there, or how many. But I didn't like it.

Fortunately, or unfortunately, the decision was made for me when the side door opened and a shadowy figure emerged. He looked both ways and spotted me, standing under the streetlight like a yellow-shirted beacon. He took off like a shot and my feet started moving. "The suspect's on the run. I'm in pursuit, headed north towards Mink Terrace. Have the car try to cut us off." I didn't wait for a reply ... didn't want to hear that I should stay put. The six-foot wooden fence at the back of my property was no deterrent for him and that's when I noticed the similarity to the shadow I'd seen the previous week. He swung over the slats easily and kept going. I did too, but only because I practise ... a lot. Drives the neighbours nuts.

The suspect didn't just bolt like a normal criminal. There was cadence to his stride, measured, precise. He wasn't one to make a quick dash and dive for cover. He expected to win in the long haul, by tiring out his pursuer. But I wasn't easily tired, so I settled in for a long chase. Because he was *not* getting away.

Flashing lights appeared to my left, coming down Mink. Apparently, the 911 operator had relayed my message. The suspect spotted them and veered right. He sailed over a chest-high hedge, leg bent like an Olympic hurdler, probably hoping it would slow me down. It did, damn it. Free jumping's not my best thing unless I can get a hand on something to push off. It forced me to stop and turn to go around the end. I rounded the corner in a skid, sneakers tearing away chunks of wet turf before I could get my footing. I heard a car door slam when I reached the next fence, and a voice. "Got your back, Beck."

There wasn't time to nod or reply, for the shadow was heading towards the thick cover of Perkins Park. I pressed my muscles for even more speed and was catching up. Yet, oddly, the man wasn't panicking. I was close enough now to see it was definitely a male, about six foot two and well muscled, with shoulder-length dark hair that was coming loose from a tie. Long sleeves and gloves prevented me from seeing skin colour, and the glimpses I got above the raised collar of the leather jacket seemed too pale to be natural. Maybe make-up.

He slowed slightly as we reached the stream as though unsure whether to cross. It seemed he knew the area well, because the rocks at the bottom of the shallow creek are moss-covered and slippery. Apparently it wasn't a risk he was willing to take because he veered again and headed towards the bike path. But that little bit of indecision on his part was all I needed. I gritted my teeth and pressed harder, closed that last gap and threw myself on him.

We rolled to the ground and I wound up on top, him face down.

"Freeze, asshole! Police!"

He started to pull away and was amazingly strong. But by then, I'd pulled the cuffs I'd been keeping with me from the case on my belt and had wrestled one wrist enough to snap it around. It took brute force and a lot of leg strength to fight his other arm behind him, but when I finally managed it he went suddenly still, like a switch had been shut off.

I began to listen for my back-up, but no sound reached my ears above my own harsh breathing and pounding heart. I got up on to my knees and started to back away, slowly, watching for any signs he was going to make a break for it.

"Do not move. You're under arrest for breaking and entering, plus flight. Don't add resisting arrest to the charges."

The reply was quiet from underneath the mass of thick dark hair, but a note of amusement made my blood run cold. "Whatever you say, Officer."

It wasn't the humour itself that widened my eyes and started my hands trembling, but that I recognized the voice.

A touch of breeze ruffled that silken hair and the pale features stood out against the ground in sharp relief. I recognized them too.

It wasn't tough or brave or even logical that I let out a shriek and back-pedalled away from the man until I was sitting on my butt in the mud. He rolled over and sat up, barely hampered by the cuffs. Familiar green eyes peered through the hair and that same little smile which used to make me punch his arm, now made me slap at the air in front of me.

"Hello, Sylvia."

"You're *dead*!" I screamed the word, my finger pointed accusingly at my former partner, Tim Meyer. It was loud enough to attract the attention of the officers who were following me. I heard a shout and the comforting sound of leather and metal rattling on quickly moving hips.

His lips thinned with a smile that didn't show teeth. "Good girl for requesting back-up. But we'll need to finish this discussion another time. I'll come by tomorrow night and we'll talk."

I saw Arellano's dark-blue uniform coming through the trees in my peripheral vision and shifted my attention for just a split second. When I turned back towards the man who looked like Tim, sparkling smoke wafted up from he'd been sitting. My ears caught the jingle of metal as the cuffs, still locked in position, clattered to the ground.

It was impossible to tell whether Arellano and Jenkins believed me when I said the suspect had gotten away. Oh, I gave a description all right, but was too shaken to reveal what I'd *really* seen and heard. That was just asking for a visit to the department shrink. We'd all been at Tim's funeral. I'd been the one to find his . . . *body* in that dark, silent alley, his throat slashed by some psycho we'd never found. I'd comforted his mother and kid sister, held them while they wept . . . while we *all* wept. To this day they consider me part of their family and invite me to holiday dinners. Tim's ashes are in an urn sitting on their mantelpiece where his mother can still talk to him. It absolutely could not have been Tim.

Except something inside of me said it was.

I got to bed after dawn. Reports, glaziers and frantic calls from neighbours and family guaranteed that. But I couldn't sleep, couldn't close my eyes without seeing his face again. Even a sleeping pill couldn't stave off the dreams. Tossing and turning might have been better because the drug made it impossible to escape the images of the past. They were already bad, but soon twisted – became tainted, nightmarish. *Hello, Sylvia.* The words came out of Tim's lifeless mouth in the alley while I tried to revive him, his ruined neck pouring blood across the asphalt. He sat up in the coffin at the service, eyes bright, but nobody else noticed. His voice whispered out of the urn on the mantelpiece, mocking me as I sat down to dinner with his family.

I woke after noon to a sharp crack of lightning hitting nearby, even more tired than when I went to bed. A hard storm had rolled in while I'd dozed fitfully. The wind, thunder rumbling and sudden flashes through the window didn't help my nerves any. Phone calls to friends and family naturally went unanswered because it was a work day. No television or Internet, either. The cable must have gotten damaged in the storm. Even my car wouldn't start. I ended up getting so frustrated that the only thing I could think to do was grab a sandwich and then crank up the stereo and clean the house.

But Tim's voice wouldn't be silenced. I could hear it echo in my brain even over the vacuum and driving rock bass. Still, I'd almost gotten to where I could ignore it by nightfall. So I shouldn't have jumped hard enough to smack my skull on the cabinet under the sink when I heard it again behind me. "You cleaned the house. I'm flattered."

As much as I thought I'd prepared myself, there was no way to really anticipate my reaction when I turned around and saw him sitting in one of the kitchen chairs. He wasn't as pale as the night before. With his hair pulled back into a tight ponytail and wearing a black silk shirt, he looked just like I remembered him.

Hug him, hit him, shoot him? A thousand emotions flew through my mind more than once. I tried to make myself believe this was just an imposter, someone playing on my memories for . . . well, I didn't know exactly why. But who else would know that I only clean when company's coming? It wasn't something I advertised.

But I believe in being safe rather than sorry, so I pulled the .38 snub-nose Taurus I was hiding in my front pocket and pointed it square at his chest. "How did you get in?" I'd locked all the doors and windows and had even put on the security system perimeter alarm and door braces.

He shrugged fluidly, seemingly not at all concerned about staring down my barrel. "Same way I got in last time."

Dammit! I backed away from him a few paces, keeping the gun steady in a teacup grip until I could flick a glance at the living room window through the doorway. It was whole, untouched. "Wrong answer."

He remained calm, leaned back slightly in the chair and braced one heel against the table leg, just like always. "I didn't use the window last time. I was *following* the guy who broke in." He sighed and draped an arm over the rails of the ladder-back chair. "Missed these chairs. They're comfy. You might as well put the gun down, Sylvia. We both know you're not going to use it . . . and even if you did, bullets can't hurt me."

I might have chuckled, but my heart was pounding like a trip hammer at the certainty in his voice. "I might not *kill* you, but a round in a shoulder or leg will certainly hurt you."

He . . . *disappeared*. Poof. Just like last night – into a swirl of sparkling smoke. It hovered, not dissipating while I tried to make sound come from my throat. But all I wound up doing was waving my gun around, searching for something solid to shoot at while backing into a corner so I had two walls behind me.

*Believe me yet? Put down the gun, Sylvia. I'm not here to hurt you.* The voice didn't come from a single source. It was like it started inside my own mind.

"You're a *ghost*! You're *dead*." My voice was high and tight, nearly a squeak. OK, fine. I was scared. But who wouldn't be?

"Not a ghost . . . a vampire."

There he was again, now sitting on the counter over the dishwasher. I turned the gun, hands shaking so hard I wouldn't have been able to shoot if I wanted to.

"There's no such thing." My head started shaking back and forth, tiny little movements that made my teeth clatter when they touched.

Tim snorted and rolled his eyes. "No vampires, but there are ghosts?" He smiled broadly, lifting his lips high to reveal extended canine teeth that came to sharp points. "These say otherwise, Syl. Trust me, I might not like it, but I know what I am."

I started to lower the gun as my brain slowly wrapped around the concept. "But your funeral . . . the urn . . . ashes to ashes." My words didn't make much sense, but he caught the gist of it.

His brows raised and he shrugged. "Not me in the urn, I'm afraid. Jolie said she grabbed me right after the memorial service. I feel sort of sorry for Mom. I'd tell her, but . . . well, you can imagine how well that would go."

So many questions, but my mouth was nearly still too dry to talk. "Jolie?"

"My sire. The one who turned me. You probably remember her . . . that little blonde hooker over on State Street? The kid we hoped had made it back home." He paused and then sighed. "She didn't."

My heart started returning to normal. This really was Tim. He was opening up, trying to let me in on whatever had been happening to him these past two years. "But why would she kill you? I thought she liked you."

"She *did* like me. That was the trouble. She remembered me." He must have noticed that my brows dropped in confusion, because he tried to find the words to explain. He moved his hands, looking around like he was searching for the right thing to say. "See, death is exactly what you expect it to be. The body starts to decay. The brain doesn't work right when we come back. All I felt, all Jolie felt, was rage. After all, we were murdered. That's the last thing we remember. Anger, rage . . . and the hunger. Damn, Syl. You can't even imagine what it's like. But Jolie . . . she was such a sweet kid. She didn't have it in her to be a predator. She needed someone to take care of her. Didn't matter if it was parents, or a pimp, or a cop who was nice to her. She thought she was in love with me. And who knows . . . maybe she was."

I set the Taurus on the counter and reached back to lift myself onto the countertop. We used to sit like this for hours, ignoring the chairs conveniently nearby. I realized abruptly I wasn't afraid any more. If he'd been going to kill me, he already would have.

"So she killed you because she had a crush on you?"

Tim nodded and hopped down off the counter. The floorboards squeaked when his weight hit them. But how then could he disconnect? Become smoke and float? It didn't make sense. "Yep. Sometimes, something is strong enough inside to remember from your old life. Most of the vamps out there are like rabid dogs. They hide, they feed and they sleep . . . forever." He paused and then got an angry look. "At least, that's what *used* to happen. But things are changing. That's why I'm here."

I waved my hands. "Not fair switching subjects until I have a handle on this. So, Jolie kills you, leaves you in the alley for me to find, but keeps track of you? Why wait until after the service? Why not just take you from the alley?"

He grabbed a chair and spun it around before sitting splay-legged on it and leaning his arms on the back. "Like I say . . . she remembered. Somehow she managed to keep her head enough to know that a cop can't just disappear without a huge manhunt. I don't know where she got the body to replace mine in the casket on the way to the crematorium, but she did. She wanted me to be *me* when I woke up and it's probably the only reason I'm sitting here. It's like amnesia. No memory at all of who you were before crossing that line into death. But if you can just *remember*, it all comes flooding back. Well," he amended with a tip of his head, "not *all*, or it wouldn't have taken me two years to show up back here."

Something was tickling the back of my head. "So how did you remember? Are you the one who's been making the crank calls to me?"

He nodded, and flushed with sudden embarrassment. He was dead. He shouldn't blush. "Yeah. I wanted you to know, but should have realized you wouldn't recognize my voice after this long. The trouble was that until just last week, I couldn't even remember your name or where you were. It's not a quick process. It's like a head injury. You remember some things, but not others. It's frustrating as hell. But Jolie actually had a good idea. She followed me around and videotaped me, or had a friend do it for her, for weeks before she turned me. She was actually a vamp for months and we didn't know it, Syl. Don't know how she managed that, but I felt like an idiot when I realized it. I mean, here I am trying to convince her to go home to her folks, when she's been dead for months."

Jolie . . . that tiny blonde waif, was smoke and teeth and . . . dead? "So you remembered you were a cop?"

He nodded. "She had videos of us responding to calls or coming out from dinner. She tried really hard to catch only me in the shot, and even had friends get shots of her touching my arm or making me smile at a joke. Everything she could do to convince me we were in love when I woke up." Tim shook his head sadly. "It almost worked, too."

It made such sense. When you have physical evidence staring at you, pictures of yourself, why wouldn't you believe it? I couldn't help but wonder what made him see the truth. "Why didn't it?"

His eyes moved from staring at the table to locking with mine. The depth of those green eyes was so intense, so hypnotic, that I couldn't tear my gaze away. He stood fluidly, with an animal grace that he'd never had before. It didn't even seem like he walked closer to me – no, more like glided. He wound up inches from my knees. When he placed a hand on either side of me on the counter, effectively blocking me in, I felt my heart in my throat. "I remembered *you*."

I suddenly felt afraid . . . not of dying at his hand, but something else entirely. "You . . . but we never." I swallowed hard, but the lump in my throat refused to move. I shifted uncomfortably on the counter, watching a tiny smile twitch his lips at my reaction. "There was never anything between us, Tim. We were just partners. You're not remembering it right."

He leaned closer and I backed up in response, hitting my shoulders sharply on the cabinet pulls. "Then why can I remember the taste of you on my tongue . . . remember the curves of your body so strongly that it makes my hands ache?" He seemed to sense what I was feeling, whether from the way I was squirming or tapping my fingernails on my jeans. He leaned closer, until I could smell minty mouthwash over cinnamon toothpaste. "Tell me, Syl."

"It was just one kiss, nothing more. We were drunk." Something we swore we'd never talk about again. He waited, unmoving, his eyes watching my every move. I stared at his neck as it disappeared into the dark silk of his shirt. I'd thought it black, but it was brown, the same rich colour as his hair. There wasn't a mark on his neck. No scar, not even a scratch to show where the wound that had killed him had been. "It was—" God, what to say? That it had been amazing? So intense that one kiss had terrified us both? "After a drug raid that went bad. We lost Bobby Tucker that night and it shook us both. We'd drawn straws to see who would handle the door ram."

He was nodding now, brows furrowed. "I remember. It was a competition to see who could take out the door with one blow."

"More than two and we had to buy a round. So Bobby always tried for one. But the door was wired."

Tim reached up and ran a slow finger through my hair. The shiver and sudden butterflies in my stomach should have made me leap down off the counter and try to get away. But I couldn't seem to move. "Your hair got singed in the explosion. Had to trim a lot of it off that night." His eyes focused again. "You liked it when I cut your hair. You kept the look."

It was my turn to nod. "You handled the scissors pretty good, even drunk." I remembered him laughing, joking around, flourishing them, hand on hip, like a temperamental French stylist.

His hands reached up suddenly and glided through my hair, triggering muscle memory that made me clench my hands into fists the same way I had that night. It had felt good . . . *too* good, and it had tipped our relationship into something new.

He didn't say a word, just lived out the memory. Gentle fingers became steel bands that locked on my head and pulled me forwards to his mouth. I couldn't stop him . . . or myself, any more than I had the first time.

Soft, but hungry, his lips and jaw devoured me, tongue searching, twining around mine. I felt my hands reach for him without permission, slide across his warm neck to let loose the band that held back his hair. Silk. I'd always wondered what his hair would feel like if left to grow long.

I ground my mouth against him with a moan that ended in a whimper, surprised and terrified at how much my body wanted this. He couldn't be a vampire. It was all some sort of mistake. Tim was really alive and here and wanting me, no longer tied to the rules of the department. No longer in fear of suspension or dismissal.

He nudged my knees apart and I let him until he was pressed against me so tight I could feel his erection throbbing urgently. No blood? No life? Not possible. Even my tongue could find no trace of the sharp-pointed teeth he'd showed me . . . until I flicked my tongue against the roof of his mouth. There they were – slender and solid, ending with a sharp point. Retractable. They were freaking *retractable*. His hand had moved to my breast now and my nipple hardened so suddenly that I jumped, felt my tongue move forwards abruptly, impale itself on the sharp point of his tooth. It wasn't any more painful than biting it accidentally, but when the copper penny taste filled our mouths, Tim tensed.

He pulled back from the kiss, his bottom lip painted red, and a new look filled his eyes. He swallowed hard and pulled his hand out of my hair to wipe his hand across his lip.

Tim stared at the smear of colour for a long moment. He shuddered and reached down to wipe it on his pants. "I've only fed once today, Syl. You have to be careful."

Blood. Vampire. Fed. A sudden surge of horror switched off my libido. "You *killed* someone tonight, before you came here?"

He shook his head quickly, and moved his other hand from my breast to rest on my thigh. "We don't have to kill, except in combat or to bring someone over. We only end up taking about a half-pint, less than someone would give at the hospital. Most people barely notice. They just wind up a little woozy."

Now I was getting angry. "But you *attack* people? Steal their blood?"

He smiled then and shrugged, apparently comfortable in his role, not the least embarrassed. "Not steal. More barter. We get blood in exchange for pleasure. An erotic high that's better than Ecstasy. There's no lack of willing donors. Trust me."

The horror settled into revulsion. This wasn't the Tim I knew. He'd been one of the few on the force who had been a gentleman. No one-night stands, no string of leggy girlfriends. He'd been waiting, he claimed, for that special someone. But now . . . "So just how many *erotic barters* have you had in two years?" My voice came out sounding more hurt and angry than surprised.

He sighed. "If you mean sex, then none." Then he tipped his head. "Well, one. Before I realized what Jolie was up to. Like I say, she nearly made me believe her. But I gravitated towards criminals. It took me a while to figure out why. I policed the streets in my own weird fashion even before I remembered I was a cop, knocking out burglars and rapists to make it easier for you guys to catch them."

I thought back, to just last week. "You mean that mugger Davis found in the alley—"

He completed the thought with a nod. "Over off Hansen Avenue? Yep. That was me."

I shook my head. "But he didn't have a mark on him. How did you—?"

He smiled again, and the teeth were back, hanging over his bottom lip dangerously. "No marks . . . except for track marks on his arm. Thought he was a junkie, I'll bet. Wound up in a policed ward for anaemia and high white count? Apparently, our saliva does that. I think it's also where the high comes from. How do you feel right now?"

I tried to think. My body was still all tingly and I had to struggle not to touch my own skin. It felt swollen and raw, and even my shirt moving as I breathed made me wet and hungry. The horror and revulsion at what he'd become couldn't make it go away. "Then why didn't you just—" Bite me. I couldn't make myself say the words, but he knew.

His voice came out soft and he touched my face, not pulling his hand away when I flinched. "Because I *remember* you. You're nobody's victim, Syl. While I know I'd enjoy it, and you probably would too, I don't ever remember you saying that you were into kinky stuff."

"I'm not." There might have been confidence in my voice, but why was I suddenly staring at those fangs and thinking it sounded like fun? The mental image of his mouth opening wide and slamming painfully into my neck was actually getting me excited. My body was aching for him, my heart pounding in anticipation.

Jesus. What the hell was in that spit?

"Crosses? Garlic? Stakes?" There had to be some way to protect myself . . . *from* myself.

He smiled, and it was just regular teeth again, the fangs tucked carefully away. "Crosses don't burn, but I haven't tried a church yet. Garlic makes blood taste weird, but it's not too bad. Stakes? Yeah, stakes are a problem. Take out the head or heart when we're vulnerable and it's curtains."

"And you're dead during the day?" Jeez, it sounded like I was trying to find a way to kill him. But I wasn't.

He shook his head, answering patiently. Trusting in his memories of me. "Sleeping, like taking a pill. You can react if you have to, but things are fuzzy. But yeah, we're vulnerable then. It's why we hide to sleep."

He said "sleep" like others say "sex". The word filled me with a warm rush of regret, and fear. Again my hands ached and I clenched them hard. I needed to get away from him until I could figure this out. But when I jumped down from the counter, he didn't move and I ran right into him, the thrill of the silk on my suddenly raw skin. It was too much for my poor body and my hands were suddenly all over him, sliding under his shirt, across the bare, taut muscles and hardened nipples. My mouth reached for him too and I was suddenly kissing him hungrily. He let me, and groaned, but didn't reach for me in return. I ended the kiss and moved to his neck, nipping and biting. Was I hoping for the same in return? I couldn't tell. My mind was too filled with fire to think clearly. I didn't even care any more if his saliva was a drug. I wanted it . . . *needed* it. I couldn't breathe past the need to have him inside me, take me over the edge while he filled himself with me, and filled me with him.

"Yes." The word was the barest whisper through his lips as I reached for his erection, pressed it tight against his stomach so I could unzip his pants. "Whatever you want, Syl. But *only* what you want."

It made me pause and take stock. His twitching member was in my hand, where I was stroking it, feeling the heat and the blood that was someone else's, keeping it hard and ready for me. What *did* I want?

My mouth spoke the truth as I dropped to my knees in front of him. "I want *you*. I've always wanted you, Tim. Dead or alive or somewhere in between. I don't care."

It wasn't his saliva, some strange drug making me do this, it was me. Me who'd kissed him three years before, me who'd struggled not to drool and stare, me who'd found excuses not to be alone with him until he died. Me who'd wept at his funeral . . . cried for the man I loved and had never told. And, as I took him into my mouth, it all came back to me, filling my eyes with tears. His groan echoed in the room and his legs shook as I pulled on him with my lips. He reached for the counter with one hand to keep himself upright and used the other to play with my hair. He whispered my name over and over as I satisfied a need I'd never gotten over. It had held me back, ended every date with a handshake, cooled any possible desire for another man.

He stood me up before we went too far and took me in his arms. I became airborne, arms around his neck, legs bent over his elbow. He kicked off his boots to hit the wall with a bang and then stepped out of his pants to carry me to the bedroom.

There aren't words to describe how Tim made me feel once he had my clothes off. Tongue, hands, lips – they all assaulted my sensitized skin, making me cry out with each new brush or lick or scrape. Neither of us could stand too much more, though. It was only minutes before he was inside me, taking that final step that I'd shied away from years before. Our cries became one as we moved together, warm flesh slapping, bringing us closer to climax.

He pulled away from a kiss and I noticed his eyes were darkening, becoming electric, even more hypnotic than before. His lips whitened, pulled back into a snarl that bared those sharp teeth. I should have been scared, but all I could feel was pleasure, a warm tension in my stomach that was quickly swallowing me whole. Grabbing my hips, he ground himself against me, then pumped furiously until I could take no more. I cried out and screamed. "Do it, Tim! Bite me now!"

He took me at my word. As my eyes were closing from the intensity of the orgasm, I saw his head dart down, saw fangs flash. Then there was pain, but the pleasure was too great and the sharp intensity in my neck became just another form of climax. My fingers dug into his shoulders as his body tensed and suddenly I was being drained and filled at once.

Just like I wanted. God help me, but it *was* what I wanted.

It was hours later that we were snuggling in bed and he finally explained why he'd come to find me.

"One of us has been taking cops off the street, turning them and then setting them loose again. I don't know why. But there are too many vamps now for an area this size. It's becoming noticeable that people are disappearing."

I snuggled in against his warm, warm skin – part of me was inside him now, keeping him as toasty as an electric blanket. "But why bring over cops? Do you think Jolie has a taste for more than you?"

He sighed. "Jolie . . . didn't survive a territory combat. She just wasn't strong enough. I'd left by then, and some nights I wonder if she didn't *want* to die."

I didn't know what to say. How would I have reacted if he'd refused me tonight, told me he had no interest? I didn't want to think about that. "So what needs to happen? What are you planning to do?"

He took a deep breath, nearly dumping my head from his chest. "We need a police force. We need to bring this, and future lawless vamps down, but with rules that we all accept and will abide by. So far, there's never been anything like that. It's been every vamp for him or herself . . . the strongest survive. But they're rising up faster than the established vamps, the ones who have created or remember their humanity, can react." He looked at me and ruffled my hair. "Except I don't remember how to do it. Faces are still fuzzy for me, and I don't remember names. I can't even recall the rules or procedures, even though I know I should. But I'm positive I could bring them back to close to themselves with a little effort. And then all us cops could keep the peace . . . just like before."

I was starting to come up with a reply when a crash sounded downstairs. We both sat up and tensed. "Wait here," he said, and disappeared into that mist again so I dropped to the mattress abruptly.

"Like hell I'm waiting here." I snorted as I whispered the words and slid out of bed to put on my clothes.

I heard a hiss and a growl that sounded like two animals fighting as I reached the hallway. I peeked into the living room.

Tim's face had turned into an inhuman mask, skin thinned to nearly glowing over hard bone. His opponent looked the same. I was surprised that I recognized him. Evan Danvers was a two-bit thug who'd disappeared a year before. We'd found him in the canal and, yep, his throat had been slashed. Danvers was a nasty-tempered waste of skin who'd caused us nothing but problems while alive. I was betting he wasn't much better dead. I was a little surprised that he was one of the people to remember their past. He didn't seem the type.

From the fangs and fingernails that he'd sharpened into claws, I realized my gun wasn't going to do much good. I retreated to the bedroom while they hissed, spat and circled on the carpet like angry cats.

What to use? What to use? I put my sidearm back in the holster as Danvers' voice drifted into the room. "You're not going to stop me, Meyer. I'll have her and she won't even remember you. She'll answer to me, just like the rest."

Tim hissed again. "Not while I live you won't."

I rolled my eyes. Talk about your melodramatic testosterone battle. While I was pretty certain Tim could take care of himself, he'd always been one to fight fair. I didn't think he'd lose, but I needed something to defend myself with, just in case.

I looked around the room, searching for something . . . *anything* to use as a weapon. And then the answer stared me in the face: the photograph of Tim and me, just out of the Academy, hanging on the wall next to my bed. Tim had framed it himself using solid burled walnut from a tree he'd cut down in his yard. While I hated to destroy it, I couldn't help but notice those nice sharp points at the end of the 18-inch lengths of wood.

By the time I'd ripped the frame apart, they were in full battle mode. It was fascinating to watch them slashing and biting, spraying blood across the floor and walls – only for the wounds to heal while I watched. But they were moving so damned quick that I couldn't figure out how to move in on Danvers without risking Tim getting wood through his chest.

That's when Danvers spotted me. He was on me before I could move out of the way. The look in his eyes was truly frightening and I felt my heart pounding as I pushed against muscles that were like steel. I'd fought Danvers before when hauling him in, and he'd been nothing like this. It made me realize that Tim had been gentle with me. I also realized his problem. No way would any of the guys on the force stand up to Danvers now. They'd all be toast and, without any memory of their former dedication to enforcement, would wind up a criminal cartel like nothing the city had ever seen. There's actually very little difference between a cop and a crook – just intent. We're all predators – intense, driven, with violent tendencies. But with nothing to channel that aggression – wow.

Tim was on him, pushing Danvers harder against me, even as he tried to pull him off. I brought the frame up between us, pushed it against his throat to keep his teeth out of mine. Unlike Tim, Evan hadn't bothered with toothpaste or mouthwash and I could smell blood and decay, like rotting hamburger left too long in the back of the fridge . . . both sweet and pungent.

Danvers threw Tim off and grabbed me by the throat. He dragged me backwards until his back was against the wall, digging nails in until I could feel blood trickle down. "That's it," he whispered. "Bleed for me, Beck. You'll be doing even more than that by the time I'm done with you."

It was when he licked a slow line up my cheek that I understood that he planned something very similar to what Jolie had. Kill me, kill Tim and bring me back as . . . well, I didn't even want to think about that. A full-body shudder pretty much said it all.

Tim picked himself up and launched forwards, but Danvers yanked my head to one side by the hair, exposing my neck. "One more step and it's all over for your girlfriend, Meyer."

He'd do it, and Tim knew it. He stopped and glared, his fangs exposed and hands clenched into fists. The wooden stake I'd been fending him off with lay feet away, and I'd just bet that

Danvers felt safe. He wasn't really watching my hands, paying much closer attention to the other vampire. Even Tim wasn't watching so it was a complete surprise to them both when I pulled the shorter frame from inside the front of my pants and used every ounce of my shoulder strength to shove it over my shoulder, point first. It hit him in the eye and paused before I slapped my other palm against the base to drive it into his skull.

He fell backwards or, more precisely, hit the wall and slid down, smearing red in a long line over the white paint.

Tim didn't waste any time. Maybe it hadn't been enough to kill him, because he bit at Danvers' neck, again and again, until it fell away from the shoulders, stake still sticking from the socket.

We were both covered with blood when Tim took me in his arms again. "God, I'd forgotten how good you are." There was a smile in that voice and I couldn't help but smile in return, pressed against his bare body happily. "That's exactly the kind of help I need."

"My name . . . or *your* name is Sylvia Beck." I stared into the camera lens, while Tim watched nervously off to one side. I opened my arms to show my full blue uniform, utility belt and all. "You're a police officer, badge 51476, and have spent the last five years keeping the citizens of this city safe from the scum of the earth. You're honest, trustworthy and kind. Oh, and—" I reached out my hand, wiggling the fingers for Tim to step into the frame. He did so, squeezing my hand, but looking nervous. "This is your sire, Officer Tim Myers. He's the man I love and I trust him with everything I am." I smiled at him then and looked back to the camera, red light blinking to show it was recording. "That's why I've decided to let him bring me over to become *you*. You're a vampire, but you're still a cop. Remember that. Remember *me*."

"Are you sure about this, Syl. You could help me just as easily by staying human."

I shook my head. "Danvers was nearly too strong. It was just his own stupidity that made him vulnerable. Next time I might not be so lucky." I touched his face and hoped the camera would show what I was feeling inside. "I won't lose you again.

And even that means I have to die and fight to remember you, it's worth it. I love you, Tim Myers. And after all, we have a city to protect, and a vampire police force to begin." I pointed at the camera. "So don't you *dare* give Tim any less than your best. I'll be watching you always, nagging at your brain to do the right thing. Remember that."

Then I nodded at Tim and squeezed his hands tight. "Let's do this." I didn't know if we could pull it off. Keep me disappeared until I recovered my memory and still retain my job. But I worked the night shift, so it *could* work. My career was important enough to try. I *had* to try. The city was counting on me . . . on *us*. It seems a little funny that my career choice suddenly included dying – but there you go.

Tim's skin paled again and the fangs came into view. His eyes were both frightening in their intensity and heartwarming in the tears that filled them. I let loose one hand and pulled down the stiff, starched collar with the pretty gold bar. "Kill me, Tim. Make me a vampire and keep me with you forever."

He was on me in a flash, throwing me to the floor so hard I hit my head – playing it up for the camera so I . . . so *she*, would understand what we'd become. He hissed at the camera and then drove fangs into me. The pain was intense, nothing like it had been in bed and I was suddenly afraid, wondering if I'd made the right choice.

But as my struggling grew weaker, his hands so tight on me that my fingers went numb, I heard his voice across my mind and it made everything better. *I love you, Syl. I'll keep you safe until you come back.*

Then there was darkness, so deep and rich that it ate away everything that was light, that was me, and I fell into a well that seemed to go forever.

Anger now. Pain and anger. The man holding me ties me to a chair, yells at me to listen and watch. But it hurts to open my eyes. He forces them open and I see myself and him. Dressed in blue, his long hair half-covering his face. Hate and fear. I can't break loose. I scream and fight, but finally give up and snarl, my teeth gnashing, slicing through my lips as I watch the shiny glass. Then a picture appears and it looks like the face in the other glass. I raise my eyebrows and tip my head and so does the figure in the glass. Is that me? I bare fangs and so does she. Fingers wiggle under the rope and so do hers. Then the woman starts to talk.

"My name . . . or *your* name is Sylvia Beck. You're a police officer, badge 51476, and have spent the last five years keeping the citizens of this city safe from the scum of the earth. You're honest, trustworthy and kind."

Blink and the woman in the glass blinks, and so does the woman on the screen. *Sylvia*. It sounds right, resonates in my head. The man who tied me up is sitting patiently in a chair on the other side of the room. "Sylvia?" My voice is the same as the woman in the picture.

The man nodded. "You're Sylvia. Sylvia Beck."

Then the same man appeared on the screen and a flash came to my head, so sharp and intense it made me yelp. Like a dream, it all came back to me – Tim's death, then Danvers and then . . . my own. I watched Tim touch my hand on the television with the same worried look he had across the room. I felt tears come to my eyes as I ran my tongue along the sharp points of teeth. Sylvia Beck. Peace officer . . . vampire. "Tim. I . . . remember. I remember you. And I remember *me*."

He smiled, and it was a wonderful thing. "Did it help? Did the tape ease the rage?"

I nodded, because it had. There were still gaps, such as I didn't know where I was exactly, didn't know how long had passed since that night, or recall the room or the names of some of the things I saw. But I recognized my uniform, and remembered Tim. It was enough, because the rest would come. "It eased the rage. But before we start a police force, come over here and kiss me, Tim. Help me remember everything."

That warm smile again, showing fangs like me, and more things flooded back . . . memories that might not be real, but *felt* real. He walked over and leaned down to kiss my lips, sending a jolt of pleasure through me. "I love you, Syl. And you'll see – we'll make it through this. Together we're going to be the greatest pair of vamps this city has ever seen, and we'll be the first of those who remember, who keep their humanity and make the world a better place."

I nodded and offered him my lips again, tucking my fangs safely against the roof of my mouth. "And we'll love, Tim. After all, that's the essence of all humanity."

# Dancing with the Star

## Susan Sizemore

There are plenty of people who come into the Alhambra
Club for the things we regulars can offer. It's a nice place,
not flashy on the inside, hard to spot from the outside. You have
to want to find the place and search for it through friends of
friends of friends. If you're a mortal, that is. The rest of us have
used it as a hangout for the better part of a century.

There's a television set over the bar, a big, flat-panel model,
always playing with the sound off. I wasn't paying attention to
it because I was engaged in seducing a handsome young man
with far too many body piercings for my usual taste. I mean, if
you want piercings, I'm perfectly capable of providing them
for you. But, he had nice eyes and a lovely voice, and the place
wasn't all that full of human patrons this evening. A girl goes
with what she can sometimes. I wasn't all that hungry, so I
wasn't trying too hard. I wasn't paying attention to the TV,
but my friend Tiana was. I was surprised when she came up
and put her cold hand on my shoulder, because she isn't
normally rude enough to interrupt me when I'm working a
fresh feed.

"Did you hear? There's been a twelve-car pile up on Mulholland."

This isn't the sort of thing that would normally interest me,
but her excitement got my attention. I shifted my gaze to the
television. It showed a scene of fire and carnage spotlighted in
beams of white light shooting down from circling helicopters. A
crawl on the bottom of the screen was showing statistics about
the dead and injured and the amount of emergency rescue

equipment called to the scene. A blonde, windblown girl reporter was excitedly talking about the same things.

Beside me, Tiana was starting to breathe heavily. I wasn't sure who was getting off on the disaster more, my friend or the reporter.

I looked back at Tiana. "So?"

Her eyes were glowing, not quite the death-eating electric blue she gets when she's feeding, but her pupils held pinprick sparks of anticipation. "You want to go have a look, Serephena?" she asked.

Normally I wouldn't have been interested, but the pleading in her voice got to me. Tiana's been my best friend for a very long time. If you know what we are you wouldn't think she and I would have that much in common. I'm a vampire and she's – well, all right – she's my ghoul friend. I feed on the living, she feeds on the energy of the dying. But we both like to shop.

"Maybe there's a dying movie star out there I can latch on to," she said. She rubbed her hands together. "A producer would be even better."

I know what that sounds like, but it really had more to do with psychic power levels than celebrity stalking. There are a lot of high-energy types in show business, a lot of people who are psychic and don't even know it.

I got up and telepathically told the pierced boy that we'd never met. "Sure," I said to Tiana. "It's been a slow night. Let's go have a look."

It was gruesome up on Mulholland Drive. Tiana ate it up – literally soaking the energy of fear and pain in through her pores. It was the scent of blood that got to me, but not in a good way. There's no fun in spilled blood. I need to take blood from the living, breathing source, to taste it fresh and hot, with the heartbeat still pulsing through it. And preferably from a volunteer, because we live in modern, humane times. Unlike some of my notorious forebears I do not get off on pain. The blood on the crash victims gave off a sick scent that roiled my stomach, but I did find hiding in the shadows and watching the emergency crews work exciting. Hey, I'm as interested in all that forensics and rescue stuff as anyone else who watches the geek-TV channels, but this was "live and direct" like Max Headroom used to say on the television show nobody but me probably remembers.

It was interesting, but after a while I glanced at the sky and sighed. The night was getting on. "Had enough yet?" I asked. "You'll outgrow your size-two clothes if you feed much longer. Besides, it's an hour to sunrise."

Tiana came out of her happy trance and turned glowing blue eyes on me. "Oh, sorry, I lost track of the time."

"No problem," I said, and took her arm to help her walk away, knowing from experience that she was drunk and dizzy from feeding.

*Help me! Where are you?*

*Here!* I shouted to the voice in my head. *Where—*

"Serephena!"

I looked up into pinpoints of blue light. Tiana. I was on my knees and she was standing over me. The fierce pain in my head blocked out most thought, but I knew that our positions were all wrong. *I* was supposed to be helping *her*.

I wanted to run into the wreckage behind us. But when I stood my legs were too shaky. I glanced back. "I—"

Tiana shook my shoulders. "We have to go. Sunrise," she said.

That was one word I understood in all of its myriad implications of pain, suffering, death. I had to go. Now. Whatever had just happened I had to get home. I took Tiana's hand and we ran together.

I have a nice studio apartment, where I sleep on a daybed in the huge windowless bathroom. The bathroom door is reinforced and has a strong lock, panic-room style, and the building, which I own and rent mostly to my sort of people, has state-of-the-art security. So normally I have no reason not to sleep very well. Normally I don't dream, either. I go to sleep. I wake up. It all happens so quickly . . . normally . . .

*The path was made of brick, laid out in a chevron pattern. It was lined with rose bushes and night-blooming jasmine. The air was so* fragrant I could taste it. The stars overhead formed a thick blanket of light brighter than I'd seen them for a very long time.

"I need to get out of the city more," I said, and continued walking towards the music in the distance.

I was wearing a dress, the skirt long and floaty and pale blue, sprinkled with a pattern of glittering crystals that mirrored the sky. This was not the slinky, black sort of garment I favoured, but it felt right, feminine, beautiful.

I was wearing, honest to God, glass slippers. Cinderella? Me? Well, it was a dream.

And my feet – my whole body – wanted nothing more than to dance.

When the gazebo came into sight, as pretty as a white confection on top of a wedding cake, I ran towards it. Something more than wonderful waited for me there.

"You!" I said, skidding to a halt at the entrance as I spied the man leaning with his arms crossed against a pillar.

"Me," he replied, a stranger with a familiar voice.

"But – you're a movie star!"

It was an accusation. I didn't expect my very rare dreams to go off on such grandiose tangents.

"And I worked very hard to become a genuine movie star," he answered, totally unashamed for showing up in my fantasy. "Would you prefer meeting a celebrity?" His gesture took in the small building. "Here? In our space?"

Our space? Yeah, it was, wasn't it?

I turned around, my skirts belling out around my legs. I could see my reflection in the highly polished, white marble floor. And his reflection as he came to join me. He moved with the grace of Fred Astaire. (I've been around long enough to have seen Fred and his sister Adele dance on the stage. I know what I'm talking about).

His hands touched me, one at my waist, one gently gripping my fingers. His warmth against my coolness. The next thing I knew we were circling the room, caught up in the music.

"We're waltzing," I said. "I don't know how to waltz."

"I learned it when I auditioned for Mr Darcy. Didn't get the role, though."

"But you learned how to dance."

"*Silver linings,*" he said.

I studied his face. There was a sweep of dark hair across his brow, high-arching eyebrows over penetrating green eyes, severe high cheekbones softened by a lush, full mouth. "*You would have made a great Darcy,*" I told him.

Of course he had the body of a god – or at least of a man who spent a fortune working long hours with a personal trainer – and now that body was pressed to mine. I liked it. A lot. The longer we danced the more I liked it.

My skin wasn't cool any more.

"*This is – nice,*" he said.

"*In a strange way,*" I answered.

"*You've noticed that, have you?*"

I nodded. His green eyes twinkled at me. We danced around in circles for a long, long time, caught up in the music and the flow of energy between us. That's what it was all about for me – flow and energy, give and take. For once I knew that I was giving as much as I was taking, and it felt good.

"*What are you – we – doing here?*" I asked.

"*Dreaming about dancing,*" he answered. His smile devastated me. "*I'm as surprised by this as you are. One moment I was floating in grey clouds – I think I was screaming, but there was no one to hear me, not even me – and the next I was here with you.*"

"*I was in blackness,*" I said. "*That's normal for me.*"

"*The grey was terrifying,*" he said. He whirled me around faster, until we both laughed. "*This is much better,*" he said. He pulled me closer. We weren't dancing any more, but the music played on and the world continued to spin.

"*No one should be in darkness,*" he said. "*Grey or black or any other kind, especially not alone.*"

I started to say that I didn't mind being alone, but being with him made me realize that I did mind. "*I've been lonely and didn't know it.*" Though I was looking into his eyes, I was talking more to myself.

Neither of us spoke for an unknowable time after that but we continued to look into each other's eyes and shared – what? Our emotions, our souls, the essences of our beings? All of the above, I guess.

"*This is such bullshit,*" I finally said.

"*But you like it.*"

My gaze flicked away from his, but I couldn't stand the loss of contact for long. "*If I could blush, I'd be blushing,*" I told him when our gazes locked again.

"*We live in a time and place that's cynical about love.*"

"*Darlin', I come from New York. People in LA are amateurs about cynicism.*"

He shook his head. "*I used to live in New York,*" he said. "*I tended bar while I went to drama school. I saw plenty of broken hearts there.*"

"*Broke a few, too, I bet.*"

"*Too bad I didn't meet you there.*"

I laughed. "*I left long before you were born.*"

"*Really? When were you there? How did you get to be—*" He looked puzzled for a moment, then said it: "*—a vampire.*"

Those in the know generally don't ask. Maybe they think it's rude, or that mystery is part of my mystique, or they are afraid of getting their throats ripped out. I hadn't told this story for a long time. "*I worked at the Plaza back in the 1930s.*"

"*The hotel?*"

I nodded. "*I was a telephone operator. There was a Mob boss that lived there.*"

"*Lucky Luciano?*"

"*You've heard of him?*"

"*I've been doing research to play him in a film.*"

"*Too bad. I hate seeing that bastard glamorized.*"

"*He did bad things to you,*" he guessed.

"*He had me killed. He wrongfully thought I'd overheard some conversations and might testify about them in court. A hit man was sent after me. It turned out that the killer was a hungry vampire. He drained me and left me for dead.*"

"*But—*"

"*But the vampire didn't realize I was one of his bloodline.*"

"*You were already a vampire?*"

"*No! My family came from Wallachia. There's some sort of genetic mutation that kicks in when a vampire bites us. Old Vlad the Impaler really is Dracula, and the king of us all.*"

"That's amazing. I'm part Hungarian. Could I be a vampire?"

"Depends if your grandmas got raped by the right sort of invaders, I guess. Do you want to be a vampire?"

He shrugged. "I want to hear more about you."

"Nice answer. The gist of it is I woke up dead and had to start over from there."

"Did you go after the one who turned you?"

"You've been watching vampire movies."

"Been in one."

"I saw it, had nothing to do with my world. But you were good," I added.

"You're lovely when you're bullshitting. What happened to the evil one who turned you?"

"I don't know if he was evil."

"He was a Mob hit man."

His indignation was adorable. "I'll concede his profession was evil."

"You've never done anything like that."

His certainty of my goodness was even more adorable. "No, I haven't," I assured him. "But after a while of wrestling with all the implications of immortality you get some perspective on good, evil, expediency, stuff like that. And no, I haven't seen him again. At least, not that I know of. I didn't get a good look at him while he was sucking the lifeblood out of me."

"But how did you survive? Didn't you have to have a teacher, a mentor? Didn't another vampire bring you into the dark world?"

I laughed and stroked his cheek. "I suppose there's melodrama somewhere, but I've never been involved in any — other than being rubbed out by a mobster, which I did find pretty melodramatic at the time."

He traced his hand up and down my back, sending tingling shivers all through me. His sympathy warmed me even more than his touch. "I'm sorry you went through such trauma. How did you survive?"

"I found the right bar and ordered a beer. Getting all the blood drained out of you makes you thirsty."

"It was a vampire bar?"

I nodded.

"Did some instinct kick in that drew you to your own kind and they taught you how to survive?"

I nodded again. He was smart and quick on the uptake. The man had many great qualities. And he could dance in a way that made me feel like I was having sex standing up, fully clothed, without ruffling a hair or breaking a sweat. Not that vampires sweat. "I've explained me," I said. "How about you? How did you get here? Wherever here is."

"That is the problem isn't it? We seem to be dancing in limbo. Though I like being here with you."

From anyone else, any other time, I would have considered that a line. But his eyes held genuine pleasure, genuine sincerity.

"I'm falling like a rock, you know," I told him.

"Me, too. Is that a bad thing?"

We both shrugged, and that became part of the dance. We laughed together, and that was part of the music.

"As for me," he went on. "I remember being with friends at their house. We played Scrabble."

I love word games. "Scrabble? Is that any way for a movie star to spend an evening?"

"Now you know why the paparazzi hate me. I lead a quiet life."

"Me too. But how did you get here?"

We danced in silence for a while. I watched as every possible emotion crossed his face.

He finally said, "It has something to do with ice cream." He looked deep into my eyes. "Is that crazy?"

"Probably," I told him. "But much of life makes no sense."

"Life and death? Am I dead?"

I pulled him close and we stood still in the centre of the gazebo for a long time, holding each other tight, giving comfort amidst the frightening questions that had no answers.

"You're so good for me," he said at last. "I don't even know your name."

"Everyone knows yours." I gave a faint, sad laugh. "No one really knows mine any more. I became Serephena back in my hippie phase."

It was his turn to laugh, at me, but not mockingly. "Oh, no, that won't do. That name isn't you. It's a flighty name. You're solid and strong and grounded."

*It was like he was giving me back myself. "Stella," I admitted.*
*"My name is Stella."*
*His smile was a blessing. It was sunshine. It was . . .*

I awoke as I always did, at the moment the sun went down. It was normally the most pleasant moment of the night. This time I woke with an anguished shout. I lay on my back with my eyes squeezed shut and tried to will myself back to sleep. That didn't work, of course. All I ended up doing was crying, and the tears that rolled down onto the pillowcase made a disgusting mess – vampire tears having blood mixed in with the saltwater.

I stripped the bed, threw the sheets in the laundry and paced around restlessly for a while wondering what the hell was going on in my head. Was I going senile? Worst of all, loneliness welled up in me and grief shook me and the heartache . . .

The heartache was a very real sensation. Physical pain radiated out of the core of my being where my shattered soul ached for the loss of half my being.

Or something like that.

I hurt. I really emotionally and physically hurt from what I knew had only been a dream. It took a couple of hours before I could get myself together enough to head off to the Alhambra in the hope of staving off the painful loneliness.

There wasn't a huge crowd at the club, but the place was jumping when I showed up. Everybody was gathered around the bar, abuzz with conversation.

I spotted Tiana and went up to her. "What happened?"

"Anton went up in flames this morning," she answered.

"Why'd he do a thing like that without having a goodbye party first?" I asked. Anton was the bartender. He lived on the second floor. Used to.

"He didn't want to make a fuss."

"How'd it happen?"

"Usual way. He walked outside to see the dawn."

It happens. Every few decades the urge to end eternity gets hold of a vampire. I hadn't succumbed to the depression yet, but the way I was feeling tonight I sympathized with Anton's choice. I wasn't sure my usual panacea of shoe shopping was going to be enough.

"Did anybody sweep up his ashes?"

"Oh, yes," Tiana answered. "He's already in a nice urn over the bar with a sticky-note reminder to sprinkle some blood on him in a year or two. The problem is what are we going to do for a bartender now?"

Blood brings us back and we are usually ready to carry on after an ash vacation. I wasn't in the mood to join in the "what are we going to do to replace Anton?" discussion occupying everyone else's attention, but I did manage to elbow my way to a seat at the bar. I found myself looking up at the television overhead.

The local news was still dwelling on last night's multi-car crash. Slow news night, I supposed. "Isn't there a gang war or a car chase you could cover?" I complained to the television. "I'm bored."

"You don't feel bored," Tiana said, coming up beside me. "You're unhappy. I don't mean to snack on your emotions," she added when I glared at her. "You know I can't help it. Why are you unhappy? Anton?"

I snorted. "May he rest in peace, but I don't give a damn about Anton." I turned my glare back on the TV screen. "What's so important about last night's car crash?"

"Four people died on scene," she said, "Everybody else is hospitalized, most of them in critical condition. But the real reason the networks are still covering it is—"

Her timing was perfect, because at that moment *his* picture appeared on the screen.

"Oh, good God!" My heart felt like a knife had been plunged into it.

Tiana's hand touched my shoulder. "I know you're a fan, but—"

"He's not dead! Tell me he isn't dead?"

I only realized I was shaking her when she shouted, "Stop it! Let go of me!"

I did. I pointed at the television. "That's the man in my dream."

"The man of your dreams? He's an actor you've got a crush on."

"I do not get crushes. And I mean he's the man that was in my dream last day. We were dancing."

"Vampires don't dream. And he was in intensive care while you were sleeping."

The relief might have killed me if that were possible. As it was, it felt like I was having a heart attack. "Intensive care? So he isn't dead?"

"Not yet, but it's only a matter of time." She glanced at the face of the reporter now on the screen. "His deathwatch is what all the media fuss is about. They're worse ghouls than I am."

I automatically patted her shoulder, knowing that this admission hurt her pride, but my mind was racing on another matter. It hadn't been a dream. Somehow, it hadn't been a dream. He'd been there and I'd been there, only where the hell was there? "How did it happen?"

"He and some friends were going out for ice cream when they ended up in the pile-up and the car went off the side of the mountain. He was the only survivor, but he's on life support and he's been declared brain dead."

"His brain isn't dead," I said. "It's been out dancing." I was sure this was true. We'd been in telepathic contact. But how?

I heard the voice in my head again that had speared into my brain back at the crash site. *Help me! Where are you?*

"Of course! He's psychic. He called out for help when we were up at the crash, and I answered him! That's how we met!" I grabbed Tiana's cold, grey hand. "Come on, ghoul-friend!"

"Where are we going?" she asked as I pulled her towards the door.

I laughed, all my depression blown away by exaltation. "To the rescue, of course!"

"We're here. Now what?" Tiana asked as we moved across the ER waiting room.

"Go up to the ICU," I answered. "And take him home."

"He's on life support. There's probably cops and private security in the halls."

"I'll take care of them. All you have to do is create a diversion."

She licked her lips and nodded. Her skin was flushed to an almost-normal human colour. This was one of her feeding grounds and she'd shown me where to sneak in. It had been easy, even with the circus in the streets.

Outside the media and fan frenzy was as thick and chaotic as I'd ever seen it in all my decades of dwelling in this town. There were news vans sprouting satellite and lighting equipment and chuffing power generators. Reporters looked solemnly into cameras as they spoke. Paparazzi were as thick as roaches in a tenement. Helicopters circled. Cops held a crowd back beyond a cordon surrounding the hospital. People held signs and candles and flowers. Some were singing the theme song from one of his movies.

I wondered if what I was doing was any less ridiculous than the behaviour of his grieving fans.

In the ER people were bleeding and screaming and crying through their own problems. It was quiet and peaceful compared to what was going on outside. No one paid any attention as we made our way through a wide doorway, down a hallway and to a door past a row of elevators. You learn to take the stairs when you want to live an under-the-radar life.

"There are three people ready to die here," Tiana said after we reached the critical-care floor and slipped into an empty room. She looked sad. Hey, she's a ghoul, but that doesn't mean she isn't a kind person.

"Can you work with that?" I asked. Hey, I'm a vampire, remember? She nodded. She prefers living off residual death energy instead of any direct involvement. "I hate doing the soul-sucking thing, but, yeah, there's nothing that can be done for any of them."

"Is my guy one of the three?" I asked worriedly.

She looked thoughtful, then shook her head. "Low energy, but stable. Now let me get to work."

I backed out of the room as she opened her mouth for one of those screams that only the dying could hear. The dying would give up their energy to the ghoul when they heard that sound.

Pretty soon there was almost as much activity on this floor of the hospital at there was outside. Alarms went off at the nursing station, crash carts were hurried into rooms. There was running and shouting, and I moved unnoticed to the room with the guard outside the door.

The guard wasn't a problem. I made him look into my eyes and he was instantly stunned.

"Is there a security camera in there?" I asked.

"No. There's a nurse," he volunteered.

"Tell the nurse to respond to the code blues. Follow the nurse and volunteer to help." I hoped that was enough of an excuse to keep the guard from getting into too much trouble when I kidnapped his charge. I rushed into his room at once.

Inside the door I stopped with my mouth hanging open. The man on the bed was hooked up to so many tubes and gadgets I didn't know how to start freeing him. I didn't have much time, so I whispered an apology for any pain I caused him and started ripping and pulling the life-support equipment off him. Trails of his blood stained my clothes when I picked him up. The scent and warmth of it was intoxicating, but I fought off the sudden bloodlust. My fangs ached like a virgin's on her first hunt as I carried him away with me.

His weight was no problem, but I'm a small woman and he's a very tall man. Carrying him was awkward, but you manage what you have to.

I took him downstairs, through the closed cafeteria and to a courtyard garden beyond it where I set him down gently beneath a squat palm tree. I sat beside him and settled his head in my lap. My fingers touched his temples.

*Are you there?*

*You came for me!* His voice called from so far away I barely sensed it.

*Do you want to live?* I asked. *You know I'm a vampire. I will try to change you if you want me to. Think carefully before you choose.*

In the long silence that followed I had to fight very hard to keep my fangs from sinking into his flesh. I'd never been so aroused by the scent of blood before, but I wasn't going to taste a drop without his permission. He had to make the choice.

*I thought I'd have to be Wallachian,* his thought came at last.

*You're part Hungarian. There's a chance you'll change.*

*It depends on if my grandmas got raped by the right sort of invaders?*

*Pretty much.*

*I'll die otherwise, won't I?*

*Yes. But that shouldn't be why you choose to become a blood drinker, a nightwalker, an exile from every part of the daylight world.*

It really isn't all that bad being a vampire, but there are difficulties and the lifestyle should not be glamorized for potential newbies. No matter how much you want to share a coffin with them.

*Can I stay with you if I change?*

My heart sang at his question. And, oh, how my fangs ached! *Yes,* I told him. *For as long as you want. For ever if you want.*

*For ever sounds good to me. Do it.*

*Remember that it might not take. That –*

*Shut up and bite me.*

I couldn't argue with that. So I did.

And I'd never had a rush like it in all my years of sucking the good stuff! I couldn't count the orgasms that shook me before every drop of him was flowing inside me.

I didn't have to share my blood with him. Some sort of enzyme in my saliva was transferred to him from the bite and the enzyme would trigger the change if it were going to happen. But, just in case, I bit my wrist and poured a few drops of my blood into his mouth. Not that he was capable of swallowing. At this point he was essentially dead. He'd either get better or I'd have to dispose of his body in a way that the marks on his throat would never be seen.

I didn't want to think about disposal. I didn't want to think of him ever being dead. I held his limp body and felt it grow heavier and colder, and I worried and cried those disgusting blood-drenched vampire tears. I don't know for how long. Long enough for my mood to turn bleak and heartbroken.

Long enough for me to be aware that the sun would be up in an hour or so.

There's an almost physical pressure on the skin the closer daylight comes. Normally I'd be starting to think about getting to cover. Instead, I vowed I'd stay here and let the sun take me if he didn't come around before the end of the night. I didn't care if my ashes blew away so far there wouldn't be anything left of me. Perhaps the fire that took me would burn him as well and our ashes would blend together.

*Sentimental, aren't you?*

I heard the thought but it took a long time before I came out of my grief enough to realize that the voice wasn't my imagination.

"You're alive!"

*Don't shout. I have a hangover. That's not right. My throat hurts. I'm thirsty. My mouth tastes like sweet copper.*

"That's my blood. You're alive," I repeated, the words whispered in his ear as I helped him sit up. "You're a vampire."

"I guess the right Cossacks raped my grandmas."

His voice was a rough croak, but the most delicious sound I'd ever heard. He struggled to his feet and insisted on giving me his hand to help me up. Living or dead, he was always a gentleman. When I was on my feet his arms came around me. He was weak enough that I ended up holding him up as we embraced.

"We could dance like this for ever," he said.

I sighed romantically. "We could." I looked around. "We could if the sun wasn't coming up soon. We need to get out of here."

He cupped my cheek and looked at me with his new night vision. "You're as beautiful as I dreamed you were, my Stella. Thank you for saving me, thank you for being with me now and for ever."

There's no way a girl can't respond to that. I kissed him, and he kissed back and it was real and deep and better than any dream.

After a while he lifted his head and gave a dry, hacking cough. "Sorry. Thirsty."

I put my arm around his waist and helped him towards the garden door. "I know just the place where we can get a beer. Now that you've changed you can find it on your own."

"I'd rather go with you."

You have no idea how much that meant to me.

Tiana met us outside the cafeteria and guided us along her secret route out of the hospital and away from the crowd. He noticed all the fuss as we drove away, he and I squeezed into the trunk of Tiana's car.

"You have no idea how happy I am to leave the celebrity era of my life behind," he told me.

"You'll miss acting."

"I'll think of a way to get back to it. Do vampires work? Do I need a job?"

"I'm a real-estate mogul. You can live off me. Wait—" I'd remembered Anton. "The place we're heading, the Alhambra Club, needs a bartender. I know the owner. That would be me. If you're interested."

We were squeezed in pretty tightly, but he managed to pull me closer. "Does this place have a dance floor?"

I laughed, happier than I'd ever imagined I could be. "It will when we're done with it, if that's what you want," I promised.

"I think dancing – being – with you is all I ever wanted."

"Me too." I couldn't stop the girlish giggle from escaping. "I guess this is a real—"

"Hollywood ending," he finished, not having to be psychic to know what I was thinking.

# Play Dead

## Dina James

E ven out here, he could hear the music.

Slowing his stroll to nearly a stop, Nikolai's crystal-blue eyes rose to the sign above the door.

THE GARLIC AND STAKE.

A wry half-smile twitched at the corner of his lips. It grew to a complete, bemused grin upon seeing the small, hand-lettered sign outside the pub, near the sidewalk, where it couldn't really be seen unless one was looking specifically for it.

VAMPIRE LAIR LOCATED DOWNSTAIRS.

Oh? Really, now.

Nikolai's eyebrows rose, and his eyes once again flicked to the sign above the entryway that displayed the vampire-themed name of the pub.

He debated about going "downstairs" just for the sheer horror of it: humans masquerading as vampires were always a good source of a night's amusement, not to mention a quick . . . bite.

If they truly knew what it was to be what they wished they were. A consciousness in a mortal form. A body without a soul. A voracious parasite, forced to live upon the blood of those they traded their soul to outlive.

There was a reason vampires were called "damned".

In no real mood for amusement, ignoring the vague promise of an evening's entertainment, Nikolai was nearly past the pub entrance when something else caught his attention.

A scent.

Soho, London was full of scents. All kinds. Some intoxicating, others repulsive.

But this . . .

He closed his eyes and breathed it in.

This scent washed over him, enveloping him as the water of a hot bath used to when he was still human.

His eyes opened just in time to catch those of a woman as she walked past him towards the glass door that led into the vampire pub.

A mortal woman.

Accompanied inside by a mortal man.

She looked away quickly, as though she didn't want to be looked at. Or maybe it was just that she didn't want to be seen entering this ridiculous "vampire lair".

Nikolai almost laughed at that thought.

But nearly as quickly as she'd looked away, she looked back again and, when their eyes connected, Nikolai felt it as a physical blow.

Stunning. That was the word for it.

Not that she was beautiful or in any way physically attractive to him.

She simply stunned him.

How strange that was. Her eyes were almost a challenge in themselves, let alone the look she'd given him. Dark-brown eyes that both demanded he leave her alone and entreated him.

*Save me, please.*

He heard it as clearly as if she had spoken to him.

She held his eyes until she could no longer do so, and then descended downstairs into the vampire lair.

What?

A woman like that? Going into . . . such a place . . . with . . . ?

"A woman like what?" he asked himself. "She's just a mortal. With an equally mortal companion. Going into an equally mortal bar to play dead."

He could hear from where he stood that the music inside was too loud. He could smell that the bar didn't observe England's uniform smoking ban. Hell, he could nearly see from here the unswept floor, the unwiped tables and the low light designed to hide both facts while making a pathetic attempt at a vampiric "atmosphere".

Humans would never understand that, while his kind shunned daylight, they found artificial light – especially the soft glow of candles – particularly appealing. They did indeed have sensitive eyes that afforded them very keen vision, but they didn't shrink from all kinds of light as they were purported to.

He didn't have any interest in this place. But *she* was in there.

She was now in that laughable vampire lair, with a weak, male human who would do little to nothing to sate Nikolai's appetite if Nikolai wanted his blood. Of course, judging from the look the woman had given Nikolai, this human man did little to nothing to sate *her* appetite either.

It would be entirely too easy to take her from him. The thought amused him, and he smiled again.

Yes.

Why not? He wanted her. For some reason he wanted *her* more than anyone he had in, well, he couldn't remember the last time he had actually *wanted*, and he wasn't sure it was just because he could have her. It seemed he *was* in the mood for amusement, after all.

However, that meant he had to follow her.

He found himself reaching for the door handle and opening the door.

Out on the street, the smell of garlic had been merely annoying. Now it was overwhelming. They must pump it in from somewhere. More of their insipid "atmosphere", he supposed. Not that the stories of garlic repelling vampires had any truth to them. Far from it.

It was repellent, period.

But that didn't matter now. He had a purpose.

Nikolai strode past the drinkers to the entrance to the vampire lair downstairs. It was a steep staircase that turned 90 degrees halfway down.

He rolled his blue eyes and debated.

He was wearing a white suit. Another hand-lettered sign at the top of the stairwell said clearly: 'NO SUITS!'

Suits. He hesitated a moment.

It wasn't the sign that gave him pause. It was the idea that he might get something foul and disgusting on his white jacket or trousers.

Contrary to Hollywood myth, he did not live in a manor house with servants who did his laundry and this suit was "dry-clean only". And if he said so himself – not that he could see for himself (the story about vampires not having reflections was as true as the garlic myth wasn't) – judging by the longing looks he had earned today from men and women alike, he looked damn good in this suit. It was a suit that was far too expensive to even consider dirtying in a dank little mortal "hangout".

As if a real vampire would be caught dead in such a place. No pun intended.

But that was an overused cliché anyways. Vampires were not technically "undead". They were very much alive, thank you. Nikolai really had to hand it to movies and folklore. Mortals would never understand that one's body could be separated from one's soul and still be alive.

Modern humans didn't believe in anything. They called themselves "advanced", though Nikolai had yet to see any proof of advancement in humans save for their technology and hygiene. They just wouldn't believe it if you told them that they all had an immortal soul. They had no clue about the war being waged over these souls or any idea about their powers. Asking them to believe that there were creatures interested in gaining possession of their souls was ludicrous indeed.

Nikolai considered the stairwell for another long moment. *She* was down there. Her heartbeat was less than 50 metres away. Even here, he could hear it. *Feel* it. Its rhythm was synchronized with his own. Did she not feel it? How could she not?

He wanted her, and he would have her, if only to satisfy his curiosity over this unorthodox desire.

The moment's hesitation gone, Nikolai descended the stairs.

Confidence bordering on arrogance.

That's all Katrina could call the look on the man's face as he entered the bar. Oh, she'd seen him outside. A *white* suit? The man seemed to be stuck in the 1980s, sans mullet (which was a mercy), though she could tell his hair was longer than most men wore it. Maybe he was just far too much of a *Miami Vice* fan, though he wasn't wearing sunglasses (thank God). Still, all criticism aside, he did wear that suit well, even if he did look a little strange in here, where everyone else was wearing black. If anyone looked out of place, it was her, with her dark-pink top and a black pencil skirt.

Of course, Dan had assured her she looked fine, though she was sure Dan would have said anything to get her to come down here. He had wanted to come here for months, ever since he read about it online on one of his vampire forums.

It was right up Dan's loud, wannabe-vampire alley.

She, on the other hand, was bored out of her mind.

One drink. She'd promised, just one drink.

Her hopes that it would be a quick drink were dashed, though. The bartender was still on his cell phone. How that guy could hear anything over the loud death-metal music was beyond her anyway.

Her eyes caught those of the guy in the white suit. He made her feel inexplicably better about her clothes. Now they both looked out of place. The way he was eyeing her made her uncomfortable though.

He looked at her hungrily. Desirously.

She looked away, both pleased and embarrassed.

She didn't . . . look like that. Feel like that. She wasn't anyone.

Certainly not anyone that – well, let's face it – deserved a guy that hot looking at her like that.

*Come on, Dan! Hurry up! Come on, bartender! Get off the phone!*

Dan was oblivious to her, as usual. He was studying the old horror-movie vampire behind glass at the end of the bar while he waited for the bartender to get off the phone.

The guy in the white suit suddenly gestured dismissively in the direction of the bartender and Dan. With a wave of his hand, he seemed to dismiss all of it. And his gesture seemed to be for her benefit alone.

Then he held that same hand out to her.

Katrina looked around nervously. No one noticed him. How could they not? He didn't look like he belonged here. Why weren't they noticing him?

But no one was looking at him.

And no one was looking at her.

Her eyes went to his again. Shy, now.

Nikolai tried not to let his impatience show.

Why wouldn't she come to him?

Wait. Wait. This was the New Millennium. Mortal women didn't respond as well to a commanding male as they used to. Well, not outwardly.

It was Nikolai's experience that they all yearned secretly for such a man, but their modern pride would not let them admit it. Modern mortal females had fought long and hard for equality and independence and respect. To confess that they truly just wanted a strong man to care for them was tantamount to treason; ill regard for the rights their foremothers had fought to give them.

Still. Semantics aside . . .

Slowly he turned the hand he held out to her palm down, as though he wished for her to take it.

Wished.

He was giving her the choice. That was what these women wanted these days, wasn't it?

To be given a choice?

Even though he didn't believe there was truly one for her to make?

This was destiny, after all.

Why wasn't Dan looking around to check on her? God, he was always so oblivious to her! To anything outside his own interests. If he ever managed to order their drinks, he would probably just start talking to the bartender and wouldn't even notice she had gone.

He didn't even notice that someone was noticing her.

Wanting her.

Asking her to come with him.

She found herself doing something completely insane. She left the sticky, rickety chair she'd been sitting in, moved hesitantly away from the safety of the unbalanced table and reached to take the hand of . . .

"Nikolai."

He said his name, answering her unspoken question just as her hand touched his. He then brought her hand to his lips and brushed her knuckles with (what could only be described as) a reverential kiss.

Why couldn't she seem to hear anything in the room other than his voice?

Why couldn't she look at anything but his eyes?

Without another word he cradled her left hand in his and effortlessly moved around behind her, his right arm encircling her waist as he guided them both out of the dark bar and up the stairs out of the vampire lair.

"Do you hunger?" he asked once they were on the street. A soft, low sound in her ear.

Oh, God, his voice! It was all Katrina could do not to melt right there.

That was one damn sexy accent.

Of course, this was Europe. All the men here had sexy accents of one kind or another. That's one thing America really didn't have much of – sexy accents. Texans were kind of cute though, with their Southern drawl, and OK boyfriends if you liked Budweiser, pickup trucks and line-dancing.

Nikolai didn't look Texan. Nor did he sound in any way American. Or English. His question alone: Do you hunger? English obviously wasn't his first language.

What a question.

Yes, she hungered, but not for anything on a menu anywhere in Soho.

She hungered for something she couldn't name.

A shake of her head was all she could manage.

Nikolai laughed richly. "You have permission to speak . . ." His words trailed off in a prompt for her name.

Not that he didn't already know it. Even he, who wasn't as adept at reading human thought as some of his soulless kindred were, had learned her name almost as easily as he knew his own.

"Katrina," she supplied without stammering, hardly even remembering that she should be protesting against his condescending offer of "permission".

"Katrina," he repeated, his tone turning her name into a caressing accusation.

His arm tightened around her waist.

Panic settled over her, but only for a moment. She closed her eyes and breathed as deeply as she could, which wasn't very deep at all. A series of disturbing thoughts raced through her mind.

What was she doing? What if he was a rapist? A murderer? A psycho serial killer?

A vampire?

"You're not a vampire, are you?" she found herself asking aloud.

Nikolai released her enough that he could look at her sternly. Then he smiled at her.

Her eyes widened as she took in his fangs.

Then she laughed. The Lair. He must be an actor, playing a role. *Miami Vice*, remember? A Don Johnson wannabe, though mercifully shaven and with neatly trimmed, if a little Renaissance-ish hair.

"The lady laughs," Nikolai said, seemingly crushed. He sighed deeply.

Katrina rolled her eyes at him. "There's no such thing as vampires," Katrina informed him, smiling back.

"Try telling that to my family. Now, let us escape this vile place and those individuals back in the bar," Nikolai said as he moved her down the street.

"So, are you going to take me down one of these narrow alleys, drain me of my life's blood and leave me to die?" she asked, somewhat teasingly even as she snuggled further into his arm. It wasn't cold, exactly, but the summer night's breeze was brisker than she was used to.

"I prefer hiding in plain sight," Nikolai answered. "Besides, do you know how hard blood is to get out of white clothing? I am rather fond of this suit."

"It looks sinful on you," Katrina said, blurting out what she'd been thinking since she'd first laid eyes on him.

"Well, my soul already dwells in hell, so I have no fear that wearing this will do it further harm," Nikolai answered, hardly thinking that he'd just voiced a truth he'd never spoken aloud before.

And he'd said it so effortlessly, without even thinking that she might not understand. Without even realizing that he was speaking to her as if she weren't human.

She just laughed.

Nikolai breathed a silent sigh of relief and chastised himself inwardly for his slip. Why? What did he intend to do with her? They were just walking along a street in Soho, like . . . like normal people. Well, like he *was* a man. They weren't walking along like predator and prey. Hunter and hunted. They were just walking along like a man and a woman. And she'd laughed at him, and told him she didn't believe in vampires.

Perhaps she didn't believe in Heaven or Hell either. Most humans didn't these days. Or if they did, they did so in a completely incorrect, awkward and befuddling manner.

His centuries of anguish and torment, his greatest shame, laughed off like it didn't happen. Like it wasn't even possible.

And it didn't matter to him. Her laughter made it . . . laughable. *Bearable.* He supposed that when the truth was spoken nakedly it *was* rather laughable.

He was a lost soul. Literally. Well, that's what they called it, anyways. His soul, along with those of others of his kind, wasn't exactly "lost". He knew exactly where it was. It was in hell, with Lucifer.

He was quite literally, damned.

Only in his particular case, his soul had been willingly given in exchange for immortality. Damned by his own hand. That truly was the ironic kick in the groin.

Others – most notably Kail the Betrayer – still thought of themselves as victims even though they had clearly earned (even asked for) the forfeit of their soul. However, Kail was unique. Kail wanted his soul back and had dedicated the whole of his immortal existence to finding a way to get it.

Nikolai wasn't unique. He was exactly the same as all the others who attempted and succeeded in making a deal with the Devil, not quite understanding what true immortality entailed.

Living off the blood of those you sought to outlive.

But Nikolai was willing to pay the price and willingly joined the most powerful of the vampire clans that wished to call him "brother". Nikolai was one of the Destrati.

And the woman beside him had laughed.

Though she ceased when she saw the look on his face, and studied him a moment as they walked.

"You really think you're damned?" Katrina asked him softly.

"Because of my actions, my soul dwells in hell," Nikolai answered, again being honest without thinking about what he was saying. "Is that not what 'damned' means?"

"You know, I don't usually get into the deep philosophical discussions until the second or third date," Katrina replied with a nervous laugh.

"I do not date," Nikolai found himself answering calmly. "My personal life is complicated. My family does not allow much time for . . . dating. I simply saw you tonight on the arm of that mortal man who is not even remotely interested in a thing like you and . . ."

A thing like her? What, was she a television? Or a laptop?

Nikolai sighed. He had no idea what he was doing, with her or with himself. She made him feel . . .

Feel? Was that it? He hadn't really felt much of anything more than indifference for such a long time. His life was composed of endurance, duty, hatred and occasional envy (but that was brief, and usually only directed towards his own kind).

And *his* kind didn't associate with *her* kind.

She was food. More than that, she was mortal and still had her immortal soul. She wasn't just sustenance. She was an enemy. The worst kind, as she was clearly undeclared territory in the War Between The Sides.

She was undeclared and unclaimed, and he wanted her.

Some of his kind took brides, and he was both old enough and high enough in rank to be afforded that privilege. He just never thought he would wish to take it. However, once the idea had occurred to him, he wanted it more than anything. Not "it" more than anything, but her, as his bride, more than anything.

But she hadn't been selected. And that would prove a problem.

"Excuse me a moment, miss," a cultured voice came from behind Nikolai. "May I borrow Nikolai for a moment? Please, if you could wait in the cafe just there. A double mocha sounds particularly good at the moment, does it not?"

Katrina just nodded, barely questioning the suggestion in her mind.

Nikolai growled through gritted fangs.

"Now, now, Nikolai. Not in front of the mortals."

"What do you want, Betrayer?" Nikolai asked as low and as dark as he could manage, given that he was held captive not only by the hand on the back of his neck, but by a power far greater than his own. Far, far greater.

"Such ill manners," came the reply. "Still the Destrati haven't moved out of the Dark Ages."

Nikolai was released, and allowed to face Kail.

The taller man in the dark suit held Nikolai's piercing blue eyes with his own pale sea-green ones. Kail's long, chestnut ponytail hung casually down his back, secured with a black strip of leather.

"Kail," Nikolai said warningly.

"It's Kyle now, actually," the older presence said with a smile. "I'd formally, and politely, introduce myself, but you already seem to know me. As I already know you. And I must say, Destrati, you were far too easy to sense."

Kyle looked toward the cafe and back to Nikolai, his point made clearly.

Nikolai looked away, scowling. "It is none of your business," Nikolai said grudgingly.

He looked back at Kyle. "And as Destrati I should kill you where you stand."

Kyle laughed richly. "Don't think I don't know your reason for being in London, or that I am unaware of exactly how long you've been here, searching," said Kyle, very amused. "I abhor destroying anyone when there are other ways of settling things. Besides, what would pretty Katrina say if I destroyed you and left her alone? I believe the term these days for a woman who is deserted by a man while on a date is 'stood up'. She would wonder for the rest of her short, mortal life where you'd disappeared to and what she had done to cause you to leave. For she would blame herself, you know. It would quite probably scar that pretty little soul of hers deeply. Such attachment in so little a time. Dare I speak the forbidden? Could she be your soul—" Kyle stepped easily out of the way of Nikolai's lunge "—mate?" He continued speaking as though nothing had happened. "It is rather too bad that your soul has already been—" Kyle dodged another lunge, again without effort "—traded for immortality, isn't it?"

"Nikolai? Are you coming?"

Katrina's voice broke into Nikolai's thoughts and immediately soothed him. He made to round on Kyle again, but the other vampire seemed to have vanished.

Oh, but he was still near. Nikolai was sure of it. But Katrina was waiting for him. How strange that felt. To have someone care where he was and if he was coming to join them.

Nikolai knew Kail/Kyle lived in London. It was why Nikolai was here. He'd been here for months, trying to find the Betrayer and bring him before the Council for justice.

The vampires – these lost souls – lived in virtual peace. Not, however, with each other.

Each vampire clan had their own Council and their own code.

Kyle was an outcast among them all.

To bring the Betrayer to justice would put him as second to the leader of the Destrati – not the largest of the vampire clans, but the most powerful. The Sovereign's second had been killed in a duel a century ago by a rival and Sarina now sat at Dominic's left hand.

It was rumoured that they were lovers, but Sarina had won the rank in a fair fight.

There was no way for anyone to ascend to her position without challenging her. And Sarina, both as second and the ranking female of the clan, would select his bride, when Nikolai announced he was ready to take one.

Brides were culled from a select group of mortal women who were suited for the burden of being soulless and immortal. Docile, doe-eyed, beautiful and worshipful women who would remain so throughout eternity, and who would never question their place or their purpose.

Katrina wasn't one of those. Beautiful, yes, but not Sarina's idea of beautiful. All Sarina's selections were the same. What did he do if he wanted to choose his own bride?

*Meet me at the County Hall at midnight and I will tell you what to do.*

Kyle's voice spoke in his mind, almost halting Nikolai as he entered the cafe where Katrina stood waiting with two mugs of a brown beverage with a white frothy top.

Oh, God, a human drink. A *vile* human drink at that. And she wondered why he didn't date.

Nikolai dared a silent reply to Kyle.

But before he asked the question, the reply was there.

*Of course you can bring her. In fact, it's a good idea that she doesn't leave your side until then.*

Nikolai was mystified and, for some reason, suddenly frightened. He hadn't been frightened in a very long time. He was immortal. Why should he be afraid of anything?

Then he realized he wasn't afraid for himself. He was afraid for her. He was afraid of losing her.

*Isn't that being afraid for yourself?* Kyle's voice asked in his mind.

*Go away, Betrayer!* Nikolai bit back silently. *I am on a date!*

Kyle's laughter was faint in his mind, but it was there.

*Wait!* Nikolai found himself shouting telepathically. *She is offering me a mortal drink! What do I do?*

*Figure it out, Destrati.* Kyle's voice was barely an amused whisper, but Nikolai got the point.

He was on his own. He sat down on the barstool and contemplated the drink for a long moment.

"You know, I am not really in the mood for coffee," Nikolai said, setting his mug back on the counter.

"Nor am I," Katrina said, looking confusedly at her own drink before she set it beside Nikolai's. "I don't even drink coffee. I don't know why I thought to come in and order them."

"Where are you staying?" Nikolai asked.

Katrina eyed him. "You move fast," she said wryly.

If he'd been a true human, his cheeks would have flushed at her insinuation. "I . . . I didn't mean to imply . . ."

Katrina smiled and brought a hand to his cheek in comfort. He looked so hurt, so suddenly crestfallen. His skin was soft and cool beneath her hand.

Her touch. How long had it been, since anyone, mortal or otherwise, had touched him for the sole reason of touching him? Oh, there were always willing women (willing men too, to be honest, if one's tastes ran to such, which Nikolai's didn't). But this was different. This touch was freely given.

Free will.

He closed his eyes, remembering what it was to have free will. Free will came from the soul.

He didn't even feel her move between his loosely parted knees, it was so effortless. His arms went around her waist as though he had held her every day of his existence.

Katrina's hands cupped his face and slid into his hair. He tilted his chin up, enjoying her touch. Then she kissed him, sweet, hesitant and entirely chaste.

"Is this a parting?" he asked, opening his eyes to look at her when she broke the kiss almost as quickly as she'd begun it.

She nodded, unable to explain. She was with Dan and not about to go to some hot stranger's place for a one-night stand. This guy had "player" written all over him and she'd almost gone for it. What had she been thinking? She hadn't been, that's what. One did the craziest things on vacation.

"I'm not," he said suddenly.

Her brow furrowed. "Not what?" she asked.

"A 'player'," he replied.

"I didn't say that," she protested immediately.

"You thought it," he said.

"And you're a mind-reader?' She pulled away from him.

"Yes."

"Then why did you bother asking me where I was staying?" she asked, patronizingly.

He just looked at her. What kind of conversation was this?

"I was being polite," he offered, almost hesitantly, as though he didn't know if that were the answer she wanted, but the only way he knew to answer her.

She rolled her eyes at him and made to leave.

He caught her hand. "Please," he found himself saying. "Don't go."

She turned back to look at him, her eyes unsure and hurt.

Why was she upset? Was his truthfulness thought dishonest? Was she afraid of him?

"It's not like that, Katrina Francesca," he said softly. "You asked how I knew. Do you want me to lie to you, like you think I'm doing anyway?"

Her eyes widened. How did he –

"—know your middle name?" he finished for her.

Instead of waiting for her to answer, he stood and looked down at her. He brought her hand to his chest and pressed it over his heart and gathered her close to him while he closed his eyes and murmured softly for a long moment.

She blinked rapidly to clear her vision. Everything was so foggy and she was suddenly cold. When she took in the sight before her, she gasped and took a step back from the railing she found herself pressed against.

It was Paris by night. They were on the topmost viewing platform of the Eiffel Tower.

"Hotel!" she gasped insensibly. "The Tower *Hotel*!"

"Forgive me," Nikolai said, though his tone held no contrition. "My apologies. All I heard was 'tower', and that's where you wanted to be. You have a fondness for France."

She barely had time to take another breath before they were back in London, in the dark shade of a pillar outside her hotel.

Nikolai's hands rubbed her upper arms slowly. "Breathe," he encouraged softly.

"That did not just happen," she managed through her shivers, trying in vain to control her violent shaking. "I drank too much, or slipped down those God-awful stairs at that horrid bar or it's all a dream. You're certainly proof of that . . ."

"Oh? Now why would you think that?" he asked.

"Well, just look at you," she said, stepping away from him a couple of paces. "And look at me. You're handsome, gorgeous. And I'm—"

"Beautiful," he interrupted with a smile. "That is what you were going to say, was it not?"

Katrina blushed. It wasn't, but he knew that. Didn't he?

"Yes, I knew that," he replied aloud. Nikolai's eyes went to the door of the hotel. "You will stay here tonight? With him?" he asked.

Katrina nodded mutely, still stunned. Then she shook her head, negating what she had just automatically confirmed.

"So you do know, and acknowledge," he said quietly as he slid a possessive arm around her waist, feeling something warm him from within.

"I don't believe in vampires," she said stupidly.

"Truth does not require belief," Nikolai replied, quoting an oft-repeated ethereal adage.

"You have—" she could hardly bring herself to use the word "– fangs."

"Yes."

"And you drink blood? Live off it? Need it to continue to live, or whatever?"

"There's more to it, but yes."

"Show me."

Nikolai was taken aback at her demand. "Here?" he asked, completely flustered.

"Well, where were you planning on doing so?" she asked. "What were you doing in that bar, anyway? Go there often? Is this a nightly thing for you?"

"I came for you," he replied, scowling. "I thought . . . I felt . . ."

"Oh, come now, don't fight, children," Kyle's voice came from the shadows. His eyes pierced Nikolai's. "Destrati. What have you done to enrage your family? Come. Quickly now."

Kyle barely glanced at them and suddenly they were both inside a large dark room. Oil lamps burned to illuminate it, casting long shadows on the elegant antique bed.

Nikolai was again in awe. Such effortlessness. Kyle displayed his power with such a natural ease. Nikolai had known he was formidable, but Kyle hadn't even needed to touch either of them to shift both him and Katrina at the same time. Kyle had also accompanied them without even a hint of the effort it always took Nikolai (and Nikolai was considered one of the best at manifestation). Such grace. He could rule . . .

"Do not even think it, Destrati."

Kyle's voice had gone flat and cold. Forbidding. Then he smiled at Katrina.

"Welcome, lady," he said, bringing her hand to his lips. "Please forgive all this confusion. The Destrati are ill-mannered. Nikolai will explain, I'm sure. Do so, won't you, Nikolai, while I see about your kinsmen that follow."

Kyle was gone before Nikolai could reply.

Katrina just looked at Nikolai, unsure of where she was.

Words would not come. The only way he could think to explain was with actions.

One hand slid to the back of her neck while the other pulled her closer to him by the waist. His thumb pressed gently into the side of her neck and, when it moved almost of its own accord beneath his touch, he bent his head and kissed her throat.

Katrina shivered as her eyes slid shut.

Nikolai kissed her sensitive flesh once more before parting her lips with his tongue. He savoured the taste of her, enjoying her trembling.

Enjoyment. That, too, had long been absent from his existence. He'd smiled more tonight than he had in a very long while, and another graced his lips before he found the pulse at her throat with his lips.

Katrina didn't even feel the bite. She knew he bit her though, and that he was drinking her blood, just like in a horror film. Why it didn't disgust her she could not fathom. Instead of revulsion, she felt a deep sense of . . . pride. She was able to provide him with something he needed. She felt wanted and beautiful, unlike anything she'd ever felt before. She never wanted this feeling to end.

She buried her hands in his hair and held him close, arching her back into his touch. She was beginning to feel weak and dizzy, but she didn't care.

"I care," he murmured against the delicate flesh of her neck. "I care so much, Katrina Francesca. You know that, don't you? Tell me you know. Tell me you feel it."

She couldn't think how to answer him. Thought itself seemed entirely too much effort. For the first time in her life, Katrina was allowing something to just . . . happen.

And, oh God, did it feel amazing. Everything. Anything. Anything he wanted, as long as it was just like this.

"You have to tell me," he urged softly. "You have to say it. Give me permission."

Oh, God. Permission? Was he kidding? Oh, that was inexplicably hot somehow. Knowing he wouldn't – *couldn't* – take this further without her permission.

Coherence returned somewhat. Her body was ablaze with a wanting she'd never known before, not with anyone. She pulled back a little. She just had to look at him.

Tormented anguish was all she saw etched upon his gorgeous face. A tiny drop of red glistened at the corner of his mouth. Her hand moved to cup his cheek automatically. She brushed the drop of her blood away with the pad of her thumb and met his eyes.

His arms tightened around her waist. Would she turn from him in horror? When he wanted her so badly?

She put one hand to her throat. She touched her neck gingerly and then brought her fingertips near the candlelight. They, too, glistened with blood.

She looked back at him. Her hand returned to stroke his face and he closed his eyes to shudder beneath her touch. He kissed her fingers as she brought them to his lips, taking the stain of blood from them contritely. Then he leaned down again and kissed the healing wound he'd made.

It was permission enough.

His hands found the bottom of her shirt and slid beneath it.

She closed her eyes as his hands caressed her skin. She'd sated his hunger, she knew. Now it was time to satisfy him.

"I care."

Nikolai's tone was dark and defiant as he faced Kyle in the latter's very formal dining room.

"That's all well and good, Destrati, but do you think that will in any way, shape or form move Dominic and Sarina?" Kyle swirled red liquid around in a crystal wine glass he held between his middle and fourth fingers.

"My name is Nikolai," the younger ethereal stated with a scowl.

"Is it?" Kyle mocked him. "You've been a Destrati for so long you don't even remember your own surname. Now you've found something worth turning on your own family for and suddenly the name offends you?"

"The way you say it offends me," Nikolai replied, glancing over his shoulder in the direction of the bedroom where Katrina lay sleeping.

" 'Recovering', more like," Kyle corrected, taking a sip of his drink. "Did you do as I instructed?"

"You know I did." Nikolai nearly spat in disgust. "Why do you ask what you already know?"

"Courtesy," Kyle replied, before draining his glass and setting it upon the mantelpiece above the fire he'd been absently watching. "Unlike you, Destrati, I have manners."

"Why are you helping us?" Nikolai asked. "Me, in particular? Your hatred of the Destrati is nearly as legendary as your powers are."

Kyle considered Nikolai a moment, and raised an eyebrow at his use of the word "us".

"Are my reasons important?"

"Very," Nikolai answered. "I remember well the lesson about not questioning the thing set before you."

"Clever lad," Kyle replied with a genuine smile that flashed his fangs. "I knew your cause would be a worthy one." He glanced meaningfully towards the bedroom and Katrina.

Nikolai understood, and nodded.

"Now, listen carefully, Nikolai, for I will only explain this once."

Sarina paced back and forth, though she tried to stop herself. There had been no news from any plane, neither mortal nor ethereal. Her dark eyes met Dominic's pale ones for the umpteenth time and, for the umpteenth time, he had no words for her, comforting or otherwise.

There was an audible sigh of relief as a messenger finally appeared at the doorway to the Council chamber of Clan Destrati. The messenger began to bow, but was stopped by Sarina's impatient gesture.

"Speak!" she commanded. "Tell us!"

The messenger looked to the doorway for his reply.

Kyle entered. He met Sarina's eyes.

"It seems the rudeness of the Destrati extends upwards through the echelons." Kyle's voice was humourless.

The messenger bowed quickly to his superiors, and to Kyle, before making a hasty exit. Kyle stepped into the room and bowed to Sarina. He inclined his head towards Dominic as he straightened.

Dominic bent his head in return, though it seemed forced and stiff. Kyle smiled and quickly withdrew his power from the back of Dominic's head.

"No need to curtsey, Sarina," Kyle said. "No doubt the centuries have robbed you of that knowledge, if ever you possessed it."

"You are not welcome here, Betrayer," Sarina hissed darkly. "You have no business in our Council chamber—"

Her words were cut off suddenly by an indifferent wave of Kyle's hand.

Sarina's hands went to her throat, as if the gesture would restore her voice.

"Of course he has business here, Sarina," Dominic said, though his own voice trembled slightly as he left the centre Council seat to stand. "Kail doesn't waste his time on trivial things or make a habit of appearing where he isn't wanted. Isn't that so, Ancient One?"

"Playing the sycophant doesn't suit you, Destrati. You both know I am no Ancient," Kyle said lightly. He gestured again at Sarina. She immediately went to Dominic's side.

"You're frightened," Kyle said aloud. "That's good. I trust I have your attention then."

The Sovereign and his lady nodded in unison.

"Since you two would not hear any other voice, I speak as an emissary."

"On whose behalf?" Dominic asked.

"Mine." Nikolai entered the room behind his emissary.

Sarina laughed. She spoke before Dominic could. "What is this?" she asked, looking from Nikolai to Kyle and back again. "You can't possibly be serious. Consorting with the Betrayer? An outcast? An outcast you yourself were hunting to bring to justice. And now he speaks for you?"

"I do," Kyle said formally. "On behalf of Nikolai Peityr of Clan Destrati, I issue a Challenge for Sovereignty."

Sarina laughed. "On what grounds?"

"Tyrannical dominance of the once-wise Council Destrati, its proceedings and even the personal lives of those who claim kinship of Clan Destrati," Kyle answered, grave and unyielding. "Not even allowed to choose one's own bride? That is more than tyranny . . . that's totalitarian lunacy, and no longer tolerable."

"Nikolai," Sarina purred sweetly. "We've all seen Kail's Power. We all know of it. It's mythic. Legend. He's a Betrayer . . . *the* Betrayer, with no clan who will claim kinship with him. Are we to believe that you are issuing a challenge of your own will?"

She turned to Dominic before Nikolai or Kyle could reply. "I propose that Nikolai is under the Entrancement of Kailkiril'ron the Betrayer," she charged, looking to Kyle haughtily.

"We are rather rude, aren't we?" Nikolai muttered to Kyle.

"Quite," Kyle replied with a smile.

"That's going to change," Nikolai said, smiling, before raising his voice that Sarina and Dominic might hear him. "Sovereign, I deny the accusation and remind Sarina that a Challenge may not be issued under Entrancement. Further, the accusation is fallacious in that, if Kyle's Power is indeed myth or legend, he would not need to resort to Entrancement to obtain his aim, if indeed he wished control of a clan. The Challenge stands."

"Let the Council of Clan Destrati be summoned," Kyle pronounced, raising his arms to vaulted ceiling.

When no one appeared, Kyle raisèd his eyebrows. "Well, that was dramatic," Kyle said ruefully. He eyed Dominic and Sarina. "You two *are* the Council then, I take it?"

"Very good, Betrayer," Sarina spat contemptuously.

"Sarina," Dominic said quietly, his tone betraying his guilt.

"I didn't realize that 'tyrannical dominance of the Council' meant that you *were* the Council," Kyle mused with a sidelong glance at Nikolai. "There should be at least ten others sitting at this table. So many attempted to separate Nikolai from his chosen lady . . . don't tell me you sent *Council* members out on errantry as well as your faithful minions. Ahhh, now I see . . . Sarina, I'm surprised at you. Well, not truly."

Sarina was beginning to look as uncomfortable as Dominic. Nikolai only looked confused.

"She fancies you," Kyle said softly to Nikolai. "And thought to keep you either unmarried or for herself when you wished a bride . . . didn't you, Sarina?"

Dominic looked at his second and, indeed, lover. Sarina would not look at him in return.

"I've done everything you wanted," Dominic said to her, deeply hurt. "Even things I didn't agree with, because it made you happy. You rule beside me . . ."

"Dominic – " Sarina began.

"Enough!" Dominic growled, silencing her with a hand held up. "A challenge has been issued. We will settle our own issue later. Provided we survive."

Dominic looked to Nikolai. "Weapons?"

"Power, and Power alone," Nikolai said firmly.

"No," Sarina said, horrified.

"Oh, come now, Sarina," Kyle said with a wicked grin. "Nikolai is a gentleman – of a sort – and wouldn't dare strike a woman. Well, perhaps if she came at him with a weapon. You should have spent more of your time learning to use less pointy means of defence."

Kyle looked to Nikolai. "The challenge is yours. I leave you to your fate."

Nikolai offered his hand. Kyle considered it, hesitating only a moment before grasping it firmly. Then Kyle took his leave, effortless and against the protections and wards set about the Council chamber of Clan Destrati. Nikolai shook his head and looked to Sarina one last time . . .

"Love. Wake."

Nikolai's voice brought Katrina back to herself. She was cradled in his arms. Funny, she couldn't remember him moving from the bed. And why was she dressed in a nightgown? Where were her clothes? What . . .

"Shh," Nikolai soothed. He reached to stroke her hair. "I know you've always wanted to be a princess," he said warmly. "And now you are, albeit of something not quite as you expected."

Katrina started to speak, and met his eyes. In one moment, she knew everything that had happened. She could hear his thoughts. It was the only way she could explain it, and knew it had something to do with him taking her blood.

Momentary panic gripped her as she realized that weeks had passed. Kyle had kept her safe while Nikolai dealt with his family. Nikolai had challenged, fought for and won leadership of his family. But what about Dan, and her family . . . her job?

Nikolai waved his hand dismissively, as he had at the bar that night.

Katrina raised an eyebrow at him.

"You were bored," Nikolai said contritely.

Katrina smiled in spite of herself. He was adorable when he was defensive. She reached to touch his face.

Nikolai looked up at her. "I can fix everything, if you like," he offered quietly.

"Why me?" she asked.

"Kyle says it is because you are the other half of my soul," Nikolai replied.

"A soul you don't have," she said, studying him.

Nikolai looked away and nodded.

"Why did Kyle help you? You were hunting him, weren't you? Isn't he an enemy of yours?"

Nikolai nodded, and then shook his head as she had the night they met. "He is no friend, but no longer an enemy," Nikolai explained. "Not truly. It was his idea that you play dead until . . ."

"Until . . . ?" Katrina prompted.

"Until he taught me to use my abilities well enough to challenge the Sovereign of the Destrati and win leadership," Nikolai continued. "It was time for a change. I, too, was bored, I suppose."

"Idle hands make mischief, my grandmother used to say," she said with a nervous giggle. "So you're Sovereign now?"

"Of the Destrati," he replied. "Not the largest of the vampire clans, but the most powerful."

"What makes them so?" she asked. "You?"

"No," he said, shaking his head. "We're united."

"United?"

Nikolai smiled. "All in time, my love," he soothed. "For now, you need to rest and refresh yourself."

"Am I a vampire?" she blurted. "You bit me!"

Nikolai rolled his eyes. "You watch too much television," he chided. "I've made you immortal, not a vampire. Why do you think my clan tried so hard to prevent me from choosing my own bride? Do you think I would damn another soul to hell? 'Destrati' means 'Destroyers'. I meant to destroy Kail the Betrayer, and found the other half of my soul instead. I mean to cherish it – cherish *you*, my beloved one – for all eternity. In order to do that, I had to destroy those who would destroy you. The Sovereign and his queen would never have let me become your bridegroom."

Katrina slid her arms around his neck. When he leaned close to kiss her, she stopped him with a finger upon his lips.

"Did you just say we're married?"

"Do you need some other formal declaration?" he asked, dumbfounded.

"No, just checking," she said, laughing a little. "Though you really need to stop the whole 'doing without asking' thing. It's a little outdated."

"The Destrati are ill-mannered," he said with a teasing sigh. "As Kyle reminds me whenever possible. Perhaps you could bring us out of the Dark Ages, Katrina Francesca?"

Katrina groaned. "Trina," she replied. "My friends call me Trina. Francesca is so old-fashioned."

Nikolai looked affronted.

Katrina laughed. "Nik and Trina," she said, shaking her head. "Won't Mom love that?"

His eyes widened. "Mom?"

# In Which a Masquerade Ball Unmasks an Undead

## Colleen Gleason

### London, 1819

"My lady, your mother is wearin' a hole in the floor," Verbena said as she twisted a final curl into place at the top of her mistress' coiffure. "She claims you'll be late for the masquerade ball if you don't hurry. And something about the Marquess o'Rockley attendin' and wantin' to see ye?"

Miss Victoria Gardella Grantworth looked in the mirror, eyeing her maid's creation in the form of a tall – very tall – coiffure. Her dark hair had been piled to an impossible height and then powdered so that her black curls looked more grey than white. A small bluebird perched at the side of her column of hair and a bejewelled comb rested at the top. Pink and yellow flowers and a variety of jewels further decorated the powdered curls.

"I don't know that Marie Antoinette's hair was ever this particular hue," Victoria said, "but I think it looks lovely. And perhaps I'd best go down before Mother comes up to drag me off."

She stood and the skirts of her gown rose with her as if they had a life of their own. Victoria was used to wearing the high-waisted, clinging skirts of contemporary styles, but these wide panniers and heavily brocaded layers of fabric at least left her legs free to move beneath without getting too caught up in the skirts. The only other benefit of the yards of material dripping from her body was that there were plenty of places to hide a wooden stake, between all the ruffles, lace and gathers. She felt for the one that rested just to the right side of her torso, cunningly hidden behind a pouf of lace.

"I do hope there aren't any vampires at Lady Petronilla's ball tonight," Victoria said, drawing on her gloves. "It will be impossible to fight them in this costume."

"But, m'lady, if there are, you'll be very prepared," Verbena told her, a sparkle in her blue eyes. "I've slipped one o' your littler stakes here in the back of your hair." She poked at the heavy mass near the back of Victoria's crown. "Just in case."

"If I pull it out, it is likely my hair will all come falling down," Victoria replied, gingerly feeling for the stake. "But in a pinch, I suppose it shall do. I only hope I'll not have need of it. I have been looking forward to one night where I don't have to make some excuse to sneak out and stake a vampire."

Verbena handed her mistress a small reticule. "Holy water an' a cross in here, my lady," she told her. "An' you look lovely."

Victoria might look like any normal young woman, just debuting into society, but beneath her gown – whether it be a fashionable high-waisted one or the retrospective costume she currently wore – she harboured a secret that made her very different from any other girl.

She wore the *vis bulla*, a tiny silver-cross amulet that gave her superhuman strength, speed and healing capability. Victoria Gardella Grantworth was a Venator, a vampire hunter descended from a long line of slayers in the Gardella family. Her duty, beyond that of her unsuspecting mother's expectation that she marry well, was to hunt the undead who lurked in the shadows of London society. And everywhere else in the world.

Victoria wasn't the only Venator. Her great-aunt Eustacia had been a powerful Venator before she became too old to hunt, and then there was Max Pesaro, another Venator, who spent more time disparaging Victoria's hunting skills than anything else. He, too, was a vampire hunter, though not descended from the Gardella line.

Victoria was rather glad that she would be attending the masquerade ball at Lady Petronilla's tonight, for Max disdained social functions and would not be there to glower at her and make snide comments about how many men had signed her dance card.

And then of course, there was Phillip.

Thinking of the Marquess of Rockley put a great smile on her face, so that when Victoria reached the bottom of the stairs and her mother saw her, she looked particularly radiant.

"Well, now," Lady Melly twittered. She was a handsome woman herself and had chosen to dress in Greek fashion as Circe. Having been widowed more than two years earlier by a man she'd cared for, but never truly loved, she had just recently re-entered society with a vengeance. "You do look lovely, Victoria dear, and it is certain that Rockley will be enchanted. That tiny little black patch on your cheek is just the most delightful touch. Although I do rather think you could do without that little wooden thing sticking out of the back of your coiffure. I vow, sometimes I wonder what your maid is thinking when she dresses your hair.'

Victoria smoothly moved out of the way when her mother reached to touch the stake secreted in her curls. "I like it, Mother. And should we not be leaving? I'm not certain how long it will take me to find Rockley, as we'll all be masked."

"Oh, I have no fear on that," Lady Melly said, ushering her daughter quite unnecessarily out of the front door. The carriage was waiting, a footman standing with the door open and the groom holding the horses. "He shall be dressed as that infamous Robin Hood, and I've made certain that he'll know who the mysterious Marie Antoinette is."

Victoria didn't bother to ask how her mother had found out how Phillip – as he'd asked her to call him – would be costumed, or how she could have informed him of her daughter's guise. It didn't matter one whit. She merely allowed her mother to muse delightfully over her machinations to have her only daughter marry a wealthy marquess.

Not that Victoria minded, for Phillip was handsome, charming and seemed to be as besotted with her as she was with him. He'd been seeking her out at every social event they'd both attended since her debut . . . and had even kissed her once while driving her through the park. That was when he insisted that she call him by his given name, despite the fact that they weren't married or even betrothed.

When they arrived at Lady Petronilla's home, Victoria had to succumb to her mother's last-minute fussing before she could emerge awkwardly from the carriage. Really, those skirts were more than a bit much, and she nearly lost her balance due to their weight and the fact that her heel caught in a hem.

She *really* hoped there would be no vampires here tonight.

Inside the ball, Victoria and her mother made their way from the grand foyer into the ballroom. The butler introduced them only as "Her Majesty Marie Antoinette and Circe", since they were masked and would remain that way until midnight.

In spite of wishing to appear aloof, Victoria found herself looking for Robin Hood. From the way her mother had wrapped her talon-like fingers around her arm, she knew Lady Melly wouldn't let her slip into the crowds until they found him.

But then a generously sized Aphrodite bore down upon them, her gown flowing behind her like a great pink sail. Lady Melly released Victoria's arm and greeted one of her two bosom friends, the Duchess of Farnham.

"I daresay, Victoria, you look absolutely lovely," crowed the Duchess, who wore a heavy necklace of garnets and a light dusting of crumbs. "Or shall I say, Your Majesty? Perhaps you ought to adjust your mask a bit," she added.

"Yes indeed," Lady Melly said, pulling urgently on Victoria's mask, unaware that a sharp edge was scraping across her daughter's nose. "It would be a shame if Bretlington or Werthington-Lyce recognized you before Rockley, for I don't know how you should get out of dancing with them."

In that, Victoria could not help but agree, for the former had exceedingly putrid breath that accompanied non-stop raptures over his bloodhounds and the latter spoke nary a word at all but spent his time leering down the bodice of her gown and treading upon her toes.

But at that moment, her mother's manipulations came to fruition. Victoria felt the presence of Phillip behind her before he even spoke. Perhaps it was the smell of the lemon-rosemary pomade he favoured, or perhaps it was merely that prickle of awareness, of attraction, that hummed between them. At any rate, she turned slowly – so as not to appear too eager, yet be sure he knew that she was delighted to see him – and immediately found his gaze behind the black mask.

His dark eyes were hooded by heavy lids that always gave him an appearance of deep contemplation, yet coupled with underlying humour and sensuality. "That is quite a magnificent coiffure, Your Majesty," he said, removing his soft, feathered hat as he bowed. "It's a wonder that your slender neck can carry the weight, especially with all of those jewels and other ornaments therein."

"Indeed, Sir Robin of the Hood," she replied. "I hope that you haven't any designs on relieving me of any of said jewels, under the guise of lightening the load for my poor little head."

"Jewels? Nay, my fair Queen" Phillip said, his eyes glinting wickedly from behind the mask. "It is not jewels that I seek from you."

Victoria could feel her mother's barely suppressed delight at this exchange, even as her own cheeks warmed beneath the mask and her stomach gave a delicious flutter.

Phillip, savvy as he was, took that moment to break off their little sally and turn to bow at Circe and Aphrodite, both of whom had eyes shining with delight and fingers twittering silently with expectation. "Good evening, my ladies," he said, again flourishing his cap. "How lovely you both look this eventide. I do hope you might forgive this outlaw if he claims the Queen for a waltz – as she refuses to part with her jewels."

"Oh, but of course," replied Lady Melly, fairly shoving Victoria at Rockley.

Fortunately, Phillip had become familiar with Lady Melly's enthusiasm due to past exchanges, and he caught Victoria's arm before she – and her mass of skirts – stumbled over his boots. "Shall we?" he asked, cupping her fingers intimately around his warm, muscular arm.

As he drew her towards the dance floor, where a country dance had just ended, Victoria passed a golden-haired man dressed as a medieval lute player. Though he wore a mask the colour of well-brewed tea, topaz eyes glittered through the holes and caught Victoria's gaze.

A little shiver tingled over the back of her shoulders and she felt a quick, funny twist in her middle. She knew him. The knowing heat in those eyes, the little lift at one side of that full mouth.

Sebastian Vioget.

What on earth was Sebastian Vioget doing *here*?

This time, Victoria did stumble over her blastedly heavy skirt as Phillip drew her into a smooth embrace, very correct, with the proper amount of space between them, and launched them into the three-count step.

Even as she was fully aware of the imprint of Phillip's hand at the back of her waist and the comforting feel of his fingers around hers, Victoria couldn't keep her attention from following the masked lute player. He was dressed in an emerald shirt with a gold tunic over it, making it easy to follow the shine of his garb as he moved smoothly through the clusters of people.

The last time she'd seen Sebastian Vioget had been at the Silver Chalice, a pub that he owned and operated in the unpleasant, dangerous neighborhood of St Giles. His clientele consisted mainly of vampires, although a few brave – or un-witting – humans also patronized the place.

Somehow, Sebastian had recognized the fact that Victoria was a Venator and he'd made his fascination clear. Then there had been that moment in his private office . . .

"My dear, you seem rather quiet tonight," Phillip said, breaking into her thoughts. "I do hope that my appearance didn't set you off any plans you might have had to add to your dance card, though I must confess, I would have battled my way through any of your admirers to claim my waltz tonight. Or, dare I hope – waltzes?"

Victoria smiled up at him, but felt a twinge of guilt. She'd had to forestall or interrupt their dances more than once when duty called for her to locate and stake a vampire. "Waltzes? I would be most delighted to grant you those, in the plural, insofar as I can trust you won't try to rob me of my jewelled hairpieces.

Such stories I've heard about you, Sir Robin Hood, and your quick fingers."

His eyes glinted appreciatively. "As I have been so bold as to proclaim, Your Majesty, it isn't your jewels that I hope to obtain."

"Something more valuable?" she asked, suddenly forgetting about Sebastian Vioget and vampires and anything other than the man looking down at her.

"Something eminently more valuable – and enjoyable."

It was at that exceedingly inopportune moment that Victoria felt a telltale chill over the back of her neck. As she was well aware, that cold prickle wasn't due to any sudden draft or change in temperature. It was her Venator sense telling her that a vampire was in the vicinity.

Blast.

Ignoring the sensation for the moment, Victoria looked demurely away from Phillip's warm gaze. He'd already kissed her once and he'd made it quite clear he intended to do so again.

"Is that so?" she replied, automatically moistening her lips before she realized how closely he was watching her. The warmth bloomed in her cheeks again and she felt a rise in her heart rate. Odd, how she felt little fear or consternation in facing the demonic undead, but when confronted with a mere man who was besotted with her, she felt more than a bit out of her element.

"I daresay you must be quite warm in that heavy gown," Phillip said, tightening his arm around her waist. "Perhaps a turn on the patio would be in order? I believe the moon is quite lovely."

She wanted nothing more than to do just that, except perhaps something a bit more private where they might share another kiss. But duty had reared its ugly head and Victoria couldn't ignore the chill of an undead. Nor could she waste any more time for fear the vampire would have the chance to woo his or her victim away.

"I should love to see Lady Petronilla's gardens, for they are always quite lovely in June. But when I tripped earlier, one of my flounces tore. I might visit the retiring room first, to see if it can be repaired."

Disappointment clouded his eyes for a moment, but Victoria continued with a gentle smile, "It will be quite dark in the gardens and I don't wish to cause any further damage to the flounce before it is repaired."

At the mention of the dark garden, and her accompanying smile that told him she fully intended to take advantage of it, Phillip relaxed a bit. "Perhaps you might be a bit thirsty? I shall find some lemonade while you have your gown repaired."

Victoria smiled with delight. At their very first meeting, Phillip had brought her a cup of lemonade when he learned that her dance card had filled up before he could claim a second turn and it had become sort of a jest between them. "Indeed, I would greatly appreciate that."

The waltz ended a few bars later, thankfully, for Victoria had delayed long enough. As soon as she and Phillip reached the edge of the dance floor, she slipped from his grip and started to move herself and her ungainly gown in the direction of the ladies' retiring room. But as soon as he turned away, she changed direction and made her way through the crush of costumed people.

Still fairly inexperienced at understanding her Venator sensibilities, Victoria wasn't certain how near the vampire was, or even how many there were. Max and Great-aunt Eustacia had assured her that eventually she would be able to tell, but for now, the chill merely signified that an undead was in the proximity.

And since a vampire couldn't enter a home uninvited, Victoria presumed he or she had arrived under a mask of some sort, pretending to be one of the invitees, which would make it even more difficult to identify the villain.

She'd pushed her way between a milkmaid juggling two – thankfully empty – pails and a doublet-garbed Romeo when she suddenly came face to face with the golden-haired lute player.

"Why, my dear Venator," he murmured, slipping his hand around her arm in the crowd, "how delighted I am that you should have followed me so quickly. Shall we slip away to finish the discussion we began at the Chalice?"

"Sebastian," she replied, tugging her arm discreetly away so as not to draw attention. If her mother saw her tête-à-tête with a man who not only wasn't the Marquess of Rockley, but was also without a title at all, she'd come barrelling over to separate them immediately. "What are you doing here?"

She didn't know much about Sebastian – particularly whether or not he should be trusted – but one thing she did know was that he wasn't the vampire she sought.

"Why, I'm attending a masquerade ball, the same as you, I presume. What a delight to see you here, *ma chère*, although I must admit that your costume could be considered in poor taste considering the fact that Her Majesty met a most unpleasant end. According to my Grandfather Beauregard, it was rather a bloody incident."

She drew back a bit. Was that some sort of warning? A renewed prickle lifted the hair at the back of her neck, reminding her that she had other business to attend. "Why are you here?" she asked again.

Those sensual lips smiled knowingly, lifting his mask a bit. "Perhaps I came simply because I knew that you would be here, and I find that masks, though obscuring, can also be quite freeing." His hand slid through the crook of her arm, easing her flush against his side – or at least as flush as he could, with inches of skirts, crinolines and panniers between them. "I noticed that you extricated yourself from Lord Rockley quite directly, as soon as you recognized me."

She realized he'd begun to guide them through the crowd, away from the dance floor and towards the rest of the house. Since that was the direction she wished to go anyway, she allowed him to think he was in charge.

After all, with her *vis bulla* strength, she could snap his grip and stop him in his tracks at any given moment, as the lascivious Mr Bendleworth had discovered a week ago when he tried to lure her into a dark corner.

Aside from that, since she didn't trust Sebastian as far as she could throw the well-padded Duchess of Farnham, Victoria felt it might be best to keep an eye on him for a bit. Especially if there was a vampire about.

As they pulled free of the party-goers and found themselves moving into the house's grand entrance, Victoria's neck grew colder, confirming that she was heading in the right direction.

Suddenly, she heard a low cry from one of the rooms beyond and she pulled free of Sebastian's grip. Heart beating, she slipped the stake from its little loop beneath a flounce and began to move quickly down the corridor. Her gown rustled, causing her to curse the fact that she'd entertained her mother's costume suggestion instead of dressing the way she wished: as Diana, in a flimsy, light gown. She would have even been able to put stakes in a bow quiver and wear it over her shoulder.

Victoria reached the only door that was closed tight, certain this was where the soft cry had come from. Her neck was still cold, but there was silence. A quick glance behind told her that Sebastian had disappeared, blast it, but she couldn't worry about him now.

She gripped the stake hard in her hand, listened again and closed her fingers around the cool doorknob. Then, she heard it again. A low, pained cry from the other side of the door.

Victoria twisted the knob and eased it open quickly and quietly. Inside, the room was dark, lit only by a fire needed more for its illumination than warmth. Shadows danced, black and red, and she darted her gaze around quickly.

There. In the corner, the shapes of a man and woman, entwined.

Entwined?

Victoria paused, her stake poised and, forever after, she would be grateful for that hesitation. For as she looked more closely, she saw that not only were there no burning red eyes or long white fangs on either of the two figures, but that one of them was dressed in the long white gown of Circe.

*Mother?*

And the other was the tall, slender figure of Lord Jellington, Lady Melly's erstwhile beau.

Victoria sucked in her breath and fairly stumbled back out of the room, deliriously grateful that they'd been much too engaged in – whatever they were doing – to have noticed her presence.

Her mother.

No wonder she wanted Victoria married off. Then she would no longer have a daughter to chaperone and could go about her own business.

Victoria hurried back down the hall and then paused, waiting to feel the temperature at the back of her neck. Yes, the chill was still there.

A broad, curving staircase rose out of the foyer in front of her. Perhaps . . .

Victoria gathered up her bothersome skirts and hurried up the steps, stake gripped in one hand and slippers silent on the treads. As she rose, her neck became slightly more chilled and she smiled in pleasure. Hopefully, she was on the right path and would soon dispatch the nuisance of the undead . . . and then be able to return to Phillip, lemonade and the moonlight.

Once at the top of the stairs, she hesitated for a moment, and then moved smoothly along to the left. Most of the doors were closed, for they led to bedchambers, but she paused next to each one to listen and feel.

The third door on the left was slightly ajar, but she was certain the prickling chill at her nape had become colder. One hand on the door, she eased it open slightly and peered inside.

A dark figure moved within the shadows of the room and Victoria caught her breath. Smiling to herself, she levered the door open further, started to move in and then realized her skirts were too wide. The light from the hallway would soon spill in enough to warn the vampire that someone was there, but he would likely think she was simply an innocent, helpless girl.

Victoria hid her stake behind the width of her gown and pushed the door open.

The man turned and light fell on his face.

"Sebastian!" Victoria stalked into the room. "What are you after?"

"So you've followed me again, have you, my dear Venator?" he asked, moving away from a chest of drawers. He looked as though he was withdrawing his hand from beneath his tunic and she suspected he'd just placed something – likely whatever he'd been searching for – somewhere inside. "A bit more private than the library downstairs. Did you find your vampire?"

"No," she replied. "What do you have in your pocket?"

His smile flashed hot in the low light. "Why do you not come and look for yourself?"

Victoria was too annoyed to be flustered by his blatant comment and she moved into the room with an angry swish of silk. "I would be delighted to do so," she said, approaching him fearlessly.

"My, you are full of courage tonight, aren't you?"

"No, indeed," she said, fully aware that the back of her neck was still cold and that somewhere, an undead was on the prowl. "I'm simply in a hurry and you keep distracting me."

"I distract you, do I?" He stepped closer to her, so close that her crinolines brushed his cross-gartered hose. "What a welcome bit of information, Victoria Gardella."

Before she could react, he reached out and slid a hand under her chin. He was ungloved, and the feel of his warm skin on the delicate flesh of her neck had her pulse spiking high. "I've always wanted to distract a Venator." His voice had dropped to a murmur and Victoria felt her breath catch in her throat.

Nevertheless, she stood firm. "You'll not keep me from my purpose, Sebastian. Turn out your pocket so I can see what it is you've taken."

"Don't you wish to look for yourself?" he replied. Even behind the obscurity of the mask and the low light from the hall lamps, she could see the beauty of his face. From the first time she met him, she thought he looked like a golden angel.

A nefarious golden angel.

"Turn out your pockets," she said again.

"You'd best do what the girl says, Vioget," came a bored voice, "or we'll be here all night waiting for her to get to the task at hand."

Victoria whirled, stepping back from Sebastian. Just inside the doorway stood a tall, dark-haired man. He wore a mask that covered the top of his face, but his dark hair and square chin were exposed, as was the annoyed expression twisting his mouth. The mask was his only concession to costume; the rest of his garb consisted of a white shirt, black coat and breeches.

"Nice costume, Max," Victoria responded. "Let me guess – a villain. No? A vampire, perhaps? Indeed, I do believe you have the look of Lord Ruthven to you."

"Definitely not Lord Ruthven," Sebastian put in. "That fictional vampire was known for a much better grasp on fashionable attire than Maximilian Pesaro."

"What are you after, Vioget?" Max asked, ignoring the comments and moving into the room with his long, graceful strides. He passed Victoria as though she was no more than a nuisance of a gnat and stopped in front of the other man, cutting between her and Sebastian.

"I have the matter well in hand, Max," Victoria said, smarting from his reaction. "Perhaps you ought to go and slay the vampire that's lurking about here. Somewhere."

Max barely deigned to glance at her. "I've already attended to that."

Victoria looked at him, and realized with a sudden surge of annoyance that he was telling the truth. The chill at the back of her neck had evaporated in the last few moments, since she'd come into the chamber with Sebastian.

Which meant that the vampire had to have been nearby for Max to have arrived at this room so expediently. Which meant that it had been merely by accident that he came upon her and Sebastian.

Firming her lips, she pushed herself and her gown between the two men and faced Sebastian. "I'll check your pocket, then, if you won't show me yourself."

Sebastian's mouth twitched. "Be my guest."

But before she could slide her hand into that deep pocket in his under tunic, the waft of a chill breeze skittered over the back of her neck again. In spite of herself, she turned to look at Max, to see if he registered the presence of another undead, and he gave a brief, annoyed nod. His lips moved in a silent oath – but whether it was directed at her, or the new vampire presence, she wasn't certain.

"Vioget. What are they after?" he said sharply.

The lower half of Sebastian's face turned crafty. "A particularly well-thought member of the ton has become, shall we say, enamoured of the undead. When he or she—" he glanced at Victoria "—and please note that I do keep my clients' confidences – last visited the Silver Chalice, a personal item was left behind. One that could identify him or her."

He stepped back, his hand beneath his tunic. "I was merely returning the item to its rightful owner, and I suspect that this person's 'enemies' – shall we say? – wished to stop me. Apparently, this individual is rather prominent and it is a cause for blackmail. The undead have many friends here in London. Perhaps more than you would imagine, my dear Victoria."

"Now that you've entertained us with your fantasy, Vioget, you might just as well get out of here," Max said, turning towards the door. "You'll be no help now."

Victoria felt Max's gaze pass over her and got the impression that he felt the same way about her. Blasted man.

"Why, I do believe I shall," Sebastian replied, moving quickly towards a window.

In a trice, he was gone.

Having nothing further to say to Max, Victoria swished past him, her stake at the ready. The new undead presence implied that the vampire had just recently arrived nearby, and it led Victoria to hope that the creature hadn't yet been able to find and isolate a potential victim.

Out in the hall, she paused for a moment and noted that the back of her neck had grown still chillier. That boded no good, implying that either there were more than one undead or that the creature was very close by. So, putting thoughts of golden-haired lute players and arrogant vampire hunters out of her mind, she gave herself over to her instincts.

Down. Something told her to go down.

The cold prickle grew stronger as she swept down the curling staircase, unaware – and uncaring – whether Max had deigned to follow her. She didn't need him.

At the foyer, Victoria pushed through a small group of costumed party-goers clustered near the entrance to the ballroom, and was just about to slip off down the corridor when she caught sight of Phillip. He was just coming out of the ballroom and carried a small cup of lemonade.

Blast.

With her tall hair, she hadn't a chance of getting away without him seeing her, and so Victoria had to rush towards Phillip in an effort to head off an uncomfortable situation.

"Oh, thank you so much," she cried, perhaps a bit more fervently than necessary. She took the cup with enthusiasm as she kept her stake hand tucked behind her.

"Are you mended and such?" he asked, edging towards her as if to take her arm. Perfect.

Victoria smiled up with genuine delight and jostled against him just as he reached for her. The lemonade splashed everywhere, even up onto her chin.

"Oh dear," she said, real regret in her voice. She hated that she had to do this, but truly, it was for his own good. And that of whomever the vampire might be stalking. The last thing she needed was for a curious beau to follow her. "How clumsy of me!"

"No, it was I, perhaps being a bit too enthusiastic over seeing the moon with you." He smiled apologetically. Phillip would like to simply pull her arm closer and ignore the spill (she was certain), so she continued: "I'll just be a moment, my lord. So the stain doesn't set." Victoria gave him a small smile.

"Of course," he replied. "And I'm certain you'll still have a thirst, so I shall occupy myself by obtaining a replacement. Do hurry," he said breathlessly into her ear before releasing her arm. "Please."

Victoria smiled up at him, warmth flushing over her face beneath the mask. "I will, Phillip. Most assuredly."

He took himself off, and she turned and nearly barrelled into Max.

"I trust you've got your affairs in order? Dance card filled? Beaus lined up in order of title and wealth?" he said blandly. "If it wouldn't be too much trouble, perhaps you could—"

She didn't hear the rest of his obnoxious comment, for she'd sailed off down the corridor, following the sensation at the back of her neck. When she came to the same door behind which she'd nearly interrupted her mother and Lord Jellington, Victoria stopped.

She did not want to open this door again.

But before she could, a soft cry – much more frightened than the one she'd followed earlier – reached her ears. It came from further down the hall, near the back of the house and the servants' area.

Victoria hesitated no longer and took herself off so quickly that she lost a slipper and her heavy coif bounced threateningly. The chill grew colder, and she heard another cry that led her to another closed door.

This time she didn't wait. The back of her neck frigid, Victoria yanked off her mask and flung the door open.

In an instant, she saw three vampires and four petrified maids. An impression of red eyes and gleaming white fangs drew her first, and Victoria lunged as well as she could in heavy skirts. She had the element of surprise, as well as that of her gender, as an advantage.

She shoved a goggle-eyed maid away from the vampire bending to her blood-streaked throat, and he bared his fangs as he came at her. He must not have seen the stake in her hand, for he left his chest unprotected and she slammed the point into his heart.

The vampire froze, then poofed into smelly, undead ash. Victoria whirled and found that the other two undead had released their victims and now started towards her. Her skirts caught up with her spin, then rocketed back in the opposite direction as she faced the undead.

One of them leaped towards her, fast and strong. But she was ready and kicked out from under layers of silk – rather more awkwardly than usual, but with enough force to catch one of them unawares. He stumbled back, crashing into the wall as Victoria spun to launch herself at his companion.

He was quicker than she'd expected and he caught her arm, slamming her against the back of a chair. The hard wood edge caught her in the belly and she lost her breath, spots flickering before her eyes. Victoria gasped and flailed behind her with the stake, then kicked one of her feet out behind her.

She smashed into something soft and the grip on her arm

released. Dragging in a ragged breath, she turned to find glowing red eyes and white fangs behind her. Strong arms whipped out and grabbed her shoulders, squeezing hard into her flesh as he yanked her towards him. Her neck was bare and the heavy tower of hair made it difficult for her to keep her head from lolling back.

Victoria kicked out again, but missed, and her foot got wrapped up in the layers of her costume. But her stake was still in her hand and, with all her effort, she slammed her face forwards, bringing all the force of her forehead and jewel-strewn hair into the vampire's face.

He cried out in surprise and she wasted no time, her arm whipping around to shove the stake home. *Poof*. He was gone.

And then there was one.

The vampire scrambled to his feet from where she'd shoved him against the wall moments earlier and Victoria stumbled after him, turning to chase him towards the door.

But Max was standing there and, before the vampire took two steps, Max's arm moved. Casually. *Poof*.

Victoria fought to steady her breathing into a regular rhythm; the last thing she wanted was for Max to see her panting while he stood there as if he'd just arrived for tea.

He'd also disposed of his mask and the expression on his rugged face was one of bald annoyance. "Whatever possessed you to wear such a ridiculous gown?" he asked. "How in the bloody hell did you think you'd be able to fight a vampire in that? Or did you think they might stay home tonight, merely because you wished to attend a masquerade ball?"

Victoria lifted her chin, infuriated despite the fact that she had already bemoaned the costume herself. "I don't see any vampires about, so apparently I managed the task just fine."

"You very nearly didn't. That one nearly had you over the chair."

"But I did. No thanks to you," she added, realizing that he must have been standing there, watching, as she and her skirts battled three undead on her own. Blasted arrogant man.

Victoria suddenly became aware of the fact that Phillip must have long been waiting for her and she shoved the stake back into its little hiding place. "If you'll excuse me," she said, starting towards the doorway blocked by Max.

"Ah, yes, waltzes and walks in the moonlight await. I do hope you enjoy your evening," he said. He stepped back to allow her to brush past, her gown catching for a moment before she made it through. "And, for the sake of the guests here, I hope that no other undead manages to breach the party."

"Goodnight." Her teeth gritted so hard her jaw hurt as she hurried along the corridor back to the foyer.

When she arrived, there was Phillip, waiting for her, holding a much-needed cup of lemonade.

"Ah, there you are," he said, his attention scoring over her in a way that made her face heat up. "Whatever happened to your mask?"

She looked up at him. "It's nearly midnight. And," she added, sweeping her lashes down demurely, "I thought it might get in the way."

Phillip pulled off his mask, then slipped his arm through hers, lining her up next to his tall body. "Indeed it might," he said. Then, pausing, he reached out to brush something from her shoulder. "Wherever did you get so dusty all of a sudden?"

Victoria smelled the mustiness of undead ash and looked up at him. "I stumbled into the wrong chamber and stirred up a bit of dust," she explained, smiling up in delight at the expression on his face.

"Indeed?" he replied, his hooded eyes dark and seductive. "Well, I certainly hope that stirring up dust doesn't become too much of a habit."

Victoria merely smiled. Little did he know.

# A Temporary Vampire

## Barbara Emrys

Thus far we had driven past Anne Rice's mansion in the Garden District, where a limo in front had caused avid but disappointed speculation, and toured French Quarter scenes approximating killings by Lestat, Louis and Claudia. In one of these, "Lestat" stalking a young woman was re-enacted. A woman dressed in nineteenth-century garments – so we would know it was not an actual attack on a tourist – strolled past a streetlight and into darker shadow. She looked over her shoulder twice, but in the wrong direction, for we had noticed the gleam of a pale face at another angle to her. She walked on, a bit faster now, but still as she passed the alley, he had her. "Lestat" drew her to him, one hand over her mouth, and she fainted away. Then there was perhaps a full minute of him feeding, the bite and then lapping and sucking. There was red paint in abundance over her blouse. Then he let her go, limp, to the ground and looked straight at us as though still hungry. While the group reacted, he seemed to fade into nothingness. Perhaps there was a swirl of sparkly mist before the last spot was extinguished.

I appreciated this "Vampire's New Orleans" tour the same way a hougan appreciates a stop at the voodoo shop with a midnight trip to the swamps. Still, New Orleans was new to me, as was the American south; many evening tours had similar themes and I found the antics of the aficionados amusing enough.

I had successfully avoided the four single women and also the lonely older couple, and stuck with a younger version of them, recently married, for whom the tour was clearly a turn-on.

Their exchanged glances and their constant bodily contact were feeding from the mild perversity. They used me as distraction that further heightened their tension and I, as it were, basked in their glow.

Then we made a final stop, end of the line, in Jackson Square. The daylight mimes had been gone long since, but one had lit her poses by torches of the sort made for patios in drizzly weather. In the intermittently revealing light she stood on a small platform draped in crimson satin, but she wore, of course, black. A softly draped dress as black as smoke. Her glorious hair spilled over it like liquid gold. She should have been too lovely to mime the vampire, but the effect was stunning. One saw the golden hair first, then the dark red mouth and the long incisors.

I realized belatedly that she was part of the tour.

Her "fangs" looked so real they must have been expensive prosthetics. Her long white arms came up slowly, languorously, and reached out to our whole group, yet to each of us alone. Her eyes looked at no one, and so everyone. When coins were tossed, she sank into a crouch and pulled her lips back. The young husband next to me gasped half aloud in sheer pleasure.

There are mimes that essentially clown and there are mimes that add to reality. For the first time that night, even in this haunted city, she made the undead real.

Except for myself, which would not have been mime. Yet as I watched her strike pose after voluptuous and feral pose, it was as though only the two of us knew, and all these others were ignorant.

By now our little group had drifted away; the younger and older couples headed for bed, the single women for the bars. None had any interest in the mime beyond momentary titillation. They tossed coins and a few bills and departed. Others had gathered, however, principally men by ones and twos, to whom she played as shamelessly as a stripper for the money they dropped into the collection box.

And yet she still was inside the role. I found it unsettling, and I waited at a small distance until she shook off the vampire and stepped down. She threw a short cloak over her shoulders and tied back her hair, then tipped the money into her bag. Perhaps she had palmed the teeth; I couldn't tell.

The change was enough that the last of the men sheered away. She cast one glance at me and, I saw with amusement, discounted me as a threat. She walked briskly away towards Canal and, at a distance, I watched her enter a car drawn up there. The motor fired and the car drew away.

I continued walking but turned through the French Market towards Café du Monde, where I took the merest taste of chicory coffee and sugar powder, and pondered what I had seen. Already I hoped she would appear again the next night.

And myself? I am the man at the far end of the bar, back to the wall, watching the rest of you. In the dim lighting you notice only the well-cut leather jacket and my distinguished silver highlights. Or else I'm the lone wolf strolling down Bourbon Street eyeing the passing parade but not entirely part of it. Hands in my pockets, shoulders relaxed, perhaps moving to the beats drifting out of clubs. Maybe you catch my eye and smile at me, and I smile back and walk on. Or maybe I stop and buy you a frozen daiquiri in a plastic cup and we walk deeper into the darkness, and in the morning you have a bruised throat or wrist or elbow, exactly like when you gave blood. You hardly remember me and vow to drink less. I have made that vow also.

Once I had a family of sorts among the living, who knew me and were not afraid, but that was long since. Once I was not alone in my rambles, but he too, my Aubrey-analogue, is gone. I have come here as people shop for a retirement home or relocation with movable employment. I walk around thinking, is this a place for me? I was undecided before I saw the vampire mime.

The next night I was early enough to watch her arrive and set up. The torches were already in place and the platform and collection box. Perhaps the tour provided them. But she spread the silken drape, removed her cloak and dropped some money into the box. I walked around the square. There was no car waiting yet. Likely it would return. As I turned back I saw her

staring into the darkness I passed through. Her body language
changed as she stared, no longer firm and purposeful, but
sinuous and sinister. Was it possible, I wondered, that she
was vampire?

As she began, I made my way through the tour group to drop
a bill into the collection. I could smell her perfume, a rich, spicy
odour, and her sweat. She was alive. She was superb. Each pose
she held perfectly as a statue, without visible muscle tension,
then shifted at the reward of money. But none of it was
mechanical or false. If she had learned not from experience
and certainly not most films, might she have learned from – a
mentor, say?

People came, saw, paid and left. She had to have noticed me
but she gave no sign at all, and I left before she was done, to
prowl restlessly through the warm night among the still-
crowded streets. I fed at last from one so totally inebriated
that any memory would seem by morning fantastic. Lying down
for the day, it was her face, gold-framed, that filled my mind. I
wanted her. Wanted her in my life. She was young and interesting. If she did not have a mentor – might she want one?

The living talk of more than one life in the same body, a concept
I never understood until I had been . . . "turned", I believe is
the current parlance. But my existence now is like that. There
was my young life before, and my mature life, and then my lives
after: my wild early years among Boston immigrants; my sober
Massachusetts years in which I much identified with the
region's historical persona of guilt and bloodlust; my family
years in Chicago with significant others, living and not; the
companion years of making my grand tour. Now there were
years alone and wandering with the impersonal intimacy of
feeding and the illusion, sometimes, of friendship that is in fact
passing acquaintance. How many more lives will I live in this
body? I wonder. Is this a new one beginning?

I walked slowly from my large hotel (evening room service upon
request) to Jackson Square in a light, misting rain. She was
unlikely to pose in it. I sought out the Pirate's Alley bookshop,

still open to sell Faulkner, Chopin and even Rice. I handled one of her novels, wondering if this had been a source book for the mime. Faulkner I've never been able to read, but if I lived in New Orleans, perhaps I would come to understand him. I met Hawthorne, who's more to my taste, and once discussed original sin with him. Nothing in the concept explains my state. No snakes involved, no fall from grace. I was not even precisely murdered, nor – at least once I understood my condition – have I often done more than steal blood. But then, I had a mentor.

The rain had stopped and the sky partly cleared. I saw at a distance the mime approaching. Her hair was covered by the hood of her cape and a man walked with her, carrying the stage and the torches. He too, I saw as they neared me, was alive, his skin as dark as sky. He set up the platform and lit the torches. I followed when he left, but he led me only to the same sedan that had picked her up before. He drove away before I could locate a taxi, but I could arrange for one by the time she left.

Tonight, walking across the square towards her back, I perceived her audience. As on the other nights, men and a few couples had gathered. I stopped in the shadows behind her and watched their faces. Lust, as I had expected, and perverse thrill. Even the women present, who perhaps wanted to be her, wanted the vampire lover too. Only one face among them did not shine with desire. One nondescript man, brown hair, pale face, unremarkable clothing, watched with predatory anticipation. I thought he had been there the first night too, but I was not sure.

He was not vampire either. Light reflected off his sweating face and, as I came nearer, alcohol breathed off him. I joined the small group and looked up at her, and her pose was off slightly, stiffened and just a bit forced. She too had noticed him and he worried her. And worried as I was also, I felt elation. Better than anyone else, better than her driver (or friend, partner, lover), I could protect her from this.

People came and went. Not much money tonight. The hunter approached her too closely, offering a folded bill as he might to a lap dancer. She went to attack pose, admirable fangs bared, nails clawing. He laughed, but stepped back, and I closed with him, a sharp point pressed to his side.

"Come with me," I whispered, and pulled him away.

Again she broke her pose enough to watch us pass into a shadowy street. Once away he turned to grapple with me and I bit him quickly, taking enough blood to render him unconscious. I took his wallet for good measure.

By the time I had cleaned my face and hands and covered my shirt front, she was gone. Stand empty, torches out, as though she'd never been there at all. The familiar isolation washed over me.

Letitia Condit, aged twenty-two, was making her move. Actually, her first move had been to go to college, even though her family, who didn't have a nickel, couldn't see the point. During the year she'd majored in theatre and gotten by on scholarships and part-time work, and during the summers, on top of a full-time job, she'd gone to what its students called the "University of Silence", the mime school.

Her mama had thought maybe she could do a cute little routine at the fair, at least until she had kids, or maybe be a clown for kiddie birthday parties. Her daddy had never had a clue what she was doing. Now she had graduated, it was time for the next step, which was professional experience. She'd always seen that her best choice was character parts, but they were more limited for women mimes. She'd avoided the sexy parts like Lady Godiva (but you have the hair for it, her teacher said) or any other role that wasn't dignified.

She had made a perfect Virgin Queen as her final project, performing it three times, once at the school and twice in the Quarter. Payment produced regal gestures and a cynical smile, and no actress had ever done them better. But through the persona trance she'd heard the audience, what there was of it, wondering who she was supposed to be and making wrong guesses, or half-assed ones: "Maybe she's that Queen – Elizabeth? Or was that Anne Boleyn?" One had actually said, "Naw, I think it's the Pope."

A sexier character, but not about sex per se, was required and so she had studied the Quarter and its hordes. And come up with the vampire. The sexual implication was there, but the power was hers, and she liked that balance. And the tour company had bought it as closure for their jaunt. They didn't care if she went on longer, after their group had broken up. They even supplied the torches and the platform, and she called Kip on her cell phone when she was ready to leave. Kip was a tour guide and too religious to approve of her persona, but he was reliable back-up.

He was what made it possible, in fact, to face down the skankier or drunker men, and feel safe walking away with up to 100 dollars a night, on top of what the tour paid her. She was making her living with her art, and this satisfied her more than anything she'd ever done. Never mind that Kevin, the jerk, had broken up with her over it. What had she ever seen in Kevin? Well, he had been good in bed. But she performed better with her bed empty anyway, even if she was lonely afterwards, back in her tiny apartment.

Some nights she was too restless to sleep afterwards, and some of those nights she concocted plans, because this was a summer gig. When the rains came, she needed another move altogether. It was possible to move the act into a bar, but that felt too close to other acts. She'd talked to a manager at one of the likelier places, but even he had suggested removing some clothing along the way.

Some nights she went for a walk into the Garden District. She always walked to St Charles and by Anne Rice's house as a kind of talisman, sympathy for the vampire. Loners, they were, outcasts, some of whom hadn't chosen their lot. All of it went into her performance. And that was where she'd first seen the guy, the one she thought of as "the Count".

He had drifted out of tree shadow into streetlight and moonlight as effortlessly as a ghost. For a second she thought she had seen a ghost – Lafayette Cemetery was only blocks away. She drew back into shadow herself, though she'd been convinced he knew she was there, even though he never looked her way. He'd been staring at the Rice house as though taking a personal picture. He stood there motionless while the usual carload of drunken kids piled out and struck what they thought were vamp poses while taking cell-phone pictures of each other and laughing hysterically. Then he seemed to be done, wheeled round and walked towards the trolley line in a brisk, human manner.

He wore ordinary clothes, too: a dark jacket, with a T-shirt beneath, and dark pants. He looked . . . Irish, actually, in that thin-faced, sad way, like a sexy mask of tragedy. He looked . . . unhappy. A touch of weariness, a bit of boredom and, most of all, loss of hope, of goals. A face that didn't want to give up, on a person that had. Lettie knew herself an acute observer, as mimes must be. Because of all this, because of the night and the place, and because he had a certain something about him, she thought of him as the real deal. The Count. Some nights his image had fuelled her performance.

And now he'd turned up in her audience. Lettie had been disappointed, actually, to see the elegant, slim man on a vampire tour. Almost disappointed that he watched her. And when he turned up again, she thought he was just another guy ogling her boobs and not noticing her art. But again there was something. Maybe it was just her imagination, but his interest felt personal. More like a talent scout than a masher. Interested in *her*. She should be so lucky.

Tonight, though, the guy she thought of as the stalker was back. Lettie had talked with other female mimes about the attention you drew and how to deal with it. That's why she'd insisted on Kip to pick her up, which he was heartily sick of doing, but even he understood the reason. After a performance she was strung up but distracted at the same time. And this one guy, she could see in his face that he thought he owned her. He was around last week, and then she thought he'd quit, but tonight he was back. She put her anger into the poses and he didn't even get it. He came up in her face, trying to break her out of the pose and into just another money-hungry woman . . .

. . . and the Count took hold of him, said something and pulled him right away. Neither of them came back. Lettie made one final pose and stepped down. She dumped the money in her bag, slung it across her chest, threw the cloak around her and walked in the direction the two men had disappeared.

No one there. She looked down alleys and side streets. No sign of them. She was just about to speed-dial Kip when she saw

to her left a body propped in a doorway. Lettie approached
cautiously, but the figure didn't stir. It was the jerk, the one
who'd been after her, but he was out cold. And on his neck and
shirt there was blood. She reached one finger out and touched
it. Sticky blood. The feel of it ran through her veins like ice. She
stood up and jogged away fast, back to the square, to the lights.

There was her platform, her torches, as though nothing had
occurred. She called Kip, who was already, he said, on the way.
She walked down the most brightly lit side of the square,
through a fog of beer and saltwater catch, towards the river.
She shivered in the car, too sunk in speculation to notice the taxi
that followed her. In her apartment, she locked herself in, no
thought of walking the district tonight. She did not see the man
with the well-cut clothing and the distinguished white at his
temples alight from his taxi and take note of her name and
address on the bell. But later, when he dialled the number he
had obtained via the concierge, her message machine recorded
his voice.

When Lettie played back the message, she couldn't help being
intrigued. It wasn't the talent-scout break she'd been hoping
for, but a freelance journalist who might get her a feature story –
with pictures – was nothing to sneeze at. And besides, he had
the most gorgeous voice, deep and resonant, that made every
word he said pack extra meaning. He wasn't from here. He
sounded like New England, maybe, but not in awhile. When he
said, "I believe it might benefit your career," she believed it
would, and so she called back.

After some phone tag late in the day, she agreed to meet him
after her performance for a very late supper. In his favour, the
restaurant he named was not a bar or a gumbo palace but a
reputable bistro that people went to for the cuisine more than the
ambiance. And he had said he would come to the performance;
she felt better meeting him first, though it might be safer to meet
him at the restaurant, entirely on her own. You couldn't be too
careful, no matter how terrific his voice sounded.

The appointment gave some extra fire to her performance that
night. No let-down going home alone, no nervous wandering in

the dark. She was making her move towards the professional
future she wanted the way a vampire wanted blood. Lettie ran
the whole range of poses she'd developed, flowing from seductive
lover to sinister embrace to bared fangs, the crouch over a body,
cowering back as from a cross, turning at bay, and back to a
come-on glance over one shoulder with just the hint of fang
showing. Maybe because she was so pumped or maybe because it
was Friday night and the tour was full, she had her best crowd in
awhile and the collection box filled up nicely.

And the Count was there. Standing as he had other nights at
the back of the group, applauding when others did, smiling with
pleasure at each pose, though he had seen them all before.
Maybe she ought to be afraid of him too, but she just wasn't. He
kept his distance, anyway. The man who'd crowded her last
night wasn't there and she'd seen no mention of a murder in the
*Times-Picayune*. The jerk had gotten into a fight, most likely.
She hoped he wouldn't be back.

By the time she finished and stepped down, her jaw ached
from the fitted fangs and from holding the positions, but she
knew she had done it flawlessly. She took out the teeth and
pulled her hair back, part of the ritual. And when she turned,
there was the man she called the Count. Lettie was tall herself,
but he was taller, and he still moved like water. When he spoke,
she realized immediately that he was her supper date.

And that put her in a quandary. Of course she knew he had
seen her perform before. But the Count had been there three
nights running and last seen in the company of the jerk who
ended up bleeding in a doorway.

She said, "Aren't you a little old for a journalist?" All her
doubt went into it.

"I believe writers are all ages, but for me it's a second career."
He shifted so that the light shone on his face. A pale face, which
inspected her caution. "I can meet you at the restaurant – or
somewhere else if you prefer."

"Junkanoo," Lettie said. "On Toulouse. In half an hour – I
want to change first.'

He knew where it was and walked away to secure a table.
Lettie made her way to a nearby poor-boy place with spacious

women's facilities. There she changed into pants and took off her theatrical make-up in favour of natural lips and just a little powder and eye liner. She folded away her persona and looked at herself. Still a bit flushed from the performance and from her hopes for publicity too. And from the fact that it was the Count, be honest. It was exciting to find out about the mystery man. She repacked her costume in her large shoulder bag, along with the folder of publicity stills she'd brought along, and walked to the restaurant.

"JUNKANOO, ALWAYS CARNIVAL" the sign read. Spicy Caribbean food, and the walls hung with costumes, photos, and masks. At lot of the masks had horns. The journalist – Nathan Court – had got one of the window tables. These were visible, but quieter and more private in terms of sound, at least. Old-fashioned manners – he got up to pull out her chair – but he asked her what was good here instead of taking command. They ordered glasses of red wine, a plate of calamari and a bowl of stew for Lettie. She regarded him across the small table. If she stretched out her arm, she could touch his long-fingered hand.

"So, you're a freelance, you said – does that mean you don't know where a story about me might appear?" She asked it just to show she was no innocent.

"It means I'm not working on assignment, yes. But there are editors I've written for before and I queried the subject as soon as I knew you'd talk to me. I've written for the airline magazine *Great Southern*. They like the New Orleans angle, but the appeal is broad enough too."

The wine arrived and Lettie took a sip. "Well, OK. What do you want to know?"

How one became a mime, where she'd studied. Predictable background. Over the calamari and gumbo, though, he asked, "Why a vampire? Is it just the Anne Rice influence?"

So she explained, even though the food cooled, about personas and the difficulty of dignified ones for women mimes.

"Vampires are dignified?"

"Sure, think of Count Dracula. Never a hair or a gesture out of place." And she explained the power angle. "The vampire's not a really inviting role, come down to it. Not the way I do it, anyway."

"Yes, the way you do it. I see the dignity. I see the danger. And the isolation of mime feeds those, doesn't it? When you're up there, I mean, you are apart."

He stared at her eyes, not her chest, and stared so intently that he ate hardly anything, but then he was also taking notes. They discussed the isolation of mimes, feeding the crowd's response not into reaction but into the strength of the poses.

"And where did you get your poses? I'm just curious. They aren't the standard movie vampires – unless you go back to Dracula. Not the camp ones, certainly."

Lettie finished her wine and refused the waiter's offer of another glass while she thought how to put it. "I saw certain movies. *Daughter of Dracula* – have you see that one? She's so deadly, but vulnerable too. And an early version of *Carmilla*. But mostly I read."

"*Dracula?*"

"Sure. And *Carmilla*, who's the first female vampire. She wanted her victims willing – at least some of them. Wanted them to be a little in love with her. And also Mina Harker in *The League*—"

"*Of Extraordinary Gentlemen*. Peta Wilson was excellent at showing the power subtly. That moment when she turns, wiping blood off her mouth—"

"Yes, that's one. I actually tried to work up a pose from it, but it's not very clear what's going on out of context and I didn't want to fool with fake blood."

"When I first saw you," he said, "I almost thought you could be vampire."

Not *a* vampire, she noted. He must read too. "I'm a temporary vampire," Lettie said, and he laughed with her. "When I first saw you," she said, "I thought you were a ghost."

He was all attention. "When did you first see me? Where?"

"One night by the Rice house," she said. "At least I think it was you. You sort of floated over to it, and watched awhile, then left."

"Ah," he said. "I do go for walks. Like yourself, perhaps? And then I write."

"A night person," Lettie said, studying him. "And you live here, in the city?"

"I live many places," he said, and Lettie heard the bitter undertone. "I've been here for a few weeks."

The waiter had brought the bill, and the room was far more subdued. Nathan Court insisted on paying it and had just begun to make an appointment to go over the draft article with her. Lettie was hoping he'd be here at few more weeks, at least. They both had grown accustomed to people passing near the bay window, and did not immediately react when a body appeared in peripheral vision, but this one stopped, inches away.

Nathan looked up and froze, and then Letitia looked. The jerk from last night, dressed like a vampire or an undertaker in stark black, turned his glare from Nathan to her, and smiled gloatingly.

And then he was gone. "That's the guy – what did you do to him last night?"

Nathan looked disturbed, but kept his voice even. "I told him to back off, to leave you alone."

"And I saw him later, unconscious in a doorway, with blood on him."

"I'm not surprised. He's a violent type."

"And you – are you a violent type?"

"Letitia—"

She got up, rummaging in her bag for the cell phone. "Do the article – do whatever you want, but leave me out of the rest—"

She was out on the street, leaving him to deal with the bill. She punched speed-dial for a cab, and almost ran for the next main street. There was a large black car parked at the corner and, as she hurried past, the driver's door opened so fast it hit her. She stumbled back against a balcony post, and he was on her, hands around her neck, hot breath in her face. "You monster's whore—"

Letitia kicked his shins and clawed at his eyes, but his fingers closed steadily and her vision shrank into one little ball of light and consciousness. She couldn't scream, couldn't get enough breath. The way he leaned towards her against the door, they could be embracing, and no one was going to . . .

Suddenly she could breathe again. She slid to the ground, panting, and watched the two men come to grips. No one could mistake this for an embrace. Her attacker, the larger and heavier man, had one hand around Nathan Court's throat, holding him off. And Nathan's body changed, as though he now were miming, heavier and more centred, but fast. Letitia began to inch backwards, away from their straining bodies, keeping her eyes on them. "Monster," the guy hissed, "you blood-sucking—"

Nathan opened his lips and the fangs showed clearly, a set that put her own to shame. He sank them deep into the wrist at his throat and there was no pretend about it. The attacker screamed in pain and, among the passers-by, someone yelled, "I've called the cops!"

It galvanized both men. Nathan let go of the hand and drew his head back again, but her attacker's hand now held a glinting blade and he drove it home in Nathan's chest. Instead of reeling back, Nathan head-butted the taller man in the nose then punched him in the throat. Almost absently, his left hand pulled out the knife. There was surprisingly little blood, less than she'd seen last night.

He was a vampire. He had blood on his mouth. She saw the tip of his tongue lick it away.

"Letitia—" He put the knife in his pocket and kept his back towards the people still watching at a distance and holding up cell phones for pictures. "Call 911. You were attacked – he's been hanging around. A bystander punched him. I wasn't here. Clear?"

He was a vampire. He saw she knew. "I can't stay. It's too close to dawn for a police station, and besides—"

Now they heard a siren. Letitia nodded, unable to make a sound. She looked away towards the flashing light and, when she looked back, he was gone. Her obvious trauma, once the police arrived moments later, convinced them more than any explanation, but by the time they drove her to the station, she had come up with one.

She was a street performer, yes. She'd answer all their

questions. With the tour, and she recited contact information. Sometimes men in the audience were drunk. Sometimes they acted out. She described the man's actions the night before, omitting Nathan. Tonight the same man had followed her from a restaurant where a journalist had been interviewing her. Yes, she had the journalist's number at home. She'd been calling a taxi when she was attacked. She described everything except the bite and who had intervened. A stranger, she said, who'd gotten a lot more than he bargained for.

Letitia knew that bystanders must have seen him speaking to her. He had said, she told the police, that he couldn't get involved. Didn't explain otherwise. Just said, "You'll be all right now," and took off. He might know martial arts. An effective fighter, anyway. The bite wound she didn't know anything about, except – the guy seemed to be nuts on the subject of vampires. Kept saying she was the monster's, uh, girlfriend. Maybe he actually believed she was a vampire. People believed all kinds of things.

At long last they released her. She had called Kip and had called the tour, and their lawyer would contact her tomorrow. Today, almost. And she was excused from performing that evening, though they hoped she'd be able to complete her contract. In an early, faint dawn she took a taxi home, and let herself into the apartment.

The first thing she saw was the note. It was stuck with tape to the doorknob. Lettie peeled it off and locked herself in. Her heart sped up the second she opened it.

Letitia

Forgive me for coming here. I was in no state to cross a hotel lobby. I apologize for frightening you. I mean you no harm and I am helpless until sundown in any case. I'll go then.

I imagine the police will want to interview me. Tell them you've left me a message – and really leave one, in case they check.

As I told you, the article is real. I'll email it to you and let you know when it comes out.

   I wish we'd had more time together before you found
out about me. You must be very shocked and I only add to
that by being here. Please use my room at the hotel – the
key is on your hall table – if you've no one to stay with
today.
   I wish . . . I wish many things.
   Nathan

She dropped the letter and darted to her bedroom. No, not
there. He had better manners than to sleep in her bed like
Goldilocks. She almost laughed. And, of course, he was in her
costume room, along with all her personas, a sewing machine
and her make-up table. He had unrolled the futon she kept in
there and lay like a corpse upon it, on one side, face turned away
from her. She noted that he'd drawn down the shades and
pulled the curtains closed as well. Of course he had.
   She tiptoed across the room. She couldn't help feeling as
though she'd wake him. She snapped on a light and sat at her
make-up mirror and looked at him. He was even more corpse-
like. Eyes closed, oblivious. Vulnerable. She could call the
police, stake him, roll him out in the yard, whatever she chose.
He had trusted her. He had saved her.
   And thinking through this, she realized she was not afraid of
Nathan Court, Yankee vampire transplanted south. What kind
of woman, after all, poses as a vampire? What kind dips her
fingers in the blood on a man's shirt front in a dark doorway?
Not the easily spooked.
   Letitia left the light on – wasn't going to disturb him – and
put away her costume. Then she creamed her face at the
dressing table, which also reflected his motionless form. Not
breathing, either. Probably didn't eat, except blood. Was he
going to need some when he woke up? Unknown whether he
could have sex like in the books. Lots of unknowns.
   Cross those bridges later. She went to her room and changed
into a long T-shirt and brushed out her hair. Made some hot
chocolate. She didn't feel alone, the way she usually did, even
though her houseguest was completely out of it. Dead to the
world, in fact. She snorted into the cocoa, and then yawned.

She set down the mug and got out spare blankets from the hall that she tucked around the curtains. Then she lay on the floor beside him, her body mirroring his. Slightly on one side, one arm under his head and half stretched out, the other curled. His body did not look relaxed into sleep. He seemed to be holding a pose impossibly long. Lettie made her own breathing minimal. The sleeping vampire: too static to perform. But she'd like to move the way he did; the suddenness and apparent lack of effort were worth her study.

If the article was real, so was the journalist. And how different was that from an agent? They both knew what sold and dealt with marketers. She would explain that to him tonight. After he'd talked to the police. It would make sense: danger had thrown them together. You found out about each other fast that way. Got involved fast. But he'd need to sleep in the other room after tonight, so she had access to her stuff. It was going to take some rearrangement. She left the door open, brushed her teeth and got into bed, and, because she was only a temporary vampire, set the alarm for noon.

# Overbite

## Savannah Russe

Who can say what shapes a man's fate? In this case it was an incisor painfully split vertically right into the gum line. The tooth was large and as dangerously pointed as an ice pick. Its owner, a slender young man with long hair, several earrings in his right ear and a dancer's slender body, looked Goth. For that reason, Sol Tytel, dentist, figured he'd probably had it sharpened.

You wouldn't believe the stuff dentists see, Sol thought as he set the guy up for X-rays. Humanity is twisted.

When Sol's answering service had called him earlier that hot July night, a mist had risen from Gowanus Bay to spread across Brooklyn. It softened the shadows of cars and stinkweed trees under the street lights. Footsteps became muffled. Old nightmares crept along the kerbs and swirled around the drains.

The chirping voice at the service said some guy had broken a tooth and wouldn't go to an emergency room. Sol's Aunt Blanche had told the guy to call her nephew, the dentist.

Sol's chubby fingers tightened around the cell phone. You didn't refuse a request from Aunt Blanche. Sol's sister Glenda Faye once brushed off a request to pick up some smoked whitefish from a store on Eighteenth Avenue, saying she didn't have time. Ten years later Aunt Blanche had gone through the reception line at Glenda Faye's wedding, given the new bride her dry hand instead of a kiss and said, "So? You are still so busy you can't spare ten minutes to help an old woman whose arthritis is killing her?"

So Sol quickly agreed to take care of the emergency, even

though it was a Saturday night, well past the witching hour. Sol didn't really mind. He had his eye on a plasma TV out in Circuit City and mentally added up what he could bill this schlemiel. It being a date night didn't matter either. Unwed and unattached, Sol was alone, again.

Not that he was a loser in the game of love. Hell no. In dental school his nickname was The Driller, and it had nothing to do with dental caries. Yet for Sol, his love life had stalled and sat unmoving in the dank, empty garage of his existence. His only option at the moment was hooking up with one of the earnest 30-something Sarah-Lawrence graduates he met at Temple.

Tits sagging, greying hair worn as a political statement, rear ends broad and soft as sofa cushions, the women had opinions about everything, from the use of feng shui for his waiting room to the dire health risks of his ordering pastrami. One by one they came on to him with biological clocks ticking and dollar signs in their eyes.

Sol Tytel did not respond. He had a desire both secret and profane that kept him from smashing the glass under the chuppah. It drove him to the news-stand at the subway station for the current issue of *Playboy*; it made him spend far too much on certain premium cable stations. The truth was Sol dreamed only of blue-eyed blondes with tiny noses and names like Bunny. In other words, his dark Sephardic eyes wished to behold goys, preferably naked.


So this particular Saturday night, with a Goth-type guy dressed all in black lying prone in the dentist chair, Sol hummed a tune from *Phantom of the Opera* and looked at the X-rays. He decided he could save the tooth, but it was going to need a cap.

With a practised spiel, the same one he had given dozens of time, Sol explained the situation to his emergency patient and talked about payment plans. But he also had a question. Should he replicate the point? Or could Sol take this opportunity to make the tooth look normal, cap the opposing incisor the same way and give him a nice smile?

Sol grinned to show him his own perfect pearly whites.

Even with his mouth stuffed with cotton, the patient let out a laugh that sounded like ice cracking. The strip of dental X-rays shook in Sol's soft hand. That's when Brice Canyon, or so he called himself, told Sol he was a vampire. He needed his new eye tooth as sharp as Sol could make it – for obvious reasons.

Sceptical, curious and at least a little fearful, Sol nevertheless maintained his professional demeanour. His mind raced. He weighed the risks, the pros and cons. Finally he spoke. "For someone such as yourself, dental health is especially critical."

"You've got that right," Brice Canyon muttered through the cotton.

"A person such as myself, an excellent dentist, might fill, pardon the pun, a need among your . . . your kind? Am I right?"

Brice Canyon nodded.

"Then perhaps we should talk," Sol said.

Brice Canyon, whose real name was Cormac O'Reilly, was an occasional Broadway hoofer and an ageless gigolo. Even with his senses dulled by several injections of lidocaine, he saw the profits that potentially lay in a partnership with the slubby dentist. Brice could recruit vampire patients, for a fee of course, and Sol could practise his trade with great discretion.

"I think you need to become a vampire yourself," Brice suggested later that night as he leaned back on a dull brown, imitation-leather sofa in Sol's office. He stretched his long, skinny legs atop the coffee table piled high with weekly news magazines. "Business-wise, it would increase the trust factor, you know."

The forbidden nature of what Brice suggested sent a delicious thrill directly to Sol's loins. He quashed the feeling immediately, ashamed. "Can't. It must be against my religion," he answered, though not very quickly.

"Don't see why it would be, but then one's perspective on piety and ancient creeds changes when one lives on the dark side," Brice said and put his hands behind his head. He gazed at the ceiling. His face took on a sly look. "However, the sex, you know, is fantastic. Women love vampires."

"They do? Why?" The words sex and women acted like the siren's song on Sol's libido.

Brice laughed his blood-curdling laugh once more. "We're forbidden, sexy and need to be saved. That's potent, dude."

A trembling came over Sol. "Let me sleep on it," he said.

But the hook had been baited. Brice knew he just had to set it.

"Sure. But why not meet me tomorrow night and let me show you around, introduce you to some friends? See what you think."

"I guess there'd be no harm in that," Sol said.

Sol slept fitfully. The next morning, he brewed some coffee, toasted a bagel and sat in front of an edifying public affairs show on television, but his mind wandered. The thought of meeting up with this vampire rattled him. He considered the fact that he had an OK life, a little dull, but maybe he shouldn't rock the boat. He could take a vacation to Miami and cure his current boredom instead of becoming the next Dracula.

Yet much that Brice had told Sol intrigued him. Sol had often dreamed of possessing the sheer physical power vampires seemed to have. The transformation into a demigod – and Brice assured him he would be – promised a faster route to six-pack abs than calorie counting and working out at the gym.

Plus, he'd have his health even if he chose to eat corned beef and pastrami daily, took up smoking Cuban cigars and relaxed every night with a potent Martini. High cholesterol and hardening of the arteries would be a thing of the past.

And he couldn't ignore the fact that financial success as "dentist to the undead" seemed assured.

On the other hand, the eternal life aspect didn't grab him. Brice insisted vampires didn't age, but Sol had an Uncle Sid who lived to be a 97. Uncle Sid wasn't a pretty sight, especially when he put on a Speedo and went to the pool in the Assisted Living Compound in Ormond Beach. But his mental state was what alarmed Sol.

"What's living another day?" the old man had griped. "Nothing more to strive for, nothing left to conquer. No interest in women or food. I'm ready for the grave."

Sol worried that eternal life might prove to be a few centuries too long in the dental profession.

But the sex part made Sol swoon. Brice had told him stories that caused him to break out in a sweat. Threesomes, group sex, anal, oral, tantric, S&M; Brice put out a smorgasbord of exotic delicacies when it came to the ways he had done the dirty. Could Sol find the same kind of sybaritic happiness?

Brice swore on his mother's life that Sol could. Somewhere in his rational mind, Sol knew the word of a vampire wasn't reliable currency, but accepting the drab reality of his life or taking a once-in-a-lifetime offer to be transformed from Sol Tytel, dentist, to an uber-cool, dark, sexy, mysterious vampire seemed a no-brainer.

Yet Sol dithered as the clock ticked off the afternoon hours, unable to make up his mind whether to venture forth into the vampire dens of the city and meet Brice – until his old friend Howie called. Howie had inherited his Upper East Side practice from his father, now retired and living in Boca Raton. Howie's clientele included power brokers and movie stars, and when it came to his conquests of willing women, he rubbed it in all the time.

He'd crow with great glee: "She practically raped me, I swear to God. I thought I'd died and gone to heaven. Twenty-six and gorgeous. She married some old goat and is bored out of her raven-tressed skull. What do I care if her boobs are silicone? My God the woman can give a blow job." On and on. Howie never did know when to shut up.

That's really what did it – Howie's bragging. Sol buried his doubts in a dark recess of his mind and left Brooklyn promptly at sundown, determined to enjoy a night among the quick and the undead.

Manhattan's vampire underworld teemed with depravity, decadence and self-absorption. In that respect, it differed little from the singles scene in that same city. In other ways, it surpassed Sol's wildest dreams – and darkest nightmares.

Sol emerged from a yellow cab to find himself on the baking cement of the city sidewalks, the heat palpable around him. He spotted Brice lounging in a doorway, like Lucifer at the gates of hell. Perspiration erupted on Sol's balding pate. The vampire beckoned. Sol took his step towards destiny and followed him inside a nightclub called Blood Lust, where the moment the door opened he could hear loud music blaring with a driving beat.

Dim lighting, dark-red painted walls and a bouncer the size of an elephant greeted Sol. Anxiety griped him like a sumo wrestler, his breath came hard and yet he found the courage to follow Brice deeper into the innards of the place.

But what scared him most of all was the smell. It was musky, bestial and thoroughly disturbing. The patrons on the tables looked human, except when they looked up and their eyes glowed red behind the pupils. It was then that Sol realized he was no longer with his own kind.

Some wraith-thin women drifted around a large room serving drinks, mostly Bloody Marys it seemed. Sol had a sinking feeling they weren't made with tomato juice. Another frisson of fear coursed through him. Panic overwhelmed him. He turned and decided to make a dash for the door and return to the street.

But Brice had grabbed his elbow and held him fast, pulling Sol towards the far end of the room. There, in front of a live band playing loudly, couples crowded on a small dance floor, gyrating under strobe lights of blue and red.

"Yeah, I know. It's retro disco," Brice said. "Let's get a table. What are you drinking?"

They sat, tucked into a corner, Brice with a whiskey and Sol with a martini. Sol picked up the tab. He tried not to stare at the coke-snorting and flagrant groping occurring between two gorgeous young girls at nearby table. No one else seemed to notice.

Sol felt out of his element. The patrons around him were all good-looking, chic and sensual. They slipped away into corners, two by two and three by three. He could only guess to do what. He thought he would have liked to have joined them.

But was this a life he could embrace? Was this a place he could ever belong? He doubted it. His mentor, Brice, looked terribly bored. His eyes roamed the room as if searching for someone. He and Sol had nothing in common but Brice's cracked incisor. Sol desperately tried to start a conversation.

"Have you been a vampire long?" he opened.

Brice dragged his eyes away from the crowd. "Centuries. Why?"

"Just being polite," Sol said and gulped his drink

"Well don't. Try being rude. It's more fun," Brice offered.

Sol finished his drink and signalled for another. Thus fortified, he tried a different tack, daring to say what was on his mind. "What's going to happen to me tonight?" His voice wavered.

Brice leered at him, showing his incisors. Sol noted that the temporary he had created looked nearly perfect. "What do you want to happen?" Brice asked.

"I . . . I . . . don't know? What are my options?"

"Let's see. If you're in the mood for an orgy, there's a back room right over there." He pointed towards a green-painted door. "If you want drugs, just take out your wallet. Or perhaps you want someone to suck your blood—"

"Ah, no to the blood-drinking and drugs. The other . . ." His voice trailed off longingly. "I do have a fantasy . . ."

"Whatever your heart desires, my man," Brice said in a smarmy voice. "But—"

The catch, Sol knew there had to be one. "But?"

"If you fulfil your fantasy, it won't be a fantasy any more."

Mulling that truism over, his brain no longer sharp and clear, having been muddled by alcohol, Sol looked up and thought he was dreaming. A sweet-looking blonde worked her way sinuously through the room, approached the table and leaned over to display her ample cleavage.

"Macky!" she squealed and gave the vampire across from Sol air kisses alongside both cheeks.

"I'm Brice tonight," the vampire responded. "I changed my name again. I've gotten a new part."

"Brice becomes you so," she cooed. Then she turned to Sol. "And you've brought fresh meat!" She smiled, showing an adorable dimple. She put out a hand. "Hi! I'm Krista."

"Sol, meet the mighty Krista, lady of song and sorrow. She sings with the band."

"Delighted, I'm sure," Sol stammered.

Krista gave Sol a slow once-over and then gave him another long stare. "Are you going to show him the orgy room? I mean is he joining us on the dark side? He looks yummy."

Sol had never been called "yummy" before. He blushed.

"That's up to my buddy here to decide," Brice answered, his sly smile back. "Why don't you join us for a drink, while he makes up his mind?"

Krista pulled a chair very close to Sol's and said, "We're shameless, you know. We love newbies. You look sweet sixteen and never-been-kissed – or bitten."

"Is that a compliment?" Sol asked.

"Not really. It's just a statement of fact. It's obvious you're merely human. Vampires are never bald, you know. Even though on you it's cute."

Sol suspected he had been insulted, but somehow he didn't care. His eyes were drawn to Krista's pouty mouth. "I don't wish to be forward," he said, "but did you know you have a serious misalignment. An overbite. Do you have jaw pain? "

Krista looked puzzled. "Not exactly. I do get migraines."

Brice made his move, smoothly, like a used-car salesman working the lot on pay day. "Sol's a dentist. The best. He specializes in discretion and no-money down."

And soon the talk turned away from orgies to the benefits of invisible braces. Before the night was over Brice had lined up 13 new patients for Sol. Dental work had been neglected among the undead. Sol felt flushed with excitement. He was in demand.

Soon everyone was calling him Doc. He had a third Martini. He felt accepted and special. Brice, too, no longer looked bored. He however finally announced he was hungry.

"Don't look at me," Sol said in jest.

"I have someone else in mind, my friend. But a certain lady seems to be looking for you."

Then, with the band taking a much-needed break, Krista reappeared with an outstretched hand.

"It's time you got your cherry popped, Doc." Her smile was

charming, despite the overbite. She pulled him to his feet and led him to the green door. Sol moved as if in a trance, his heart hammering and his passion soaring.

In the orgy room, Krista and another pretty woman licked him like he was ice cream and he did more than just licking back. They were joined by a young man, which gave Sol pause, then another sweet young female. This was an orgy after all. Bodies entwined, moved and pumped. It was luscious, sinful and then satisfying. But in the end came terror.

Lying against some cushions in post-coital exhaustion, thinking he could use a glass of water and pondering the logistics of getting up and going home, Sol found Krista back at his side. His smile at seeing her faded instantly.

Her expression was no longer sweet. Her eyes had turned hard and glittering, her nails had turned to menacing claws and her incisors had grown very long. Fear spiking through his veins, Sol said he had to be going and tried to find his jeans, which were somewhere nearby. He didn't find them before Krista leaped on his chest.

Now an Amazon as strong as ten men, she pinned Sol down. His heart raced. His eyes grew wide. His skin turned clammy. He realized this excursion into the underworld was all one big mistake. But it was too late. With practised skill, Krista sank her sharp eye teeth right into his carotid artery. He screamed, but overpowered and thinking none too clearly (what with the Martinis and the carnal workout), he swooned.

Consciousness left him and Sol Tytel knew no more.

Sol didn't remember getting home, but he awoke the next morning in his own bed. He was alive, at least, he thought. But when he sat up, the blood loss had left him with his worst hangover since he and Barry Cohen stole a bottle of Chivas Regal during Jeff Silverman's bar mitzvah.

He staggered into the bathroom, where the sight of a stranger in the mirror startled him. He jumped back. Then he moved closer to see better. He stared. He gaped. Instead of a balding thirty-something dentist with rather small brown eyes and a blotchy complexion, Sol saw an Adonis.

He looked even more carefully. With astonishment, he discovered his hair was thicker, his belly flatter, his face leaner and his incisors . . . were definitely longer.

Wonderment overtook him. The fright of Krista's attack was forgotten. Sol was changing from Brooklyn dentist – *interest-free financing available, new patients welcome* – to a fully fledged, amoral vampire, as promised.

Weeks passed. The hot New York summer season slid effortlessly into autumn. The Yankees won the pennant. October brought cool nights.

And Sol had two private sessions with Krista in his examining room to complete his transformation while she was fitted with the latest in invisible plastic braces. By the time her overbite was noticeably better, he had became a new man – no longer human and undead to the core.

The benefits were visible. Sol's hair grew lush, black and wavy. His waist shrank to a size 28. He began to favour tight black jeans, loafers with no socks and Armani shirts.

His sister, Glenda Faye, marvelled at his transformation. He told her he had had a hair transplant, hired a personal trainer and seen a nutritionist. She immediately wanted to introduce him to one of her friends. He knew who she meant and deftly refused. Even Aunt Blanche phoned him one evening, wanting to fix him up on a blind date with the daughter of a friend. But Sol had some backbone now. Regretfully, he said, he must decline. He was far too busy to date.

And he was. From that first momentous week in July, new patients had poured into his office in an unending stream. He hired a receptionist willing to work at night, since daylight appointments were out. He found a cute dental hygienist with a fondness for the late shift. And he worked from sundown to sunup, every night but Friday, at which time he didn't venture out but fell asleep exhausted in front of the new plasma TV. And so, despite his drastic transformation, Sol's life – except for his shrinking from sunlight, aversion to garlic, and need for infusions of blood – didn't seem much different than before.

In other words, Sol had no time to get back to the Blood Lust club. He hadn't attended another orgy. And, while he did take blood donations in lieu of payments for services occasionally, he was getting restless. He was both horny and bored.

He called Brice for advice.

"Have you hunted down a human yet?" Brice asked, knowing full well that Sol had not.

"I don't even own a gun," Sol said appalled.

"Not that kind of hunting," Brice countered. "I mean stalking, pouncing and saying 'I vant to drink your blood'."

"You really do that?" Sol asked.

"All vampires do," Brice said. "I'll show you the ropes."

The lesson took place on a cold, overcast night in late October. Sol met Brice in a dark park along the Hudson River, on the Upper West Side of Manhattan.

With his wide mouth a sensual sneer and his eyes heavily lidded, Brice was as dissolute looking as a young Mick Jagger. He wore a black leather trench coat and tight leather pants. He walked with a swagger.

Sol didn't look too shabby himself, even though he felt more comfortable with his black jeans and tight Armani shirt under a nice, warm, down parka.

"Just watch me. Do what I do," Brice said and began walking north along a lighted footpath.

A lonely wind howled. The damp seeped into Sol's bones. The only footsteps to be heard were their own. No sane person would be out alone in this dark and lonesome place. Sol thought Brice might be better off hunting humans in Times Square.

Suddenly Brice pulled Sol off the path and stationed him in the shadows. A fish jumped in the river behind them. A tugboat whistle sounded. Sol blew on his hands to warm them.

"Shh," Brice said and pointed.

A young woman stopped to light a cigarette not fifty feet away. In the flare of the lighter's flame, Sol could see tear stains on her cheeks. A fight with a lover had sent her outdoors, he guessed. How foolish, he thought.

Brice stepped out of the shadows into the path. Sol hung back and observed. The girl looked up startled. She turned to flee, but Brice was faster. He caught her by the arm and turned her around. Her pretty eyes widened in terror. But she didn't scream. She simply stared.

Brice said something Sol didn't quite hear. The women smiled and stepped into the vampire's arms. Brice brought his mouth down on hers in a kiss. She went limp in his embrace. He dragged her off onto the lawn behind some shrubbery. His incisors grew sharp and gleamed in the lamplight. He bit her white throat and drank. When he was done, he left behind a small puncture in her throat and a thin red thread of blood.

"I don't know if I can handle that," Sol said as he looked closely at the prone body of the young woman, sprawled on the lawn with her head thrown back.

"She's not hurt, you know," Brice said. "I could have been a mugger. She was lucky."

Sol looked at her again. "She has a wide gap between those front teeth. Maybe I should leave her a card."

"Not a bad idea," Brice agreed. "Now, let's find a victim for you."

Sol's first target was a buxom blonde out walking her Yorkshire terrier. She smiled when he approached. He stopped and asked her the time. She said she'd be glad to show him the time and then some. Why didn't he come back to her place?

Once he got over his surprise, he thought: where was the terror? Where was the chase? He shook his head and declined. He retired to the shadows, where Brice waited, stamping his feet and sucking on an Altoid mint.

"Give it another try," Brice advised.

It took Sol a while to get it right. He finally bit a long-haired Asian student with a tattoo of a coiled snake on her ankle. She swooned right into his arms and he drank his fill.

It was interesting, it was titillating and Sol was left physically sated. Emotionally, however, he remained unsatisfied and empty inside. With uncharacteristic boldness, Sol decided he and Brice needed to have a heart-to-heart conversation. He needed to do better in the sex and romance department than his old friend Howie. He needed to be able to boast of his conquests. He needed to meet the girl of his dreams.

A few days later, on the Saturday night right before Halloween, Sol looked over towards the door of an East Village pub for the hundredth time. Another young woman dressed entirely in black with piercings in every visible orifice pushed her way into the steamy interior of Mac's Pit and didn't give him a second glance.

None of them is my type anyway, Sol Tytel thought getting miffed. He was also disappointed. He had wanted to become a vampire to become irresistible to women, to have the girl of his dreams in his bed. But Brice's stern directive to use this particular bar tucked on a side street off Second Avenue in Manhattan for Sol's first solo into the underworld of seduction and bloodsucking was a bust. It had not produced an introduction to any bite-worthy sweet young things whose flesh smelled of strawberries and whose tits would fill his hands like melons.

Sol checked himself out in the mirror behind the bar. He was gorgeous; he was a hunk. But nothing was happening for him. Maybe he was giving off the wrong vibes. He considered calling it a night, but he ordered another Martini instead, determined to give this, his maiden voyage as a fully fledged vampire on the prowl, his all.

At exactly 12.10 a.m., right after a third gin with just spray of vermouth, the door to Mac's Pit opened once more.

Sol swore he heard a drum roll because his head snapped in that direction.

There she was. Beneath a faux mink jacket, she had on a pink bustier with the straps pushed down to leave her shoulders bare and she wore a black micro mini above slender, tanned legs. As she stepped into the bar's interior, she lifted her head high, showcasing her long neck and making her hair, tawny blonde and sun streaked, flow down her back like silk. Her cornflower-blue eyes scanned the room.

Sol's heart nearly seized up in a cardio infarction when this nubile vision marched right over to put her perfect size-two, well-shaped ass on the bar stool next to his.

Heart going like a trip hammer, his body responding like a soldier snapping to attention, he turned to her. "Buy you a drink?" he asked. His eyes clung to the curve on the top of the bustier where white breasts peeked up in a tantalizing swell.

"Oh, I'd love that," the blonde said and asked for a gin and tonic. Her cherry-red lips parted in a dazzling smile. Sol saw it at once. She had a bit of an overbite, not as bad as Krista's. This could be easily corrected and he had to admit, although he tended to be critical about a woman's teeth, this misalignment was sort of cute.

"Do you come here often?" he fumbled, trying to think of something witty to say.

She swirled the ice cubes with her swizzle stick. They clinked against the glass. She lifted it and drank. Sol watched with hungry eyes while she swallowed. "My first time," she said.

"Me too," Sol admitted. "I guess we have something in common."

The blonde gave him a meaningful look, holding his doe-soft eyes with her lapis-lazuli ones. "I believe we do." She smiled wider and her razor-sharp eye teeth gleamed.

Sol's heart raced. His breath caught in his throat. She had clearly given him a signal. "Ah, errr, when you finish your drink, do you want to go back to my place? I live in Brooklyn. It's a short subway ride, but better yet, I'll spring for a cab."

The blonde scrutinized him again. She couldn't possibly be disappointed. He was a vampire now, strong of jaw and virile of expression. An odd look flickered across the young woman's beautiful face but only for a nanosecond before she answered, "I can't think of anything I'd like more."

They fondled each other in the cab. They rushed, breathing hard, to his front door. They kissed in the hallway. They tore off each other's clothing in Sol's bedroom.

"Please say your name is Bunny," Sol whispered as he tongued her neck.

"No, it's London, like the city," she answered nibbling on his ear. "But my friends call me Sunny. Will that do?"

"Oh yes," Sol moaned.

A ray of moonlight came dancing through the window. And somewhere in the New York sky, Sol was sure, stars fell.

After a heated encounter using every position Sol could remember, he felt satisfied, quite exhausted and yet the tiniest bit disappointed, something he refused to admit. The coupling had been good, but no more imaginative than some of the romps he had at college back in the day when he was younger and still 100 per cent human.

Sunny sat up in the bed letting the sheet slip to her waist. She had a great set of knockers, Sol thought, and promptly forgot everything else.

"Do you mind if I smoke?" she asked.

Sol had never started smoking the Cuban cigars he had fantasized about. He discovered he didn't like the aftertaste of tobacco or the nasty smell. He started to say he did mind but, as his eyes roamed over Sunny's skin, which was as smooth as golden ivory, he murmured, "Go ahead."

He watched her stand up, walk to his dresser, where she had left her purse, and spill out the contents while she rummaged around for her pack of Camels and a lighter.

He devoured her with greedy eyes as she leaned her hip against the dresser, her head tipped back while she inhaled deeply, making her bosom rise and fall. Her nails were painted red. The toenails of her narrow, beautiful feet were red too. A gold ring pierced her perfect navel.

Sol's chest felt so tight with longing he thought he was drowning. She was a goddess, an Aphrodite. He loved her. It was kismet.

"So, how long have you been a vampire?" she asked blowing out a cloud of smoke.

Sol turned on his side and leaned his weight on his elbow. He tried to make his eyes heavy lidded and sensual like Brice's. "A long time," he lied. "And you?"

"A couple of decades. I was touring Italy after graduation and met this Florentine count. He seduced me, bit me and abandoned me. The rest is history. You like the life?" She drew deeply one last time on the cigarette before looking around the dresser for something to use as an ashtray. She found a plaster cast of an upper jaw, turned it over and stubbed out the butt on the palate.

Sol felt a brief annoyance until he became distracted by the smooth curve of her buttocks.

Her voice held a trace of irritation too when she spoke again. "I said, do you like the life? You know, the restrictions and all. I have to use artificial tanner now. I used to love the Hamptons." She sighed and gazed somewhat forlornly at the beige bedroom wall.

"I'm OK with everything," Sol answered, fixating on the pink top hat of her right nipple. "It's been a great boost for my dental practice and I was always a night owl anyways. You ready to come back to bed?"

The night began to fade away and the horizon became a bright line in the East over the roiling waters of Gowanus Bay. Sol felt panic stir in his stomach. He couldn't bear to let this nymph, this Venus, this peaches-and-cream tidbit for his love bites leave his arms.

"Er," he said as the blonde lay on her back staring at the ceiling, her expression unreadable. "I know this will sound a bit sudden, but—"

She turned her head on the pillow to look at him. "But?"

"It's nearly daybreak. Why don't you hang out here for the rest of the weekend. I just bought a new plasma TV and I own an extensive CD library. It's quite impressive."

"OK," she said, her voice curiously flat. She studied him for a moment and squeezed her eyes shut. "Sol," she said. "How do you feel about me? Tell the truth."

Sol's tongue felt too big for his mouth. "The truth? To tell the truth I'm crazy about you. I hope it doesn't scare you off. I . . . I don't want you to ever to leave."

The blonde sat up and turned her lovely back towards him. She slipped out of bed and went to the dresser to retrieve another cigarette. Her fingers with their red tips seemed to shake a little as she pulled a Camel from the pack. She scrabbled among the spilled contents of her purse for the lighter, then flicked it, the flame lighting up her face. Her blue eyes glittered as she turned back to Sol.

"I'll have to bite other guys, you know." Her voice was a challenge. "A girl has to eat."

"No problem! Me too, I mean I guess me too. It's just a meal. We can work it out." His brown eyes lit up with hope. "Are you saying—"

"Yes? Yes. I'm saying yes. I mean in this life it's hard, difficult, to find somebody with the same – the same outlook. You know what I mean?"

Sol didn't, but nodded. He gaze had fallen to the intriguing darkness between her thighs and his attention had drifted to other things.

"What I'm saying is," the blonde continued, "we only just met, but sometimes you know right away that this is it. This is the one. Is that what you're saying to me?"

Sol dragged his thoughts back from her crotch. "Bunny, I mean, Sunny, you are the woman I have dreamed about," he said with total candour. "Whatever you want, it's fine with me. Are you nearly done with that cigarette?"

She stubbed it out and moved languidly; her movements were fluid, graceful and erotic as she came back to the bed and stretched herself next to Sol. She wound her arms around his neck and kissed him, her tongue probing his mouth. He briefly thought of her overbite: new invisible plastic braces, the best ones on the market, will fix it. Then Sol stopped thinking of anything.

Later, in the dim light of a gathering dawn, London also known as Sunny – or if Sol preferred Bunny (she had made the names up anyway) – spoke again, her tantalizing lips just inches from his. "Solly," she whispered and his heart fluttered. "I need to know, are you really making a commitment to me. Me, nearly a perfect stranger?"

"I feel as if I've always known you. I've dreamed of you. Longed for you." For Sol that was as close to poetry as he had ever come. "I'm yours. For ever if you want me. Whatever you want I'll give you." He was a man who had lost his heart. Reason had flown. He was driven by a primal need to merge and release the hungers gathering in his soul.

The blonde smiled, her teeth very white. "You know, I think I want to rearrange the furniture in the bedroom. I'm very into feng shui," she whispered.

"Huh?" Sol's eyes fluttered a little as he felt her fingers move over his belly.

"But later. Right now, take me, you mad fool." She giggled and spread her legs to receive him once more.

The bed shook. The walls vibrated. The dresser holding the blonde's purse rocked. A business card, which had been resting precariously on a tissue, tumbled to the floor. It lay there face up and, if Sol Tytel had not been occupied elsewhere, he could have read:

Blanche Stein, Matchmaker
'I will find someone perfect for you.'
Brooklyn, New York
212-555-1212

*Author's note: Any similarity to real persons living or dead is purely coincidental and that includes all my relatives in Brooklyn and Florida, especially my cousin Glenda.*

# Hunter's Choice

## Shiloh Walker

"*S*hit."

The cold wind cut through her clothes like she wasn't wearing anything, blew her hair into her face, made her eyes water and generally made it twice as hard to do what she needed to do. But she didn't look away from the couple in the alley and, other than that quiet curse, she made no noise, made no movement.

She held a crossbow in one hand, kept the other on a pair of military-issue binoculars with night-vision capabilities and a built-in digital camera. She was more used to using the cross-bow than the binoculars, but up until a year ago, the only time she'd ever used the crossbow was out on a shooting range.

That had been another lifetime ago.

Before 22 February 2007.

The day her life changed for ever – the day her twin brother and his wife, Sara's best friend, were found murdered in their hotel room while on their honeymoon.

Joseph and Darla had been the only family she had left and to lose them would have been devastating, no matter what. But to have them so brutally murdered and to live with the gut-deep belief she'd never know who'd killed them, made it so much worse.

The question of *who* would go unanswered. But Sara knew *what* had killed them. A creature that couldn't exist, that shouldn't. A monster that looked just like a man, acted, walked, talked, sounded like a man. She'd been watching this one for a week now. Something about the way he moved, the way he watched people, had set off an alarm in her head.

He shifted a little, lifted his head away from the woman in his arms. The lighting in the alley was too damn dim but Sara was used to it. These freaks never made a move unless it was someplace dark and shadowy. Through her night-vision binoculars, Sara watched as the woman unbuttoned the man's shirt, pressed her lips to his bared chest.

The man's head fell back and Sara grinned with feral satisfaction as his lips parted, revealing exactly what she'd suspected.

Two sharp, ivory fangs.

"Got you," she muttered, snapping a picture, then setting the binoculars aside and lifting her crossbow. The woman was about to get a very rude awakening but Sara figured it was better the woman see somebody get shot in front of her than have some bloodsucker drain her dry.

Behind her, the wind kicked up. Her ears caught a strange rustling sound, a quiet, muffled thump, and then she heard a voice. A familiar voice.

"Not a good idea, Sara."

She spun around, keeping the crossbow aimed and ready, as she faced the man she hadn't seen in a year. Wyatt Cooper. Blood rushed to her face and a sick sensation of panic exploded inside her.

Stunned, she blinked and squinted at him in the thin light, but there was no mistaking that face. With her heart racing, she lowered the crossbow to her side. "Wyatt?"

He glanced over her shoulder and she had the weirdest sensation that he knew exactly what she'd been doing. Her heart kicked up a few beats, slamming away at her chest wall with a force that left her breathless.

A faint grin tugged at his lips. "Fancy running into you here." His gaze lingered on her crossbow. "Weird place for target practice."

"Ahhhh . . ."

"I seem to recall you being a bit more talkative than this." He cocked his head, still watching her with that faint, amused smile on his lips.

"Yeah, well, you caught me a little off-guard. What are you doing here?"

Wyatt shrugged. The cold wind's knife-edge didn't seem to bother him as it blew his hair back from his face.

He looked incredibly out of place, she realized, but Wyatt was the kind of man who would always stand out. Under the open trench coat, he wore a dark shirt, which shimmered in the faint light, and dark trousers. During the one week they'd spent together, he always looked like he'd stepped off the pages of *GQ*.

Well, when he hadn't been naked and on top of her. Or under . . .

His shoes were more suited to pacing the floors of a boardroom than a busted-up, litter-strewn rooftop in the Chicago's West Side. But he moved across that rooftop like he did it every day of his life, unconcerned by the cold, by her weapons or the way she watched him.

"What are you doing here?"

He slid her a look as he approached the hip-high brick wall where she'd spent the last two hours. "Looking for you."

"Looking for me." *Shit*. Alarm bells started to sound. Time to make a run for it. Her binoculars and one of her bags lay just a foot away. She could grab them. Grab them and get the hell out. "Why are you looking for me?"

"I'll answer that question after you answer one for me." Crossing his arms over his chest, he stared down into the alley.

From the corner of her eye, Sara followed his gaze. Her heart sank to her feet as she realized he'd distracted her at the worst possible time.

Down in the alley, the vampire was feeding. The woman stood still, almost passive, in his arms and there was a look of utter rapture on her face.

*Damn it, damn it, damn it!* Jerking the crossbow up, she aimed quickly, knowing she'd only have a second . . .

Less. There was no time to aim before Wyatt moved, grabbing the crossbow out of her hands with uncanny strength.

"Give it back!" Sara reached for it, but he slipped away. "He's going to kill her."

If she thought her words might have had some sort of impact on him, she'd thought wrong. "No, Sara. He's not. He isn't going to hurt her."

"You don't know what in the hell you're talking about."
Fine. Screw the crossbow. She reached under her shirt, pulled
out the Glock holstered at the base of her spine, watching him
from the corner of her eye as she aimed. Again, she never even
saw him move until he was pulling the gun away.

"Unfortunately, Sara, I do."

Something cold and ugly moved through her and she lifted
her head, watched as Wyatt moved to stand in front of her.
He studied her face with grim eyes. If her instincts hadn't
already been screaming at her, they would have started, just
from that look.

"What are you doing here, Wyatt?" she asked again, her voice
hoarse. She asked – even though a part of her already knew the
answer. "How did you know I was here?"

Last year, just days after Joey had been buried, Sara had met
a sexy stranger with eyes the colour of amber, silken black hair
and a wicked smile. She wasn't the type to pick up men in bars,
wasn't the type to go back to a hotel with a guy she'd known
only hours. But she'd done so with Wyatt. And she remembered
it all in vivid detail.

She'd spent one week with him, one week in which they
rarely left his hotel room. On the seventh day, she'd slipped out
of the room while he'd been in the shower and she hadn't seen
him since.

She'd thought about him way too often for her peace of mind
and what few dreams she had that weren't nightmares had been
centred around him – hot, sweaty dreams that left her aching
and needy and lonely when she woke in her solitary bed. They
left her wishing she could be different somehow, that she could
move past the mission she'd set for herself.

She thought of him – wondered if he ever thought of her and
figured the uber-sexy man had long since forgotten her.

But now he stood before her, watching her with that grim
look on his face. "I'm here because of you, Sara."

"Why?" She inched backwards, deciding she'd forget about
her bag. The gun. The crossbow. She could get new weapons.

His lids drooped and, when he looked at her again, terror
wrapped an icy fist around her heart. His amber eyes glowed.

When he opened his mouth to speak, she barely heard him say, "I think you know why."

She was too busy staring at his fangs.

Talk about taking one for the team, Wyatt thought with disgust as Sara back-pedalled away. Her pale-green eyes were wide with shock, her pretty face had gone pale with fear and he could hear the rapid beat of her heart from five feet away.

Five feet and growing. Her hand slid to her waist and then fell back to her side as though she just remembered he'd taken her gun. A seriously mean-looking gun. Wyatt had little use for weapons, but he knew his way around them and the ones he'd taken from Sara weren't the kind used for recreational purposes.

They were a soldier's weapons. A fighter's. A killer's.

It hurt his heart to see what grief and rage had done to her. Wyatt's memories of that one week last year were crystalline. He could recall it in such acute, exquisite detail. The way her lashes fluttered right before her eyes went wide as she came, a feline smile curling her lips as she cuddled into him afterwards.

The way those pretty green eyes had misted over with tears she tried to hold back. The reluctant way she told him that her twin brother had been murdered, along with her best friend.

Even then she'd had secrets in her eyes, some hidden knowledge she hadn't given voice to. Thinking back, Wyatt knew he shouldn't have let her slip away as she had. And not just because he could have happily spent the next 50 years in bed with the woman.

When she'd slipped away from him, he had almost gone after her. Almost. But he'd been sent to make sure she would be all right – not fuck her brains out. He'd ended up doing both, and the guilt he carried was lightened only a little by the knowledge that she'd needed him. And he did prefer to think it was *him* she'd needed, and not just anonymous, comfort sex. A man was allowed a few delusions, after all.

That guilt was back though. He'd been thinking with the wrong brain and now they were both caught in a mess.

"You're one of them," she whispered. There was a stricken

look in her eyes that was going to linger in his mind for a long, long time.

"Sara, I'm not going to hurt you."

She laughed. It was an ugly, brittle sound that echoed through the night. As it faded, she stared at him with a mixture of disbelief, hurt, anger and fear. "Don't give me that line, Wyatt. I know what your kind do. Hurting people is all you know."

"If I'd wanted to hurt you, I could have done so last year."

She flinched as though he'd slapped her. Wyatt held still, when all he wanted to do was reach for her, pull her to him.

"If you don't want to hurt me, then what in the hell do you want?" she demanded.

Her voice dripped with sarcasm and he knew she didn't believe him. It hurt. But he'd come into this knowing he'd get bloodied – figuratively speaking. Getting his heart ripped out again, much like what happened when he realized she'd walked out on him, was much better than the alternative. That didn't even bear thinking about.

Focus on the problem, Wyatt, not the consequences of failure, he told himself.

"I just want to keep you from making a mistake." He jerked his chin in the direction of the alley but didn't look at her face. "He wasn't hurting her. He doesn't believe in it."

Sara's lip curled. "Yeah. I bet. You know, this vampire-with-a-soul bit has already been done. Buffy and Angel pretty much covered that storyline."

Despite himself, Wyatt grinned. "Buffy and Angel are Hollywood, love. This is real life." His smile faded and he pushed a hand through his hair and sighed. "Sara, vampires aren't demons any more than humans are. Yes, some are monsters . . ." He slanted a look in her direction and added, "But then again, I've seen my share of human monsters, too."

"Humans didn't kill Joey and Darla."

"No." Wyatt faced her levelly. "You aren't mistaken in that. They were attacked by vampires. But not all vampires kill, Sara."

She gave him a hard smile. It matched the look in her eyes. Hard. Emotionless. Empty. "Sorry, not buying it."

"If all vampires kill – how come you're still alive?"

For a second, she looked unsure. Wyatt pressed his advantage. "Did I hurt you once, Sara? Do anything you didn't want me to do?"

"Just because you didn't then doesn't mean you never would, lover."

He gave her a narrow look. "Sara, darling, it's a bit insulting to imply I'm a cold-blooded murderer and then call me 'lover' in the same breath."

She sneered at him. "Don't tell me you've been harbouring fond memories, Wyatt."

"Fond?" His lids drooped over his eyes. Unable to stay away any more, he went to her, moving quicker than mortal eyes could track. Her eyes widened, her heartbeat kicked up and her apprehension scented the air.

The predator in him stirred, the hunger rousing.

But the man ached. He reached out and hooked a hand over her neck, moving against her so that their bodies were pressed together from chest to knee.

"Fond memories? That doesn't describe it. I remember the way you moaned in my arms, the way you smiled when you woke up and smelled coffee. I remember the way you taste."

Lowering his head, he buried his face in the curve of her neck and shoulder. She tensed and tried to jerk away. He breathed in the scent of her, let it flood his system and then he let her pull back.

"I remember the way you cried yourself to sleep while I held you. I remember you walking out on me."

He blew out a breath and shifted his gaze away from her. This was hard, even harder than he'd thought it would be. How could those few nights have left such a mark on him?

He hadn't been with another since her and the sexual frustration alone was murder. But he didn't want any other woman. He couldn't see a pretty brunette without remembering her, remembering the way he'd buried his hands in her silken hair as he kissed her. The way it had spread over them like a blanket as they slept.

"I've got fond memories of fishing with my dad. My first dog. My first woman." He slid her a look and added gruffly, "But 'fond' doesn't even scratch the surface when it comes to you."

No. "Fond" was for barely recalled memories of his youth, memories of the life he'd planned to live until fate intervened. "Fond" was something he might enjoy reminiscing about, but nothing he'd spend his life missing. He'd missed Sara every day. Woke thinking of her. Dreamed of her. Thought about her. Ached for her.

Sara was one of those things "not meant to be" that he usually was able to move past. Like the life he had once so carefully planned. The fiancée he'd been forced to leave behind. His job. His home. His parents. Things, people he'd loved. But he'd been able to move past them.

He couldn't say the same about Sara and, as he studied her face, he knew he wasn't going to be able to tuck her neatly away in some niche. She might be a "not meant to be", but he couldn't accept it.

She started to squirm, her gaze moving away, as though his attention made her uncomfortable.

When he took a step towards her, her eyes swung back in his direction and, although she kept her expression blank, he could feel the fear in her. He didn't stop though and she didn't back away from him. "You're afraid of me."

Her chin angled up. "I'd be stupid to *not* be afraid."

Wyatt cocked a brow at her. "Why? When have I ever done anything to hurt you? To make you think that I might?"

Curling her lip at him, she gestured towards his face, her eyes lingering on his mouth. Although he knew there was nothing sexual about the look, his body responded as though she had pressed a kiss to his lips rather than sneered at his fangs. "Those aren't there for ornamentation."

With a shrug, Wyatt said, "No. They aren't. They serve a purpose. But I decide what purpose they'll serve, Sara. I didn't lose my humanity when this happened – and I didn't *choose* for it to happen."

Her lashes flickered. He'd like to think he was actually reaching her but Wyatt hadn't ever been much for optimism.

"Leave me alone, Wyatt."

She glanced towards her things, but she didn't try to get them. Instead, she backed away until she reached the rickety fire escape, watching him as though she expected him to pounce on her. The idea had its appeal, although not for the reasons she seemed to think. But Wyatt just stood there and watched as she swung her legs over the edge of the roof and disappeared from view.

"That didn't go well."

The wind slammed into him as he stood there in the darkness, debating his next move. For now, the vampire Sara had been targeting was safe, as were any others in the area (she'd left her weapons behind).

Wyatt tucked her gun into his waist, turned to look back at her other things. With a sigh, he started to pack them up only to stop and look back in the direction had Sara had gone.

It was midnight and Sara was a woman alone. He'd follow her, make sure she got wherever she was staying unharmed. His train of thought slammed to a halt as his body whispered a warning. An icy-cold touch slithered down his spine and every instinct he had went on red alert. His head flew up and he turned his head, following a summons few could hear. Death. Blind hunger.

He hadn't lost his humanity when he became a vampire. But some had.

There were monsters out there preying on humans and, right now, one of them was on the hunt.

Sara couldn't hear the footsteps and, when she turned to look, she saw nobody behind her. But she knew she was being followed.

Hell. Screw *followed*.

She was being stalked.

The skin on the back of her neck crawled, her gut knotted and blood roared in her ears. Her fingers itched and if she'd had her gun, she would have been holding onto it like a security blanket. She wanted to run. Desperately. But the calmer part knew that running was a bad, bad idea. Very bad. Things that ran got chased. Things that got chased too often got caught. No thanks.

Then there was another part of her that whispered she needed
to get back to Wyatt. *That* voice, for some reason, was harder to
ignore. She had no logical reason to think that anything about
Wyatt promised safety – even if he had just let her walk away.
Even if he hadn't tried to hurt her.

"Where are you going, pretty girl?"

It was a low, amused voice – deep with a Southern accent, soft
and quiet. Not at all threatening. But she felt the threat.
Sending a glance over her shoulder, she looked for him, but
saw nothing. Picking up her speed, she focused on the sidewalk
in front of her. And ploughed right into him.

Instinct kicked in and she drove the heel of her palm upwards, but he moved away, evading her strike with pathetic
ease. He grabbed both her arms. His fingers were hard, the chill
of them seeping through her clothes and freezing her to the
bone. "Where are you going in such a hurry?" he asked,
smiling.

Sara said nothing.

The smile faded away and he cocked his head, studying her
face. "You aren't screaming. Why aren't you screaming?"

Again, she said nothing.

His fingers tightened on her arms and he jerked her close.
Sara craned her head away from him when he pressed his mouth
to her cheek and he started to laugh.

"There, that's more like it. It's more fun when you fight."

"Then this is going to be a lot of fun for you."

The sound of that voice was about the sweetest sound she'd
ever heard, Sara decided. So what if she had all but run away
from him a few minutes ago? Angling her head, she tried to
follow the sound of his voice, but the man holding her moved,
dragging her into an alley at their right.

He moved with a speed that left her head spinning. Fear had
blood roaring in her ears. She thought she heard them talking
but their words didn't make a whole lot of sense. At least not
until a hand fisted in her hair and jerked her head to the side.
"Unless you want me to rip her throat out in front of you, you'll
stay the hell back."

*That* she heard, even though she wished she hadn't. The

vampire lowered his mouth to her neck, running his teeth along the arch. "Come any closer, Hunter, she dies."

She focused on Wyatt's face. She could see him now, moving through the alley, a smirk on his lips. Light and shadow played across his face and those piercing, pale-amber eyes of his glowed. "You know how this ends, boy. Let her go. I might even give you a head start. But that's your only chance."

The man at her back tightened his hand, forcing her head into an unnatural angle which hurt. Shit, it felt like he was going snap her neck before he could bite her. "I know what happens if I let her go."

Wyatt smiled. It was a mean smile, full of threat and menace. "That's going to happen anyway. You just get the choice – painfully slow or mercifully quick."

Behind her, the vampire tensed. His arm came up, angling across her upper body and his hand spread across her neck, gently, almost lover-like. "I got a better choice."

"Like hell," Sara snarled and reared back with her head. He either wasn't as quick as Wyatt or he'd been fooled by her silence, because he didn't move out of the way in time. She hit him with a force that left her head spinning, but she heard bone crunch. At the same time, she lifted her foot and brought the heel of her booted foot down on his.

What happened next was too quick for her to process. One minute he had her, and then she was flying, careening through the air and hitting the wall with jarring force. Her head smashed into the brick and brilliant lights exploded behind her eyes.

Distantly, she heard her name. Wyatt. There was a roar. A rush of wind.

The pain in her head throbbed, blocking out anything, everything else. Hands touched her face. Gentle. Soothing. "Sara, look at me."

Too hard. Opening her eyes just took too much effort. But he brushed his fingers down her cheek and she realized she had to see him. Lifting her lashes, she stared at his face, watched as it swam in and out of focus. His amber eyes were dark with worry, anger. Despite the pain radiating through her, she had to smile.

He actually looked like he cared.

But vampires couldn't care.

Wyatt sat in the chair by the window, brooding as he watched the sun sink below the horizon. As time passed, some of the stronger vamps could tolerate ever-increasing amounts of sunlight. Just a few seconds at first, but their tolerance improved slowly. Wyatt's Change had been nearly 80 years ago and he could take enough sun to watch as the sun made its disappearance.

His skin itched and burned, just like it would from sunburn and it felt like there were blisters forming. But as the sun's rays faded, his body started to repair the damage.

He knew when she woke, heard the subtle change in her breathing, in her heartbeat. Still, he wasn't prepared for the low, throaty sound of her voice. "I didn't think vampires could handle sunlight."

Closing his eyes, he steeled himself to see her face before turning to look at her. She was pale, but alive. The past 13-plus hours had been awful. He'd fought his body's natural instincts, remaining awake throughout the day to watch her.

Watch.

Worry.

Brood.

And worry some more. It had been more than 80 years since he'd graduated from medical school and saying that things had changed was putting it mildly. Still, a concussion was fairly basic and that was all she had. One thing about being a vampire: if she had been bleeding internally, he would have scented it.

She was still staring at him wide-eyed. Wyatt sighed and glanced over his shoulder at the darkening sky. "Most of the mythology surrounding vampires is either pure nonsense or highly exaggerated."

"Like the sight or scent of blood turns you into a maniac?"

Wyatt shrugged. "Older vamps have better control than that. A new one? Possibly. But new vamps are supervised until they have some sense of control."

"You make it sound like there are laws."

"There are." Wyatt didn't bother elaborating. She wouldn't care about their laws, about his purpose, about anything.

"Apparently the laws aren't serving much purpose," she said, her voice bitter.

Gently, Wyatt pointed out, "Humans have laws. But humans still kill, still steal, still rape. The law gives us a way to punish the guilty but as long as free will exists, there will be those who break the law. Mortals and vampires."

She looked away from him but not before he glimpsed the pain, the anger in her gaze. "The law failed your brother and his wife, Sara. I'm sorry for that. But you can't continue on this mission of yours. It's going to get you killed."

Her laugh was soft and bitter. "You think I don't know that." She paused and looked back at him. "These laws – somebody has to uphold them, right? Can somebody find justice for my brother? His wife?"

"Sara." He waited until she looked at him and then he slid off the chair. There wasn't anything he could say to take this pain from her, even if he shared all he knew, nothing would undo the pain. This much, though, he could give. He knelt in front of her and wished he could touch her, wished she could want his touch. "It's already been done."

She blinked. Her throat worked as she swallowed. Her tongue slid out to wet her lips and, even though it was an innocent gesture, Wyatt's blood warmed and hunger flared to life. He had to focus to even understand her next words.

"Already done?"

He couldn't not touch her, Wyatt realized. She'd pull away, he'd feel a fool, but he had to do it. Lightly, gently. All he did was brush her hair back from her face, a quick caress that lasted just a heartbeat. Her breath froze in her lungs and he braced himself. But she didn't pull back. She didn't flinch. Her eyes didn't freeze over with disgust. Her eyes lifted and met his. Slowly, Wyatt reached out, cupped her cheek in his hand. "Done. They were dead before the sun set the next day."

Sara slumped, dropping her head down. "Dead." She was motionless for a minute and then she stood, brushing past him to pace the room. "Dead. You tell me they've been dead for a year. And you expect me to believe you. Just like that?"

Rising, Wyatt tucked his hands into his pockets, watched her long strides. "I don't expect you to believe me, Sara. Not over this. Not over anything."

She came to an abrupt halt and turned, facing him. "Then why *do* I? Why do I trust you? How come I look at you and I don't have this urge to run when I know I should?" There was naked emotion in her eyes, confusion. Doubt.

And need.

The need hit him square in the gut, because it seemed to echo the emotion inside him. His voice was rusty, hoarse as he said, "It's your brain telling you to run, Sara. But some other part of you realizes I'm no danger to you."

"How can you *not* be?"

A fist closed around his heart. Wyatt took one slow step in her direction. Followed by another. Another. He was close enough to reach out and touch her, but he wouldn't let himself. "How could I? How could I possibly hurt you?" Instead of touching her, he reached behind him and pulled the Glock from his waistband. Then he allowed himself to touch her, but gently. Only her wrist. Wrapping his fingers around it, he pushed the gun into her hand and then lifted it, pressed the muzzle to his chest. "Can you hurt me, Sara? It's still loaded. If you really believe I'm a soulless monster, then you should pull that trigger. I've faced my share of monsters and believe me, I don't hesitate."

She jerked against his hold, but he wouldn't let go. "You're crazy," she whispered. "You think I won't? Think I can't?"

Wyatt smiled sadly. "Oh no. I know you can pull the trigger. I know you have. And if you really believe I'm nothing but a monster, then you need to pull the trigger."

Her breath hitched in her chest. Her gaze lowered to the gun pressing into his chest. At this close range, there was no way the bullet could miss his heart. He'd be dead before he even hit the ground, just like a mortal.

"No." Her voice came in a harsh, broken whisper.

She pulled against his hold and this time he let her go, watched as she put the safety back on, carefully . . . oh, so carefully. Then she laid the gun on the bedside table and rubbed her hands down the front of her pants. "No.'

"Why not?"

"Because I can't." She shook her head and turned to face him. "I can't."

There was a look in her eyes that might have made him do something that would have totally humiliated him – like reach for her; like tell her that he'd spent the past year wishing things could have been different, wishing that he could have spent it with her. That he had thought about spending the rest of his life with her, after just one week together – and what a fantasy that was.

She was mortal. She'd die in a handful of short decades. He was vampire. He could die and, sooner or later, he would. But the odds were that he'd be walking the earth long after Sara went to meet her Maker.

Yet even that ugly fact wasn't enough to keep him from touching her. No. What stopped him was the slow, careful way she backed away from him. What stopped him was the blank, expressionless mask that crept across her face with each step she took away from him. By the time she was at the door, the look on her face was as smooth and blank as a doll's. She reached behind to open the door without looking away from him.

He was tempted to just let her leave.

He'd known this was an exercise in futility, but he couldn't just let her walk away. And it had nothing to do with orders from the damned Council, either.

As she eased the door open, he moved quickly, crossing the floor. Her eyes went wide and his ears picked up the telltale skip of her heart as he reached over and pressed a hand to the door, keeping her from opening it. "You can't leave just yet, Sara."

Her chin angled up. "Why the hell not?"

"Because what you are doing has to stop."

The fear he sensed inside her had already faded and she shoved past him. Her elbow dug into his side and, automatically, he rubbed it. *Mean little brat.* "We have laws, Sara. Laws to protect innocent people – *and* innocent vampires. They do exist."

She rolled her eyes. "Yeah, right. Because bloodsucking doesn't actually hurt people, right?"

Reaching out, he stroked a hand down her neck and said, "Actually, you're quite right. It doesn't have to hurt, and there's no reason to kill."

She smacked at his hand. "Don't touch me."

The ice in her voice stabbed at him, cutting into more than just his pride. He eased a little closer, but whether he was trying to soothe wounded pride or something deeper he didn't know. Advancing on her, he followed her as she backed away until she bumped into a narrow table.

"I remember when you begged me to touch you," he whispered. He pressed his finger to her lips and remembered her taste.

"Don't remind me."

"Do you need a reminder?" Wyatt asked. "I don't. I remember all of it. Every . . . last . . . detail."

Her sea-green eyes darkened to jade and her breathing hitched. He heard the acceleration of her pulse, scented the change in the air around her. "You remember too, don't you?"

The thick fringe of her lashes fluttered, shielding her eyes. But he didn't need to see them to know the answer. He slid his hand down, curving it over her neck, his thumb resting the shallow notch at the base.

"I'm the same man now that I was then," he told her, his voice harsh. "The same man you picked up in a bar, the same man you followed to his hotel, the same man who made love to you and held you when you cried. If I didn't hurt you then, why would I do it now?"

Her body shuddered and Wyatt tore away with a curse. He stalked away but the sound of her footsteps on the floor behind him made him pause. "Sara—" He turned, certain she'd be running for the door again.

But she wasn't. She took another step towards him. Another. Another. "You can't expect me to unlearn everything I've believed since my brother died, Wyatt," she said.

"I don't."

She didn't even seem to hear him. "I'm not an impulsive person. Or at least I didn't used to be. I didn't pick up men in bars. I didn't go to hotels with strangers. I never would have believed I could develop some bizarre *Buffy* obsession and start hunting for monsters that can't exist."

*Am I doing this?* Without a doubt, the answer was yes. And it was what Sara had wanted to do from the time she opened her eyes and saw him sitting in a chair, his gaze focused on the setting sun. She'd watched as his face flushed red, as though burned, watched as blisters formed and then faded moments later as the sun disappeared.

If she'd harboured doubts over what he was, they would have died in that moment. But even the knowledge of what he was didn't stop her.

She doubted anything could.

There was no reason for what she was doing. Couldn't be. Nothing rational, nothing sane, but she still didn't stop. She took another step and this one brought them so close, their bodies all but touched. "And I also wouldn't have thought, even a few hours ago, that anything could change my mind about what a monster is. And what a monster isn't."

She lifted her head, stared into his eyes. "I'm not willing to change my mind on it. Not yet. Maybe never. I don't know if I'm ready to give that up."

Reaching up, she traced a finger across his lips and whispered, "But I can't change my mind on you either." She pressed lightly on his bottom lip and he opened his mouth, slowly, just a little, as though he didn't want to at all. His fangs weren't showing, but she could remember how they looked, found herself wondering why they weren't visible now. "Even with these."

Sara thought back. He could have hurt her at any time during the day while she slept. Or on any number of occasions a year ago, and he hadn't. Deep inside, she knew he wouldn't . . . couldn't. As strong as her grief and rage was, her belief in him was even stronger. Her knees went weak as his lips closed around her finger, sucking lightly, nipping on her fingertip as she slowly pulled her hand back. "I dream about you and I know I'm not ready to give *that* up."

His pupils flared, a harsh breath escaped him. Pushing up onto her toes, she pressed her mouth to his.

For the next 30 seconds, he stood almost frozen as she kissed him. Still, so still she was starting to develop a complex but then his hands came up, grasped her waist.

"What are you doing, Sara?" he whispered against her lips.

"Can't you tell?" Tipping her head back, she smiled at him and slid her hands under his shirt. "We did it plenty last year. I thought you said you remembered everything."

The hands at her waist shook, a convulsive, involuntary tightening that drew her closer. "Are you sure about this?"

"No," she replied honestly. "But I am sure about you. You wouldn't hurt me. I've spent the past year dreaming about you and I'm tired of dreams." Holding his gaze, she pushed up onto her toes and pressed her lips to his.

And this time he kissed her back. His arms banded around her, pulling her off the floor. The room spun as he pivoted, walking backwards to the bed and falling down on it, taking her with him. The time spent apart ceased to exist as they fought free of their clothes. His body was hard, cool against the warmth of hers, but with every passing minute, his body heated until his skin seemed to burn as hot as hers.

His hands raced over her, touching her with a desperate greed that she recognized. It seemed as though Wyatt was as greedy for her as she was for him. He nipped her lower lip, kissed his way down her neck, took one aching nipple in his mouth. As he suckled on her, he wedged his hips between her thighs and pressed against her. She moaned out his name, fisted her hands in his hair and tugged until he brought his mouth back to hers. His taste – it was like nothing she'd ever known. She loved it. It was addictive.

Just like his touch. Just like his hands and his body. The way he looked at her, the way he stared at her as he played with her hair, the way he whispered her name as she drifted off to sleep in his arms. All of him. Everything.

He pushed inside her and she tore her mouth away from his to suck in a desperate gasp of air. His lips brushed against her cheek, to her neck. He kissed a hot, burning path down to her neck, across her collarbone, before he pushed up onto his hands and stared down at her as he started to move. "You wouldn't believe how often I've wanted to do this," he rasped.

She reached up, brushed her fingers across his upper lip, lingering at the faint bulge of fang just underneath. He tensed, tried to turn his head away, but she slid her hand behind his neck, tangled her fingers in his hair. "As often as me?" she asked, tugging his head down towards her. "Kiss me."

He did, but it was careful. Cautious. She hated it. Instinct drove her and she deepened the kiss, took it rougher. She felt the response inside his body, in the hard, driving rhythm of his hips against hers. Not enough, again. It was instinct that had her pulling back from his kiss – just a little. Just enough. Enough so she could sink her teeth into his lower lip and bite. He froze. A smug smile curled her lips as she met his eyes.

A rough growl escaped him. His eyes dropped to her mouth and he swore, crushing his lips to hers. At the same time, he slid a hand down her side, palmed her bottom and lifted her. One deep thrust, then another. Another. It hit hard, fast, hot, slamming through them with hurricane force. Tearing her mouth away, she cried out his name while he buried his face in her neck, groaning.

Heart pounding in her ears, struggling to breathe, she closed her eyes. He rolled off her and pulled her up against him, stroking a hand up and down her back. "Are you OK?"

"Hmmmm." Sara couldn't quite find the energy to lift her lids, but that was OK.

"Not an answer, damn it. You've got a concussion. What in the hell was I thinking?"

Heaving out a sigh, she forced her eyes open and reached up, pressing her fingers to his mouth. "Stop. I'm fine. Tired. But fine."

Very, very tired, actually. Her lids felt weighted and she didn't bother fighting it any more. With his hand stroking up and down her back, and his body warm and strong against hers, she felt more at peace than she had in months. Since the last night with him.

Sleep dropped down on her hard and fast.

She could have been asleep for two minutes or two hours. Sara didn't know. All she did know was the warmth and security she'd felt while she slept in Wyatt's arms was abruptly gone and she was unceremoniously shoved off the bed, hitting the floor on the far side.

"Stay down," Wyatt growled.

Blinking, trying to force her brain to wake up, she peered up over the side of the bed as the hotel door flew open. The vampire standing there was the one who'd grabbed her the night before. He flicked her a glance, a wide grin spreading across his face and then he looked at Wyatt. She saw his hand come up. Saw her crossbow.

She screamed.

Wyatt dodged away, evading the other vampire with ease. Sara scrambled across the bed, reaching for her gun. A cold hand grabbed her ankle.

Wyatt snarled. "Let her go."

She kicked out, connecting with a belly that felt as hard as iron, but he didn't let go. He tugged and she lunged, made another grab for her gun – and this time, she got it. Because he'd let her go – or rather, been forced to let her go. Drywall cracked as Wyatt threw him into the wall.

Sara turned just in time to see Wyatt reaching for the other vampire and the other vampire lifting her crossbow. Time slowed down to a crawl. There was a scream trapped inside her head, one that couldn't break free. But as the silver-tipped bolt pierced Wyatt's chest, Sara jerked her gun up, sighted and pulled the trigger. The muffled *pop* sounded terribly loud, although logically she knew nobody outside the hotel room could have heard it.

Blood, bone and more grisly matter exploded and the other vampire slumped back. Dead. Totally dead, his body limp, the top half of his head gone.

But Sara didn't care. She was too busy moving for Wyatt, catching his swaying body before he could crash to the floor.

Under his weight, she fell onto the bed, clutching him against her. "Wyatt . . ."

His amber eyes turned blindly towards her. Blood trickled from the corner of his mouth. "Get out of here, Sara. Somebody . . . probably called the cops." He started to cough and more blood stained his lips when the fit passed. "Get *out*."

"Not without you."

His lids lowered. "Can't. Too close to the heart. I'm not going—" his body arched and shuddered "—anywhere. Not strong enough right now."

Desperate, Sara shoved him off her lap, braced his weight on her side. "You're not dying. I'm not leaving you here." She closed her hand around the bolt and jerked. It wouldn't budge. "Help me, Wyatt."

"Get out of here, Sara!" he rasped, his voice harsh, but weaker.

"You want me out, you help me."

He swore, but reached up, grabbed the bolt and ripped it out. It fell to the bed beside him as dark, dark red blood flowed from the wound. "Get out, Sara."

She barely heard him. She was too busy staring at the silver-tipped bolt. *Her* bolt. *Her* weapon. He was going to die because of her.

*No.*

His voice came back to haunt her as she stared at the bloodied arrow. *Most of the mythology surrounding vampires is either pure nonsense or highly exaggerated.*

Most. Not all. She barely remembered reaching for the arrow. Didn't remember pressing the barbed, sharp edge to her wrist or slicing her flesh. Didn't remember anything until she wound a hand in his hair and guided his mouth to her wrist.

He jerked back. "No."

"Yes."

Wyatt grabbed her wrist and shoved it away. "*No*. Get out of here, Sara. Get out, now."

"You want me gone you'll have to make me. You can't do that if you die."

He shook his head, but even that took too much effort.

She went cold, somehow realizing that he was out of time. Sliding off the bed, she knelt so he could see her face. "Don't die on me, Wyatt. Please don't die. I haven't spent the past year dreaming about you because the sex was good. I need you."

His lashes barely flickered. Breath rattled out of his lungs. All but blinded by her tears, she shoved her wrist to his mouth once more. He brushed his lips against her wrist. His lashes lifted and she stared into his eyes. "Please."

He struck.

It didn't hurt. That was all she could think of as his mouth worked at her wrist. It didn't hurt – and it didn't last more than a few minutes. Still too much time though, because, as he shoved off the bed, moving far too slow and stiff, she could hear the wail of sirens in the distance.

"Get out of here," he muttered, turning his head to look at her.

The hole in his chest was no longer pumping out blood but he still looked too damn pale. She grabbed her shirt from the floor, her jeans and hurriedly put them on. "Sure. You're coming."

His lids flickered. But he nodded, stumbled towards the door, then outside. Stark naked. Sara followed along behind him and just barely thought to grab the keys from the table and his shirt. On the way outside, she wrapped it around her wrist in a messy, cumbersome bandage.

"Benz," he mumbled.

She got the door open and he collapsed inside. She ran around, climbed in, started up the car.

"Don't speed," he said, his voice thick, slurred.

"I won't," she said and forced a smile. "I've been evading the police off and on for close to a year now."

The next 30 minutes were silent. Too silent. She kept sending him looks, terrified he wasn't going to make it and a few times she almost started to panic, because he wasn't breathing. Did he even have to breathe? But then his lids would move, he'd shift and her heart would start to beat again.

When he spoke up, his voice was strong, cutting through the silence. "Pull over."

"Why?"

"Because I'm sitting here buck naked. Sooner or later somebody might notice."

A familiar blue sign reflected back at her as her headlights splashed across it. "There's a rest stop in a mile. I'll pull over there."

He was quiet. Didn't speak at all as she pulled over at the rest stop or as he reached behind the seat and grabbed a bag, hauled it up and dressed. He managed to do so both gracefully and silently – not easy considering he was sitting in the passenger seat of a car. Luxury car or not.

"We ready?"

"Not quite." He grabbed her and hauled her into his lap, his eyes focused on her face. His fingers closed around her wrist, unwrapping it. Tossing the bloodied, ruined shirt aside, he lifted her wrist and studied the gash. "You shouldn't have done that," he whispered, lifting her wrist to his mouth. She hissed as he licked it, and she automatically tried to pull away.

"Be still," he said.

"You're licking a very sore open wound," she said drily.

"Hmmm. It will help it heal, keep it from getting infected." From under his lashes, he shot her a look. "Why did you do this?"

She went still. "I . . . I don't really know. But I had to. I couldn't stand to think about you dying."

He brushed his fingers across her cheek. "You said you needed me. How can you need me? I'm a vampire. We've spent exactly eight days together. One week last year. And today. How can you need me?"

She licked her lips, leaned in and pressed a kiss to his cheek. "I don't know, but probably for the same reason that I couldn't hurt you. Probably for the same reason you told me to leave you there to die." Looping her arms around his neck, she cuddled against him. "You're OK, right? You're not . . ." A sob escaped her lips and she buried her face against his shoulder.

"Shh." He stroked a hand up her back. "I'll be fine. Thanks to you."

She wasn't going to cry. She wasn't. Wasn't. Wasn't. And after about two minutes and dashing away her tears and sniffling, she almost believed it. Lifting her head, she self-consciously wiped the damp tear tracks from her face before looking at him.

"So now what?" he asked.

"I think maybe you should take me with you – wherever you're going. After all, I'm not exactly safe to let out around you vampire types."

A faint smile curled his lips even as he shook his head. "You don't want that, Sara."

"Why not?"

"You come with me, I won't ever let you go." He sighed, laid a hand on her cheek. His flesh was still cool, too cool.

Laying her hand over his, she whispered, "Promise?"

His eyes glowed, for just a second, reflecting golden light back at her. "Sara, you're asking for trouble."

"You're trouble. Sexy. Broody. Not entirely truthful when we first met. *Vampire*. And I'm asking for you, so yeah, I am asking for trouble." She pressed her lips to his, forgetting that he'd had his lips pressed to her bloodied wrist. By the time she remembered, she didn't even care.

"We don't really even know each other," he muttered against her lips.

"So? We've got time, right?"

He laughed softly. "Yeah. We've got time."

# Remember the Blood

## Vicki Pettersson

*I*na moves through the crowd as if leashed and muzzled, careful to make eye contact with no one, to touch no one. Sensuality is her perfume – as it won't be long now – so she can't fault the people around her from undressing her with their eyes. She can barely refrain from touching herself. Although knowing better, yesterday she opened a door she shouldn't have, entered a club packed with people desperate to start their New Year's celebration early and paid the price in mounting frustration. Dozens of bodies had ground against her, hands sliding over her waist, across her belly; seeking, too, the outer curves of her breasts, her ass. Fingers had pressed and kneaded, searching for something they'd never possess, begging with wordless, tensile strength, as if Ina were a living talisman.

The crowd tonight is different. No one dares to touch her at a black-tie event. Not even at a New Year's Eve gala, when Dom flows as freely as water. Not even when she's dressed in silk so thin it outlines her nipples. Not even though she's so aroused she's sure some of them can smell it on her.

Still, they watch. She feels their thoughts – pretty fireworks going off behind curtained gazes – rising into the air to explode with coloured lust and hopes and dreams. And that's just the women.

Being at the centre of a desire that borders on worship is hard to describe and, if someone had asked her to, the closest Ina could come is this: she is more than woman; she is goddess. There are others like her, but she is uncommon enough to be idealized, the humours at such perfect balance inside her bodily vessel that she is at once both at peace with eternal life and kissing cousins to lumbering death.

And yet, and yet . . . Ina has found herself unexpectedly living in a world that worships girls. All of a sudden, to open one's thighs is to declare yourself a woman, and to capture it in video or print is to make it true. If she'd known how lonely this would cause her to feel, displaced rather than elevated, an eidolon rather than a deity, she may have chosen to remain an innocent, ignorant girl herself.

She slips from the vaulted arcade of the museum and into the horticultural gardens of the Cuxa Cloister. She holds her champagne glass aloft, like she belongs there, but no one is around to see. It's cold in Manhattan, and elsewhere bodies are tightly packed in a manic bid to stay warm and connected. Here, however, Ina freefalls into the darkness, with only torches to light her way as her heels clip-clop against 900-year-old stone never meant to see the New World.

Russell is waiting where the note said he'd be, leaning against the rampart of the west terrace, with Fort Tryon Park dropping down the hill behind him and, beyond that, the Hudson. Ina's first instinct upon sighting him is to flinch. He's pretty in that unearned way; a strong chin inherited from someone who may or may not have been strong and a physique built in front of mirrors, where grunting loudly and breaking a sweat while some pop tartlet's video plays in the background means a good day's work. He has done his work for the day, and showered since, but it's the stench of his motives and thoughts and past deeds that helps Ina pinpoint him in the dark.

The scent is so strong, so perversely recognizable, that it takes a moment for her to notice the two women slumped on each side of him. Perfume and beer and desperation assail Ina as they both shift upon seeing her, and she can tell they just came from that twisting, gasping mass of humanity at the core of this city, which will soon pulse as one.

As if, she thinks, the entire world is one giant heartbeat pumping for her.

Russell laughs when Ina licks her lips. Clearly she has made the mistake of telling him in some previous "lifetime" that in the eleventh hour every human she passes is a dusky red temptation. Thus, the women.

"Ah, lovely Ina. Fucking ravishing . . ." His eyes trail her body like he knows it. "Though it looks as though you've been stealing kisses from nefarious places."

Ina doesn't smile, and his companions look disturbed that he should actually know her. Russell leans against ancient brick, enjoying the reaction. Ina imagines he's said the same thing to her every year for the past eight. She both wishes she can remember and gives thanks that she can't.

"Let's go," she says shortly. Even had she wanted to converse with him, she'd have trouble doing so. For the past three weeks she's had trouble completing thoughts, much less sentences. She is now so distracted by the impending hour, so *obsessed* with crossing into the next, that she wants to jump from her own skin. Hunger and desire, her sharpest weapons, are now turned against her. She knows it was the same last year because she'd written it down in a pained, sharp scrawl.

Russell gifts her with an oily smile. "Come, Ina. Stay awhile. Perhaps you'd like something to drink?"

He's fucking with her. She'd written this down too. *He will fuck with you. He always does.*

Russell frowns when she doesn't react, which would be enough to cause her to smile, but the shadow that cuts across the torchlight like a falling axe widens it on her face.

"The lady said move."

The voice is silken death. It belongs to Alexander. And he is hers.

He is wide, shoulder to thigh, muscled beneath the denim, menacing even as he drops a light palm to her shoulder. Her memory of him may only reach back a dozen months, but she knows that touch anywhere, and can tell it's the same for him. The heart always recognizes its twin, even when the mind is forced to forget. Ina looks up, watches the light flickering in his black hair like it's kindling there. She likes to tease that the threading grey is as golden as the sun. It makes him snarl, which she loves.

Russell jolts upright and the women flanking him actually flee, probably unaware it's a prey's instinct causing them to do so. Russell recovers by sucking on the neck of a dark bottle, scowling at the departing women. They had stifled their screams, but the squeals and relieved giggles fly over the rampart walls once they deem themselves safe. There's nothing more reassuring than the receding effects of adrenaline.

Meanwhile, Russell soaks in the alcohol like a sponge. A foul, weak human with poisoned blood, he's a natural disaster, but that's why they chose him all those years ago, and it's what makes him perfect for the task. That, and that he can be so easily bought.

Recovered from the jolt Alexander has given him, Russell jerks his head. With drink-induced bravado he leads them back through the gardens and along the covered walkway, past brightly lit rooms filled with music and laughter and medieval treasures a man such as Russell shouldn't even be allowed to breathe upon. But Russell is ignorant of real treasure and more intent on slipping through the narrow stone arcade before them, then down the dark stairs and into the ageing park. Ina sidles up to Alexander once their soles hit the winter earth, and when he takes her hand she's almost warmed.

Still, right now Alexander reminds her of an ancient warrior, his gaze distant and trained on an unseen threat. He belongs in armour, palming shield and sword while he screams murderous intent to the skies. The only time that distant gaze melts into focus is when it's turned upon her face, and this is what brings out Ina's warrior side. That softening gaze makes her feel powerful as well, like she could crush a man with no more than a smile.

Russell keeps the lead all through the park, alternately swaying and swaggering as he steers them over the dormant heath and ivy clinging to the gently sloped hillside. A running monologue of curses and bullshit streams from his mouth like sewer water, which neither of them care to, or even can, concentrate on. They remain so silent that every few yards Russell has to look back to make sure they're still there. Perhaps he's hoping they're not.

But despite his bluster and bravado, the path he carves towards the Hudson Parkway, where they first met, is unfailingly direct.

It's New Year's Eve and he wants to be done with this dark, chilling business, and get back to the light and warmth of those who age. The beer has made him boisterous and the night giddy, and he laughs too loudly in the silence of a park that has been abandoned for places that glitter and wink. It seems everyone in New York is indulging in the fantasy that tomorrow life somehow really will be different.

Ina smirks knowingly. For her, this is actually true, but even as the thought fans the embers of her hunger, she remains cynical. It's hard to be expectant of a future when you never possess a memory beyond a dozen months. Still, cynicism or not, there's no way to stop that ticking clock, or to convince others that their hope for the future – now rising like impotent prayers in the empty night – is fragile, misplaced, unheard. Better to hope one simply lives through the night.

Ina grimaces as she swallows back blood-tinged saliva, her attention abruptly drawn to the artery in Russell's neck. It pulses like cascading neon, beckoning and bright against the pitch-black park. He turns, thinks she's smiling, and smiles back.

"Yo, Alex," he calls, somehow knowing Alexander hates the grating of that single syllable on his foul tongue. "Your girl wants me."

He laughs and laughs and Alexander grips Ina's hand so hard he breaks the bones in her pinky finger. The pain gives her something to think about and takes the edge off her hunger, though it's only a temporary solution, like putting a numbing ointment atop a flesh wound. But it's her turn to calm Alexander now – thank God they alternate their little breakdowns; she thinks it's one of the things that makes them so good together – and she keeps her tone light as they turn that final corner around an oak being strangled by ivy. The three of them slip under the recessed bridge like a series of dark tides. "Don't you ever shower, Russell?"

"Wants *me*, Alex," Russell sing-songs again, walking backwards and pretending to shoot at them with unloaded fingertips. "Bad."

"Kindly retrieve the chains." Alexander's voice skirts beneath the bridge like wind-whipped gravel, and Ina shudders in pleasure. God, even his voice moves her. "Do her first."

Russell is unhinged by the threadbare sound too, but he's done this eight times before, and dismisses any threat of danger as he turns away, giggling something about freaks and peepshows and shit. His boots slap at the grime-caked concrete, reminding Ina of flippers or clown shoes, and she snorts. She likes clowns. Alexander tightens his grip again and, though she quickly sobers, she doesn't mind his small show of temper. He's doing this for her, after all. For them.

So she thinks of Alexander's footsteps instead of Russell's, the light and assured way in which he walks through this world . . . beside her. She's written before about how the sight of him always calms her, and it does that again as she gazes up to find him backlit in grey silhouette, a three-dimensional cutout against a two-dimensional world. In artificial light he is unremarkable, if tall, and he comes from an age that valued a close shave at pate and neck, fortunate that it is fashionably classic. But in the dark, where he is at home, those smooth features blur into a block of unyielding stone.

Alexander follows his own whim; he is wearing wireless rims he doesn't really need and still sporting a light accent he adopted in his time spent in Louisiana before finding himself, and Ina, in New York. She only knows this because he was keeping record even then.

Yet while no bald evidence of discomfort plays across that stoic face, Ina sees he isn't entirely settled. There's a midnight knowledge of the deed to come lurking behind his eyes, a carnal flinch as Russell calls Ina forwards, though Alexander never even blinks.

Ina joins Russell at the midway point, where the darkness narrows into a span of only eight feet, the light from each end of the tunnel flickering like tapers losing fuel. It's not a proper bridge, mostly meant for run-off from the park, but it's solid and remote and this perfectly suits their purposes. She drops her handbag along the incline of the wall where shadows eat it whole, while flicking a cursory glance at the sacrifice, already there, slumped in the tunnel's concave centre. It's a woman and it has dull brown hair that's muddy and matted, jagged finger-nails and a bottom lip split from an unnecessary blow.

Ina slips her back to the wall, ignoring the way Russell feels her up on the way to manacling her wrists. She can't help but bare fangs when he grinds against her, but Alexander, more controlled, glares at her. She swallows her fury and stares out over Russell's greasy head. His foul breath billows up like a garlic cloud around her as he laughs. Garlic. Yeah, that's really fucking funny.

Russell isn't so far drunk on drugs and power that he forgets Alexander, unchained, at his back, and he doesn't linger over Ina. She imagines he'll come back once they're both tightly secured. Ina's knees had been caked with the alley's dirt at her rebirth this year. The previous year, she'd written about semen in her hair. It's thinking about this, and about all the indignities she can't remember, that makes her start to shake.

Be strong, Ina tells herself, strong like Alexander. See how he seeks Russell's gaze, his own expression carefully blank? See how compliant he is when his wrists are shackled at his side? There's more strength in one of those beautiful hands than in Russell's entire body, yet he has pulled it back, hidden it deep and done it for you. No, Alexander has the hardest, lowest task by far. The least Ina can do is tolerate Russell's prodding fingers.

Finally Alexander is bound too and his iron chains clank gently as he tries their hold. Russell turns back to her with a glint like acid rain sparking in his eye, and he steps over the sacrifice like it's a part of this wasted alley. He can go away now, his job done, his financial life, his mortal life, secured for another year. He doesn't need to stay for the rest, and indeed – even though they're both shackled to chains that'll only give three feet in any direc-tion – it'd be safer for him to be long gone by then.

But Ina has a feeling Russell never leaves. She feels that he's the freak he was giggling about under his breath earlier. He's the one who likes his peep show.

"Tell me more about the build-up, Ina. Tell me about how you can feel the year folding up around you—"

*Folding up around me like a black silk scarf.*

Oh, God. She'd told him about that. Ina swallows hard, a reflex, unable to keep from glancing Alexander's way. He is indiscernible against his wall, but she knows he isn't happy. He hates surprises.

Russell nudges the sacrifice with a toe, but he only has eyes for Ina. In the dark, they are mere pinpricks, even with Ina's strong sense of sight. "You'll do anything for it, won't you? Like some bitch in heat—"

"Fucking cliché." The insult escapes as if on its own accord. She hates clichés, and this capacity to hate silly things is one of her weaknesses. Alexander hates nothing, therefore he cannot be moved to anger like this. He loves her, however, which Ina supposes makes *her* his weakness.

She hangs her head at her bad behaviour, but not before she sees Russell's chin lower, the pinpricks tightening upon themselves. "Oh, because you bloodsuckers don't deal in cliché? Shit." Russell is pacing now, working up his mad, as they say in Louisiana. "You approached *me*, remember? No, of course you don't."

And the forgetting, at least, wasn't cliché. No paperback or Hollywood flick had ever gotten that right. They just glossed over the compensation required to stay forever young, beautiful and strong. Odd that it wasn't obvious. It makes perfect sense to Ina that mortals age under the weight of the memories – all they've done and, even more, what they *haven't*. It is these regrets that make them old and wrinkled, wistful and bitter, weak and dusty. The only thing Ina has in common with them is that her death-day marches down upon her as their birthdays do, wanted or not. However, instead of waking each year to a new wrinkle, she wakes to a literal stranger in the mirror.

That, Ina thinks, she can handle. But Alexander as stranger? She looks over to where he is draped shapelessly in shadows. That she cannot.

Meanwhile, the ignorantly ageing Russell is still ranting in front of her. "You *need* me, you bloodless husk. You need me to set all this up, find the sacrifice, chain both you fuckers apart in order to keep you together. And you'll do exactly what I say if you want to get it."

"Remember your humanity," Ina warns, though she's chained like the bitch he compared her to.

"Remember the 'man' in that humanity, whore." He is fast with his words. His mind could have gotten him far if he'd been a lawyer or a doctor or a comedian, and not a lazy, second-rate crook skilled only at turning his own luck bad. "I know all your homicidal secrets. Bite me and you're lost to each other in the next lifetime. And for ever." He has reassured himself at least, and he stands before her, straight-spined, in a practised pose, and within reach. "Now, tell me what it feels like right now. How you lose control and start licking and sucking everything in sight."

If it were anyone else, she might, because that isn't it at all. Simple lust can't describe the way emotions are suddenly spun like silk, the textures soft, but so multi-layered and startling that when Ina finally feels the weight of them she wants to weep. It is this awakening need to *feel* that is the true hunger, and Ina becomes so addled that she even puts food in her mouth. (Her favourite is chocolate on the tip of her tongue, its contrast and silkiness as it melts to coat the back of her throat. It is lovely all the way up until she pukes.) She eats this unnecessary subsistence, sightless and slightly manic, until colour suddenly blooms on her tongue. She looks down to find her finger in her mouth, blood on the tip. Her blood, but no matter. Hunger soars like a bird of prey in flight.

But explaining nuance to Russell would be like reciting algebra to a dog. Besides, he's right. He holds the keys to their fate, which probably explains his hard-on. He's the fucker who demands they meet on the very last night, when decisions must be quick and absolute, and when he has someone more powerful than he'll ever be by the metaphorical balls. It is the only time of year – and probably in his pitifully short human life – when he knows he can *squeeze*.

"Hope you took good notes this year, Ina, baby."

"Don't call me that."

"What? Ina?" he asks, with oily innocence. "But it's your name, isn't it?"

He tilts his head. His hair, greased into perfection, doesn't alter, but the move exposes his neck. "Or is it?"

Alexander jerks his head once. Ina bites back her reply.

"'Dear diary'," Russell mimes a cursive hand in the icy air. "'Please don't let me forget my true love after I suck the life out of my last victim of the year. Please let us stay together for ever. I really like the way he fang-fucks me.'"

"Fuck you," Ina says before she can stop herself.

"Now there's an idea." Russell smiles crookedly. "But not a very novel one."

An admission now that they are both shackled and he knows she'll soon forget. He looks at his watch and pushes a button so the face lights up, then flashes her the time. Two minutes to midnight. In other parts of the city, party-goers are swilling drinks with bubbles, wearing shiny hats, hoping the mania they feel now will be a strong enough tide to ferry them across the threshold of the new year.

"But I have a better idea this year. Why don't you let me read that little book you two pass back and forth? I want to see what you remember. I want to see *how* you remember. It's in there, isn't it?"

He points to Ina's bag. He knows they must have it close. Their own belongings are the first things that call to them upon their rebirth, so it's important to keep it all together and keep it near. That's how it works. Find Russell, the fleshly guide who will bind them, ensuring they stay where they are and share in the same blood without killing one other. Then bring along the written guide so they may find themselves after and, finally, rediscover each other. Russell clearly knows all this, though again, Ina doesn't recall telling him.

"Don't touch it," Ina warns as he does just that. He leans low and, when he rises again, he swings the bag side to side in the air, laughing and nearly stepping on the sacrifice that currently divides, but will soon reunite, Alexander and her.

Russell is rummaging around inside the handbag now. It is packed as Ina instructed three years ago. She is only surprised it has taken him this long to think of it. "Where is it, you bloodthirsty bitch?"

Ina grits her teeth, holding in the now-strained silence. Far off, a chorus of cries is swept along in the wind like summer stalk, but it is Russell's scream that blooms like a thick stem with thorns. A smile widens Ina's face, stretching it, though her teeth are still clenched tight. The razors are sewn in every silken fold, every pocket. And while the scream is gratifying, it's the scent of his elixir, fouled though it is, that causes her appetite to rear. Suddenly a film is lifted before her eyes, like she's wearing a gauzy veil, and the entire world is instantly reduced to a two-toned wash of soothing sepia.

Alexander shifts into view and Ina gazes at him for clarity. Indeed, he smiles back steadily, completely in control. She loves that about him, and is wishing she could take a long, refreshing sip from that calmness when she is slapped.

"Fucking whore!"

Fucking idiot. Russell leaves blood smeared on her cheek. She feels the smile on her face alter. A lone man's premature holler fills the sky. Without willing it, Ina leans forwards, testing. Her restraints hold, but Russell backs from the strike zone, suddenly careful to keep her in view. *Goddamn straight.*

She hisses.

The sacrifice screams in sepia.

"Where is it?" Russell tries to sound like he is still in control.

"I have it." And though the words were whispered, it is Alexander's warrior's cry.

Russell's eyes widen but it's too late. Even the realization of death is a future event he won't live to see. Just like the New Year that will soon chime in the sky. The abrupt way life abandons him is jarring, but fascinating, like a pile-up on the freeway. Pain firecrackers across his gaze, then falls and fades and disappears.

The sacrifice shrieks when Russell's larynx lands at its feet, then it scrambles backwards until its bonds catch. Ina thinks it should be grateful it gets to watch the man's demise, and she thinks of kicking it into silence, but its cries join the other, more joyful ones now hanging prettily in the city sky, and Ina doesn't think anyone will know the difference.

Besides, she knows she can't touch it without latching on, and Ina must share. Sharing its blood is what will connect her to Alexander. It is the last blood of the year, and the first of the new, which allows them to recognize one another when all else is forgotten. Alexander – clever, bold, imperturbable – thought of it years ago.

"Careful," Ina warns, because she can see that Russell is long gone and Alexander is still tearing at the torso. She hopes it's in anger and not need. Russell's blood may be bitter, but subtlety fades when they gorge. Tonight, of all nights, the blood has to be sweet. "You don't want too much."

If Ina's heart could beat, it would be racing at the sight of that beloved dark head lowered over that rotted shell. She'd read an article this year that proved even the mortal scientists had realized that transfusions could affect personality. She half expects Alexander to glance up at her with Russell's low gleam sparkling in his own eye and mutter, "Shut up, bitch," before draining the man dry. That fear is what's kept them from daring this before.

But Alexander does stop, tossing the husk aside with such force its bones crunch wetly against the curved concrete. Then he wipes a sleeve over his mouth, holds up Russell's watch and smiles like a kid on Christmas morning. If possible, she falls more in love with him in that minute. It is the last.

Laughter bubbles up inside of Ina as Alexander cuffs himself to the wall with real shackles, pushing the ones he planted there before aside. The pure, clean blood has to be calling to him, racing as it is in the sacrifice's veins, tied in silky red ribbons to those futile screams, but he is all tranquil self-assurance.

"Tell me again about the first day we met," she says, once he's settled across from her.

"In which lifetime?" he whispers. The sound rumbles like velvet thunder, the voice of the gods, reverberating in her chest.

Ina sends a sigh skittering back, shaky and vulnerable. "The only one that matters."

"OK." But his voice is suddenly wounded with regret.

He doesn't want to forget.

The sacrifice doesn't want to die.

Want, Ina thinks, has nothing to do with it.

"What time was it?" she encourages softly.

Now that beautiful, stained, marble mouth twitches. "You were there. You know what time."

But she needs to know *he* still knows and, seeing her want laid bare, Alexander sobers instantly. "It was just past midnight, but it wasn't this cold. The night had fallen softly, as if the sun was dragging its heels as it was pushed from the sky—"

"The fucker."

His smile was brief. He was used to her: her language, the cadence, the way new words ran across that old tongue. "Then I saw you."

"Saw me where?" she said coyly. He indulges her. He knows coy is reserved solely for him.

"Chained where you are now, of course." His voice was proprietary; he was the one to discover her. He also knows she secretly wishes cats didn't fear her, that she sometimes makes herself sick on fruit juice for reasons she can't name and that she has dreams which place her across the Atlantic – ones that cause her to wake screaming. "The darkness was just one long stroke between us. It slid over my chest—"

"My breasts." Which she caresses for him.

"And down my belly—" His fingertips play over it.

"Igniting the hunger," she whispers, eyes trailing downwards.

The hunger is the worst. No one apart from Alexander can understand the irony that spikes in those final moments, the fear that giving in means giving up. That if she sips and lives, she might also lose the only one who makes her want to live at all. She knows it's not true, that the forgetting will erase even that want and that the throbbing in her veins now is merely the elixir of the last blood calling to her, but as she feels fogginess cloud her clear mind, she panics. She looks down and discovers her knuckles are bleeding. She's been wrenching them against her restraints without realizing it. The blood starts a rapid-fire reaction. Her jaw throbs, her mouth waters and her gums itch, eliciting a groan.

A movement distracts Ina and she suddenly remembers they have an audience. She shifts, eyes the warm body eyeing her and recalls – probably for the last time – the sacrifice who'd ushered in this year. He hadn't been as young as this one is, but he'd been sweet and hopeful and alone. All requirements, and all guaranteed to be met with Russell choosing the sacrifices.

So it'd been perfect and, in the end, Ina liked to think the boy had been grateful to be a part of something as large and meaningful as everlasting love. His blood infused them with new life, but their purpose gave him a life beyond the flesh.

Ina gazes down at this year's sacrifice, wanting it to know its fortune in being chosen. The overwhelming wonder of little miracles couples with the late hour and her hunger to bring tears to her eyes. She hisses her joy. Alexander responds, his elation deepening his growls. But the sacrifice screams louder at the sight of their fangs and Ina's giddiness is snuffed by annoyance.

So as the sepia fades to black and the old year and life is rubbed out by the new, Ina holds on long enough to allow Alexander to lunge first. Even though numbness whips along her limbs to freeze her core, her love for him is so great she allows him to break the skin. She doesn't know if it's the buzzing in her ears that drums out the screams or if they just suddenly stop. All she knows is physical satisfaction and profound relief as she surges forwards and – together – they drain the sacrifice dry.

They tell Ina she is impatient and impulsive and she grunts because it's dead on. Alexander is supposed to be cool-headed and implacable, and if that's true she could see why she would love him. She watches him read, the way his brow draws down, deepening his features. Then he looks up and shrugs, an almost embarrassed smile touching his lips, touching her. Ina's heart dips, the first plummet. That smile says he might be willing to believe . . . if she is.

She offers a tentative one in return.

"This is how you'll learn to love me," he told her the first time he handed her the guide. She reads about this account, apparently written while their limbs are intertwined and he's living deep inside her, a warm coal waiting to be stirred to life.

They had written it all down before meeting with Russell, what they'd done and why, and that they'd have to find someone new to help them in this year's end. It reads like fiction to Ina and she can tell it does for Alexander as well, which must be why they left little clues in the text, breadcrumbs only known to them.

"I already love you," is what she reports herself as saying, and she can imagine that, even as she scents lovemaking on the turning pages, even as she knows it is probably deliberate. She's betting that would be her idea. Get to the mind through the nose, the body, the instinct, the appetites. In spite of all they forget, their own core personalities remain constant and, while she may not know another soul in this world – she may have to fight to re-know this Alexander year after year – she knows herself well. She is selfish, stubborn, temperamental, insatiable and – if what she reads here is true – always uncaring about anything else when Alexander is in her arms. She looks up. He is biting clean through his lip. It's a mannerism she thinks she can learn to love.

Realistically, though, the attributes listed are true of most of their kind. It's why they move and live alone, and run solo. Unions aren't unheard of, of course, but when you have to begin your life anew at the dawn of each year – something none of them have to be told, something they each feel as plainly as the turn of the planets – it's best to refrain from unnecessary attachments. But Ina and Alexander have apparently found necessity in keeping record, not only of their own liaison, but of the others as well. Daniel and Marcus, for example, who have also found one another year after year. It's written down in black and white, at the place in the guide that they've marked for themselves as the beginning.

While Ina can't be sure of Alexander yet, she knows this is a good approach to take with her. She is more willing to listen and believe a story about someone else's happily-ever-after than she is about her own.

*Ever* is a long time.

Daniel and Marcus have somehow managed to find one another year after year without a guide. But then, Alexander reports, at the beginning of last year, Daniel moved from town before they could reacquaint, and the guide tracks Marcus' resulting deterioration. It says in February he begins a manic quest to collect every blood type, which he hangs in a silver vial shaped like a cross around his neck. In March, he runs out of blood types and stops going out altogether. By May he is drinking milk and Clorox and even liquefied vegetables just to taste something new.

Have they a need then, even in their ignorant forevers, to partner up? When you've tasted it all and there's nothing new on earth, is true love really what they thirst for in a life without end?

Ina considers this as she walks with this beloved stranger along the streets of Washington Heights, silent and as if they have a destination in mind. They attract little attention from the giddy pockets of people still drinking and yelling in the frigid night. Their heads are bowed over their book, this written lifeline into the past, and they take turns reading.

In the fall just past, Ina consented to Alexander's absence for two whole weeks – something she'd apparently never allowed before. The plan was to lure Daniel back to town with Alexander as bait, set up an accidental introduction between Marcus and him and let chemistry take over from there. It is Alexander's soft spot for the idea of true love that does Ina in. The romance of his temporarily putting aside his love so two others might experience it makes her want to turn and immediately start memorizing his features. But Alexander is still reading, and the last word written on the Daniel and Marcus saga is that Ina and Alexander are invited to brunch with the couple the following week. They, too, now share their sacrificial kill.

It is the most romantic thing she has ever heard.

Ina is hungry again by the time they finish their walk, but eating is a personal thing and, despite the way they woke, the idea of Alexander watching unnerves her. Instead, they return in silence to the apartment they share. The number has been written in bold black lettering in the guide. Ina recognizes the handwriting as her own. Keys are pinned to their underclothes.

Except it isn't an apartment. It is an abandoned Asian restaurant; lettering like smashed spiders sprawled across the walls, spices baked into the plaster. It looks deserted from the outside, is boarded up and reinforced by steel on the inside, and the appearance of dilapidation continues until a corner rounds out the view, provided anyone would wish to stop, reconsider and peer in. Alexander and Ina take the corner soundlessly, which makes her gasp stand out like an exclamation point in a poetic stanza.

The kitchen has been made into a library, with wall-to-wall shelves of shining oak, custom carved by a carpenter's hand with built-in lighting, and packed from ceiling to floor. History books, memoirs, true crime – all hardcover, all pristine – some so old they'd make curators weep. There is only one chair in the room, an oversized leather monstrosity with a giant ottoman parked in front, a handmade cashmere throw at the back and a side table at each arm. She knows which table is hers. There is a small Indian box, marble with inlays of mother-of-pearl and gold, and an unmarked bottle scented with sandalwood and white tea, things she instinctively loves.

There is something else she instinctively turns towards – the large, commercial refrigerator, the stainless steel walk-in door softened by a curtain of wood and glass beads that jangle like wind chimes as Ina passes through. The walls inside are softened with diaphanous panels, a swirl of colour like the frothy ends of pastel clouds. The floor is littered with silken pillows, batik sheets and shawls with fringing like moth's wings. The door locks from the inside.

Ina returns to the kitchen, lets her eyes wander over the volumes of history books, and wonders if she'll recognize the actions of the few females within. It shouldn't matter. The past is dead and one should live in the moment. It is what it is, all you have is the now: clichés, but valid because they were true. They were also the golden rules of their race. If Ina's personal history is inscribed in the makeshift book Alexander is loath to put down, these hated prosaisms are etched on her soul. She is grateful for the eternal life she's been given, the youth and vitality that are the rights of immortals, but what she wouldn't give or pay for just one true memory of a lifetime already lived. Yet living requires forgetting, and because Ina clings to life like an infant to the breast, she can handle wondering about herself.

But she looks over at Alexander, unconsciously running his thumb along the leather cover of their guide, along a soft spot already showing there, and suddenly knows she doesn't want to wonder with him too.

"If we didn't have the guide, this would be unimaginable." She means the apartment, the shared life, the planning of the sacrifice year after year . . . all of it.

"And that's why we do it. We knew we'd need the proof of the thing." Even though proof enough was in their mingled scents, covering every square inch of that kitchen. It smelled to Ina like perfect madness.

"But knowing nothing more than you do now, do you think we'd have felt the lack, like Marcus?"

A frown mars that perfect brow for a long moment as Alexander thinks hard, considering the depth of emotion that would have to exist for a creature such as himself to feel such a thing, to care so deeply. He finally nods. More importantly, he says, he wants to remember. He believes the memories lie like stakes in the pockets of those who hunt them, no less dangerous for being hidden. Perhaps more so.

And Ina? Alexander looks at her with an expression she's already beginning to recognize – one brow cocked in challenge while his chin lowers shyly – and he asks the unanswerable. What, of importance, does she believe?

Ina is silent for so long, light threatens the sky.

Ina believes truth lies in the blood.

Long ago, in a time when the streets of New York were filled with cobbled streets, horse shit layering them, soapboxes cornering them, dice games hidden among them, she was a factory girl with roughened hands and a back that was beginning to bend. She remembers this clearly, this and the way the entire world seemed intent on reaffirming she was no one special – from the foreman who would palm and pinch her for 14 hours straight, to the important men in carriages who ignored the pale, hunched girl trodding home in the gutter. Then there was the gaggle of urchins waiting for her care when she got back home, none of them her own. The experiences of her short mortal life are seared in her grey matter like an anchor into humanity and are the only ones she would willingly cut loose.

But beneath the grime and helplessness and the resentment only beginning to form, her blood was sweet. Or sweet enough to attract one more monstrosity into her life. She never saw him coming, and had barely felt his arm wrap around her body before the twin needles pierced her, causing her to jerk with rigour. But, in spite of the pain, that unknown immortal did not let one red drop hit the pressed dirt beneath her cheek, and despite the long, insistent tugs on her life, she'd been aware that this marked her as special enough.

After that, there is nothing. There is this morning. There is this stranger she supposedly loves, Alexander, standing across from her with a shyly raised brow.

The irony between the lack and poverty and pain, which she can remember, and the love and joy and acceptance that she cannot, makes her want to curl into herself. The only thing that stops her is the miracle of what she and this kindred stranger seem to have done. They've created a net for themselves, something that suspends them not only above humanity, but above the rest of their kind. They live in their own universe. How many couples, immortal or not, are able to claim the same? Ina thinks most simply go through the motions, doing what and who they've always done simply because momentum and habit carries them that way. She believes most spouses wouldn't be able to answer in the affirmative if asked if they'd choose their partner again today. Now. This minute and moment. This second. This life.

Monsters.

"What did his blood taste like?" she asks suddenly.

No matter that they forgot something as vital as pure love. They always remember the blood.

"As you'd think." Alexander lowers himself into the leather chair and looks away.

She knows what she thinks. It tastes like the air after the fireworks have died. Like petrol freshly touched by flame.

Ina runs the tip of her tongue across her incisor, nodding slowly.

"There will be no one to help us this time," she mutters before realizing what she's just said. She looks at Alexander sharply, nicking her tongue, but he's gazing at her with a new look on his face.

"We possess a year to find someone else," he says, eyes on her lips and tongue as the puncture wound closes and she licks the blood away. Ina feels herself go light-headed. She has already noted that Alexander's speech – he has told her he hates to be called Alex – is closer to the old tongue. To her, looking at him is like gazing at a living portrait. She has adopted the new – language and style and mores and dress – and she wonders if he minds.

Fuck it, she thinks and opens her mouth to ask him just that, but a child's voice rings through the new night, sharp through the open window, though it's at least two blocks away. Another shoots back like a bottle rocket, the sound crisp. It's too late for them to be out, their mother should know better. You never know what lurks in the cradle of night.

"Hungry?" Alexander asks her. Is it a simple question, or is he concerned for her?

"No, they're just annoying." Ina's watches him for a moment, wonders if it's only hunger that has him licking his lips or if the fouled blood has affected him after all, coating his mouth with the fumes of spent fuel.

"Stay inside." Alexander says, rising like a sail. "I'll go tell them to be silent."

"No, I'll go with you." Somehow she already knows she must stay with him every possible second. A year is a very short time. She joins him with equal fluidity. "Besides, I like children."

Ina does eat in front of Alexander and he in front of her and, later, when they're back in their kitchen, nestled among pillows with the door locked tight, she thinks that watching him feast was perhaps the most erotic thing she has ever witnessed in her life. She has gorged to the point that she might burst with one more drop, and she drapes her arm across her belly only to find

Alexander's is already there. She touches his hand and finds it's too warm as well. They have each been chasing a hunger they're still afraid to name.

Surely it's only the shared blood. She decides that by to-morrow's sunset they will be in control again. They will part. They will inhabit their own universes.

But curling into Alexander's too-warm side, Ina already knows this for a lie. It's like those mortals who cheat on good spouses, opening themselves up to appetites best dampened and flesh that doesn't belong to them. They start out in control, thinking they'll be satisfied with just one smile, one caress, one kiss, one fuck, maybe once a year. Until their motto alters from "just this once" to "you only live once".

But Ina, not even able to claim the same, knows they're wrong. Even without memory she knows that when it comes to the passions, once is never enough.

A hunger like this never dies.

# The Sacrifice

## Rebecca York

*K*ing Farral of Balacord had prayed to the gods for a son to secure his succession. When his wife presented him with a daughter, he named her Morgan in defiance of her sex.

Twenty-seven years later, Morgan knew her father was still disappointed in her. He had planned to marry her off to the prince of a neighbouring kingdom to secure a military alliance. Since they had not come to satisfactory terms, she was still unmarried and well past the age when most girls had made a match. She knew that, in her father's eyes, the fault was hers.

But that problem had receded into the background now that the kingdom was under siege from the northern barbarians. Two hundred people were crammed inside the castle walls. Their food supply was dwindling, even with pitifully short rations. And the enemy had beaten back the royal troops time and again.

As Morgan watched and worried, she came up with a desperate plan to save her people – if she had the courage to see it through.

It was night when Morgan tiptoed towards the door of her chamber.

Nedda, the old nurse who had raised her since she was a baby, sat up on her straw pallet. "Where are you going, child?"

Morgan kneeled beside the grey-haired woman. "To the mountain stronghold we talked about."

Nedda grabbed her skirt with a trembling hand. Her voice wheezed out of her when she spoke. "No woman has ever come back from that terrible place."

"But I have to try it. It's our only hope."

"Can I change your mind?"

"No."

Her old friend hugged her hard. "Then the gods be with you, child."

"And with you,' Morgan answered, feeling heartsick at this parting, fearing she would never see her faithful guardian again. "Go to sleep now. And when they ask you where I've gone, say you don't know."

Stepping outside her room, she stole down the corridor, towards a small door that led to the cliff on the riverside of the fortress.

Inside the castle, the air was fetid with the stench of fear and too many people huddled together in too small a space. Outside, on the ledge above the river, the night wind was a welcome balm.

She looked up towards the narrow slit of a window where light shone out into the darkness. It was her father's room, where he paced and raged over the fate of his kingdom, and maybe of his people, too. Because if they were dead, how could they serve him and pay him tribute?

"Forgive me, Father," she said, with a quaver in her voice. "I have never pleased you. I hope I will make it up to you now."

Quickly, she bound up her long golden hair in a net, then stripped off her clothing and stood in her shift, moonlight streaming over her slender curves. She stuffed her clothing and her sandals into the leather bag she had brought, the outside of which was smeared with grease to keep the contents dry.

Moonlight glimmered on the water far below. It was a long way down. She had never dived from this height before, but she had seen boys dive off the cliffs into the river and she knew the deep pool where you could hit the water and not break your body on the rocks. Well, at least she hoped she knew it.

At the edge of the cliff, she looked down, her heart pounding, and her mouth as dry as old parchment. She might die in the next few minutes, but if the barbarians, the Digons, took the castle, they would surely rape and murder the king's daughter.

Tonight she had a chance to choose her own fate; a choice she had never been given by her father.

Before she could lose her nerve, she tied the bag by a cord to her ankle, then took a deep breath and dived.

Hitting the water was like slamming into a stone wall. Then she went down into the depths of the pool, so far that she thought she would never come up again. But she was a strong swimmer, and she kicked upwards, stroking with her arms to give herself more momentum.

When she thought her lungs would burst, she broke the surface and dragged in a lungful of air, then let the current carry her downstream. Away from the castle. Away from the barbarians who were determined to capture her father's kingdom and enslave his people.

When she finally climbed out, the wind blew against her skin, raising goosebumps. After rubbing her arms to bring the blood to the surface, she hurried into the forest, where she pulled out the boy's trousers, shirt and sandals she had brought. After hiding her hair under a leather cap, she strapped a knife to a sheath at her waist and set off towards the East – towards the mountains where the monster dwelled.

The monster of legend – Garon.

She had heard whispered tales about him. And days ago, she had slipped into the room in the castle where the books were kept and read what she could. It was said that, long ago, he had come to the aid of Balacord. And he had extracted a terrible price. Was he still alive? Would he help them again?

She knew her father didn't give credit to those old stories, or he would have acted on them. But she believed. And people like Nedda believed.

So she walked eastwards, past cottages and farmyards filled with the stench of death, where the Digons had slaughtered the people and the animals. When her feet ached and her legs refused to carry her further, she found a tangle of brambles where she could rest.

After a meagre meal from her provisions, she set off again, more cautiously than before. It was dangerous out here with the sun up. But she knew that the further east she travelled, the less likely she would be to meet anyone. People stayed away from Garon's stronghold.

She travelled for three days, singing war songs to keep up her spirits and thinking about her parents and her younger brother, Kerwin. If he survived, she believed he would make a better king than her father. When she let herself think about the monster, she almost lost her nerve. But somehow she kept walking into the mountains.

Gradually the trees grew shorter and more scraggly, and the low vegetation more compact. The sun was dipping behind a tall peak when she came to a place where the ground was scorched and rocky. The old legends said that this was where Garon lived and they told what she must do to make herself acceptable to him.

What form would the monster take? She had heard he might look like a man. Or maybe some fearsome creature. But whatever his appearance, she must throw herself on his mercy.

She retraced her steps to a mountain stream she had crossed, then pulled off her travel clothing and washed her body in the cold water. Colder than the river. She used the shirt for a washcloth, with a bit of soap she had brought along, then dried herself with the pants.

When she was clean, she opened her bag again. With trembling hands, she took out the other clothing she had brought – the white gown that Nedda had sewn for her wedding night. She pulled it over her head, feeling the silky fabric cup her breasts. The waist was snug, with the skirt flaring out over her hips. She had seen herself in this gown. She knew her nipples showed indecently through the cups of the bodice. And the skirt did nothing to hide the golden triangle of hair at the top of her legs. Only her husband and her serving women should see her like this, but here she was, out in the open air.

Next she pulled out a gold chain, with the King's crest of a laurel branch and a sword worked onto a flat disc. Quickly she slipped the token around her neck, so that the crest lay flat against her chest.

Would she please the monster?

Would he accept her as a sacrifice?

Her heart pounding wildly inside her chest, she went back to the scorched earth and continued on to a little field where the rocks were small and sharply pointed, covering the ground with a treacherous carpet. The legends said she must slip off her sandals now. But her hands trembled as she untied the straps.

Teeth clenched, she took a tentative step onto the shifting surface. A sharp rock dug into her sole, but she took another step, and another, ignoring the pain. She was halfway across the terrible field when a voice stopped her in her tracks.

"Who dares approach this place?"

She looked up and saw a man standing stiffly at the opposite side of the rocks, about 20 yards away, with his back to a mountain cliff. He was tall, with dark hair and dark eyes fixed on her like a hawk watching a rabbit. He wore black trousers and a black shirt open at the neck.

She raised her chin. "You are Garon?"

He made a dismissive sound. "What of it? I asked who *you* are."

"I am Morgan of Balacord."

His voice turned derisive. "What half-cracked father would give his daughter a man's name?"

"King Farral of Balacord. I am Princess Morgan."

His gaze drilled into her. "Well, Princess Morgan, you should not be here – dressed like that."

"I have come in the old way – to ask your help for my kingdom."

"You won't get it. Go back before it's too late."

She would not simply turn around and go home. Defiantly, she took another step forwards, then another.

"I can smell your blood. Leave this place," he said in a harsh voice.

She looked down at her feet, then back at the bloody foot-prints she had left on the rocks. Ignoring him, she kept walking forwards until the pain was so great that she wavered on unsteady legs. She swayed to the side, and he sprinted forwards, his boots crunching on the rocks. Swiftly, he caught her before she fell and gathered her into his arms. She felt his body tremble. Looking up, she saw his face, pale and rigid above her. Clenching his teeth, he turned and carried her the rest of the way across the rocks and into an opening in the side of the mountain.

Beyond the doorway was a cave, but like no cave she had ever seen. The rock walls were squared off. Tapers flickered in candelabra set about a huge room with beautifully carved furniture and marble statues on low pedestals. The rugs were richly patterned and the walls were lined with tall shelves full of more books and scrolls than she had ever seen in her life.

He laid her on a couch, looking down at her feet.

"Your blood . . ." he said in a thick voice.

"Take it. I have come to make the sacrifice demanded for your help."

She saw his nostrils flare as his hot gaze swept her, travelling over her neck, her breasts, her hips and down to her bleeding feet.

She tried to lie still. Tried to keep her body from shaking. But she was frightened now. More frightened than she had ever been in her life.

He knelt on the rug beside the couch, taking one of her feet in his hand, lifting it to his lips.

In a kind of haze, she watched his tongue flick out and stroke over the sole of her foot, taking the blood with it. His tongue was rough and it sent a tingling feeling over her foot where it laved her. But it did more than affect that one spot. Other parts of her body responded. She felt an ache kindled high up between her legs.

She had heard stories of this creature who craved mortal blood and she had hardly believed them. But she had come here hoping that they were true.

He turned her foot to the side and found a place where the sharp rocks had cut her deeply. He sucked at the wound, drawing more blood from her, increasing the frisson coursing through her body. She felt his small, sharp fangs graze her skin as he licked at her blood. Then he swabbed his tongue over her wounds before placing her foot back on the couch.

As he broke the contact, she made a sound low in her throat. He raised his head and looked up at her, then clasped his hand around her opposite ankle before stroking upwards with his long, delicate fingers to her calf, then her inner thigh, leaving a trail of heat.

Once again, she watched him lick at her wounds before finding a place where the puncture was deep. When he sucked strongly, the pull increased the fire in her body. He drew on her for long moments before licking at her wounds.

She looked down, seeing that blood no longer flowed from her cuts. In fact, her skin felt whole – as though she had never been injured.

He raised his head, his eyes bright as he stared down at her. When he started to stand, she reached out and grabbed his hand, holding him where he was.

"I must leave you," he said in a thick voice.

"No," she answered, as she gathered the courage to hold him there, to make him finish this. Lifting his hand, she brought it to her breast and rubbed his fingers against her through the delicate fabric of her gown. As she felt a dart of sensation, she heard his indrawn breath.

His gaze bored into her. "What do you know of this?"

"Nothing. I am a virgin. But I know what I feel now."

"And I am a monster who has just taken of your blood. What do you say to that?"

"That you are also a man who will give me pleasure." She said it boldly, not even knowing if it was true.

"You are much too . . . forward."

"I have been told all my life that I do not know how to obey the rules."

"You have displeased your father, the King?"

"Many times."

"And you have been punished for your wilfulness?"

"Yes."

Defiantly, she dropped her gaze to the front of his pants. She had never seen a naked man, but she had heard the maids whispering and giggling about what they did with their lovers. When she reached out a trembling hand towards him, he jerked away from her and moved back until he was standing a few feet away.

His voice was harsh. "If we go any further with this, no man will have you for his wife."

"I know."

"You don't understand what you're doing."

"I do."

As she watched, he suddenly changed – from a man to a creature with horns, a long thin face, claws instead of hands and a forked tail that whipped back and forth across the rug.

A devil. From the legends. And from the nightmares of her childhood.

Morgan gasped and pressed back against the sofa cushions, her heart pounding as she fought to catch her breath. She knew that he was trying to frighten her into fleeing, but she wasn't going to do it. Not when she had come this far. Gathering her courage, she sprang off the couch. With her eyes closed, she reached for him, clasped him in her arms and held tight.

He roared his anger, but she stayed where she was. She felt him changing again, to a creature with skin that was rough and scaly. Again, she kept her eyes squeezed closed.

This time, when he roared, his face was inches from hers. And she felt his breath turn hot, burning her cheek.

Still, she held on to him.

And then he changed a third time. Feeling the shape of his body, she could tell he was a man again.

"You are brave," he said, awe in his voice.

"I have to be," she answered.

As they spoke, his embrace changed. He had been holding her in a punishing grip. Now his touch was gentle as he stroked his hands up and down her back. He took her by the shoulders, rocking her breast against the rough fabric of his shirt, making her nipples ache.

Overcome, Morgan pressed her face to his shoulder. One of his hands found her chin and tipped it up so that his lips could come down on hers. Earlier, his mouth had sent powerful sensations through her body, but that was nothing compared to what he was doing now. He moved his lips against hers, brushing, sliding, settling.

"Oh!"

She felt him smile as his tongue slipped into her mouth, playing with the line of her teeth and the sensitive tissue on the inside of her lips.

While she was absorbing the sensations, he picked her up in his arms again and carried her further back into his dwelling, through a massive door, which he shut behind them, closing them into a bedroom lit by more of his candelabra. In the flickering light, he set her down beside a wide bed, then pulled her gown and the gold chain over her head and dropped them on the floor so that she stood naked in front of him.

When he pulled off his shirt, her breath caught. His chest was magnificent, well muscled and smooth.

As she watched, he worked the buckle at the top of his pants. When it was opened, he pulled his trousers down and stepped out of them. Her gaze settled on his male part. In all of her 27 years, she had never been alone in a room with a man, except her father and her brother. And certainly not with a naked one. She forced herself not to gasp as she took in the size of him. She kept her head bent, unable to look him in the eye and show him her fear.

And because she couldn't simply stand there, she stepped forwards and clasped her arms around his shoulders.

He made a rough sound as his arms came up to cradle her body against his.

Electricity arched between them. But his words tore at her.

"You should be afraid of me. Why are you not afraid?"

"I want to be your lover," she managed to say.

"I haven't done this . . . in a long time. Perhaps I'll be too rough. Perhaps I'll hurt you."

"You won't."

When he started to speak again, she brought her mouth back to his, moving her lips the way he had done to her, then playing with the seam and sliding her tongue into his mouth.

He made a surprised sound as she imitated what he had taught her. He stroked his hand down her body, then cupped her bottom and pulled her against the hard shaft rising between them.

When she swayed on her feet, he eased her onto the bed and came down beside her. Sighing deeply, he rolled her on to her side. Looking into her eyes, he slid his hands over her body, stroking her arms, her neck, her breasts. When she arched into the caress, he bent to take one distended nipple into his mouth, sucking strongly, drawing on her.

Letting the hot, needy feeling envelop her, she raised her hand, touching his body, awed to be playing her fingers over his broad chest. Leaning forwards, she circled one flat nipple with her tongue, pleased at the way it beaded in response.

His indrawn breath made her feel powerful.

In the next moment, he reached down to touch her where no one else had ever dared touch, his fingers tangling in the triangle of blonde hair at the top of her legs before slipping lower, into her moist folds. The sensation made her gasp.

She gasped again as his finger dipped inside her and circled, then moved all the way up to the place where her greatest sensation resided.

"I want . . ." she gasped.

"What?"

She felt her face heat. "I don't know how to say it."

He watched her face. "But you've felt sexual climax?"

"What is it?"

"The ultimate pleasure for a woman. And for a man."

Was that the word for it? The secret, forbidden pleasure. She couldn't meet his eyes as he rolled her on to her back and continued to stroke her, angling his hand so that he could press against the throbbing place of greatest sensation as his finger stroked the inside of her.

She felt her tension climbing, climbing.

"Let me make you come," he whispered, then bent to tease her breasts with his mouth again.

She felt the explosion gathering inside her.

"Garon." She called out his name in wonder as waves of pleasure vibrated through her – more pleasure than she had ever known in her own, lonely bed.

And as the waves began to recede, he covered her body with

his and plunged inside her. There was a moment of pain. But she was so relaxed that she hardly noticed.

He bent his mouth to her neck, and she felt another small pain as sharp teeth pierced her flesh. His mouth sucked at her as he stroked in and out of her, his being vibrating with tension. Then she felt him go rigid, felt him suck more strongly as his body jerked and went stiff.

She lay breathing hard, overwhelmed by what they had just done. He eased off of her and rolled on to his back. She knew very little of what happened between men and women, but she suspected that what they had done had been extraordinary.

When she turned her head, she saw her blood on his mouth. Maybe that should have horrified her, but she only felt limp and relaxed.

She had come here to save her people, but they had receded into the background as he fulfilled a longing she didn't know existed within her. She wanted to tell him what making love with him had meant to her, but was afraid to reveal too much.

So she only said, "You gave me great pleasure."

"And I took your blood."

"I gave it to you," she answered.

He sat up and looked down at her. "You knew I drank blood?"

"Yes," she whispered. "I read the old stories. They said the cuts on my feet would tempt you."

"You read?" he asked in surprise.

"Yes."

"Who taught you?"

"I taught myself."

"Well, if you read about me, you know I don't just drink blood. I live on it."

She nodded, then asked in a small voice, "Where do you get enough to sustain you?"

"I have a herd of deer that feed me. They come when I call them. They are my friends."

His friends. She tried to imagine how lonely he must be. Emotions welled inside her. She felt something for this man that she had never felt before and didn't understand now.

She only knew that her heart seemed to swell inside her chest.

"Human blood tastes better," he said, then looked away. "So I must stay away from the communities of men. If I take too much from one person, I kill him. Or her."

"You didn't kill me."

"I could have."

"I think you've learned control."

"I frighten humans. With good reason. You were very brave or very foolish come here," he said.

She lifted her chin. "Call it what you want, but I feel better than I ever have in my life."

Ignoring her words, he added, "Your journey to this place should be rewarded. You said your people needed my help."

"The Digons have laid siege to my father's castle. They are barbarians. They will kill our men and rape our women and make them slaves. And they will take the kingdom for their own."

"And you think I can save your people?"

"Yes."

He stood up, strode to the door of his bedroom and pushed it open. From the mouth of the cave, she saw the dawn coming.

"I must sleep," he said.

"But . . ."

"We will talk when I wake up. But first, I will get you food and drink." He walked into the front room and vanished.

She got up and pulled on her gown and the gold chain, then hurried to the place where he had been. While she was trying to work out where he had gone, he reappeared, holding a tray of meat, fruit, cheese and bread and a crystal goblet of cold water.

Her eyes widened. "Where did you get that?"

"From the other side of the mountain."

"So quickly?"

"Yes."

He walked back towards his bedroom. "I will sleep until the sun is low in the sky. You are welcome to stay here. Or not."

He swept his hand towards one of the rugs and she saw the sandals she had taken off on the other side of the sharp rocks. He had brought them to her, so she could walk back the way she had come. Before she could tell him she had no intention of running away, he closed the stout door between them, leaving her alone in the beautiful room.

She ate some of the food and drank from the goblet, then wandered around, taking in the details of the room. It was wonderful, with more treasures than she could ever have imagined. Diamonds, emeralds and rubies sparkled in a silver bowl. A large crystal globe had images of the moon and stars embedded inside it. There were tables of what looked like scientific instruments. Some, like a telescope, she recognized; others were a complete mystery to her. And beside them were quill pens, inkwells and stacks of notebooks where he had written in a language she could not read.

Enthralled by everything she saw, she drifted around the room, inspecting his treasures. Tables held shells from the sea, crystals, bottles of coloured glass, boxes carved of stone and wood, and cunning images of animals, some real and some from stories. She found a beautifully carved dragon, a unicorn and a bear that was completely white.

She left the best for last. On the shelves was a treasure trove of books and ancient scrolls, beautifully illuminated. She opened books on history, philosophy, science, geography and language: all the subjects she had longed to study when she had been forced to join the other women of the castle learning weaving, embroidery and how to sew clothing, because that was all females were good for. That and marriage and having babies.

Now she attacked the riches of the library, pulling out volumes that interested her and carefully putting them back before she picked up another.

She could stay here for a thousand years, she thought, reading. And learning from the man who lived in this remote place. He was no longer a monster to her. He was like no one she had ever met – not her parents or her brother or the people of Balacord, who spent their lives working for the good of her father's household. She saw that he had curiosity and the leisure time to learn all the disciplines of the world. And that he had travelled from this place and brought wonderful things back to enrich his life. Yet he must be lonely living here alone.

Time sped by. When the door to the bedroom opened, she blinked. Garon stepped out. He was dressed in black, as she had first seen him.

"You're still here."

"Of course."

"I must eat."

She stiffened, wondering if he was going to take her blood again, but he walked past her, out into the night, and she realized he was going to his deer herd. A pang of guilt assaulted her. She had lost herself in his books and her people were still in mortal danger.

When Garon returned, she went to him.

"Will you help me now?"

"It might not come out the way you expect."

"Why not?"

"You must see that for yourself."

"How?" she asked.

"You will come with me."

There was no other choice. "All right," she answered immediately.

"You might yet lose your nerve."

"I hope not."

"You said you were from Balacord. I know the place." He tipped his head to the side and looked at her. "What do you know of the legends?"

"That when the people needed a boon from you, they brought a virgin sacrifice to your mountain."

Garon considered her answer. "Those women were brought here against their will. You came on your own."

"I had to."

"Few people would do it."

He sounded so grave. And she heard herself ask, "What did you do with them? The virgins."

"I took them to the other side of the mountain, where I bought them husbands."

She stared at him. "I thought . . ."

"What?"

"That you ravished them and . . ."

"Killed them?"

"Yes," she whispered.

"I made love with them. But I do not kill for pleasure. I do not kill the deer. There are enough of them to feed me without killing."

"But you will kill the barbarians?"

Garon was silent for a long time, and she felt her heart pounding as she waited for his answer. "Yes. For you. Because you had the will and the courage to ask."

"Then we must hurry. They have laid siege to the castle. The people cannot hold out for much longer."

"We will make you ready to leave."

Morgan felt a pang. She didn't want this time with him to end. He had listened to her, really listened. And he had shown her more regard in a few hours than she had ever experienced in her whole life. She felt the sadness of that and struggled to push it away. She had work to do, and she must not let her own needs distract her.

He walked further back into the cave and returned with a shirt and pants and a set of leather armour.

"Put this on."

"Why?"

"Because you are going into battle."

Morgan swallowed and turned her back so she could take off the gown and pull on the shirt and pants. Then she picked up the top part of the armour, turning it in her hands. "I don't know how to fit it to me."

"I'll help you." He slipped the upper piece over her head and hooked it together under her arms. "Put your hands on my shoulders."

She did, closing her eyes as she clung to his strong body, wishing they were back in bed together. And when he fitted the leg guards over her thighs, she fought a surge of heat.

Maybe he felt it too, because she heard his breath catch.

"How did you find armour that fits a woman?" she asked, trying to distract herself.

"Magic," he said, his voice thick.

He picked up the helmet from the bed and fixed it on her head, carefully tucking her hair out of sight. Then he pulled back a drapery and turned her around so that she could see herself in a long mirror.

She stared at the warrior confronting her. "I look . . . fierce."

"We'll see if your heart matches your appearance. Come outside."

She followed him out of the bedroom, through the room with the wonderful books and then into the night. The moon was so bright that the rock outcroppings cast shadows.

"Stay there while I change," he said.

"To what?"

He stepped back, a few feet from her. Then he began to grow and transform. She gasped as scales covered his body. His neck and head elongated. His arms turned into wings and his feet became talons. In seconds a terrifying dragon stood before her, towering twenty feet in the air.

In the moonlight, he arched his neck, lifted his head and roared. Along with the mighty sound, a stream of fire shot out of his mouth.

If he was trying to scare her again, he had succeeded. But she managed to stand her ground. She had come too far to run from him now. He looked dangerous. No, he *was* dangerous. But not to her. She knew he would never hurt her. Not on purpose.

His voice roared out of him, as he crouched low to the ground. "Climb on my back. Use my scales to pull yourself up."

Teeth clenched, she climbed onto the dragon's massive back, straddling him like a great horse. There was a kind of saddle for her to sit on and his shoulder blades stuck up like two handles. It seemed that he had shaped his back so she could ride easily and hang on. She grabbed on with her two hands.

"Are you ready?" he boomed.

"Yes," she answered, wondering if it was true.

Garon leaped into the air, his great wings flapping as he gained altitude, carrying her up and up, high above the forest and into the black velvet night where she thought she might touch the stars.

She had envied the freedom of birds that could fly away to a new place any time they wanted. Now she looked down in wonder, awed by the moon-silvered view below her.

It was cold. She was glad of the armour's protection but still the wind stung her face as they flew high above the forest.

His strong wings beat the air, eating up the distance. She had taken three days to walk to his mountain lair. The moon had barely moved in the sky when she saw the castle and the barbarians camped around it.

"Press yourself down and hold on," the dragon boomed as he dived towards the invaders. She flattened herself against his back and dug her fingers into his shoulder blades as he hurtled downwards.

Below on the plains around the castle, she heard men shouting and pointing towards them. Soldiers in the castle were shouting and pointing, too. Some of the barbarians aimed their bows into the air. Arrows flew past Morgan only to bounce off the dragon's scales.

Garon plunged downwards towards the Digons. When he was almost on them, fire shot from his mouth, enveloping the camp below. Tents went up in flames. Men's clothing caught fire, and they ran screaming towards the river. Their cries and the smell of their burning flesh rose into the air.

Morgan turned her head away. She didn't want to see the death of these men, but she knew what they would have done to her people if they had won. So she hung on as the dragon wheeled and dived, scorching the men and the land around the castle.

The barbarians left standing scattered, running for their lives. The dragon hunted them down – picking them off one by one. When he was finished, he landed on the field, in the middle of the destruction.

Morgan looked towards the castle. Men inside cranked the gears that lowered the great drawbridge and raised the gate. She expected her father to come out with cries of thanks.

Instead, archers rushed through the opening, firing at the dragon as they charged him.

Morgan screamed.

Garon bellowed in anger. Whipping his head from side to side, he sprayed the soldiers with fire, then rose into the air with his rider still clinging to his back.

Arrows followed them upwards but fell back to earth.

Morgan pressed her face to the dragon's back, hot tears stinging her eyes. He had saved her father's kingdom and this was his reward. Reaching for the chain around her neck, she pulled it over her head and flung it into the air, watching it plummet towards the ground. The soldiers would find it. And maybe Nedda would understand that she had not died after all. That she was all right.

They flew back the way they had come. Back to the mountain cave. And when they landed, she slipped to the ground.

The dragon backed away from her, transforming once more so that the man she had come to know was standing before her, his face hard and set.

"You saved them and they tried to kill you," she cried out.

"They fear me."

"You knew what would happen," she accused.

"Not for certain. But it was my guess."

"And you wanted me to see."

"Yes."

"Why?"

"So you will go back where you belong."

"How can I?"

"I can give you proof that you brought the monster that saved them."

"What proof?"

"You can carry back scales from the dragon."

She didn't hesitate in her answer. "I don't want to carry anything back. I want to stay here."

"You are human and I am not. There can be nothing more between us."

She felt his words like physical blows. But she stood her ground. "You would send me back to my father?"

"Yes."

"No. I do not belong with him. He has never cared for

me or my happiness. He only wants to use me for his own good."

"Yet you came here to save him."

"I came to stop the suffering of his people. In a few years, my brother, Kerwin, will be the ruler, and he will be a good king. But I do not want to go back to Balacord."

"Then I will take you to the other side of the mountain and buy you a husband."

His voice dismissed her but she ran to him and clasped her arms around his waist. "Let me stay with you. I feel closer to you than any man I ever met."

He was so much stronger than she. He could have wrenched himself away, but he stayed in her embrace. His voice was low and sad when he answered. "You cannot."

"Why?"

"I am old. Hundreds of years old. I am not human. And I live on blood."

"I do not care about that."

"You will grow lonely in this place."

She raised her head and met his gaze. "I will not grow lonely. I will have you to teach me all the things you know and all the things I have longed to learn." She let her joy shine in her voice. "We will argue about politics and religion and philosophy the way educated men do. And we will discover new things in science together."

For a moment, she saw her joy echoed in his eyes. But it quickly faded. "You are human. And you will grow old and die."

She gave him a cocky grin that welled up from the depths of her soul. "And you are magic. You will keep me young."

"You have too much faith in my magic."

"We'll see. We can figure it out. Together. And if my life is shorter than yours, I will be content. For it will be the life I have chosen for myself. A life of freedom, not the narrow existence my father planned for me."

His voice was gritty as he asked, "Where did you get such wisdom?"

"From the place inside myself where I spent most of my time, because that was the only escape for me. Until now."

He stared at her in wonder. "You are so different from the other virgins they brought here. They were frightened. And shallow. They had no thirst for knowledge. They only craved safety and comfort."

"I'm older than they were. I am a king's daughter. And I have been punished many times for being . . . different."

"Thank the gods you are."

She clasped the back of his head and brought his mouth down to hers for a long, hungry kiss. She felt his response. Felt her desire leap to meet his. And she felt the armour she was wearing vanish.

By magic.

He began to kiss her as he ran his hands over her body. And all the passion she had held in check burst forth.

They staggered together into the cave and managed to make it as far as a thick carpet before they fell in a tangle of arms and legs, kissing and stroking, and driving each other to the peak of need.

Then he was inside her, staring down at her in wonder, moving in a rhythm that fuelled her desire, building the intensity to a level neither one of them could sustain for long.

They spun off into space together. And when his teeth pierced the flesh of her neck, climax rolled through her, through them.

He was still inside her when he lifted his head. "I took only a little of your blood. Just enough."

She reached to stroke his damp face. "And I gave it gladly. Out of love."

She saw a flash of disbelief on his face. "Love?"

"Oh yes."

"You don't know what I am."

"Of course I do. You went to great pains to show me the worst that you could think of." She smiled up at him, touching his lips, where a small red drop glistened. "But I saw more than you intended. Much more. Your power is so much greater than my father's, yet you use it wisely. He is a petty ruler. But you are truly noble."

His face registered his shock. "How can you call me that?"

"Because it's true. That and more. Your wisdom stretches

beyond the reach of any man. You have sacrificed much, but you do not always know what is best for yourself. I pray that I can teach you."

With that, she clasped him tightly, knowing it would take time for him to accept everything she offered.

But they had the time. And she hugged that knowledge to herself, even as she clasped him.

Her monster. Her devil. Her dragon. Her teacher. And her lover.

# The Midday Mangler Meets his Match

## Rachel Vincent

". . . and we've got your weather report coming up in minutes, so stay tuned for a list of area schools expected to be closed this evening. But first, the morning headlines . . ."

I groaned and glared uselessly at the television, looking up from my history book. I didn't want current events. I just wanted to know whether or not school had been cancelled, because if it had, I'd have a reprieve from the first chapter on Global Conflict the Second.

On screen, a flawlessly composed and impeccably dressed woman sat at a desk behind an open laptop, her eyes on the camera, the pristine points of her fangs pressed into a plump lower lip.

"Early last night, area police found the charred remains of another child, the latest target of the Midday Mangler, in the parking lot of the Gateview Mall. Like previous victims, she had been drained, then bound and left exposed to a deadly dose of morning sunlight. There's been no official word on the child's identity, but inside sources say the body is almost certainly that of nine-year-old Phoebe Hayes, who was reported missing after school two nights ago."

*What?* I'd heard about the other bodies, of course. We all had. But Gateview Mall was only ten minutes away. The Midday Mangler had been practically in my backyard.

"This makes the fourth disappearance and grisly murder of a child in the last month, and the first in the metropolitan area.

Police are urging parents to supervise their children closely and check in with them often. And, of course, if you see anything suspicious, call the police immediately."

The school closings forgotten, I hit the power button on the remote in disgust. What kind of *sick fuck* would feed from another person, much less a *child*? And leave their bodies to fry in the sun? That just added insult to injury, and robbed the poor parents of one last glimpse of their child resting in peace.

And really: the "Midday Mangler"? The national media had obviously run out of good serial-killer nicknames (which worried me almost as much as the fact that they needed them).

"Ewww, sick!" a high-pitched voice cried from the back of the house. I looked up from my work again, worried for a moment that Luci had heard the news report. "She *bit* the little girl?!" My sister giggled, and I relaxed.

She hadn't heard.

"Yeah, because the kind old woman was really an evil witch," Oscar said, his still-changing voice deepening with the drama of the story. "What'd you *think* she was going to do? Pat the kids on the head and send them on their way?"

I dropped my book on the couch and stood, my homework momentarily forgotten. When Oscar and I were little, our mother had told us that same story over and over. It was our favourite. Especially the part where the little girl shoved the witch out of the door into the blazing sunlight, where she was scorched to a crisp, black shell. Then the girl freed her brother and they waited out of the deadly sun until dusk, when they could escape into the safety of the dark woods.

Lucinda giggled again, and Oscar continued as I snuck down the hall, my bare feet silent on the carpet. "Now do you want to hear the rest of it, or are you gonna talk all morning?"

"OK, I'm done!" she cried. "Tell me the rest."

I peeked around the door frame to see Luci sitting up in bed, her purple-print comforter pulled up to her waist, white curls brushing the shoulders of a frilly yellow nightgown. The bedside lamp threw dim light over her, shining on pale-blue eyes, glinting on the points of tiny, sharp incisors bared in delight.

Over her shoulder, a thin beam of sunlight shone through a hairline seam in the plush, purple-upholstered shutters covering her window, where moonlight had streamed an hour earlier.

Oscar sat in a ladder-back chair by her bed, reading the familiar lines of the fairy tale from a worn, leather-bound book that had seen its best days before our parents were even born. "The old witch held Gretchen immobile, her lips locked on the little girl's throat, her fangs piercing thin, fragile skin. She sucked hard, pulling blood from Gretchen's body again and again, filling herself with it until the girl began to weaken and finally fell to the ground, motionless. Her eyes closed, her heart was still."

I frowned as Oscar ran one pale hand through his stiff blond spikes. I didn't remember Gretchen collapsing.

"When the little girl was dead, the witch turned to her brother, who still sat in the cage, staring at his sister's lifeless body in horror. Handel knew he was next."

Luci's eyes widened, and her lower lip quivered.

My jaw clenched in aggravation. I stomped into the bedroom and snatched the book from my brother, smacking the back of his head with my free hand. "Don't ad-lib with her, you moron!" I scowled as he whirled on me, irritation bringing a drastic flush to his enviably pale cheeks. "She's six years old! Give her the children's version and save your horror stories for your idiot friends," I snapped.

"It's not a story, Kez." Oscar's pale-green eyes blazed with conviction. "It's a morality tale, and the message is 'don't take candy from strangers'. How is she supposed to learn anything if the story doesn't illustrate the possible consequences?"

He reached for the book, but I stepped back. "First of all, it's not *your* job to educate her. But beyond that, appropriate consequences for a first-grader do *not* include cannibalism and death. Leave the lessons to her teacher and go finish your own homework before I tell Mom you went all gruesome on Luci again."

Oscar scowled, but plodded into the hall without argument. Mom was still mad at him for the D he'd pulled in maths. It wasn't that he couldn't do the work – he'd skipped both second and fifth grade, and was now the youngest freshmen in the school by nearly two years – but that he had no interest in sitting behind a desk all morning. And until he figured out how to get an A without doing homework, he couldn't afford to piss her off further.

"And you . . ." I smiled and settled onto the edge of Luci's bed, plucking a pink bear from the pile stacked against the headboard, his plush fangs stark white and glittery. "It's past your bedtime, and you're keeping Petals up."

"Did that really happen?" Luci scooted down under the covers as I pulled them up to her chest.

"Did what really happen?"

"Did that witch really bite Handel and Gretchen and suck their blood?"

"Of course not." I lifted one corner of the blanket and tucked Petals in beside her, his rounded, white-on-pink ear nestled in a tangle of her sweet-smelling curls. "Handel and Gretchen aren't real. It's just a story, and Oscar told it all wrong. In the version Mom told us, Gretchen kills the evil witch and saves her brother. And they both live happily ever after."

But Luci wouldn't be placated by my happy ending. "Oscar says people used to bite all the time. That that's how we used to feed ourselves, instead of cutting meat with a knife and fork and drinking blood from a carton."

"Well, Oscar's full of crap. And you can quote me on that."

Luci grinned. "So we never drank blood from each other? Then why do we have fangs?"

*Damn it, Oscar!* He was always telling her half-truths and leaving me to sort the facts from the bullshit. Medieval use and abuse of fangs was *not* something I wanted to explain to a first-grader.

"OK, here's the deal on fangs, but listen up, 'cause I'm only going to say this once. OK?"

She nodded solemnly, wrapping one small arm around Petals.

"Do you know what vestigial organs are?"

Luci shook her head.

Of course not, I thought. She's six. "Vestigial organs are the parts of our bodies we used to need a long time ago. But we've evolved over time and now we no longer need them. Like wings on a bird that can't fly. Or like your tailbone, which doesn't really do anything because people no longer have tails. Our fangs are like that."

Her grip on Petals tightened. "So we *used* to use them to drink blood?"

"Well, yes. A long time ago."

Her eyes widened again, and her pale brows dipped in concern. "Did people eat kids?"

"No! Feeding from other people – including children – has *never* been OK. Even when we all lived in caves. We ate animals then, just like we do now. Only back then we didn't have refrigerators to keep the blood and meat from going bad, so we had to drink and eat straight from the source. But there was no evil witch who drank from children. That's just Oscar's version of a story Mom used to tell us."

"Why didn't Mom tell *me* that story?" Luci asked, and I stifled a groan. She had a knack for asking the hard questions. *Because since Dad left, she's working two jobs and barely has time to sleep, much less tell stories.* But I couldn't say that.

"Because she's really busy right now. But I'll tell you a story any time you want."

Her eyes brightened a little at that, and she hugged Petals closer to her chest.

"You ready to sleep now?" I asked. Luci nodded, and I tucked the covers in tight around her. With a twist of her lamp switch, the room went dark, but for that slim crack of light from the window, nowhere near enough to hurt her.

I was almost out the door when she whispered, "I love you, Kez."

"Love you too, Luce." I left her door open an inch, then trudged into the living room where Oscar sat on the couch in front of the television, *not* doing his homework.

"What's this?" I dropped onto the cushion next to him and kicked his feet off the cluttered coffee table.

"Bloodclot. Live." On screen, a tall, thin man screamed at the crowd through lips painted a gruesome shade of red, reminiscent of drying blood. His make-up-whitened skin was crowned by a shocking thatch of long, jet-black hair. "Ruben Bensch is a *demon* on the guitar. I'm gonna get my hair darkened just like his."

I snorted. "You're dreaming. Mom will never go for that." And even if she did, dying his hair black wouldn't help Oscar's social life. Considering his larger-than-average brain and his smaller-than-average build, it would take a miracle for him to fit in. Black hair was no miracle.

"She will if I get an A in maths."

"Like I said . . ."

Oscar kicked my ankle, but before I could retaliate, the front door opened. I twisted on the couch, squinting against the assault of harsh daylight as our mother rushed through the door. The sun was bright and made my eyes water, but thanks to the covered porch (built so Luci – the most sensitive of us to sunlight – wouldn't be burned even if she was still awake at eight in the morning), no direct rays blazed inside.

Mom shut the door and stomped snow from her boots onto the mat. "Sorry I'm late again, guys." She flipped the blue-velvet hood back from her head, untied the strings, then pulled her cape off and hung it on a hook to the left of the door. "Is Luci in bed?"

"Yeah, but she's probably still awake if you want to go say good morning."

"Thanks." Mom kicked her boots off and tugged her blouse down over a recently thickening middle. She set her purse on the end table next to Oscar, then headed towards Luci's room.

She was back in minutes, plopping down on the couch between us.

"Hey, Mom, if I get an A in maths this semester, can I get my hair dyed like Ruben Bensch?" Oscar pointed at the television, where Bensch was now yelling in painful disharmony with the rest of the band.

"Absolutely not." Mom stared at the screen in mild disgust. "That's unnatural. You'd scare the shit out of Luci."

"Too late," I said, grinning as Oscar scowled. "He's already improvised a new ending to 'Handel and Gretchen'."

Mom frowned at him. "No more not-so-happy endings, Oscar. Not while that real-life monster is still on the loose."

And this time I didn't think it was just Luci that was scared.

My alarm went off at 6 p.m., as usual, and I started to smack the snooze button. But then I remembered Mom had to work early again – on weekdays she answered phones and fetched luke-warm white cells for an attorney downtown – and I would need to wake Oscar up and get Luci ready for school. So I rolled over and glanced at the sliver of light shining through the crack in my shutters.

It dimmed a little more each second. Dusk was well under-way, and by the time I'd showered it would probably be safe to open the shutters and wake Luci with a healthy dose of moonlight.

Oscar would just get the overhead bulb flipped on as I passed his room.

Twenty minutes later I ran a brush through my dripping hair on my way to Luci's room. Next door, Oscar was groaning and mumbling because I'd thrown his pillow into the hall when he tried to use it to block the light from his face.

"Luciiiiinda . . ." I sang softly, walking past her bed to the window. Luci rolled over and pulled up her blanket. I flipped the latch on her shutters and folded them back to reveal a beautiful starlit night beyond the glass. "Come on, Luce! Time to get up."

As I twisted the switch on her lamp, my baby sister sat up reluctantly, blinking huge blue eyes at me, her irises so pale they were nearly colourless. I'd always been jealous of those eyes. Mine had more colour than was fashionable. But then, so did my hair. Luci and Oscar had nearly translucent curls, like our mother. But my hair was so dark and coarse it was practically yellow. It was my father's hair, and every time I saw it I remembered him. And wondered where in the hell he was.

He'd been gone for three years, and Luci barely remembered him.

"Come on, hon, let's get you dressed and fed before we have to fight Oscar for the bathroom mirror."

I dressed her in two layers, because the note Mom had left on the fridge said it would probably dip below freezing near midnight. Again. I was so ready for spring, in spite of the shorter nights it would bring.

With Luci clothed, pigtailed and at least half awake, I aimed her at her usual chair in the kitchen and continued to the fridge, from which I pulled a package of sausage links and a carton of eggs. The sausages I stuck in the microwave, set to a precise 98.6 degrees. A degree cooler, and Luci wouldn't eat them.

While the sausage warmed, I made breakfast smoothies. One egg and whole blood for Luci; two eggs and red cells only for me. I was watching my waistline.

Oscar joined us several minutes later, his curls straightened into the usual white points. He topped two slices of toast with congealed pig blood and popped open a can of platelets.

I turned the television on while we ate. The evening anchor for *Headline News* appeared on screen, listing the top stories of the night. The first one, naturally, was the charred body found in the mall parking lot.

Sometime during the afternoon, she'd been positively identified as Phoebe Hayes, and with the confirmation of her identity had come the first break in the case. Two of Hayes' classmates had seen her get into an unfamiliar, pale-blue sedan after school on Monday morning.

I nearly choked on my smoothie when the screen showed her school photograph. I'd known the Hayes girl was only nine – the morning anchor had said that much – but somehow, seeing her staring at me as I ate my breakfast made the reality much harder to accept. Or even comprehend.

"I don't like sausage." Luci poked at one untouched link with her fork.

"You liked them yesterday," I said, my glass halfway to my mouth. And suddenly I was glad her chair faced away from the television.

"Today they're gross." Luci rolled her meat into a thin puddle of blood. "I don't like them cold."

I rolled my eyes and speared a link of my own. "They were warm when I got them out of the microwave." My gaze wandered over her head to the screen, where the reporter was giving a brief bio of the dead girl.

Phoebe Hayes was a fourth-grader at an elementary school across town. Luci couldn't possibly have known her, which meant I wouldn't have to explain the ritualistic murder of small children to her in our mother's absence. Thank goodness.

"You want some toast?" Oscar held his last slice out to her.

Luci's eyes lit up, and she dropped her fork on her plate. "Yeah. But no pig's blood. I like lamb. Smooth, not chunky."

Oscar just stared at her for a moment. Then he shoved the last of his breakfast into his mouth and got up to fill her special order. Mom would have made her eat the sausage. But Mom wasn't there, which was probably part of the problem.

I pulled into the student lot, braked to avoid some idiot on rolling shoes and parked in my assigned spot. The lot was illuminated by at least a dozen, huge, automatic lights, beneath which students loitered in groups, bundled against the plummeting temperature.

"Look at them," Oscar spat, staring out the windshield. "Like bugs drawn to the light."

I followed his gaze to the largest gathering, a loose knot of students clustered around Amelia Garrison and her new car. No one was obviously fawning, but everyone seemed to find a reason to touch the car, or talk to Amelia.

"It's disgusting," Oscar continued, shoving a textbook into the backpack propped between his feet. "And the worst part is that it isn't really their fault. We're biologically programmed to be attracted to a certain physical ideal, to a combination of features that speaks to us on a cellular level, telling us a potential mate is healthy, and will probably produce healthy children."

I blinked at my socially challenged brother. What kind of twelve-year-old talked about biological programming and healthy offspring? "You know, *this* is why people make fun of you. It's not because you're short; it's because you're weird."

He scowled. "I'm serious. I mean, *look* at her."

I looked.

Like the rest of us, Amelia had the usual pale hair, skin and eyes – all the result of millions of years of darkness gradually eliminating our need for pigment. But Amelia Garrison was the embodiment of that evolutionary ideal. There was less than a shade's difference between her irises and the whites of her eyes, and her hair was practically clear. To emphasize that enviable trait, she brushed some kind of glittery gel through her mane every morning, so that she virtually glowed beneath any light that shone on her. Rumour had it she'd even had her fangs surgically augmented. I wasn't prepared to swear by that bit of gossip, but I knew for a fact that her cuspids hadn't been that long – or that *white* – the year before.

"You're just jealous." I shoved my car door open, and bitterly cold air curled around my ankles.

"I'm not jealous. I feel sorry for them. They don't even realize they're at the mercy of urges and instincts they can't control. I'd rather take a morning stroll than run that particular rat race."

No wonder Oscar wanted to dye his hair when everyone else was bleaching. Not to blend in, but to stand out. To separate himself from a world he both envied and despised.

"Just do me a favour and don't say stuff like that where anyone can hear you." I did *not* want to have to rescue him from another pounding.

"You think I'm stupid?" He lifted one pale brow, then shoved his own door open, tossing his bag over one shoulder. "Don't wait for me after school. I've got science club."

"You got a ride home?" I slammed my door and eyed him over the roof of the car.

"I can find one."

I frowned for a moment, then nodded, knowing damn well that his ride would come from the faculty adviser, not from any fellow student. "OK."

He took off towards the building and I grabbed my backpack from the rear floorboard, glancing at the seat to make sure Luci hadn't forgotten her lunch when I'd dropped her off.

The back seat was empty except for my phone, which I grabbed and flipped open. The display said I'd missed a call from Titus ten minutes earlier. But my phone never rang. I started to call him back, then spotted him walking across the lot towards me.

I kicked the back door shut and shoved my keys into my pocket, dropping my bag higher on one shoulder as I leaned against the car.

"Evening, beautiful." Titus dropped his bag next to mine and bent down for a kiss.

I pressed myself against him, loving the contrast between the delicious warmth of his body and the cold metal at my back. His lips met mine and I opened for him, everything else forgotten with his taste in my mouth, his tongue teasing mine.

The points of his fangs brushed my lip, not hard enough to break the skin, but firm enough to threaten. A thrill shot up my spine, tingling all the way into my fingertips at the hint of danger. At the possibility those barbs – those evolutionary remnants – represented.

Kissing Titus gave me biological urges Oscar wouldn't understand for several more years. They made me want to do things (to let Titus do things) that I'd told Luci were unacceptable.

And in polite society, they were.

But we weren't in polite society. We were in the grip of a desire untempered by age, unspoiled by experience. And from the perspective of youth and passion, with the tips of his fangs on my skin, the cravings of our ancestors didn't seem quite so savage.

They seemed . . . *yummy*. The most pre-eminent delicacy and the ultimate penetration all rolled into one. But we'd resisted the urges, content with teasing each other so far, because the taboo was inescapable, with good reason: psychos like the Midday Mangler had rendered the consumption of fresh blood forever synonymous with brutality, debauchery and death.

Those bastards really ruined it for the rest of us.

Finally, Titus pulled away, and I let him reluctantly. "You know you're the only reason I come to school," he said, his voice gruff with need, as his hand wandered up from my waist.

I smiled and pushed his hand down. "After school." I grabbed my bag and tugged him towards the building. "Hey, did you call me?" I asked, as he fell in next to me.

"Yeah, before bed this morning. And thanks for returning the call, by the way. It could have been an emergency." He smiled to let me know he was joking and I shoved him with the hand still holding my phone.

"Whatever. I just got the missed call. What'd you need?"

"A summary of chapter fifteen in the history book." A stray chunk of white hair fell into Titus' face as he blinked at me innocently.

I rolled my eyes at him, well aware that I was a big sucker. "Worldwide economic ramifications of Global Conflict the Second. It's mostly just the same stuff she talked about yesterday in class."

"Yeah, and if I hadn't slept through that, I might have some idea what you're talking about."

"That's what you get for playing video games all day instead of sleeping."

"Sleep is overrated." He pulled open the front door and held it for me as I passed under his arm, then glanced back at him, smiling.

"Well, passing grades aren't."

The rest of the night was uneventful. Boring, even. So when the last bell rang, I was ready for a little excitement.

Titus didn't have a car, so I drove to his house (his parents wouldn't be home until shortly before dawn). My shirt hit the floor the minute the front door closed behind us. My pants lasted until we got to the hall, and my bra fell onto the dresser as I passed it on the way to Titus' bed. I dropped my phone on the nightstand and turned to look at him.

He was still dressed, because I liked to help him out of his clothes. It was like unwrapping a present. A very yummy present. And I was never very careful with the wrapping.

His lips found mine as we fell onto the bed, my head sinking into a soft feather pillow that smelled like his shampoo. He held himself up with one hand, while the other roamed my body with frustrating self-control.

I wasn't so patient.

My eager fingers urged him on. My body arched into his touch. My mouth sucked at his, my tongue flicking lightly over the points of his fangs, teasing us both. All it would take was a little bit of pressure. Just a scratch. Somehow I knew that a single drop of my blood in his mouth would be all the prelude either of us needed.

Titus pulled away from my mouth, staring down at me with heat smouldering behind his nearly white eyes. "Do you want to?"

He'd asked before – he was a guy, after all – but never like this. Of course, I'd never spent quite so much time molesting his cuspids before, either.

I thought about it. I mean, I *really* thought about it. Part of me did want to. Rumour had it that several girls in the senior class had tried it. Just a drop was supposedly enough to make run-of-the-mill sex extraordinary. If it could do *that* for pedestrian lovers, what could it do for us? Because *ordinary* had never been our problem.

But in the end, I couldn't do it. The idea of bloodletting was *incredibly* hot. Erotic. But that was in part because it was taboo. And it was taboo for a reason.

I shook my head, and Titus smiled. He was OK with waiting, because he viewed every no as temporary, and I was never inclined to argue with that assumption. It had held up so far.

He kissed me again, exploring my mouth with renewed eagerness, as if to assure me he was OK with my decision. My fingers trailed down his back as he positioned himself over me. His muscles flexed beneath my hands. His knee parted my thighs and my legs wrapped around him.

My eyes closed as he entered me. That part was new enough to still be special. And as we moved against each other, I knew I wanted it to always be like that. Always special. And always Titus.

He made a sound of contentment against my cheek as he withdrew, only to plunge forwards again, grinding against me with delicious earnestness, and . . .

My phone chirped, signalling a new voice message.

"Ignore it," he begged, watching me as he withdrew again.

"I can't." I reached for the phone, and he groaned, collapsing against me to one side. "Sorry. Oscar's ride probably fell through." I selected the new message and held the phone to my ear, more than a little excited by the knowledge that Titus was still inside me while I performed so routine a task as checking my voicemail.

There was a new message from my mother. Only it sounded like she'd actually left it at least a couple of hours earlier.

"Keziah, I have an office meeting late this morning, so I need you to pick up Luci from school. Love you, sweetheart, and thanks!"

"Dammit!" I shoved Titus off me harder than I'd meant to, and winced at his hurt expression. "Sorry, but I have to go."

The elementary school got out ten minutes earlier than the high school, and Titus and I had been at his house for at least fifteen minutes after the last bell, which meant Luci had been on her own for almost half an hour. She probably thought we'd all forgotten her.

"What's wrong?" Titus asked, pulling me close.

"I gotta go get my sister, and I'm already late."

The disappointment on his face was blatant, and more than a little flattering. I smiled to soften the blow. "I'm sorry." I pulled my boots on in front of the door and grabbed my keys from the floor where I'd dropped them. "But hey, my mom won't be home before dinner. Meet me at my house in twenty minutes, and I'll get Oscar to watch Luci."

He nodded reluctantly, and I kissed him on the way out of the door. I jogged down the driveway to my car, deftly avoiding several solid sheets of black ice. My clunker protested with a mechanical groan when I slammed the gearshift into reverse and stomped on the gas.

The crosswalk in front of the gym barely registered as I drove through it, and a girl in tight jeans and a puffy, quilted jacket leaped back onto the sidewalk just in time to avoid my front bumper. She hissed and bared her fangs at me as I roared past. I silently cursed my second-hand cell phone.

*If Dad had stuck around, we could afford shit that actually works!*

I wasn't really worried about Luci getting lost. Her school was only four blocks from our house, and she'd been driven that route every school day for the last year and a half. But it was awfully cold, and she always forgot to zip her coat. And if she got sick, Mom would have to take time off work to watch her all night, which meant her cheque would be short next month.

However, as I drove, our financial worries slipped to the back of my mind, replaced by a much grimmer possibility. What if something went wrong? Six years old was too young to walk home alone, even in a kid's own neighbourhood. Especially with some psycho out there draining children and exposing their bodies to fry at dawn.

Suddenly my errand seemed much more urgent, even as I told myself that she was fine. There was no way the school would let her walk home alone.

I ran two stop signs and one yellow light on my way to the elementary school and, when I finally got there, my heart seemed to sink into my stomach, anchored by fear. The parking lot at the rear of the school was where kids usually waited for their parents. They stood on the sidewalk next to the building, watched over by a selection of teachers until their parents' car made it to the front of the line wrapping around the school.

But when I got there, there was no queue of cars and no children lined up on the sidewalk. Instead, a single adult presided over at least a dozen kids fighting for a basketball lit from within by a flashing LED.

I didn't bother inspecting the children. The lot was well lit and Luci was not among the players. Even if I hadn't known what she was wearing – and I *did* since I had dressed her myself – I knew she hated basketball.

My keys jangled as I pulled them from the ignition and shoved them into my front pocket. I kicked the car door shut and crossed my arms over my chest to hold my jacket closed as I ran across the narrow strip of crunchy grass and shoved open the rear entrance.

The halls were a maze of mostly closed doors and walls covered in student artwork. An antiseptic smell permeated the air as the custodians cleaned in the children's absence, and it took every bit of self-control I had left to keep from running full-out to the front of the school.

I settled on a fast walk instead, my shoes squeaking on the tile, my heart pounding at least three beats per step. Logically, I knew Luci was most likely perfectly safe. Probably sitting in a chair in the principal's office, snacking on whatever they had handy, filling in pages in a colouring book. But every moment that passed without Luci throwing herself into my arms and pouting over how late I was, deepened the sense of panic rapidly tightening my chest.

Something was wrong. I was sure of it.

I rounded the last corner and the office came into sight, its two windows covered by white mini-blinds, blocking the view from within. I jogged the last eight feet and pulled the office door open much harder than I'd intended to.

Inside, all heads turned my way. Two secretaries stood between a tall credenza and a broad, dark window with a view of the front parking lot. In one corner, a teacher's aide was making photocopies on an ancient, rumbling machine. But there was no little girl with soft white curls. The child-size bench across one wall was empty.

"Lucinda Cartwright," I said, panting from exertion I hadn't even felt until that moment. "Where's Luci Cartwright?"

"She's . . ." One secretary looked to the other for assistance, tapping a stack of papers on her desk to even the edges, then turned back to me when the other woman merely shrugged. "She's gone. All the children have gone for the day except for the after-care kids playing ball outside."

*Oh shit.* Fear traced my veins like ice, and my panic suddenly felt justified. "Where'd she go?" I demanded, laying my palms flat on the credenza, crinkling a volunteer sign-up sheet.

"I don't . . ." That same secretary looked to the aide then, whose tag read "MS CYNTHIA".

Cynthia cleared her throat and flashed small, delicate fangs in a smile designed to placate small children and calm worried parents. I was neither, and her smile didn't do jack-shit for me.

"She was picked up with the other children, about fifteen minutes ago," Cynthia said.

I turned my full attention to Ms Cynthia, whose left index finger now hovered over a green button on the photocopy machine.

"Who picked her up?"

"I didn't see." She shrugged. "But she was gone before the last student left."

My hands clenched at my sides and my jaw tightened. "You don't *know* what happened to a six-year-old placed in your care?" She started to answer, but I cut her off. "So, you either let her wander off on her own, or you sent her home with someone who didn't have permission to pick her up. I know this because my mother and I are the only ones who have permission to take Luci from school, and *she* just called and asked *me* to do it. So for the last time, *where is my sister?*"

"I don't know," Cynthia finally admitted, her copies now forgotten.

*Damn it.* I spun towards the secretaries again and felt my upper lip curl back from my teeth, exposing my fangs in what I hoped was an obvious and terrifying threat. "Call the police." No one moved, so I slammed my hands down on the desk again. "Now!"

The secretaries jumped, and one snatched the phone from its cradle, already dialling when I whirled on the aide in the corner. "My mother works for one of the largest law firms in the state, and if anything happens to my sister, she'll name you *personally* in a lawsuit. By the time her boss is done with you, you'll wish you were born on a beach at high noon."

With that, I pulled the door open so hard it slammed into the wall, and I was racing through the halls again. There was no time to be awed by my own nerve, because I was busy being amazed by their incompetence.

How could they let a first-grader just wander away?

With any luck, she'd simply walked home on her own. I'd go home, and she'd be on the couch, munching on blood pudding and watching cartoons. Or maybe she hadn't made it home yet. Maybe I could still catch her . . .

The back door of the school slammed shut behind me, and heads turned my way from the basketball court, where another aide was now rounding up the children to herd them inside. Moonlight glinted off the windshield of my car – the only one in the lot – as I pulled open the door and slid behind the wheel. I backed out carefully, watching for stray children in the red glow from my tail lights.

I went one block east then turned and flicked on my high beams, driving slowly as I scanned both sides of the road for Luci. I saw several children, most a little older than my sister and walking alongside older siblings or parents. They were bundled against the cold, their faces blurred by the darkness, except where the streetlights shone. But by the time I was two blocks from home, they had all reached their houses and gone inside, except for one trio of kids playing flashlight tag several yards down.

The street was practically deserted, as if people knew something bad was coming. The tightness in my chest had spread to both arms, filling me with an impending sense of danger, as if dawn loomed just over the horizon.

But the clock in my dashboard said it wasn't quite three in the morning, and we had nearly four blessed hours of darkness before the sun would blaze a trail across the city, chasing everyone inside.

A block and a half from home, movement on the opposite sidewalk caught my eye, something flashing in the edge of the glare from my headlights.

I squinted, looking closer, and a small form came into focus. She had long white curls and wore pair of fuzzy pink pants with lace around the hem. *Luci*. Thank goodness. The flash was from the silver bangle our father had given her the month before he'd left, as if he were already planning to disappear. I hadn't seen her slip that on last night, but that was no surprise. She wasn't allowed to wear it to school because Mom was afraid she'd lose it, but Luci had snuck it into her backpack more than once.

And I'd never been more thankful for her willingness to break the rules.

I rolled down the driver's side window and stuck my face into the shocking cold. My mouth was open to shout her name when another car turned the corner from the opposite side of the street. It drove between us, and I waited for it to pass.

But it didn't pass.

The car slowed, and finally stopped in front of Luci. I could barely see her pigtails through the other car's windshield. The man behind the wheel leaned across the seat and said something to my sister that I couldn't hear. A second later, her head bobbed. The man shifted into park, slid across the seat and leaned back to open the rear door.

To my absolute horror, Luci climbed inside. And that's when I noticed the colour of the car. It was a light-blue, four-door sedan.

"No!" I shouted through my open window, and the man looked up. For a moment, his eyes met mine from 100 feet away. Then he slid back across the seat and shoved the car into drive. He hit the gas, and the car rolled forwards.

It happened too fast. I couldn't think. But I saw Luci very clearly. She waved to me from the back seat, her smile wide, tiny white fangs glinting in my high beams.

*No!* I stomped on the accelerator and twisted the steering wheel to the left as hard as I could. My car lurched across the street, perpendicular to the road, and hit a light pole. My skull bounced off the headrest and my forehead smacked the wheel. An instant later, the other car smashed into my passenger side, and this time the side of my skull hit the window.

I'd been T-boned in the middle of the street by what could only be the Midday Mangler, a block and a half from home. Where, I realized hazily, Titus' car sat in the driveway.

Trying to clear my vision, I shook my head and fumbled with the handle until the car door swung open. I was up in a flash, wobbling as I ran around the rear of my car to where my passenger side was now bent around the other car's much stronger grill.

Screams split the air behind me, and seemed to cleave my throbbing head in half. The kids playing flashlight tag. Their footsteps pounded on concrete and a door slammed shut. Distantly, I heard them yelling for their mother.

"Let her go!" I shouted at the driver, but my voice sounded weak and frail. I'd hit my head hard – twice – and my vision was blurry. There were two Lucis staring at me now, their identical mouths open in surprise and fear, and two kidnappers, both of whom were shoving open a double set of driver's side doors.

My vision finally merged, and the Midday Mangler stood in front of me, tall enough that I had to crane my neck to see him. He flashed yellowish teeth and a stained set of fangs in the instant before his fist flew. I barely had time to register the motion before it met my head.

Then everything went blissfully, frightfully dark. And quiet.

I woke up with Luci. That was the upside. The *only* upside, in fact. Luci was crying and shaking me and my cheek was wet with her tears.

"Kez, wake up!" she sobbed, and I opened my eyes to see her face hovering over mine. For a moment, I couldn't remember where we were, or how we'd got there. But then the throbbing in my head slammed into agonizing focus and I remembered the driver of the other car, who'd apparently knocked me out.

"Calm down, Luce." I pushed myself into a sitting position and let my head rest against the cold wall at my back. "What happened? Where are we?"

"I don't knoooowww!" she howled, shoving damp white curls back from her face. "Nobody got me after school so I walked home and a man said Daddy told him to pick me up and bring me to him, so I got in the car 'cause I miss Daddy."

The Mangler had certainly gotten lucky with *that* line.

"Then I saw you, and the man's car hit your car, and you got out and you were walking funny, and the man *hit* you! And you fell dooowwwwnnn!" Her terrified summary dissolved into even more terrified tears, and I pulled her close, taking in our surroundings for the first time.

We sat on thin, rough carpet in a small, empty room with solid white walls. The only window was covered in what looked like steel shutters, padlocked shut. No beam of light split them. It was still dark.

I reached into my pocket for my phone. I was irate – though not really surprised – to find it gone. "Where did the man go?" I asked, eyeing the door.

Luci wiped tears from her face with the tail of her shirt. Her jacket lay on the floor, wadded up as if she'd used it for a pillow. "I don't know. He put you in here and said if I didn't go in the room with you, he'd k-kill you. Then he closed the door. I tried to open it, but it's locked."

Of course it was locked. If he would lock the shutters, he'd lock the door. But I checked anyways, just in case.

The door wasn't just locked; it was bolted. I could probably have broken a flimsy twist-lock, but I could do nothing against the deadbolt.

I inspected the window next. The shutters were steel, as were the hinges. And the padlock. We weren't going anywhere until someone let us out.

Unfortunately, having seen the news recently, I was pretty sure I knew what would happen then.

I bit my tongue to keep from frightening Luci with a display of my anger and fear. Then I sat against the wall and she curled up with her head on my lap. I covered her with her coat and stared at the door, willing it to open.

I needed a plan.

But even worse than that, I needed a weapon.

The next couple of hours passed very slowly. I heard nothing from outside our prison room and, as far as I knew, whatever house we were in was completely empty besides us.

But even worse than the silence, broken only by Luci's gentle sleep-breathing, was the steady lightening I could see between the halves of the shutter. At first I thought I was imagining it. But as the minutes continued to slip through my fingers, I knew it was real. Time had not stopped, and dawn would come.

And I was pretty sure we'd have a fantastic view.

Around 6.45 a.m. (based on the colour of that murky splinter of light), something creaked outside our room. A door opening, or maybe closing. Either way, we were no longer alone.

"Luce, wake up," I whispered, but she only turned over. I shook her shoulder, and she groaned, her eyelids fluttering. "Wake up, Luci. Someone's here."

She blinked at up at me. "Kez? What . . . ?" Comprehension surfaced behind her eyes and she sat up so fast her forehead hit my chin, snapping my teeth together. Her hand clenched around mine in terror, and she started to shake. I don't know how much she'd heard about the dead children the police had found – four so far within a fifty-mile radius of the city – but she knew we were in danger, even if she didn't know precisely how much.

"It's OK." I stroked her hair as I'd seen our mother do. Then I set her on her feet and stood between her and the door. "Just stay behind me." I had no idea what I was going to do, but if we were going to die, I would do my best to take that kidnapping, child-murdering bastard with us.

Floorboards creaked beyond our room as footsteps grew closer. Then metal scraped wood as the deadbolt was pulled back slowly. The doorknob turned, and Luci's teeth began to chatter behind me. Her hands gripped the tail of my shirt, pulling it taut around me. I reached back with one hand and patted her, comforting her as best I could with that brief contact.

The door swung open. The Mangler stood in the doorway, framed by what little I could see of the room beyond. He wore jeans and a dark sweatshirt. And he held a gun.

The gasp at my back said Luci had peeked.

"I'm sorry for the pistol." The man waved the gun at me. "It seems so impersonal, I know, but you were a bit of a surprise, and I wasn't sure how much trouble you'd be."

I remained silent, unwilling to converse with our captor.

"I started to simply get rid of you – after all, your *vintage* is a bit aged for my average customer – but then I realized I might have a use for you after all." His eyes wandered south of my neck, and I shuddered in revulsion.

"Not gonna happen."

"Oh?" The man smiled, again showing me his stained teeth. I couldn't suppress a chill at the knowledge that the latest discolourations had probably come from Phoebe Hayes' veins. "Then I guess I can skip the pleasantries and just shoot you right here. In front of your sister."

Luci sobbed behind me, clinging even tighter to my shirt. "No," I said, at least as much for her as for me. I did not want my death to be the last thing she saw.

The man stepped to one side and motioned towards the larger room behind him. "After you."

I turned and knelt beside Luci, tilting her chin up until her eyes met mine. "It'll be OK," I said, desperately hoping I wasn't lying to her. "Just stay here until I get back. OK?"

She nodded, tears trailing down her face, and I hated that bastard all the more for scaring her. If I got a chance, he was gonna pay.

"Come on." The man grabbed my arm and hauled me backwards, away from Luci, who cried harder. He shoved me out of the door into what should have been a family room, but came closer to resembling a torture chamber. "See that?" He tossed his head towards the centre of the room where an odd metal table took up most of the floor space. I recognized it from a special on the forensics channel. It was a fucking *autopsy* table.

*What kind of sick freak has an autopsy table in his living room?*

"That's where we drain the little morsel and bottle the contents to be shipped all over the world. They go for quite a pretty penny online. But I get to sample the product first. Quality control, you know." His eyes gleamed with excitement, and my stomach roiled.

"You psychotic bastard!" My fist slammed into his head before I'd even realized it was in motion. My vision blurred with fury and unspent tears, and I could think of nothing but beating him senseless, grabbing Luci and running for our lives.

I hit him again, but I'd lost the element of surprise, and this time my fist only glanced his left cheek. Dimly, through the glaze of my wrath, I saw him raise the gun.

But then something else streaked across my vision: a small, pastel-coloured blur, moving fast and furious.

*Luci.*

A primal shriek tore free from her pink flower of a mouth, and she ran with her arms outstretched.

"Luci, no!" I thought she'd go for a direct hit – like tackling Oscar when they wrestled – and she stood no chance of knocking over a grown man. But she grabbed his wrist instead, mere inches above the hand holding the gun.

Her small hand wrapped around his arm, her grip white with tension. Her head dipped. Her mouth flew open, tiny fangs bared. Her expression was vicious, and her teeth were all business.

She clamped her mouth onto his wrist and bit down so hard that the delicate muscles in her jaw bulged with the strain.

The Mangler screamed. He let go of me and shoved at Luci's head, his other hand still somehow clenching the gun by its grip. "Let go, you little demon!" he shouted.

She tossed her head, her mouth still clamped onto his wrist, and finally the gun thumped to the carpet. I wanted to grab it, but it had fallen behind them and I couldn't get past. So instead I jumped onto his back and wrapped both arms around his neck, letting my weight choke him.

He stumbled backwards with the pressure on his windpipe and tore his arm from Luci's grasp. Blood poured everywhere, arcing from his ruined wrist onto the floor until he clamped his free hand over the wound.

And still he screamed.

The Mangler stepped back again, swinging around wildly, trying to dislodge me without letting go of his other arm. He couldn't do it. But he didn't have to. The first time he slammed me back into the wall, pain shot through my spine. The second time, I nearly passed out.

The third time, he brought both arms up and used his free hand to prise my arms from his neck. We were both slick with his blood by then, and I could barely hold on to him.

With my grip broken, I slid to the floor. He spun and kicked me in the ribs. I crumpled to the carpet in the fetal position. When my eyes opened, I saw my sister standing in the bedroom doorway staring at me, her face streaked with tears and blood, both trailing to her ruined shirt.

"Run, Luci!" I shouted. Only it came out more like a whisper, because he'd kicked most of the air from my lungs.

But she heard me.

Luci nodded once, then took off across the living room, on the opposite side of the autopsy table. The Mangler started to lunge after her, but I grabbed his foot. He went down hard, smacking his wounded arm on the edge of the metal table. I could tell at a glance that it was broken.

Luci twisted the deadbolt and threw open the front door, then screamed and recoiled in horror. I didn't have to look up to see the problem. Light had poured in the moment she'd opened the door.

The sun was up, and we had nowhere to run. We were stuck inside some psychotic gingerbread house with a wicked witch who just happened to have a bad case of five a.m. shadow.

"Hide!" I shouted, with what little breath I'd regained. But Luci didn't move. She cowered behind an armchair, the only normal piece of living-room furniture I'd seen so far. It was the only thing between Luci and a deadly dose of morning sunshine.

The rays shone in through the glass storm door, over and around the chair, passing a scant three inches above her hair. If we didn't close the door before the sun got much higher, her curls would start to smoke.

At her age, even indirect UV light stung and a direct hit would blacken her skin in seconds.

I could take a little more, but not much.

On the floor the man moaned and shoved himself to his feet with his good arm. That got me moving. I tiptoed around the edge of the room, sticking to the shadows. I was almost to Luci when a hand tangled in my hair from behind and jerked me back. I staggered, but he held me up.

"OK, bitch, let's see how well you tan."

He shoved me forwards, towards the front door. Light fell across my feet, and I was more grateful than ever for my boots, even if they didn't give me much purchase on the carpet.

Another shove and the light slanted up my jeans. I had to

throw my arms into the air to keep them above the rising line of light. One more push and I'd be extra crispy.

"Kez!" Luci shouted from behind us. That was all the motivation I needed. I was *not* going to let my sister see me fried alive.

I threw my arm back, hissing when heat raced across my exposed hands. My elbow connected with the Mangler's ribs, and he grunted, caught by surprise. I swung myself around and pulled him with me, shoving him between myself and the glass door.

He screamed, and smoke rose from the back of his neck. His good hand scrambled for a grip on my arm, but we were both slick with the blood Luci had drawn from him.

I threw my leg up and kicked him in the chest as hard as I could. He flew backwards and crashed through the glass door onto the porch. When he tried to get up, smoking all over by now, he tripped and fell down the steps into a viciously sunny patch of light.

My hands still burning, I swung the wooden door closed and slid the bolt into place. I watched through the keyhole as the Mangler burst into flames. Only then could I look away. Only once I was sure he wasn't getting back up.

That's when I let myself slide to the floor, my back against the solid wood standing between me and an agonizing death. "Come here, Luce," I whispered, and she looked up hesitantly. "It's OK. Come here."

Luci crawled to me and climbed into my lap. She put her head on my shoulder and looked up into my face, now just as tear-streaked as hers. "Is he . . . gone?"

"Gone for good, hon." I hugged her as tight as I could, only relaxing my grip when she yelped. "Now we just have to find a phone—" I had a feeling mine was gone for good "—and wait for the police." But we wouldn't have to wait long; the first sirens were already wailing in the distance, probably summoned by one of the horrified neighbours who would later tell reporters that the Mangler had seemed so *normal*.

Outside, a car door slammed. The sirens weren't close enough yet. My pulse jumped, and I clutched Luci harder.

"Kez! Are you in there?" a familiar voice shouted. I gasped, and my heart beat in excitement and disbelief now.

I stood and pulled Luci with me as I peered out of the peephole, squinting against the cruel daylight. A figure stood on the sidewalk between the Mangler's charred corpse and Titus' beat-up compact, parked on the street. He was covered from head to foot in a purple cape with a deep hood and huge dark glasses covering his face.

"Step back," I said, guiding Luci behind the door as I opened it and stepped aside with her. "Titus?"

He stepped over the body and raced up the walk, pulling open the busted glass door. The first cop car arrived, followed immediately by several more and an ambulance, as Titus stepped inside and swung the door almost closed. He pulled his hood and glasses off in the safety of the shadowed interior, and his eyes relaxed the moment they met mine. "I thought that bastard had killed you."

"Nope, but not for lack of try–" I never got to say the rest, because his lips met mine, sucking the words right out of me. Along with my breath.

When he finally pulled away, I frowned at him, as the commotion rose outside. "How did you find us?" I asked, my hand on his arm. I wasn't willing to stop touching him. Ever.

"Police scanner," he said, tossing his head over his shoulder in the direction of his car. "I heard the address, and I guess I was closer than the nearest units. So, what the hell happened?"

Luci tugged on my sleeve then, and we glanced down at her to see her looking up at Titus. "I bit him," she said. "Just like the witch in Oscar's story."

And I'd cooked the son of a bitch, just like the witch in our mother's version.

"That's right, hon." I stroked her hair back in spite of the pain in my hands, streaking it with blood neither of us had lost. "You did great."

She smiled at us then, and her teeth were smeared with blood, dainty little fangs and all.

Vestigial, my ass, I thought. Then I started to laugh, and was still laughing when the first cops burst through the door.

# The Music of the Night

## Amanda Ashley

Cristie Matthews couldn't believe it, she was actually inside the Paris Opera House. It was everything she had ever imagined, and more. Try as she might, she couldn't find words to describe it. Beautiful seemed woefully inadequate. Awesome came close, but still fell short.

She owed her fascination with the Paris Opera House solely to Andrew Lloyd Webber – or to be more exact – to her fascination with his amazing production *The Phantom of the Opera*. She had seen the movie, of course, but it didn't hold a candle to the stage play. She had seen the play once, and once had not been enough. The music had enthralled her; the plight of the Phantom had touched her every emotion from joy to despair, and she had eagerly joined the ranks of those who saw the play again and again, never tiring of it, always feeling emotionally drained when the Phantom's last anguished cry faded away.

She had become obsessed with all things Phantom. She had collected everything she could find with that world-famous logo: music boxes and posters, ads in the paper, books and magazine articles. If it related to the Phantom, she simply had to have it: dolls and figurines; snow globes and playing cards; picture frames and jewellery; Christmas ornaments and collector plates; every version of the music on tape or CD that she could find.

Before coming to Paris, she had researched the Opera House online and found a wealth of information. The Opera House had been built by Charles Garnier (at that time a young, unknown architect). Completed in 1876, the Palais Garnier was considered by many to be one of the most beautiful buildings on earth. The theatre boasted 2,000 seats; the building's seventeen storeys covered three acres of land. Seven levels were located underground, among them chorus rooms and ballrooms, cellars for old props, closets and dressing rooms, as well as numerous gruesome objects from the various operas that had been produced there. It was rumoured that these grisly effects had sparked the idea behind Gaston Leroux's *The Phantom of the Opera*.

And now, after scrimping and saving for three years, she was there, in the Phantom's domain. Alone. Shortly after the final curtain, she had hidden in one of the bathrooms. If she got caught wandering around, she would simply say she had lost her way.

Which would not be a lie, because she really was lost. There were so many hallways, so many doors, she no longer knew where she was.

Her footsteps echoed eerily in the darkness as she climbed a set of winding stairs and then, to her relief, she found herself inside the theatre.

She sank into a seat near the back of the house and gazed around, wondering if this had been such a good idea after all. It was dark and quiet and a little bit spooky sitting there all alone.

Resting her head on the back of the seat, she closed her eyes and music filled her mind – the haunting lyrics of "The Music of the Night"; the Phantom's tortured cry when he sees Christine and Raoul pledging their love on the roof top; his heartbreaking plea when he begs Christine to let him go wherever she went; his anguished cry as he takes her down to his lair; his rage and anger and the faint glimmer of hope when he demands she make her choice; the last haunting notes when he declares it is over.

There was a never-ending discussion on any number of web sites about whether Christine should have stayed with the Phantom, and also surveys asking whether the listers themselves would have stayed with Erik (the Phantom) or gone with Raoul. Poor Raoul, he seemed to be disliked by one and all.

There had never been any doubt in Cristie's mind that she would have stayed with the Phantom. She knew what it was like to be left for another, knew the pain and the heartache of unrequited love, knew there was more to life than sweet words and a pretty face.

Sitting there, with her eyes closed, she seemed to hear Christine's voice, but of course, it was only her imagination.

Still, it seemed so real. Opening her eyes, Cristie stared at the stage, blinked and looked again. Was there a figure standing there? A figure wearing a hooded cloak and a red scarf? Cristie rubbed her eyes. Not one figure, but two. A dark shape wearing a black hat with a long, curling black feather stood beside the cross on the cemetery wall. A long black cloak covered him from neck to heels. Was that a staff in his hand? Canting her head to one side, Cristie heard him sing ever so softly and sweetly to his wandering child.

Cristie sat up straighter and leaned forwards. It wasn't possible. She had to be dreaming. She rubbed her eyes again. The figure of Christine seemed transparent, ghost-like, but the Phantom . . . She was certain he was real.

Fear sat like a lump of ice in her belly, and then she realized that what she was seeing was probably just some star-struck member of the cleaning crew, or a night watch-man wearing one of the Phantom's costumes, or . . . Of course, it was an understudy who had stayed late to rehearse. It was the logical explanation, except it didn't explain the ghostly Christine.

Suddenly, echoing through the empty building came the Phantom's cry of rage as Christine turned her back on him and left with Raoul. Fireballs spit from the Phantom's staff to light the stage and the image of Christine disappeared. But the figure of the Phantom remained standing near the cross, his shoulders slumped in defeat, his head bowed.

It had always been one of her favourite scenes, one that had never failed to move her to tears. This performance by some unknown actor was no different. With a sniff, she wiped the dampness from her cheeks . . .

. . . and found herself pinned by the gaze of the man on the stage. Even through the darkness, she could feel those black eyes burning into her own.

Her mind screamed at her to leave, to run from the theatre as quickly as possible, but try as she might, she couldn't move, couldn't tear her gaze from his.

It took her a moment to realize he had left the stage and was walking rapidly towards her. He moved with effortless grace, the long black cape billowing behind him. His feet made no sound; indeed, he seemed to be floating towards her.

And then, abruptly, he was looming over her. The half-mask gleamed a ghostly white in the darkness.

"Christine?" His voice, filled with hope, tugged at her heart.

She shook her head, her eyes fixed on the mask that covered the right side of his face. No, it couldn't be. He wasn't real. He didn't exist.

He took a step closer, and then he frowned. "Forgive me, you are not she."

Cristie tried to speak, but fear trapped the words in her throat.

"You are very like her," he remarked, a note of wonder in his voice.

His voice was mesmerizing: a deep, rich baritone, haunted, tinged with pain and sorrow and a soul-deep loneliness.

Caught in his gaze, she could only stare up at him, her heart pounding a staccato beat as he reached towards her, his knuckles sliding lightly over her cheek.

"Who?" Her voice was no more than a whisper. "Who are you?"

"Forgive me," he said with a courtly bow. "I am Erik."

She swallowed hard. "Erik?"

A slight nod, filled with arrogance. One dark brow arched in wry amusement. "Some people know me as the Phantom of the Opera."

Cristie shook her head. No, it was impossible. She was dreaming. She had to be dreaming. Soon, her alarm clock would go off and she would wake up in her room at the hotel. And she would laugh.

She looked up into his dark haunted eyes and wondered if he had ever laughed. Wondered if she, herself, would ever laugh again.

"And your name?" he asked.

"Cristie," she said, and fainted dead away.

He caught her before she slid out of her chair.

She was quite lovely, he thought, light as a feather in his arms. Her hair was a rich auburn, soft beneath his hand. What was she doing here in the Opera House long after everyone else had gone?

A soft laugh escaped his lips as he carried her down the aisle, turned left and disappeared through a secret door.

Down, down, down, he went, until he reached the boat by the underground lake.

He placed her gently in the stern, then poled across to the other side.

"Cristie." He spoke the name softly – reverently – certain it was short for Christine. He wondered if, this time, he might be blessed with a happy ending.

Cristie woke to the sound of music. Sitting up, she glanced at her surroundings. She didn't have to wonder where she was. She knew. She had seen it all before: the organ, the masked man sitting behind it with his head bowed over the keyboard, the boat rocking gently in the water beyond, the flickering candles.

She was in the Phantom's lair.

He continued to play, seemingly unaware of her presence. The music was darkly sensual, invoking images of sweat-covered bodies writhing on silken sheets. The notes poured over her, making her skin tingle.

She studied his profile, though she could see little but the ghostly mask. Was he as hideous as he was portrayed on stage and in the movies? If she were Christine, she would rise from her bed and tiptoe towards him. She would wait for the moment when he was so caught up in the music he was composing that he was oblivious to everything else, and then she would snatch the mask from his face.

But she wasn't Christine and none of this was real. She had to be dreaming. It was the only answer.

The music ended abruptly and she found herself staring into his eyes.

He inclined his head in her direction. "Welcome to my abode, my lady." His voice was like warm whisky, smooth and intoxicating. Would he sing for her if she asked?

Feeling suddenly uncomfortable at being in his bed, she threw his cloak aside and gained her feet. "I'm sorry," she stammered, "I must have fainted."

"Would you care for breakfast?"

"What? Oh, no, thank you." She forced a smile. "I really must go."

In a lithe motion, he rose from the bench and glided towards her. "So soon?"

She nodded, struck by the beauty of the unmasked portion of his face. And his eyes, they were dark, so dark.

He gestured towards a small table. "You may as well eat." He lifted a white cloth from a large silver tray revealing plates of sliced ham, fried potatoes and soft-boiled eggs. The scent of coffee wafted from a silver carafe. A crystal pitcher held orange juice; a white basket held a variety of muffins and croissants.

Her stomach growled loudly. She hadn't eaten since early last night, after all. "Well, I guess it would be a shame to let it all go to waste."

"Indeed."

He held her chair for her. "Please," he said, "help yourself."

"Aren't you going to join me?"

A faint smile played over his lips. "I've eaten. Please, enjoy your meal."

And so saying, he went back to the organ.

It was the strangest meal she had ever eaten – her sitting at the table, him sitting at the organ, the air filled with music that soothed her soul and excited her at the same time.

She studied him surreptitiously, noting the way he swayed ever so slightly to the music, the graceful play of his long, tapered fingers over the keys, the intense yet faraway look in his eyes. His white shirt emphasized his broad shoulders. The ruffled front should have looked feminine but there was nothing feminine about this man. His black trousers hugged well-muscled thighs. And the mask . . . It drew her gaze again and again as she imagined what lay behind it.

Glancing at her watch, she took a last sip of coffee and pushed away from the table.

As though pulled by a string, he turned towards her, his fingers stilling on the keys.

"Thank you for breakfast," she said, looking around for her handbag. "And for putting me up for the night."

"My pleasure." In a fluid movement, he rose and moved towards her.

"You don't really live down here, do you?" she asked. "I mean . . . do you?"

"It has been my home for many years."

"Do you work for the opera?"

He laughed softly, the sound moving over her like silk warmed by a fire. "No."

A sliver of fear trembled in the pit of her stomach. No one knew she was here. If she disappeared, no one would know where to look.

"Would you like a tour?"

"Some other time," she said, backing away from him. "I really have to go."

He moved to close the distance between them. "Christine—"

His nearness played havoc with her senses. "It's Cristiana, actually."

"I'll see you up," he said.

She nodded, suddenly finding it hard to speak.

He plucked his cloak from the bed and settled it on his shoulders in an elegant flourish that would have made any Phantom worth his salt proud.

"My purse . . . ?"

He found it on the floor and offered it to her with a slight bow. "Shall we?"

He handed her into the boat, poled effortlessly across the lake, escorted her up a long, winding stone staircase and out a narrow wooden door into a dark alley.

Cristie gasped, surprised to find that it was night when she had thought it was morning.

"Will I see you again?" he asked.

"I don't think so. I'm leaving for home in a few weeks."

"You don't live here?"

"No, I live in the States."

"Ah."

'You don't really think you're the Phantom of the Opera, do you?"

"No, my fair lady, I don't think it. I am indeed he."

"But that's impossible. You'd have to be . . ." She lifted one hand and let it fall. "I don't know, over a hundred years old."

He nodded, as if such a thing was perfectly natural.

"Very funny." No doubt about it, she thought, he was quite mad.

A hint of anger sparked in the depths of his eyes. "You don't believe me?"

She shrugged. "I'm not sure the Phantom was real."

"I'm quite real, I assure you."

"And you're over a hundred years old? How do you explain that?"

"Quite easily." He smiled, revealing very sharp, very white fangs. "I'm a vampire."

She stared at him and then, for the second time in as many days, she fainted.


Cristie woke in the Phantom's lair again. It was becoming quite a habit, she mused. Only this time the organ was silent and she was alone. She glanced at her watch. The hands read six o'clock, but she had no way of knowing if it was morning or evening.

Rising, her heart pounding, she found her handbag and hurried towards the lake, only to find that the boat was gone. Chewing on the inside of her lower lip, she glanced at the water. How deep was it? Did she dare try to swim across? The water looked dark, forbidding. It was said that there were alligators in the New York sewers and, while she had never heard of any alligators in Paris, who knew what other dangers might lurk beneath the dark surface of the lake?

Retracing her steps, she sat at the table, only then noticing that the dirty dishes had been taken away. A clean cloth now covered the tray. Lifting it, she found a thick ham and cheese sandwich on white bread, a bowl of onion soup, still warm, and a pot of tea.

Never one to let anything go to waste, she picked up the sandwich, wondering where her host was. No sooner had the thought crossed her mind than she sprang to her feet. Good Lord, he was a vampire! How had that slipped her mind? She had to get out of there before he returned! Vampire. Had he bitten her while she slept? She lifted a hand to her neck, relieved when she felt only smooth skin. No bites, thank God. And she wouldn't wait around to give him another chance.

Grabbing her handbag, she ran to the water's edge, her fear of the man who called himself the Phantom of the Opera stronger than her fear of the water. She removed her shoes with a sharp stab of regret at the thought of leaving them behind. Manolos were hard to come by, especially on a teacher's salary, but her life was worth more than a pair of shoes. Stuffing her handbag inside her blouse, she waded into the water. It was dark and cold and she had gone only a few feet when she realized she had made a horrible, perhaps fatal, mistake. Not only was the lake deeper than she thought, but a swift current ran under the water's calm surface. She shrieked as it caught her, carrying her away from the Phantom's lair, sweeping her along like a cork caught in a rip tide. Helpless, she flailed about as the waterway grew narrower, darker and as the light from the Phantom's lair grew faint and then disappeared.

Weighed down by her clothing, her arms and legs quickly tiring, she screamed for help one last time before she sank beneath the dark current.

Erik cursed as the sound of Cristie's cries reached his ears. Foolish woman. Why hadn't she waited for his return? Foolish man. Why had he refused to let her go? And yet, how could he? Her face, her voice – so like Christine's of old, and yet uniquely her own. He had lived in solitude for so long. Surely he deserved a few years of companionship? If she would but stay with him, he would grant her every desire, fulfil her every wish. If she would love him. He laughed bitterly. There was little chance of that. A woman like Cristie, so young and so beautiful, could surely have her pick of handsome men. Men who walked in the sun's light without fear.

He raced towards the lake with preternatural speed. He had no need of illumination to find her. He followed her scent and when he found her, floating face down, he plunged into the lake and drew her into his arms. Relief surged through him when she coughed up a mouthful of water. A thought took him to his lair. A wave of his hand lit a fire in the hearth.

Cursing his selfishness, he placed her on the bed and quickly removed her sodden clothing. If she died – no! He would not let that happen. Wrapping her in a thick quilt, he gathered her into his arms and carried her to the rocking chair located in front of the fire. Sitting down, he held her close, his hands massaging her back, her arms and her legs. The scent of her hair and skin filled his senses, the throbbing of the pulse in the hollow of her throat called to his hunger, tempting him almost beyond his power to resist. But he would not take advantage of her, not now, when she was helpless. Nor, he realized, could he let her go – not when Fate had been kind enough to send her to him; not when she knew what he was (though if she told the tale, he doubted anyone would believe her).

Awareness returned to Cristie a layer at a time. She was warm. It was quiet. Soft music filled the air. A gentle hand was stroking her brow –

With a start, Cristie came fully awake to find herself cradled in the Phantom's arms, staring up into his dark eyes.

*Vampire.*

"Please," she murmured tremulously. "Please, let me go."

His knuckles caressed her cheek. "Please stay," he urged softly. "Be my Christine, if only for a little while."

Fear made her mouth go dry. What would he do if she refused to stay? She closed her eyes for a moment, remembering how she had always hated Christine for leaving the Phantom and going away with Raoul. Cristie frowned. Hadn't she always said that if she had a choice, she would have stayed with the Phantom? But this wasn't a play, and this Phantom was a vampire.

His voice rumbled against her ear. "A month, my Christine. Won't you stay with me that long? The world you know will still be there when you return."

"And if I refuse?"

He had meant to keep her against her will, if necessary, but looking at her now, seeing the fear in her eyes, he knew he would not. "No harm will come to you," he said. "I will take you back to the theatre where I found you."

Relief washed over her, but only for a moment. How could she refuse him? Never before had she seen such pain, such utter loneliness, reflected in anyone's eyes. And yet, how could she stay? How did she know she could trust him to keep his word? What if he only wanted to drink her blood, or worse, make her what he was? The mere idea filled her with revulsion.

"I will take nothing you do not wish to freely give," he said quietly. "I want only your company for a time."

Cristie glanced at her surroundings. She had come to Paris looking for excitement. Was she going to turn her back on it now? She was in a place no one else had ever been, with a man no one believed existed. Think of the stories you'll have to tell, she thought, ignoring the little voice in the back of her mind that warned her she was being a fool to accept the word of a vampire.

"Will you stay?"

"Yes." The word seemed to form of its own volition. "Yes, I'll stay."

He smiled at her then, and she thought she would promise him anything if he would only smile at her like that again.

They were sitting side by side on the bench in front of the organ. At Cristie's request, Erik had played The Phantom's score for her; played it with such fervour that she had seen it all clearly on the stage of her mind.

Such a beautiful, bittersweet story. With a sigh, she glanced at Erik. "How did you come to be here?" She lifted her hand to his smooth left cheek. "What happened to you?"

"Three hundred years ago, when I was a young man, I ran into a burning building to save a child. A wall fell on me. It burned the right side of my face and most of that side of my body. They took me to the hospital where the physician said there was nothing they could do. I was dying. Late that night, a woman came into my room. She said she could save me, if I was willing, and when I agreed, she carried me out of the hospital and made me what she was. Years later, I came to this place while it was in the last stages of construction. It has been my home ever since."

"But the Phantom. He's not real."

"Men were more willing to believe in ghosts a hundred or so years ago. It was easy to convince the owners of the theatre that the Opera Ghost lived, easy to convince them to do my bidding."

"But the play—"

"—is based in part on my life."

"And Christine? Was she real?"

"Yes."

"What happened to her?"

"She married Raoul, lived to a good old age and passed away."

"You loved her."

"Yes." He lifted a hand to his mask. "But after this, I never saw her again."

"So she never had to choose between you and Raoul?"

"No. I made that choice for her."

"And you've lived alone ever since?"

He nodded.

"But—" A rush of heat warmed her cheeks. She wanted to ask if there had been other women, but couldn't quite summon the nerve, any more than she could ask how and when he fed, and what became of those he preyed upon.

"I am not a monk," he said, surmising the cause of her flushed cheeks. "The managers pay me quite well. On occasion, I have entertained courtesans. As for those I prey upon, I pay them handsomely."

"I didn't mean to pry."

"Ask me what you will. I will hide nothing from you."

"Do I look very much like her?"

He smiled wistfully. "Yes. And no."

Later that night, as she lay in his bed, she thought of all he had told her. Only then, as sleep crept up on her, did she stop to wonder where he took his rest.

It was the first thing she asked him the following night.

"I have another lair deeper underground," he replied. "And, while it is not quite so elegant as this one, it serves its purpose."

"I've put you out of your bed," she murmured.

"I will find comfort in your scent when you are gone."

"Erik—" Why did his voice have such power over her? Why did she long to take him in her arms and comfort him? She scarcely knew him, yet, waking or sleeping, he was in her thoughts. There was much she still wanted to see of Paris but she was content to stay down here, in this twilight world, to bask in the love that shone in the depths of his dark eyes, to lose herself in the music he played for her each night, to listen to his voice as he sang the hauntingly beautiful songs of the Phantom.

As the days went by, Cristie found herself yearning for his touch and with that yearning came a growing curiosity to see what lay beneath the mask. But each time she started to ask, her courage deserted her.

One night, he took her up through the tunnels to watch the play. Close to his side, Cristie saw it all through his eyes. She felt the Phantom's hurt, the pain of Christine's betrayal, the loneliness that lived inside him, the anger that resided deep within him. She cringed when the Phantom killed Piangi and wondered if his death was based on the truth, as were some other parts of the story.

But, fearing the answer, it was a question she did not ask.

She quickly accustomed her waking hours to his. In his underground lair, time lost all meaning since there was no way to tell if it was morning or night. She didn't know where he obtained her meals and, reluctant to hear the answer, she never asked how or where he found those he preyed upon.

He was an intelligent and interesting companion. He spoke several languages and entertained her for hours with tales of his travels around the world. He had seen it all: the wonders of the Old World and the New. He read to her from the classics, his beautiful voice bringing the stories to life. They spent hours discussing the works of Brontë and Shakespeare, as well as the horror novels of Stephen King and Dean Koontz.

The days and weeks went by swiftly and with each passing day her affection for Erik grew deeper as she came to know him better. How sad that he was forced to live in this horrible place, shunned by humanity because of his appearance, when he had so much to offer.

One day, while she was wandering around his lair, she discovered a small door at the far end of the room. Driven by boredom and curiosity, she plucked a candle from one of the sconces. When she opened the door, she found herself in a large, cavernous room filled with a veritable treasure trove of paintings and works of art. Scattered here and there were weapons – a rusty sword, an old pistol, several knives and daggers. A jewellery box held a number of exquisite pieces – a diamond necklace, a ruby pendant, a bracelet set with emeralds.

Moving deeper into the room, she found another, smaller door. This one opened onto a stairway that descended into a pit of blackness.

Heart pounding, she tiptoed down the stairs. The candle cast dancing shadows on the walls as she descended the stairway. At first, she saw nothing but an empty room. And then she saw it: a black coffin sitting on a raised platform. The thought of Erik lying inside, his hands folded on his chest, his long black hair spread across white satin, sent a shiver down her spine.

She stared at the casket for a long moment, then she turned on her heels and ran up the stairs, any lingering doubts she might have had about what he was vanquished by the sight of that solitary coffin.

She could tell by the look in Erik's eyes when she saw him that night that he knew she had seen where he took his rest. Though he didn't speak of it, the knowledge hung there between them.

*Does it matter?* He didn't speak the words aloud, but she heard them clearly in her mind.

Did it matter? To Cristie's surprise, she realized it changed nothing between them. At any rate, it was of no consequence now. Her time in this dark, almost magical world was almost at an end.

As the last few days went by, Cristie found herself increasingly reluctant to go. How could she leave him there, alone, in his dark underground lair? But, of course, she couldn't stay. Her old life, friends and family, awaited her at home. They did not speak of the fact that their time together was almost over, but she saw the awareness in his eyes.

Their last night together came all too soon. After dinner, Cristie asked him to play for her, and as he did so she sat down on the bench beside him and kissed his cheek.

Startled, his hands fell away from the keys. "What are you doing?"

"I . . . nothing. It was only a kiss."

"Only a kiss." He repeated her words slowly, distinctly. "No woman has willingly touched me in over three hundred years."

She blinked at him. Three hundred years? It was inconceivable that he should have lived so long. "I should like to do it again, if you don't mind."

He stared at her in profound disbelief. "You don't mean it?"

"But I do." She kissed his cheek again, and then, very lightly, she kissed him on the lips. They were warm and soft, untouched by the fire. Her gaze searched his. "Let me see your face."

"No!" He drew back as if she had slapped him. "Why would you ask such a thing? No one, no one, should have to see it."

"You said you would grant me anything I wished. I wish to see your face before I go."

He stared at her, his eyes narrowed, his breathing suddenly erratic. "Very well." He ripped the mask from his face and tossed it aside. "Is this what you wanted to see?" His voice was almost a snarl.

It was horrible. The skin on the right side of his face and down his neck was hideously puckered where it had been ravaged by the fire. Did the rest of his body look the same? She couldn't imagine the pain he must have suffered, the anguish of seeing people turn away from him in revulsion. No wonder he hid in this place!

"Are you satisfied?" he asked brusquely.

"Do you want me to run screaming from your presence?" she questioned him.

"You would not be the first to do so," he said, his voice tinged with bitterness.

Cupping his face in her hands, she kissed him again. "I expected you to be a monster, but you've treated me with the utmost kindness and respect. You could have taken me at your pleasure, yet you did not." Rising, she took his hand in hers. "This is our last night together. Let us have something to remember." Pulling him to his feet, she led him towards the bed.

He followed her as if in a trance, unable to believe that any woman would willingly give herself to him. He was no stranger to women. He had bedded many in his lifetime, but never had a woman come to him so willingly, or made love to him so tenderly. Never had he allowed any of them to see him without the mask, nor did he let them caress him. His lovemaking had been one-sided and accomplished in total darkness, assuring that the women couldn't see his ruined flesh.

Sitting on the edge of the bed, they undressed each other. Erik held his breath, certain she would be repulsed when she saw him, but if she found him repugnant, she hid it well. She kissed each scar and, as she did so, they no longer seemed important. She explored his body as he explored hers and, when they were poised on the edge of fulfilment, he asked for that which he craved.

"A taste," he whispered, his voice husky with longing. "Let me taste you."

She stared up at him, her eyes wide. "Will it hurt?"

"No. It will only heighten each touch, each sensation." She wanted to refuse, he could see it in her eyes. "Please, my sweet," he begged softly. "One taste, freely given."

With a sigh, she closed her eyes and offered him her throat.

It was the most generous thing anyone had ever done for him. Whispering endearments, he trailed kisses along the length of her neck before his fangs gently pierced her tender flesh. Ah, the joy, the ecstasy, the wonder of that first taste! Warm and sweet, it flowed over his tongue like the finest nectar, filling him with the very essence of life.

Cristie sighed as pleasure flowed through her. In spite of his scars, his body was beautiful. Long and lean and well muscled. His skin was warm and taut beneath her questing fingertips. She ran her hands over his broad shoulders, his chest, his belly, loving the way he quivered at her touch. She had never known such pleasure, such wonder. She moaned as his body merged with hers. He was a gentle lover, his touch almost reverent, his words soft, poetic, filled with an aching tenderness that tugged at her heart. She prayed he would not ask her to stay longer, knew she could not bear to tell him no.

Sated and content, she fell asleep in his arms.

He watched her all through the night. Their last night. And as he did so, he knew he could not bear to tell her goodbye, could not abide the pain of parting, of watching her walk out of his life. So, in the dark of the night, while she slept, he dressed her, then carried her out of the theatre, his heart aching with every step.

Cristie woke to the warmth of the sun shining on her face. Opening her eyes, she squinted against the brightness she had not seen in weeks.

Sitting up, she glanced round, surprised to find herself lying on her bed in her hotel room with no recollection of how she had got there. Had it all been a dream?

She lifted a hand to her neck and felt the sting of tears when her fingertips encountered two tiny wounds. It hadn't been a dream.

"Oh, Erik," she murmured, "couldn't you at least have let me say goodbye?"

She had her answer with the asking. He had left her before she could leave him.

She grieved to leave him, but how could she stay? Her life was in the States. She taught kindergarten in an upscale school in Boston, she had a family in the city, lifelong friends, a home of her own. Erik had no life outside the bowels of the Opera House. He had no friends or family, no home other than his underground lair. How could they have a life together? She could not live in his world and he could not live in hers.

With a sigh, she went into the bathroom to shower and dress. Thank goodness she had paid for her room in advance, she thought, and then frowned. How had Erik known where she was staying?

Leaving her room, she went downstairs for breakfast. She had another three weeks of vacation. Determined to see as much of Paris as she could, she went sightseeing. She visited The Arc de Triomphe, which had been built to honour the men and women who had died fighting for France. She visited the Eiffel Tower. She toured Notre Dame, which had taken 170 years to build, walked around The Pantheon, which had been built as a church by Louis XV, but was now the final resting place of such notable French thinkers as Rousseau, Voltaire, Hugo and Zola, as well as scientists Pierre and Marie Curie. Amazing places, all of them, but no matter where she was, Cristie's thoughts were on Erik. With every moment apart, the realization grew that she had fallen in love with him – with his kindness, his tenderness, the sound of his voice, his rare smiles and laughter.

Though they had never spoken the words, she was certain that he loved her in return. But was love enough? Could she go on without him? Did she want to?

She went to the theatre that night and every night for the next week, hoping he would seek her out. She scanned the balconies, the dark corners, the shadows, but there was no sign of him.

On her last night in Paris, she hid in one of the bathrooms in the theatre again, then spent two hours wandering the corridors trying to find the door that led to his lair. She called his name, but to no avail.

She spent a miserable night sleeping in one of the seats. In the morning, she asked a startled member of the cleaning crew to let her out.

Defeated, she returned to the hotel, packed her bags and took the next flight home. She moped for days, her heart heavy with despair.

Cristie was glad when school started. She'd spent the week before getting her classroom ready, eager for the new year, eager for anything to take her mind off of her Phantom. But even the excitement of a new year failed to lift her spirits.

Her steps were heavy when she returned home after the first day of school. She had once found joy in teaching. Where had it gone?

She was unlocking the front door when she felt a rush of wind and then, to her astonishment, Erik appeared beside her.

"Cristie." Just her name, but it held a wealth of emotion.

"Erik! How did you find me?"

"Your blood," he murmured, his dark gaze searching her face. "It led me to you."

"I didn't think you ever left the opera house."

"I would risk anything to see you again."

"I missed you, too," she said and, taking him by the hand, she drew him into the house and shut the door. "I tried to find you."

"I know."

"Why did you hide from me?"

He shrugged, an elegant shifting of one shoulder. "I thought it best to let you go, but I realized my life has no meaning without you. And so I came here, to ask you to be my Christine for always. Will you share my love, Cristie, be part of my life?"

She knew what he asking. Being a vampire had once seemed repulsive; now it would open the door to an eternity with the man she loved.

With a nod, she went into his embrace. No words were necessary. Gazing up into his dark eyes, she canted her head to the side, granting him access to her throat.

Murmuring her name, the Phantom enfolded his Christine in his arms and, with one sweet kiss, he joined their lives together, forever.

# The Day of the Dead

## Karen Chance

"I'm looking for my brother," the girl repeated, for the third time. Her accent was terrible, New Jersey meets Mexico City, making her difficult to understand, but Tomas doubted that that was the problem. The largely male crowd in the small cantina weren't interested in the *gaba* with the sob story, even one who was tall and slim, with slanting hazel eyes and long black hair.

Japanese ancestry, Tomas decided, or maybe Korean. There might be some Italian, too, based on the slight wave in her hair and the Roman nose, which was a little too prominent for her slender face. She was arresting, rather than pretty, the kind of woman you'd remember, although her outfit would probably have ensured that anyway. He approved of the tight cargo pants and the short leather jacket. But the shotgun she wore on a strap slung over her shoulder and the handgun at her waist took away from the effect.

"He's nineteen," she continued stubbornly. "Black hair, brown eyes, six foot two—"

The bartender suddenly snapped to attention, but he wasn't looking at her. His hand slid under the counter to rest on the shotgun he kept there. Tomas hadn't seen it, but he'd smelled the old gun oil and faint powder traces as soon as he walked in. But the man who slammed in through the door was merely human.

"*Hijole*, Alcazar!" the bartender shouted, as the room exploded in yells of abuse. "What do you mean, bursting in here like that? Do you want to get shot?"

The man shook his head, looking vaguely green under the cantina's bare bulbs. "I thought I heard something behind me," he said shakily, joining a few friends at an already overcrowded table. "On the way back from the cemetery."

"You shouldn't have been there so late," one of his friends reproached, sliding him a drink. "Not tonight."

"I lost track of time. I was visiting Elia's grave and—"

"*¡Aguas!* You will do your daughter no good by joining her!"

There was frightened muttering for a moment, and several patrons stopped fingering their weapons to actually draw them. Tomas had the distinct impression that the next time the door opened, whoever stood there was likely to get shot. Tension was running far too high for good sense.

Then the bartender suddenly let out a laugh, and slid another round onto the men's table. "I wouldn't worry," he said heartily. "From what I hear, even your Consuela doesn't want you. Why would the monsters?"

The room erupted into relieved laughter as the man, his fright forgotten, stood up to angrily defend his manhood. "She ran off with some wealthy bastard," he said, shooting Tomas an evil look.

Tomas calmly sipped mescal out of a reused Coca-Cola bottle and didn't respond. But he wished for about the hundredth time that he'd given a little more thought to blending in. His reflection in the chipped mirror behind the bar, while not Anglo, stood out as much as the girl's. The high cheekbones and straight black hair of his Incan mother had mixed with the golden skin and European features of his Spanish father, resulting in a combination that many people seemed to find attractive. He'd always found it an inconvenient reminder of the domination of one half of his ancestry by the other: the conquest of a continent written on his face.

He couldn't honestly blame the locals for mistaking him for a wealthy city dweller, despite the fact that he'd been born into a village even poorer than this one and was currently completely broke. He'd picked up his outfit, a dark blue suit and pale grey tie, at an airport shop at JFK. He'd needed a disguise, and the suit, along with a leather briefcase and a quick session with a pocket knife in front of a men's room mirror, had changed him from a laid-back college student with a ponytail to a 30-something businessman in a hurry.

He'd eluded his pursuers, but with no money he'd been forced to use a highly illegal suggestion on the clerk. Since then, he'd lost track of how many times he'd done something similar, using his abilities to fog the minds of airline employees, customs agents and the taxi driver who had conveyed him 100 miles to this tiny village clinging to the side of a mountain. Every incident had been a serious infraction of the law, but what did that matter? If any of his kind caught up with him, he was dead anyway. He just wished he'd thought to find something else to wear after landing in Guadalajara. There weren't a lot of locals in 1,200-dollar suits.

Tomas couldn't see the outfit that helped him stand out like a sore thumb, because an altar to the souls of the dead had been placed in front of the mirror. Hand-carved wooden skeletons in a variety of poses sat haphazardly on the multi-tiered edifice, each representing one of the bartender's family members who was gone but not forgotten. One hairless skull seemed to grin at him, its tiny hand wrapped around an even tinier bottle of Dos Equis – presumably the man's favourite drink. A regular-sized bottle stood nearby, a special treat for the spirit that would come to visit this night. It was El Dia de los Muertos, the Day of the Dead.

A particularly fitting time, Tomas thought, for a vampire to return home.

At least resentment of the city slicker gave the men something to talk about other than their fear. They didn't relax, being too busy shooting suspicious glances his way, but most of them let go of their weapons. Which is why everyone jumped when a shot exploded against the cracked plaster ceiling.

It was the girl, standing in the middle of the cantina, gun in hand, ignoring the dozen barrels suddenly focused on her head. "My. Brother," she repeated, pointing the gun at the bartender, who had lost his forced joviality. "Where is he?"

"Put your weapon down, *señorita*. You have no enemies here," he said, eyeing her with understandable concern. "And I told you already. No one has seen him."

"His car is parked by the cemetery. The rental papers have his name on them. And the front seat has his handprint – in blood."

She threw the papers on the bar, but neither they nor her speech seemed to impress the bartender. "Perhaps, but as I told you, this is a small town. If he had been here, someone would know."

The glasses on the shelf behind him suddenly exploded, one by one, like a line of firecrackers. The gun remained in the girl's hand, but she hadn't used it. Tomas slowly set his drink back down.

"Someone here does know. And that someone had better tell me. Now." Her eyes took in the bar, where most of the men's weapons were still pointed at her. That fact didn't seem to worry her nearly as much as it should have.

"I saw a stranger." The voice piped up from a table near the door, and a short, stocky man, dressed in the local farmer's uniform of faded jeans, cotton work shirt and straw hat, stood up. "He was taking photographs of the ceremony, out by the graves."

"He's a reporter," the girl agreed. "He was doing a story on . . . something . . . but said he'd meet me here."

"I told him to go away," the man said. "This is a day for the dead and their families. We didn't want him there."

"But he didn't leave. His car is still there!"

The man shrugged and sat back down. "He said he was going to photograph the church, and I saw him walking towards town. That's all I know."

"The church is the white building I saw driving in?"

"Yes." The bartender spoke before the man could. "I can show you, if you like." He motioned for the boy who'd been running in and out all night from the back, clearing off tables and wiping down the bar. "Paolo can take over for me here."

"You're going out?"

"But it's almost dark!"

"Are you mad?"

The voices spoke up from all directions, but the bartender shrugged them off. He brought out the shotgun and patted it fondly. "*Ocho ochenta*. It's only a short way. And no one should go anywhere alone tonight."

The murmuring didn't die down, but no one attempted to stop him. Tomas watched them leave, the bartender solicitously opening the door for the girl. His broad smile never wavered, and something about it made Tomas' instincts itch. He gave them a couple of minutes, then slid off his stool and followed.

There was little light, with the sky already dark overhead, the last orange-red rays of the sun boiling away to the west. But his eyes worked better in the dark and, in any case, he could have found his way blindfolded. The village looked much the same as it had for the last three millennia. Many of its people could trace their ancestry back to the days when the Mayan Empire sent tax collectors here, to reap the benefits of the same plots these farmers still worked. The 500-year-old village where he'd grown up in what was now Peru seemed a young upstart by comparison. It was gone now, bulldozed to make way for a housing development on the rapidly expanding outskirts of Cuzco. But although he hadn't been back here in almost a century, nothing seemed to have changed.

A trail of bright yellow petals led the way to a small church with crumbling stone steps overlooking the jungle that floated like green clouds against the mountains of the Oaxaca. The church was still draped with the *flor de muertos*, garlands of marigolds, from the morning service. He went in to find the same old wooden crucifix on the altar, surrounded by flickering votive candles and facing rows of empty pews. He edged around it and paused by the back door, where the sweet, pungent smell of incense mingled with the damp, musty odour of the jungle. Beyond it, out in the twilight, he caught a whiff of the girl's perfume.

The church faced the red earth of the town's only street, but behind it the jungle washed up almost to the steps, except for the area where a small cemetery spilled down the hillside. It had never been moved despite each summer storm threatening to wash the bodies out of their shallow graves and into the valley below. Tomas picked his way down a marigold-strewn path to the cemetery gate, pausing beside a statue of

La Calaca. The skeleton lady was holding a placard with her usual warning: "TODAY ME, TOMORROW YOU". In many such villages, families stayed all night at the graves of their dead, waiting to welcome the spirits that returned to partake of their offerings. But not in this one. Only four people stood among the flower-decked crosses and scattered graves, and only two of them were alive.

There was little light left, other than a few burning votives here and there, shining among the graves. But Tomas didn't need it to recognize the new additions. The wind was blowing towards him and it carried their scents clearly: Rico and Miguel, two thugs in the employ of the monster he'd travelled 1,000 miles to kill.

"I saw her. She shattered them with some kind of spell." The bartender was talking, while Rico held onto the girl.

"Why carry all this?" Miguel held one of the girl's guns negligently in one hand, with the rest tucked into his belt. "If she's so powerful?"

"I'm telling you, she's some kind of witch," the bartender said stubbornly. "That mage I sent you this morning was her brother. She came looking for him."

"Where did you take him?" the girl demanded, her voice full of cold, brittle anger.

Everyone ignored her. "Her aura feels strange," Miguel said, running a hand an inch or so above her body. "Not human, but not exactly mage either."

"What are you girl?" Rico demanded, his breath in her face. She didn't flinch, despite the fact that she had to be able to see his fangs at that range. If she hadn't known what the villagers feared before, she certainly did now.

"Tell me what you've done with my brother or I'll show you." She sounded no more concerned about her predicament than she had at the bar. Tomas couldn't tell if that was bravado or stupidity, but he was leaning towards the latter. Her heart rate had barely sped up, despite the obvious danger.

"What about me?" the bartender demanded. "You said if I brought you the mage, I was safe. I want my nephew's safety in exchange for this one."

"That will depend," Rico said, jerking her close, "on what she can do. You had better hope one of them is what the master wants, or we'll be taking out the price for our inconvenience in your blood."

Tomas didn't move, didn't breathe, a lifetime's habit keeping him so still that a small bird lit on a tree branch right in front of his face. But inside, he was reeling. It wasn't the cavalier kidnapping that surprised him. The men's master, a vampire named Alejandro, had been organizing hunts on the Day of the Dead for as long as Tomas had known him. While families across Mexico were busily collecting delicacies for the dead – chocolate for *mole*, fresh eggs for the *pan de muerto*, cigarettes and mescal – Alejandro was collecting treats of his own. Strong, smart, cunning – they'd all had some advantage that made them attractive prey. Assembled together, they were always told the same thing: last until morning or escape beyond the borders of Alejandro's lands and win your freedom. They were given flashlights, weapons and maps showing the extent of the ten-mile square area he claimed. Then, at midnight, they were released.

No one ever lived to see dawn.

The participants had changed over the years, from Aztecs to conquistadors to local farmers sprinkled with the occasional American tourist. But one group Alejandro had always left strictly alone was magic users. He liked a challenge, but not prey capable of bringing down the wrath of the Silver Circle, the guardian body of the magical community, on his head. He was twisted, cruel and sadistic, but he wasn't crazy. At least, he hadn't been before. It seemed that some things had changed around here, after all.

"I told you to let go of me." The girl's heart rate had finally sped up, but Tomas didn't think it was from fear. Her complexion was flushed and her eyes were bright, but she wasn't trembling, wasn't panicking. And there was something wrong about that, because even if she were a witch, at three to one odds, with two of the three being master vampires, most magic users would be more than a little intimidated. His estimate of her intelligence took another dive, just as what felt like a silent thunderclap exploded in the air all around him.

A shock wave ran through the ground, shivering through his body like a jolt to his funny bone. It shook the surrounding trees and caused the dusty soil to rise up like steam. The little bird took off in a startled flutter of wings and Tomas made a grab for the limb it had been sitting on, catching hold just as the ground beneath his feet began to buck and slide. Within seconds the slide became a torrent of red earth heading for the side of the mountain – and a drop of more than a mile.

The bartender lost his footing and went down, hitting his head against the side of a massive oak. It must have knocked him out, because the last Tomas saw of him was his body tumbling over the cliff, still as limp as a rag doll. The two vampires jumped for the trees on the opposite side of the path, out of the main rush of earth. They made it, but the girl wasn't so lucky. She fell into the crashing stream of rocks, foliage and dirt, her scream lost in the roar of half a mountainside sluicing away.

Tomas hadn't wanted to get close enough for the vampires to scent him, but it meant that she was too far away for him to grab. She managed to catch hold of a tree stump in the middle of the sliding mass, but she was getting pounded by a hail of debris. Tomas tried to tell himself that she could hold on, that he didn't have to risk being seen by Alejandro's men on a dangerous rescue attempt. He didn't mind the thought of dying so much – considering what he was about to face, that was pretty much inevitable – but he was damned if he wasn't going to take Alejandro with him.

Then the church bell began to chime, its plaintive call cutting through the sound of the earthquake, reverberating across the valley only to be thrown back by the nearby hills. Tomas glanced behind him to see the back end of the old building hanging precariously over nothing at all, its foundation half gone in the landslide. With a shudder and a crack, the church broke in half, the heavy stones of its colonial-era construction beginning to crumble. Some of them were ancient, having been looted by the builders from nearby Mayan ruins, and weighed hundreds of pounds apiece. Even if the girl managed to hold on to her precarious perch, they would sweep her over the mountainside or break her into pieces where she lay.

Bile rolled up thick in his throat. Alejandro had wanted to make a monster of him, a carbon copy of himself. But he'd probably be pleased enough at the thought that he'd turned Tomas into someone who would stand by and watch an innocent die because saving her might cost him something. He might never live to kill that creature, but he wouldn't give him that satisfaction.

Tomas let go of the limb and leaped for the one spot of colour in the darkness, the girl's pale face, using her as a beacon to guide him through the hail of falling debris. He reached her just before the first of the ancient stones did, grabbed her around the waist and leaped for the side of the path that remained half stable. It was the one where his old associates were trying to scramble to steadier ground, but at the moment, that seemed a minor issue. Despite senses that made the falling hillside look as if it was doing so in slow motion, he couldn't dodge everything. He twisted to avoid a stone taller than him, and slammed into a smaller one he hadn't even seen. He heard his left knee break, but all he felt was a curious popping sensation, no real pain – not yet – and then they were landing on a surface that wasn't falling but was far from steady.

Tomas rolled and got up on his good knee in time to block a savage kick from Miguel. He'd hoped that, in the confusion and danger, his old comrades might not have recognized him, but no such luck. Miguel hit a nearby tree hard, but flipped back onto his feet almost immediately and was back before Tomas could regain his stance.

Powerful hands choked him, setting spots dancing in front of his eyes. He grabbed his assailant's arms in an attempt to keep his throat uncrushed. He pushed Miguel's arm the wrong way back until he heard the elbow crack. The vamp didn't let go, but his hold weakened enough for Tomas to twist and get an arm into his stomach, using all his strength to send him staggering into the path of the falling church. One of the tumbling pews caught Miguel on the side of his head, knocking him back against the newly created embankment, where the heavy wooden cross from the altar pinned him with the force of a sledgehammer.

It wasn't quite a stake, but it seemed to do the trick, Tomas thought dazedly, right before something long and sharp slammed into his side.

"So the traitor has come back at last," Rico hissed in his ear, twisting a shard of wood so that it scraped along his ribs, sending stabs of hot pain all up and down his midsection. "Allow me to be the first to welcome you home."

Tomas jerked away before the sliver could reach his heart, but his knee wouldn't support him and he stumbled. He felt the hillside disintegrate under his foot and then he was falling, tumbling halfway down the side of the embankment. He grasped the top of a coffin, one of many now sticking out of the newly churned earth, to save himself, and the lid popped open just in time to intercept another slice from Rico's stake. A pale, silverfish-grey arm flopped out of the tilted casket, and Tomas sent its owner a silent apology before breaking off the limb to use as a makeshift weapon.

He spun to see Rico a few feet away, his hand raised as if to strike. Only the blow never fell. Rico jerked once, twice, then he dropped, falling along with the last of the debris into the valley below. For a moment, Tomas didn't understand what had happened. Then a cascade of spent shotgun shells tumbled down the embankment, rattling against the coffin lid like bones, and he looked up to see a pair of slanting hazel eyes staring down at him.

"Are you all right?" The girl's blood was dripping onto his face, a soft wet plucking like a light rain.

"I should be asking you that," he said, struggling to get back over the edge with only one good leg.

He felt it when his skin absorbed her blood, soaking it up like water on parched earth, using it to begin repairs on the damage he'd suffered. But it wasn't enough to do much good. What he needed was a true feeding, something he hadn't taken time for recently. It had cost him in the fight; he couldn't afford to let it lessen his already slim chances against Alejandro.

He paused by Miguel's impaled body, still full of the blood he'd recently stolen, some of it already pooling in his eye sockets. The sight worked on Tomas the way the smell of a feast would on a starving human. His mouth began to water and his fangs to lengthen without any conscious command from him. He would have delayed it, would have gotten rid of the girl first, but he couldn't risk having the blood coagulate and lose the energy it contained.

"I have to feed," he said simply.

Instead of recoiling as he'd expected, she merely took in his injuries with an experienced eye. "Yeah. Heroics have a way of coming back and biting you in the ass. But when you're done, we need to talk."

He nodded and hunched over Miguel so at least she wouldn't have to watch. Tomas couldn't remember the last time he'd fed from another vampire, but he quickly recalled why it wasn't a common practice. The reused blood nourished him, the light-headed rush of feeding giving the same almost narcotic high as always, but the taste was like metal in his mouth. He forced himself to finish, trying to concentrate on the feel of his cracked ribs knitting, on the tear in his side mending and on the grating sensation in his knee slowly fading. The healing of wounds, especially if done so quickly, was excruciating and this was no exception. Tears had leaked out of the corners of his eyes by the time he was finished, forced out by the pain, but Tomas didn't mind. Pain was good. Pain meant he was still alive.

"I hate it when that happens."

Tomas looked up to find the girl scowling around at the cemetery. Or what was left of it. A huge swathe had been carved out of the middle, where nothing but slick red earth remained. On either side, coffins stuck out of the ground like bony fingers, with a few marigold crosses scattered here and there haphazardly. Up above, on the crest of the hill, the remaining half of the church swayed dangerously on its ancient foundations. One last pew teetered precariously on the edge of the abyss, half in and half out of the structure, while inside the church, a single candle still burned.

"You handle yourself pretty well in a fight," she continued, as Tomas rose from Miguel's exsanguinated corpse.

"I've had some practice."

She gave a sputtering laugh, short and mocking. "Yeah. I bet."

Tomas pulled himself over the edge and examined her. Amazingly, she seemed to be all right. There was a shallow cut on her forehead and few scrapes and scratches here and there, but nothing serious. It was little short of miraculous.

"We need to talk, but we ought to get out of here," she said, slinging her shotgun over her back again. He'd heard her reloading while he fed. "Half the village is likely to be here any minute."

Tomas sat down on the edge of a stone bearing weathered Mayan hieroglyphs. "I doubt it," he said wryly.

She studied him silently for a moment, then plopped down alongside. "Want to fill me in?"

"This is the Day of the Dead. And in this area, that term has always had more than one meaning." He spent a few minutes sketching out for her Alejandro's idea of a good time, making it as clinical and unemotional as he could. It didn't seem to help.

"Let me get this straight. That son of a bitch has taken *my brother* to use in his stupid games?"

"Possibly," Tomas agreed. "Although I can't understand it. He never took magic users before."

"Maybe he got bored. Wanted more of a challenge."

"Does a cat get tired of playing with lizards or mice, and attack the neighbourhood dog instead? Preying on weaker creatures is Alejandro's nature. But if your brother is a mage, he wouldn't fall into that category."

"His type of magic isn't likely to help him much," she said curtly.

"I don't understand."

"You don't need to." She stood up. "Just tell me where I can find this guy."

Tomas shook his head. "I can't do that.'

"Why not? Based on how his vamps treated you, I got the impression you weren't all that close."

He smiled at the understatement. "We aren't. But helping you commit suicide won't aid your brother."

"Tell me where to find this Alejandro, and the only one dying will be him."

Tomas got slowly to his feet, gingerly putting his weight on the injured knee. It held. "For what it's worth, I've come to kill him. If I succeed, it may cause enough chaos to allow your brother to escape. Wish me luck."

He started to go, but a hand on his arm stopped him. "I'll do better than that. I'll go with you."

"I told you – that would not be wise."

"Really? And you think you'd have survived just now without me? It sounds like you going alone isn't so wise, either."

Tomas turned to face her, already exasperated. He had enough on his plate tonight. He didn't need this. "You may be good with a gun, but that won't keep you alive. Alejandro was once my master. I know what he's capable of."

"Uh-huh. And can he break off half a mountain because he loses his temper?"

Tomas regarded her narrowly. "You're saying that was you?"

"That's what I'm saying. I'm a jinx."

"I beg your pardon?"

"Jinx. J-I-N-X. A walking disaster area. Fault lines love me. Of course, so does just about anything else that can go wrong."

"An inconvenient talent."

"And an illegal one. If the magical community ever finds out a jinx as powerful as me is walking around, they'll kill me. Which is why I got really good at protecting myself – and other people – a long time ago. This vampire has bought himself more trouble than he knows."

"Bringing down a mountainside won't help your brother. If he's where I think he is, it would only bury him as well."

"I can control it. And this isn't exactly my first time at the rodeo. I can take care of myself."

Tomas hesitated, instinct warring with dawning hope. "I tried to draw someone else into this recently, and almost got her killed," he finally admitted. "I swore that I'd never do that again. This is my fight—"

"It *was* your fight. Once that bastard took Jason, he made it mine." When Tomas just stared at her, trying to think of some way to get rid of her that did not involve actual violence, the ground grumbled beneath him. The precariously perched pew gave up the struggle and slid down the hillside, only to go sailing off into the void like a huge wooden bird. "Look, I'm not asking you, I'm telling you. You think you've got troubles now? Try leaving me behind. My brother is all I've got, and he is *not* dying tonight."

"It will not be easy," he said, wondering how to even begin to explain what they were up against.

The girl snorted. "Yeah. I kind of got that." She held out her hand. "Sara Lee. And no, I don't cook."

"Tomas."

"Well, Tomas. We gonna stand here exchanging pleasantries all night, or go kill a vampire?" Tomas didn't say anything, but he slowly took her hand. She grinned. "Well, all right then."

"Jason is a reporter for the *Oracle*," Sara said, as Tomas hot-wired her brother's rental car. Hers had been parked in the part of the cemetery that hadn't survived and was currently explor-ing the bottom of the valley. "We were supposed to meet up in Puerto Vallarta for a vacation, but when I got to the hotel, he'd already left. All I found was a note telling me he'd got a lead on a story and asking me to meet him here."

"If Alejandro has started kidnapping magic users, it would be front-page news," Tomas agreed, as the engine on the old subcompact finally turned over. "Or your brother could have found out about one of his other businesses. He controls every-thing from magical narcotics to weapon sales in much of Central and South America."

"I know. I've dealt with his people before." At Tomas' sideways look, she shrugged. "I can't buy weapons from legit-imate sources, not in the quantities I need. The authorities monitor that kind of stuff."

"Why would you need huge quantities of magical weap-onry?"

"Why do you want to kill your old master?" she countered. "I didn't even think that was possible."

They bounced out onto the main road through the village, with only the weak light of a quarter moon to see by. "It wouldn't be, if he were still my master. I challenged him to a duel a century ago, but he wouldn't face me. He brought in a champion, a French duelling master, instead. But rather than kill me as Alejandro had wanted, after Louis-Cesar defeated me, he claimed me as his slave. I only recently escaped."

"And came straight back here."

"Yes."

"That's very . . . heroic."

Tomas didn't think it qualified as heroism if he had nothing left to lose. But he didn't say so. Her tone made it clear that the word she'd really been searching for was "stupid".

"Alejandro killed the entire population of my village. There isn't anyone else." If the dead were ever to be avenged, it was up to him to do it. And after 400 years, they'd waited long enough.

"So you came back alone." She shook her head. "People like you are bad for business."

"You're a mercenary." Tomas supposed he should have figured it out before.

"We prefer the term 'outside contractor'."

"I couldn't afford to hire a team," Tomas said, turning onto the pitted road leading into the mountains. "And you also came here alone."

A dark shape suddenly loomed in front of them, forcing Tomas to squeal tyres and practically stand the car on end to avoid hitting it. The shape resolved itself into a tall, gaunt man, with the brilliant eyes of a fanatic set deep in the hollows of his craggy face. "Not so much," Sara said, climbing out of the car. "Boys, glad you could make it."

"Looks like we already missed some of the fun," another man commented, stepping out of the jungle that hedged the road on each side.

Tomas stared hard at the new arrival. He hadn't heard him approach, and that was unacceptable. Unless he was a mage using magic to mask his breath, the sound of his heart beating, his footfalls – all would have alerted Tomas to his presence. But he didn't look like a mage. He had a jagged, ugly scar on his right cheek, as if someone had dragged a fork with sharpened tines over his skin. It was the sort of thing that could be fixed by magical healers or covered by a glamourie. Unless, of course, its owner preferred to look like an extra from a horror flick.

"Meet my knife and gun club," Sara said, slapping the man on the back. "At least the ones close enough to get here in time for the festivities."

The men didn't greet him, and nobody offered any names, but they also didn't demand to know what Sara was doing with some strange vampire. Of course, she didn't give them much of a chance, launching directly into an explanation of the problem. If Tomas had had a doubt about their profession, it would have been quieted by their reaction to the news that they were about to raid a vampire stronghold.

"Can I keep the bones?" the fanatic hissed, speaking for the first time. "They're useful in some spells."

"Knock yourself out," Sara said, shrugging. "But no collecting until we have Jason, understood?"

The man gave a quick nod that reminded Tomas of a lizard or some other kind of reptile. It wasn't a human movement. The other man didn't say anything at all, just switched over a couple of the weapons in the collection draped over his body for several others he drew from a pack on his back. Then everybody got in the car.

Tomas pulled off the road a few miles to the north, where a burbling stream snaked its way through the dense jungle. "We walk from here," he said, pushing the car off the road in case any of Alejandro's men were out a little early.

"I don't see a house." Sara had pulled night-vision goggles out of her associate's pack, and was staring around.

"There isn't one. Alejandro lives underground."

"Come again?"

"There are some Mayan ruins near here, with a maze of underground passages beneath them. He's lived there for centuries."

"Great." She sounded less than enthused.

"What is it?"

"Nothing. What about guards?"

"Normally, the entrances are all watched. That's why I picked tonight to return. They will be open for the hunt, as the prisoners' first challenge is to find their way out of the maze. Many never do."

"We need to reach them before they're released then. Otherwise, they'll be scattered in the tunnels, in the jungle – we'll never find them all."

"I thought the plan was to rescue your brother."

"Yeah. Like I'm going to leave you and the rest to be prey to that thing."

Tomas glanced at her, but it was difficult to see much of an expression behind the absurd goggles. She'd sounded sincere enough, though. And he couldn't let her go in thinking that way. "I know where they used to keep the prisoners. We'll go there first. And if we're lucky enough to locate your brother alive, you need to take him and go."

"I don't abandon a colleague in the middle of a mission. We go in together, we leave together. That's how it works."

"Not if you want to stay alive!" Tomas grasped her arm. "I have the best chance of reaching Alejandro alone. If you stay to help me, both you and your brother will die. Not to mention that you will almost certainly cause me to fail at my task."

She stopped, looking from the hand on her arm to his face. He released her, but the steady stare didn't change. "If you don't want my help, why are you taking me along?" she demanded.

"Because you wouldn't find your brother alone. Not in time."

"And why would you care about that? You don't even know him."

"I might not know your brother, but I've known plenty of others." A thousand faces, ten thousand, he'd lost count over the years. All of those eyes begging him to help them, to save them. They'd seen his face, the one that had prompted Alejandro to nickname him "my angel", and assumed he was their saviour. Only to realize with horror that he was one of those hunting them.

"What?"

"Alejandro forced me to help with the hunts," Tomas said bluntly, "because he knew how much I hated it." Telling her was unnecessary, but it was probably his last chance for confession. He didn't remember the last time he'd talked with a priest, not even the last time he'd wanted to, and she couldn't absolve him anyway. But then, considering some of the things he'd done, he doubted that anyone could. "I've killed thousands just like Jason," he added, trying to keep his voice neutral. "And the only mercy I could show them was to make it quick. For once, I'd like to help someone survive. And to have Alejandro be the one wallowing in his own blood."

"That's a plan I can get behind," she said, fingering her automatic.

Tomas shook his head and didn't comment. Once she saw what was waiting for them, her bravado would fade. Just like everyone else's always did. The two men didn't say anything. But when he and Sara stepped into the undergrowth, they followed.

The next hour was taken up with slipping through a jungle in which no paths had ever been carved, followed closely by a damp cloud of mosquitoes. Sara managed it better than Tomas had expected; it wasn't easy going even for him. Alejandro had left the jungle intact for exactly that reason: it formed an added layer of protection. It also added to the fun of his hunts, watching mere mortals flounder around in the endless green sea until he chose to put them out of their misery.

They finally reached an old temple on the edge of Alejandro's lands. The place was beautiful, silvered with moonbeams, the stones seeming to glow with a delicate light just bright enough to pick out shapes. Weeds and vines had half obscured the entrance and small trees were growing out of the tumbled stones over the lintel. A crop of wild orchids had moved in, settling among the ruins like nesting birds, their white and orange petals spotted with brown, like freckles. Tomas reached out to touch one and found it softly furred beneath the pad of his finger – like skin. A sudden shiver flashed up and down his spine, before twisting like a snake in his gut. For a moment, it felt like the last century had never happened, like he was returning from a mission for his master with blood on his hands, and all the rest was merely a dream.

"This it?" Sara asked briskly, breaking the mood.

"Yes," he said, and for some reason it hurt to talk, like he was scraping the words out of his throat.

They ducked under deeply sculpted reliefs and entered the main hallway, which led to a chamber with a stone altar. Like his own ancestors, and unlike the Aztecs, the Maya had rarely practised human sacrifice. It was far more common for their priests and kings to use their own blood as the sacrifices their gods required, letting it flow when crises occurred or when the auguries deemed it necessary. Tomas had always been proud that he came from a people who understood the real nature of sacrifice – and it wasn't having someone else bleed for you.

The altar sat in front of a raised dais, behind which was a small room where he supposed the priests might have once readied themselves for ceremonies. It was empty now, except for a set of rock-cut stairs leading down into darkness. Below were a series of *chultuns*, old underground storage chambers for water and food, and beneath them the reason Alejandro had chosen this site in the first place: naturally occurring limestone caverns that even Tomas had never explored in full. It was like an underground city, part of which the Mayans had used as a refuse dump, part of which had some type of mystical significance, with carvings on the walls showing ancient ceremonies and still partially covered in moulding paint.

"This is one of the lesser-used entrances," he told them, as Sara drew out a flashlight. "But we shouldn't risk the light. Alejandro's men don't need it and, if they see it, it will only draw them to us that much faster."

She nodded, but didn't look happy. Tomas wasn't surprised. Descending into an unknown labyrinth that to her eyes must have been pitch dark would have upset most people. But there wasn't much to see, unless she liked the look of striated stone and deep, dark holes branching off here and there. That was all until they reached the populated areas. And then, she was probably better off if she couldn't see what lay ahead.

The four of them entered the tunnels, and almost immediately Tomas found himself struggling to breathe against a thick, smothering pressure, voices rising like a tide in his head. He'd killed before he came to Alejandro, fighting against the men who had come across the sea to steal his homeland. But those deaths had never bothered him: he'd never lost one night of sleep over them, because those men had deserved everything he did to them. The ones he'd taken in these halls were different.

Taken. It was a good word, he thought bleakly, seeing with perfect clarity the bodies, pale and brown, young and old, faces spattered with blood, bodies cracked and split open. They had bled out onto the thirsty earth because the ones who hunted them had been so sated that they could afford to spill blood like water. And none of it had been due to the hand of God, through some natural, comprehensible tragedy. No, they had died because someone with god-like conceit had stretched out his hand and said, *I will have these*, and by that act ended lives full of hope and promise.

More often than not, Tomas had been that hand, the instrument through which his master's gory commands were carried out. He hadn't had a choice, bound by the blood bond they shared to do as he was bid, but that had somehow never done much to soothe his conscience. He had known it would be hard to return, but he hadn't expected it to be quite this overpowering. Four hundred years of memory seemed to permeate the very air, the taste of it thick and heavy, like ashes in his mouth.

He glanced at his companions. Forkface had an utterly blank stare, as cold as ice, while the fanatic kept muttering silently to himself and fingering a necklace of what looked like withered fingers. Sara was looking a little green, as if something about the atmosphere was getting to her, too.

He swallowed, throat working, and said roughly, "Are you all right?"

She nodded, but didn't try to reply. He decided not to press it, struggling too much with the weight of his own memory. They silently moved forwards.

It was deeply strange to walk through the familiar halls, the bumps and jagged edges of the lintels stretching out claws of shadow that even his eyes couldn't penetrate. He'd done so much to try to forget this place, but he'd been branded by

Alejandro's mark too long to succeed. The feeling of familiarity grew with every step, like each one took him further into the past. He kept expecting to meet himself coming around a corner, as if part of him had never left at all.

Tomas wondered what he might have been like if he'd never been taken. Or if his first master hadn't decided to show off his new acquisition at court, where Alejandro had chosen to claim him. Once, he'd yearned for freedom with everything in him, hungered for it as he never had food, lusted for it as he never had any woman. But it didn't seem to matter how long he waited or how much power he gained, the story was always the same. He'd had three masters in his life, but had never been master himself. The idea of being free was like an old photograph now, faded and dog-eared, and Tomas didn't think he could even see his face in it any more. All he wanted now was to end this.

Sara stopped suddenly, breathing heavy, her hand gripping the wall hard enough to cause bits of limestone to imbed themselves under her nails. She saw him notice and tried to smile. It wasn't a great attempt.

"God, it's hot." She ripped off her jacket, tying it in a knot around her waist, and gathered her hair into a riotous ponytail to get it off her neck.

Tomas hadn't noticed much of a fluctuation in temperature. Usually, the caves were cooler than above ground, not the reverse, although at this time of year the transition was less noticeable. But patches of sweat had already soaked through her shirt and glistened on her skin, and her hand left a wet print on the wall where it had rested.

"This way," he said, leading them into one of the outermost rooms branching off the main hallway before stopping dead.

"What is it?" Sara had noticed him tense, instantly aware of a change in the atmosphere.

"Something's wrong," he said softly.

"Like what?"

The three mercenaries had drawn up in a defensive wedge and were scanning the room, their weapons in hand. But there was nothing to see except a few rat bones and a scrap of ancient material.

"There are supposed to be mummified bodies here."

"Great," Sara muttered. "For the extra creepness this place was missing."

"This was where Alejandro kept the remains of ancient Inca kings," he explained.

Alejandro had acquired them as trophies shortly after following Pizarro to the New World, and had brought them along when he finally decided on a permanent residence. Once they were settled in, however, they'd largely been forgotten, left to mildew in dank, underground cells.

Tomas had been one of the few to ever visit them. They had been venerated by his people even after death, remaining in their palaces, supported by their lands, just as they had when alive. Each new Inca monarch had to wage his own wars of conquest to fund his rule, because what had been his ancestors' remained theirs and beyond his control. Legions of servants had daily draped their withered corpses in the finest of garments and prepared lavish meals for them. On important occasions, they had been brought out to sit again in court, giving council to the living and presiding over the festivities.

There had always been something uncanny about them – brown, almost translucent skin stretched over old bones, empty eyes and hollow mouths, with shadows inside like parodies of human organs. Tomas had come this way knowing it was usually avoided by the court. That still seemed to be the case, but for some reason it worried him that the kings weren't there. It made something cold go running along his spine.

"I'm more concerned about the living," Sara said, eyes on his face. "Are we close?"

Tomas swallowed. He was imagining things. The kings had just been moved, that was all; or perhaps Alejandro had finally decided to rid himself of his macabre trophies. "Yes. The old cells are down there." He pointed out a small hole in the wall, about two feet square.

"Down there?" Sarah peered into the darkness, her hand tightening convulsively on her gun. "You're kidding, right?" She sounded hopeful.

"No. There is another way in, but it involves going through much more populated areas. This is safer."

"Safer." She didn't look convinced. She peered inside the small, dank, black hole for another moment, then muttered something that sounded fairly obscene. "Stay here – keep watch," she ordered her men. Then she stowed her gun in its holster and went in head first, on hands and knees. Tomas followed close behind.

The tunnel slanted sharply downwards, leaving behind the mildewed plaster of the *chultuns* for true caverns. Tomas could sense the room's emptiness almost as soon as they entered the small tunnel – there were no whimpers, no cries for help, no rapidly racing heartbeats. But before he could tell Sara, she was already out the other side. He emerged in a dark cave half-filled with ancient garbage, with deer bones and pottery shards crunching under his weight. His foot slipped on an old turtle shell, causing him to almost lose his balance, and then there was a rumbling that set half the room's contents jittering.

"There's no one here!" Sara whirled on him, her face livid.

"They must have moved them."

"A convenient excuse! I swear, vampire, if you've lied to me—"

"To what end?"

"To get me down here alone—"

"I had you alone in the cemetery," Tomas pointed out, with barely concealed impatience. The rumbling just got louder, with rocks and small pieces of pottery stirring uneasily. "If I meant you harm, I would have acted then."

"You said they would be here! That you knew where they were!"

"If Alejandro had followed the usual practice, the prisoners *would* be here," he replied, trying for calm. "But the contents of the room above were moved, and if they changed one long-standing practice, they may have changed another. I haven't been back in a century—"

"Something you might have mentioned before now!" She was sweating harder, with a few drops glistening along her hairline before falling to stain her shirt.

"We will find your brother," he told her. "I swear it."

"Why should I believe you?" She sounded frantic.

"Why shouldn't you?" Tomas asked, bewildered. "What reason do I have to lie?" A crack formed in the ceiling overhead, raining dirt and gravel down on them. "I thought you said you could control this!" The caverns weren't entirely stable, as multiple cave-ins had demonstrated through the years. If she didn't cut it out, she was going to bury them both.

Sara looked around, as if she honestly hadn't noticed that the entire room was now shaking. "I can! Usually."

"Usually?"

"I'm a jinx. My magic isn't always . . . predictable. I've learned some control through the years, but it's harder when I'm angry." She paused, her breath coming hard. "And I really don't like being underground."

"You're claustrophobic?"

"I have a small problem with enclosed spaces." There was a badly concealed edge of panic in her voice.

"But you're a mercenary! Surely—"

"I'm a mercenary who prefers to fight in the open!" she snapped, her face scrunching up with effort. The shaking didn't noticeably diminish.

"You might have mentioned it!"

"Very funny."

The crack widened, dirt and rock exploding inwards, peppering them with pieces of rock as sharp as knives.

"Do something!"

"I'm trying!"

She was almost doubled over in effort, pain written on her face, but whatever she was doing wasn't working. A huge crack reverberated around the small space, knocking them both to the ground, hands pressed against their temples. A moment later, a chunk of the ceiling the size of a sofa broke away and came crashing down, missing them by inches. Tomas stared at it for a split second through a haze of dust before grabbing her around the waist and dragging her back to the entrance.

"Hurry! Back up the tunnel!"

"It won't help." She'd braced herself against the wall. Her face was pinched and white and her eyes wide and panicky as they met his. "Hit me."

"What?"

"I need a distraction! Something else to think about. Pain sometimes works."

Tomas could feel the pressure building in the room, like a storm in the distance, about to break. "Sometimes isn't good enough! I can put you under a suggestion—"

"No, you can't."

"I assure you—"

"I'm a jinx!" she repeated furiously. "My magic doesn't work like most people's! I'm not susceptible to suggestions, vampiric or otherwise. Now hit me, goddammit!"

"No," he said, and kissed her.

It was an instinctive reaction, something unexpected that might shock her enough to stop this without actually hurting her. But then she shuddered slightly and her mouth opened under his and her hands clenched on his shoulders and somehow he was kissing her savagely, this woman he barely knew who might be the last person he ever touched, the last warmth he ever felt.

Sara's heartbeat was hard against his hand, the urgent thump resonating through his body. They stumbled back into the cavern wall, Tomas cradling the back of her head to save her from a concussion, trying to remember to be careful when his hands were so hungry that he couldn't hold them still. Sara was shaking almost as hard as the room and, for a moment, it was the most natural thing in the world to be kissing her desperately, both hands locked around her head now, the long hair coming loose under his fingers, while the mountain threatened to fall in around them and death lay waiting, sure and inevitable, only moments away.

Tomas hadn't realized fully until that moment how certain he'd become that he wouldn't survive the night. He felt the knowledge settle into him now along with her breath, and instead of sadness or regret, he found himself just overwhelmingly grateful that, if this was the end, at least he wasn't facing it alone. It was, all things considered, more than he deserved.

And then Sara pulled away, her eyes wide open, shocked and angry, and struck him hard across the mouth. It was enough to rock his head back, to make him taste the rich, metallic tang of his own blood. He wiped a smear off his lip with a thumb as she pushed at him, hard.

"I said *hit* me! Are you deaf?" She didn't wait for an answer, but launched herself towards him, fist clenching.

Tomas caught her hands, effortlessly holding her away from him. "Vampires don't get in fights with humans unless we intend to kill. You're too vulnerable, too easily broken."

Another rock hit the floor, hard enough to send bones and debris flying. Sara looked around wildly. "If you don't, we'll both be broken! Nothing else works!"

He grabbed her by the hips, swinging her against the wall, slamming her backwards into it. Startled out of fighting for a moment, she just stood there, panting and staring up at him as he pressed against her.

"If I misjudge, there will be no one to stop this hillside from erupting just as the cemetery did. You'll be unconscious or worse, and we'll both die – as will your brother."

His hands were busy as he spoke and, with a sharp tug on the hem of her blouse, he sent the buttons flying. By the time he'd pushed the cloth out of the way, getting his fingers on the living warmth beneath, her nipples had gone tight and pebbly and she was gasping, her hands fisting in his shirt. But she wasn't pushing him off. She was kissing him brutally, lips and teeth savage, pressing hard against his body while her hands clawed at his back.

"Are you distracted yet?" he breathed, as she ripped open his shirt, pushing his undershirt up to his neck and biting at a nipple.

"I'll let you know," she said roughly, dragging their lips together again.

Her mouth tasted of the sharp sweet tang of mescal, or maybe that was him. Her lips were sweet, but her body was shaking and her eyes were darting everywhere as if certain this wasn't going to work. And it wasn't, if he couldn't get her mind off the room and onto him – and keep it there. The room was coming down in chunks around them and the only thing that kept running through his mind was that it would be truly typical to come 1,000 miles to die in some deserted ante-room.

He was breathing hard, adrenaline pumping through him, as he managed to get a hand between them. He dipped his head for another kiss, hands slipping away from hot, damp skin to tug impatiently at the button on her jeans, to work at the zipper. He pushed the maddeningly tight material down her thighs, his hand clenching on the soft flesh of her hip, rounded and warm for his palm. He pulled her closer, fixed the angle between them, and pushed into her.

Her legs wrapped around his thighs, clenching, as he began moving. He'd been careful because he hadn't prepared her, but she gasped out, "I won't break," her voice low and rough, and he began thrusting hard and fast, the way his body craved. His only concession to her comfort was his fingers working between her thighs roughly.

Within moments she was shuddering, her breath fracturing into harsh, quick gasps, panting, "*Harder*, damn you!"

"Make me," he growled.

In one quick movement she shoved him back, her foot behind his, tripping him, sending them both falling to the floor and driving herself onto him. Tomas barely noticed the hard floor or the pottery shard that was gouging him in the back or the unstable ceiling hanging above him. He was too busy watching her face. He kept his hands on her hips, guiding her, but not giving in to her gasped commands. Instead, he deliberately slowed down, then abruptly stopped, waiting.

"Tomas!"

He ignored her, even though she wouldn't stop squirming, pushing the jagged pot shard further between his shoulder blades. She shifted, pulling back enough to rip open his shirt, to rain biting kisses all along his neck, to lick the hollow of his collarbone and mouth, his shoulders. Tomas' hands scrabbled desperately at the rubble beneath him, but he didn't move. He just lay there and took it, amazed at how much he needed this, until she let out a frustrated scream and raked her nails down his chest. "Move, damn it!"

He just stared up at her, at her glittering eyes and sweat-drenched, dusty hair, her blouse open and her jeans around her knees, giving him a view of the dark stain of his hands against the pale skin of her hips. He wondered how he'd ever thought her less than stunning. She glared at him and then pulled further back, letting him almost slide out of her, then suddenly forced herself back onto him. She did it again and Tomas bit back a groan, but he held himself completely still.

"Some help here!" she demanded, and did something with her hips that made his eyes roll into the back of his head.

He slid his hands down the curve of her back and tightened them on her slim waist. He could feel the tremors in his frame the longer he held on and knew he'd soon have no choice but to move. And she knew it, too – she was laughing when he finally gave in, an exultant sound that ran like fire through his veins. He let her have her moment of triumph, before suddenly stopping once more. It took her a second to notice, then she stared down at him, momentarily speechless.

"That's inhuman!" she finally hissed.

He grinned. "So am I."

She wrapped her hand around his tie and jerked him upwards, the new angle forcing a moan out of them both. "Finish this or I swear—"

Tomas was moving before she completed the sentence, ignoring caution this time, fast and furious, glad that he didn't actually *need* to breathe because she hadn't let go of the tie. And then her hips were jerking in a way that was making it hard for him to focus, her gasps loud in his ears, her body's pleasure doubling his own. He felt her shudder, her release and the clenching of her body triggered his, making them both groan deep in the back of their throats – and a great mess of pebbles and dust poured out of the ceiling.

It took Tomas a few seconds to realize that he wasn't trapped beneath a ton of dirt and rubble, that this wasn't a cave-in, just the result of one final tremor. He dug himself out to find Sara staring about room, which was, surprisingly, mostly still intact. It was also blessedly quiet.

Those hazel eyes came back to rest on him and she smiled a

little crookedly, teeth a shock of white in her dirty face. "OK. I guess that method works, too."

Instead of having to fight their way to the centre of the complex as Tomas had expected, their path was unobstructed, the halls echoing, silent and empty except for the carved faces of long-forgotten gods staring down from the walls and lintels. That was more than strange – it was unprecedented. And very bad. Tomas had always known that his only real chance was that he knew this place, and its master, better than anyone. But nothing had gone as planned all night, and he honestly didn't know what to expect when they finally made it to the huge natural cave that Alejandro used as an audience hall.

He brought them in through a little-known side tunnel that let out onto a set of steps about a storey above the cave floor. There were guards at the entrance, finally, who Tomas dealt with by simply ordering them to sleep. He was a first-level master; he hadn't been worried about them. But the creature sprawled on the throne-like chair at the head of the room was first-level also, and far older than he.

As usual, Alejandro was dressed like a Spanish nobleman of the conquest period, which he'd once been. He didn't look like a monster, with an attractive if florid face and bright, intelligent black eyes. But then, the worst ones never did. Seeing that face again brought a sudden, miserable lurch, a shuddering memory of centuries of heartbreak and horror and nauseating fear. Tomas had to clutch at the door jamb, feeling the rock crumbling beneath his fingers, to keep silent.

Nobody else said anything either. Tomas had warned them that even a whispered word was likely to be over-heard, as beyond the excellent acoustics of the room itself was the small factor of vampire hearing. So Sara was quiet as they surveyed the scene spread out below, although her face was eloquent.

Tomas now knew why they hadn't met anyone on the way. The prisoners should have been downstairs, the vampires getting ready to disperse throughout the property for the hunt. Instead, the entire cavernous space was crammed with people, mostly human, but with a ring of vampires circling them. It took Tomas a moment to realize what was happening, because none of this was normal.

A young Mexican man stumbled forwards, pushed by one of the guards, to land near a small group of others. There were five bodies lined up in a row at the front of the hall, their throats slashed down to the bone, white gleaming through red flesh in wide, jagged lines. The floor there was not the chipped, angular surface of the outer halls, but worn to a smooth, concave trough by generations of feet. A small stone altar had been found when Alejandro moved in, leading to speculation that this had once been the site of sacred rights. Blood from the corpses had run down the central depression, looking like a long finger pointing the way to the altar and to his throne above it. Standing to the side of the carnage were two men and a woman, each human, with expressions ranging from dazed to disbelieving to horror-struck.

Tomas felt a hand grip his arm, and looked down to see Sara clutching it hard enough to bruise had he been human.

"To the right," she mouthed, and nodded to indicate the tall, lanky young man at the end of the line-up, his face dead white and smeared with blood. He looked like he'd put up a struggle, but there was nothing of that spirit visible now. He was swaying slightly on his feet, mouth slack, and blinking slowly behind his glasses like a sleepy owl. Shock, or close to it, Tomas thought; so much for hoping he could run on cue.

"You want to save the life of this man?" Alejandro asked, addressing the young brunette on the other end of the line. "Because you know what I want."

Instead of answering, the young woman giggled, a nervous, high-pitched sound that warned of incipient hysteria. It reverberated oddly in the high vault of the room; laughter wasn't a sound that lived here, and the echoes came back with sharp, mocking edges. She stopped, cutting it off abruptly.

"We told you already," the older man next to her said, his salt and pepper beard quivering more than his voice. "What you ask is impossible. Even if we could create that many – which we can't – keeping them under control would be—"

"They're zombies!" Alejandro screamed, cutting him off. He gestured savagely to a row of odd-looking spectators assembled behind his throne. The missing kings looked out with dead, empty eyes onto the crowd, assembled once more in an audience chamber, as if to give their advice. "They'll have no more mind than these! A child could control them!"

"If the child had multiple souls," the older man snapped. "We're necromancers, not puppeteers! To raise a zombie, we must lend it part of our soul – that is the only way to direct it. I can create one or two zombies at a time – no more. An especially gifted *bokor* might be able to manage as many as five, but a whole army?" He gestured to the mass of waiting humans. They were there, Tomas realized with a sickening lurch, to be turned into more troops for Alejandro's growing megalomania. Troops who wouldn't question his orders, wouldn't challenge him as Tomas and a few others had dared. "You ask the impossible!"

Alejandro didn't move, didn't blink, but Tomas knew what was coming. A flick of a guard's wrist broke the man's neck, his body tumbling to the floor to join the others. The young man who had been intended as the next victim fainted and was dragged back into the waiting throng.

"Do it," Alejandro told the girl, who was staring at the body of her fallen colleague as it was arranged in line with the others. "Now."

She transferred her stare to the creature on the throne, and Tomas knew she couldn't do as he asked. It was written on her face, along with horror and revulsion and abject terror. She was shaking, just standing there, and he doubted she could concentrate enough to remember her name at this point. Much less how to manage a complex spell.

"She'll fail," Sara said suddenly, "and my brother will be next."

Tomas looked around frantically for any sign that she had been overheard, but there was nothing. The closest vamps, two guards a few yards away at the bottom of the stairs, never even flinched. They were watching one of the captives who was busy vomiting up his dinner, the gasping, wet sounds followed by painful dry gasps. Tomas glanced at Sara, who nodded at the fanatic. He was clutching his bones and murmuring something with a distracted air, as if everything below wasn't enough to hold his attention.

"Silence shield," Sara explained. "Have any suggestions, or do you just want to wing it?"

Forkface had taken off his bulging pack and was systematically tucking stoppered vials into his already weapons-filled belt. It was pretty obvious how he was voting. Too bad they'd all be dead within half a minute of an attack.

"This is Alejandro's power base," he said, struggling to explain in terms a human could understand. "In addition to his own, he can draw power from every vampire in the room. A frontal assault will not be successful."

"Any idea what will?"

Tomas' eyes were on the woman necromancer, who was crying and chanting at the same time, with theatrically raised arms but no discernable effect on any of the bodies. "Can he do a spell to allow you to move through the crowd unseen?" Tomas nodded at the fanatic.

"The best he can do in full light is a shadow spell to make us less obvious. It works on humans by redirecting attention away from us. But I don't know what effect it will have on vamps." She glanced at her colleague, who was still muttering to himself but was now staring at an old inscription in the rock. She kicked him.

"Yes, yes. Will not work on master-level, but all else, yes."

Tomas nodded. "I'll distract Alejandro. While he is occupied with me, slip through the crowd and get your brother."

"That won't help everyone else."

"If I can defeat him, his position will devolve onto me and they'll be safe." But the odds were a lot less in his favour than he'd hoped. Catching Alejandro somewhere in the tunnels or the jungle, alone except for a few of his closest attendants, he might have stood a chance. But nowhere in his plans had he figured on anything like this.

His voice must have reflected some of his doubt, because Sara narrowed her eyes. "And if you can't?"

"Once they see me, the court will likely have eyes for nothing else. Get as many people out as you can while they are distracted."

"Distracted killing you, you mean. Bullshit."

"I came here knowing this was the likely outcome."

"Another little thing you forgot to mention. We're gonna have to work on our communication."

Tomas decided he couldn't waste more time arguing. The woman necromancer had failed and Alejandro's power was boiling through the room, hot on his neck. He was furious. And when he lost his temper, people died – a lot of them. It would be perfectly within character for him to simply order every human in the room put to death. As if in response to Tomas' thoughts, the guard behind the woman started forwards, hand raised.

Tomas was grateful for vampiric speed, which allowed him to reach her before the guard could snap her neck. He caught the vamp's arm, but he needn't have bothered. The room had frozen.

"Tomas." The voice was the one he remembered, echoing inside his head like cool silver, but crawling under his skin like something alive. However, the power behind it, the force compelling him to do Alejandro's will, was gone. For the first time, Tomas had reason to be grateful for his current master. As much as he hated the man, Louis-Cesar's ownership ensured that Alejandro's unspoken command exerted no more pull than that of any other first-level master. A rank he currently shared.

Tomas opened his hand and the guard retreated in an undignified scramble. The rest of the court was moving closer, not attacking, yet, but on high alert. No one had any doubts about why he was here.

Apparently, neither did Alejandro, because the moment Tomas made a move in his direction, a strong force pushed against him, like a hundred invisible hands holding him back. Make that 200, he thought, glancing about at the family he'd once called his own. The fifteen feet to the bottom of the stairs felt like miles; he had to fight for every inch with eyes burning into his spine like acid and a thick, roiling nausea in his gut. He had a moment of vertigo, swaying on his feet like a drunk trying to dance, and someone laughed, high and cold and mocking. It wasn't Alejandro. His eyes were glittering dangerously and he'd lost the faintly amused smile that was his usual armour.

The stairwell leading up to his throne had twenty steps. By the time Tomas reached them, he was panting like he'd run a mile.

"I challenged you once before," he said around the mass that had risen in his throat, huge and cold and sickening. "But you were too cowardly to face me. I have come—"

It was a good thing he hadn't worked too hard on his speech, because he never got to give it. The vampires had closed in on every side, jostling each other, trying to get up the courage to attack him. Tomas had hoped that Alejandro's pride would force him to fight his old servant himself, especially with the odds so heavily in his favour. But Alejandro remained seated, letting his men get more and more worked up until, finally, two broke away from the crowd and dashed in, snarling.

They came from opposite sides, and while Tomas was dealing with the one on the left, turning his own knife back against him, the one on the right smashed something heavy against his leg. It was the one he'd injured earlier, the one that had yet to completely heal. He fell to his hands and knees, the jar of landing on the shattered kneecap turning the whole room white hot with blinding pain.

He pulled the knife out of the first vamp, who retreated back into the crowd, howling and clawing at his wound, and rolled in time to slash at the second's throat. He missed because the vamp dodged, lightning fast, at the last minute, but Tomas didn't need weapons to crush his throat, only an application of raw power. The vamp was young and that effectively put him out of commission. But it also used up power Tomas couldn't afford to lose, and there were doubtless dozens of others that the family would consider expendable if their deaths served to further weaken him.

Tomas dragged himself back onto one leg, momentarily crippled while his system fought to rebuild torn cartilage and shattered bone. Alejandro leaned forwards, still not bothering to get to his feet. "Do you really believe you will make it all the way up here, Tomas? Because I believe I will sit here and watch them gut you as you try."

Four more vampires rushed him, all from the same side, and although he dealt with them and with the low-level master who had waited on the other side for them to distract him, he missed the axe that someone threw from the crowd. Alejandro made a small gesture and the assault halted, for the moment, while Tomas shuddered and leaned his forehead against the slick, cold surface of the third step, a buzzing uproar surging all around him. On the third or fourth or tenth try, Tomas managed to take a couple of shallow breaths. He brought up shaking hands and tore the weapon out of his belly.

"Really, Tomas. I'm disappointed. I remembered you as better than this." Alejandro had finally bothered to get out of his seat, but he didn't come any closer. "And to think, I was contemplating offering you a position at the head of my new army. I really will have to reconsider."

Hot tendrils of agony shot out from Tomas' stomach wound as he tried to stand. At least he couldn't feel the throbbing in his leg any more, Tomas thought, and laughed to cover the scream that wanted to tear out of his chest. An all-out assault on Alejandro was the only chance he had. If he hurt him badly enough, the family might back off, waiting to see the outcome before they risked attacking the man who might be their new master. Slogging slowly up these steps, one by one, being battered from all sides and buffeted by Alejandro's power, was a sure recipe for disaster. But it was also the only hope the humans had.

He couldn't hear anything from the back of the cave, from the mass of 400 or 500 hundred people who had been corralled there. And there was no way so many could remain silent while witnessing something like this. Not unless they were being shielded and hopefully guided out. But it was a long way through the maze of hallways, as countless mortals had learned to their terror, and even further to the town beyond. He had to give them time if they were to have any chance at all. And in this slice of hell, time meant pain.

Pain wasn't a problem, Tomas decided, looking into Alejandro's amused black eyes. He'd brought it to enough people through the years. It was his turn.

"Still a coward posing as a gentleman," Tomas gasped, and threw the gory axe straight at Alejandro.

His old master turned it aside with an elegant wave of his hand, but anger and surprise caused his attention to waver slightly, allowing Tomas to make headway against the stream of power opposing him. He made it to the tenth stair before the world spun around and dropped out from under him, and he hit something hard and unyielding. Only when the pain receded a fraction did he realize he'd been dumped on the floor by another axe, this one to the spine.

And master or no, no one healed a wound like that instantaneously. Suddenly, his limbs didn't work: his arms and legs flopped uselessly around him, his head fell back into a puddle of his own blood. Alejandro waved off the guards who were rushing in to finish Tomas, as he slowly descended the remaining stairs.

He stopped directly in Tomas' line of vision, his booted feet just touching the bloody pool. He unsheathed a rapier, good quality Cordoba steel instead of wood, making it obvious that this wasn't going to end quickly. "How the mighty have fallen. That is the phrase, isn't it? From my lieutenant to this, all because of ambition."

Tomas tried to tell him that ambition wasn't the point, that it never had been, but his throat didn't seem to work either. Although that might have been because of the sight that suddenly loomed up behind his former master. At first, Tomas was sure he was imagining things. But not even in a pain-induced near faint could his brain have come up with something like that.

Behind Alejandro, a withered arm encased in a few rotting rags appeared, a tracery of thin blue veins pulsing under the long dead skin. A head followed, cadaverous and brown, but with two enormous, glittering eyes rolling in the too-large sockets. They stared at Tomas for an instant, full of terrible, ancient fury, before the arm caught Alejandro around the neck and a mouth full of cracked and yellowed teeth clamped onto his neck.

Alejandro gave one sharp gasp before the others were on him, a crowd of dry, old bones and tanned leather skins that glowed slightly from the inside, like someone shining a flashlight through parchment. And although Alejandro's power still surged around Tomas like a hurricane, they didn't seem to feel it. There was a crack, a thick, watery sound, and then silence – except for the ripping, chewing noises coming from the middle of the once-human mass.

The kings had returned.

Another pair of feet came to rest beside him, just brushing his hair. Tomas looked up to see Jason, slack-jawed no longer, but with a quiet intensity his eyes. It seemed Alejandro had kidnapped one necromancer worth his salt, after all.

"You brought them back," Tomas managed to croak after a moment.

Jason didn't look away from the creatures and their meal. "They brought themselves."

Tomas didn't have a chance to ask him what he meant, because the earth began to move in a very familiar manner. Jason grabbed him under the arms and pulled him backwards down the stairs. No one tried to stop him. It was as if the court was frozen in place, staring in disbelieving horror at the sight of their master being attacked by supposedly harmless sacks of bones.

They made it to the edge of what had been the holding pen before Alejandro's power suddenly cut off, like someone throwing a switch. A ripple went through his vampires as they felt it too and realized what it meant. They came back to life with a vengeance, but too late; half the roof collapsed in a cascade of limestone.

Sara and one of her men ran up, dirty-faced and panting. Forkface grabbed Tomas, yanked the axe out of his back and threw him over a shoulder. Then they ran.

The doorway collapsed behind them, dust billowing into the air while rocks and gravel nipped at their heels. The entire tunnel system was buckling, floor heaving, ceiling threatening to crush them at any moment. His helper lost his footing and they both went down, Tomas managing to catch himself on arms that, while unsteady, actually seemed to work again. He grabbed Sara, attempting to shield her, at the same time that she grabbed for him. And amid stones falling and dust clouds choking them, they braced together, Sara saying things that Tomas couldn't hear over the roaring in his ears. But their small patch of ceiling held and, after they limped across the boundary from the caves to the old temple, the rumbling gradually petered off.

They emerged at last into the jungle, where a mass of dazed people huddled together in small groups under the dark, star-dusted sky. Forkface dumped Tomas unceremoniously beside a small pool just inside the temple, where people were scooping up water in hats, hands or flasks. It was green and it stunk, with slimy ropes of algae clinging to sides, but nobody seemed to mind. Some were hugging, more were crying and one, amaz-ingly, was laughing. Tomas blinked at them, disbelieving, seeing for the first time in 400 years the Day of the Dead celebrated in this place by the living.

Jason brought him some water in an old canteen and, while Tomas didn't particularly need it, he drank it anyway. The fanatic came over to join them after a moment. It seemed he'd been delegated to lead the way out while Sara and her remaining associate remained behind to rescue Tomas. He seemed perturbed that they hadn't brought him any bones, and eyed Tomas speculatively for a moment before moving off, muttering.

Tomas' whole body hurt and he was ravenously hungry, but he was alive. It didn't seem quite real. "How did you do it?" he finally asked Jason.

"I didn't. I only woke them up."

"I don't understand."

"The Inca kings were believed to watch over their people, even after death, and to demand good behaviour of the living. Any who defied them soon learned that they also had within their power to reward or to punish."

"That's a myth."

Jason smiled, an odd, lopsided effort. "Really. It seems strange, not to mention expensive, to tie up most of the revenues of the state in the care of creatures who have no ability to hurt you." He shook his head. "The ancient priests prepared the royal dead well. I only had to give them a nudge."

"You mean—"

His eyes went soft and dreamy. "They said they had been watching Alejandro for a long time. And they were hungry."

"Well, they'll have the whole court to snack on now, once they finish with him," Sara commented, stopping by after locating enough local people to serve as guides for everyone else.

Tomas had a sudden image of vengeful Inca monarchs pursuing Alejandro's vampires through the halls where they had once done the same to humans. He smiled.

"Attacking that thing on your own was insane," Sara said bluntly. "I like that in a person. Want a job?"

Tomas just looked at her for a moment. He was a first-level master, one of only a handful in the world. Others of his rank were either sitting in governing positions over his kind or were powerful masters with their own courts. They were emphatically *not* running around with a motley crew of mercenaries carrying out jobs so crazy no one else would touch them. He'd killed Alejandro, or close enough by vampire law. He could assume his position, round up whatever vampires had made it out before the cave-in, and claim to be the new head of the Latin American Senate. That would put him beyond the jurisdiction of the North American version – which wanted him dead – and his master – who wanted him back in slavery. He could rebuild Alejandro's empire and walk these halls once more, this time as their master. He would be rich, powerful and feared . . .

And, in time, just like Alejandro.

"Well?"

Sara didn't seem to be the patient type. It was something else they were going to have to work on. They weren't touching, but she was standing so close that he could smell the vestiges of her perfume mingled with gunpowder and sweat. It was strangely comforting, like the lingering warmth of a touch even after it's gone. Tomas looked up at her face, surrounded by stars, and, for the first time in longer than he could remember, he saw a future.

"Where do I sign?"

# Vampire Unchained

## Nancy Holder

### In the tunnels beneath Central Park, New York City

High midnight, vampire's delight; black as a coal mine or an empty mirror; the wind shrieked like the bringer of the one true death. It was raining hard enough to soak through gravestones, and the damp, slimy brick tunnels stank like a bog. Vermin squealed in the candlelight as the vampire nest of 16 waited for Andrew Wellington, their sire. Firelight from twin, old-fashioned wooden torches set in sconces on the wall flickered on glowing red eyes and jewelled fangs. Fear and bloodlust floated in equal measures through the tunnel like a miasma.

And yet, it was a better place than the city above them. New York was a war zone, overrun by Supernaturals – rival vampire nests; voodoo *bokors* with their zombies and *loa* gods; succubi and incubi . . . the list seemed endless. A group of human magic users called the House of the Blood had ripped the veil between good and evil and the world writhed in chaos.

All I wanted to do was give our people safe harbour, Liam Cadogan thought. He was Andrew's second-in-command, and there was a good chance his life – such as it was, for he was a vampire – was about to end.

Struggling against the grip of the nest's four strongest enforcers, Liam bared his fangs in futile rage. He hissed and snarled, his vampiric nature taking over; he was cornered and he was in fatal danger. A few of the nest laughed; others stared on in horror; a few more drew back into the shadows – the guilty ones, his allies.

Then Elizabeth, the sire's consort – she went by Liz these days – glided from the darkness with a prize in tow. It was Claire Rossi, his woman. His *human* woman.

Liam's knees buckled at the sight of Claire, captive and afraid. Her auburn hair hung in sopping ringlets past the shoulders of her black raincoat. Her eyes, the colour of dark chocolate, stared out at him beseechingly from her heart-shaped face. Her breath puffed like steam as she panted, whether from the cold or terror he had no idea.

"No," Liam whispered, heartsick.

"Yes. Oh, yessss," Liz replied with a cruel chuckle. "Come on now, Liam. After all those years at his side, you know you can't hide anything from Andrew. Especially not someone as fetching as your whore."

Liz's waist-length white hair dangled at the small of her back as she tossed her head, showing her jewelled fangs in the torchlight. Whatever they had planned tonight, Liam would drink them all dry before he let them hurt Claire.

So he supposed he was a traitor, as his sire insisted.

Liz's long scarlet fingernails pressed deeply against Claire's beautiful neck. He wondered if Claire was wearing her crucifix. Little would it matter.

Liz didn't draw blood; that wasn't her place. The other vampires watched on in silence, resembling Liz far more than he: bone white in the flickering flames; eyes glowing like red embers; fangs long and heavily decorated. Though almost all of them wore modern clothing – both sexes favouring black leather trousers and jackets, the same as Liam – he was the only one who looked completely human. Liam was pale, yes, but not bone white; his hazel eyes gleamed red when the bloodlust was on him, but at no other time. And his hair was the same chestnut brown it had been on the night he'd been changed.

Andrew had told him that the centuries would leach his skin. That his fangs would grow and his eyes would glow crimson. But he'd been a vampire for over 150 years and as far he could tell – from videos and pictures of himself – he looked the same as ever.

Andrew had been wrong on a number of counts lately.

Flanked by torchlight, Claire's trip hammer heartbeat pummelled Liam like physical blows. He wanted to tell her she wouldn't die. He had lost one beloved woman; he would not lose another. Nor would he allow them to drag her into this twilight world of blood and death. She was a daughter of the sun, and she would remain so.

But to what purpose? he thought miserably. Demons cloud out her sun. Wraiths scream and caper like packs of animals. Heaps of garbage line the streets; whole city blocks are on fire. If I could take her away from all this, I would. But where could we go?

Liz grinned a challenge at him and rippled her fingers against Claire's neck as if she were playing a cello, her favourite musical instrument. Her other favourite instrument was a cat-o'-nine-tails, and she'd asked Liam more than once if he would care to play with her. He suspected Claire was paying for his constant refusals. Liz didn't take rejection well.

As if she could read his mind, Liz hissed at him and pressed harder. Claire whimpered, and some of the vampires chuckled. She was wearing black wool trousers and boots, and the neck of a red turtleneck sweater poked from above the black coat. She was exquisite, as always. A breathtaking woman, warm and passionate, far more sensual in her humanity than the wanton sexuality of female vampires.

Overhead, thunder rumbled. Liam heard the distinct howls of the werewolves that had overrun Central Park, and the flapping of vampire minions' wings as they clustered beneath the venerable old bridges.

Then he heard the familiar footfalls of his liege lord, his sire, Andrew Wellington.

For Claire and him, the nightmare was about to get worse.

He gazed steadily back at her as a ripple moved among the vampires. The men not restraining him dropped to one knee and all the women curtseyed. Liz stayed as she was, keeping Claire prisoner. Liam's four nestmates held him tighter, as if they thought he would bolt and attack Andrew.

A wise precaution.

"Ill-met by moonlight, Liam Cadogan," Andrew said as he appeared in the black circle of the tunnel. His deep voice echoed. He loomed tall and alabaster white, with white hair and eyes that swirled like blood and long fangs that were not only jewelled at the tips but carved with elaborate Chinese-style bats, like pieces of elephant ivory. He wore a black turtleneck sweater and black jeans.

"Andrew, may the blood run red," Liam said, inclining his head. There was no sense antagonizing his sire.

"Don't pretend," Andrew flung at him. "It's done. We're . . . done."

Liam heard the pain in Andrew's voice, and felt it, too. If only he could make Andrew see why he had done it – why he had parlayed in secret with the House of the Phoenix, seeking a treaty, an alliance. The Wellington Nest could never hope to survive the chaotic hotbed of New York if they walked alone. The luxury of isolation was over.

Andrew jerked his head at his four minions, who squeezed Liam's wrists and elbows so hard he thought the bones would shatter. The four – James, Steve, Lars and Thor – had been bodybuilders, bouncers and construction workers in their mortal lives. They were young as vampires and still in love with their own strength. Or maybe they wanted to hurt Liam to prove their loyalty to Andrew. Or maybe, like most of the others, they wanted to hurt Liam because they hated him.

"Chain that traitor to the wall," Andrew ordered.

"No," Claire whispered under her breath. Andrew's eyes flicked her way and Liam gave his head a quick shake. Best she keep silent.

Liam's dark hair grazed the filthy tunnel wall as the four pushed his wrists and legs into manacles set into the mossy brickwork. He remembered the cuffs from their time living here, after the massacre of 1857, before Andrew moved them to a beautiful brownstone in the Upper East Side, where they still lived. They would chain humans here until they were ready to feed; though once they'd killed those responsible for murdering his wife and children, Liam partook as seldom as he could, and found no joy in it, no taste, no life.

James hissed and checked the fasteners on the manacle around Liam's thick left wrist. Lars checked the other. Steve and Thor checked his leg chains, which bit into Liam's heavy motorcycle boots.

Liam could still smell the blood on the chains. The metal was rusted and weak, and it wouldn't hold him long. Andrew surely knew that.

The four vampires moved away, signalling to Andrew that Liam was secured. With fangs fully bared, Andrew stepped forwards and grabbed a handful of Liam's plain black T-shirt and ripped it off his body. Liam didn't move; he stared hard into the ruby-red eyes of his sire. He knew the thick scar across his chest was visible for all to see. It was three inches wide, purple and white. Scars dealt in human life didn't heal after one rose from the grave.

"Seneca Village," Andrew said in a murderous tone as he pointed to Liam's scar. "It was the first village where free men of colour owned homes. Germans lived with them and some Irish. Irish like Liam Cadogan, his wife and three children. From the Olde Country but three months, and already living the American dream of home ownership. Not so, Liam? *Creid in ádh na nÉireannach.*"

"Believe in the luck of the Irish," Liz said. She had been there then, with two others who had since turned to dust, staked by humans.

"His wife and children died that night. Do you remember, Liam, how they screamed? Moira, your lovely Irish lass. Seamus, the little boy, still swaddled. And Liam would have died, from that stripe across his chest, except that Liz and I came to him."

Liz tapped her head against Claire's and smiled prettily.

"I asked him if he wanted vengeance. I asked him if he would become their enemy. If he would spend eternity feeding on them, for feeding off the likes of him."

He whirled on the nest, baring his fangs at them. All the vampires drew back, their eyes glowing from the shadows like magical rubies.

All except for Liz, who took a step forwards, dragging Claire with her. The temperature changed; the tension ratcheted up. Something was about to happen.

"Liam said yes," Andrew told the group. His eyes blazed like hellfire. "*He. Said. Yes.* Swore to me—"

"Times have changed," Liam said evenly, hoping to divert Andrew's attention while he tried to find a way out of this debacle. Claire looked glassy-eyed, as if shock had overtaken her.

"But *they* have not changed," Andrew retorted. "Humans have not. They're the same as they ever were. Greedy, barbaric and duplicitous."

Andrew was 600 years old. He had seen many wars, ethnic cleansings, ritual killings – cruelty and narrow-mindedness raised to a high art. He, Liam and Liz, together with the growing Wellington Nest, had watched both World Wars, Vietnam and the Middle East. Humans *were* far more violent than vampires could ever be. Worse, they fed off each other. A vampire who attacked another vampire wouldn't live to see another night.

Andrew spread wide his arms. "You all know this place as Central Park. We've hunted here many a night. But when Liam came into this life, it was Seneca Village, a little outpost in a swamp no one else wanted. Just a few huts, a store and three churches. The people here weren't hurting anyone. They were free at last, just like the speech."

Andrew's gaunt, porcelain face grew hard.

"But the rich swells of New York wanted a city park. So they razed it and killed Liam's people."

Gleaming scarlet eyes ticked towards Liam, studying the purple-white scar across his chest – his death wound.

"Now the humans *say* they want our help—" Andrew continued.

"The humans in the House of the Phoenix," Liam cut in. Claire's house. Her people. Her family.

Andrew snorted. "The House of the Phoenix is an illegal, renegade organization, created by a man who's been declared an outlaw," Andrew scoffed. "Jean-Marc de Devereaux. A magic user. Such wielders of magical power call themselves the Gifted."

There was a stirring throughout the nest. Most of them had

never heard of the Gifted. Liam had told only a few what he had learned.

"The Gifted are even worse than normal humans – what *they* called 'Ungifted' humans – like Liam's lover. This woman's people have crept into the castle courtyard like a pack of serfs, seeking the great lord's protection." Andrew raised his chin and stared coldly at Claire.

"Back in those days, I was a knight in service of such a lord. We used those serfs as cannon fodder. Then, when our enemy tried to starve us out, we slaughtered all those extra hungry mouths."

Claire narrowed her eyes. "Not everyone would have done such a thing," she said.

All vampiric eyes gazed first at her, and then at Andrew, who guffawed.

"I see the attraction, Liam," he said. "She's got hot blood." He mockingly swept a bow in her direction. "And her naïvety is touching, given how cynical we've all become."

"Other vampires have already joined the House of the Phoenix." Claire's voice quavered, but she did not falter. "All of us are treated equally, whether we are Gifted, Ungifted or Supernatural."

"That won't last long." Andrew's voice was icy. "My dear girl, you are so very expendable."

Without warning, he darted forwards, grabbed Claire's hair and jerked her head backwards, exposing her neck. Liam jerked on his restraints as Andrew and Liz bared their fangs, hissing in anticipation.

Liam got ready to spring.

"What I think is missing is the bloodlust," Andrew mused, inspecting Claire's neck as if it were a ripe pear. "Liam never really wanted what we have. He is not a lover of the night, a connoisseur of blood, a hunter. Like us."

He lowered his fangs towards Claire's neck, and now Liam hissed. Andrew didn't break her skin; he jerked up his head and nodded at Liz.

"Chain her beside him." He moved aside and folded his arms over his black sweater.

Liam watched as Liz yanked Claire forwards and threw her against the wall. *Click, click, click, click* and Claire was pinioned. Liam could hear her heart racing even faster. He could smell her fear.

"Liam," she breathed.

"You have to love the night now, Liam," Andrew glided towards Claire as if he couldn't stand to be away from her; as if she were irresistible. Liz watched with narrowed eyes and bared fangs.

"You have to be a hunter or you're no good to anyone, not even your lass here." Andrew's smile was panther-like, and Claire pushed hard against the wet, mouldy brick. "The peaceful times are over. This war is like no other."

"Which is why we need allies," Liam argued, his instincts urging him to strike. But he knew that if he attacked his sire – or any other member of the nest – his and Claire's lives would be forfeit.

"Allies, not users," Andrew retorted, as he left Claire and faced the nest. "I'm your sire," he reminded them. "I've lived longer than any of you, including Liz. I know what we're facing. And I know we can never, ever depend on humans for anything but treachery."

He looked over his shoulder at Liam. "You buried your common sense at Seneca Village, Liam Cadogan."

"Times have changed, Andrew," he said again.

"You repeat a feeble argument." Andrew's gaze lingered on his lieutenant. "We had a good run, you and I. I'll miss you."

"You don't have to do this," Liam said, though he had no idea what "this" was.

"We'll leave you now," Andrew announced. "Once we've left the tunnels, some humans I've hired will spread crosses and communion wafers across each of the exits. You won't be able to leave, Liam. You'll be stuck in here with her."

Andrew held up a finger. "If you send her out alone, we'll be waiting. And if you Change her, I'll stake her myself."

The other vampires stirred uneasily, glancing at each other, at their sire. Rail-thin Sanguine who had once been a Goth, tried to catch his eye. He was one of Liam's followers, believing that they needed the strength of the House of the Phoenix behind the nest. Liam didn't acknowledge him. If he did, Sanguine would suffer, too.

"You just said you would never harm another vampire," Claire said. Liam's nestmates gaped at her temerity. Maybe she wanted to die now and get it over with.

"Times have changed," Andrew said, not to her, but to Liam. "But the longest a vampire has ever lasted without feeding is a week."

He reached out his hand for Liz. She curled possessively around him and glared at Claire. Liam saw the hatred there; he had spurned Liz a hundred times and taken a despised human as his lover instead. And Andrew liked her; perhaps wanted her.

"You'll find your bloodlust, Liam. I have no doubt of that," Andrew continued.

"The House of the Phoenix will come after you," Claire said, struggling in her chains.

Andrew cocked his head; then he sauntered up to her and pressed the length of his body against hers. It was sexual and dominant, and Liam set his jaw, forcing himself not to react. He couldn't win this round.

"I can hurt you badly without killing you, you know," he said slowly, as he rocked his pelvis against her. "I can maim you. Disfigure you. I can make you beg to die."

"*There's* something to brag about," she shot back. Her voice shook. She took a breath and clamped shut her mouth; Liam was afraid she was going to spit at Andrew. What would he do then? Slash her throat? Gouge out her eyes?

Instead, Andrew cupped her breast. She gave a little cry, blinking her eyes. Then he released her with a sneer.

"Have a good feed, Liam, and let the old dream go. When next we meet, you'll finally, truly, be one of us."

Seething, Liam watched as Andrew took Liz's hand and walked back into the darkness. In ones and twos, the others followed. Sanguine was last.

"*I'll go to them for help,*" he mouthed.

Liam made no expression.

And then they were alone.

The torches flared but stayed lit as he broke free from the wall with a couple of sharp pulls and kicks. Chunks of brick clattered to the floor, into a pool of standing water. Then he unpeeled the manacles and let them fall, too. A rat squeaked and scurried away.

"Andrew restrained me for dramatic effect," he announced. "Or to humiliate me."

"I didn't think they'd hold you," Claire replied, looking down at her own chains.

He slipped a finger between her wrist and handcuff and bent it outwards as if it were made of butter. Making short work of her bonds, he reached for her and she sank into his arms. Her damp, pliant body moulded against his and he smelled the spice of her blood. She was warm as only the living are, and the pulse in her neck beat wildly.

"I'm sorry," she murmured against his chest. "You told me never to come to you. That it wouldn't be safe. But I got a note. It said you needed to meet me under the Gothic Bridge. And they were waiting."

"A note," he said. "Who gave it to you?"

"A vampire in our safe house named Giselle. She joined us six months ago."

He was alarmed. There had been no one in the Wellington Nest named Giselle. Andrew had gone outside to recruit someone new. He wondered if Liz knew about her. Although both Liz and Andrew took lovers, their loyalty was to each other.

"Giselle has to be a plant. Andrew's infiltrated the House of the Phoenix." He pulled her away gently. "How can your Gifted leaders not know?"

"Maybe they do know," she said hopefully. "Maybe I've been followed, and they're going to attack."

"Wouldn't Andrew know that? He would be bringing the fight to the nest," Liam ventured. "Why?"

Before she could answer, he began to pace.

"If he's allied himself with someone else, someone stronger, who could take out the House of the Phoenix, who would *want* to take out Phoenix . . ." He froze. "Jesus, Joseph and Mary," he murmured, alarms detonating like bombs. "The forces of darkness? The House of the Blood?" He shut his eyes, sickened on behalf of his nestmates, and unable to believe that Andrew would do such a thing. Vampires were Supernaturals, but they weren't evil.

"That could be the real reason he brought us down here – to get rid of me so I couldn't tell the others. He may assume I know – or that I'll find out – because I've been talking to the leaders of your House."

"We have to get out of here," she said. She gripped his arms tightly and looked up. "Hello?" she called. "Can anyone hear me?"

"Can the Gifted read your thoughts?" he asked her, wondering, too, if they could read his.

She nodded. "Some of them can." She bit her lower lip and searched his face. "What if they *do* come and they fight Andrew to try to rescue us? Can they beat him?"

Bring it on and we'll see, he thought. Then he looked at her and was filled with shame. He had to protect her at all costs.

Andrew was right; despite everything they'd been through, he and Andrew were done. Liam was no longer part of the Wellington Nest. He was a renegade like Jean-Marc de Devereaux, the Gifted leader of the House of the Phoenix. He, too, had clashed with the others of his kind; he, too, had struck out on his own to protect his loved ones.

Liam peeled off Claire's wet raincoat, slipping her arms through the drenched sleeves. Then he took off his black leather jacket and draped it over her shoulders. Putting his arm around her, he eased her over to the torches.

"You need to get warm," he said. "You're freezing. It will sap your strength."

The scent of her fear increased.

"You didn't answer my question," she said.

A war over our heads. A possible attack on my loyal confederates. My sire, turning on me. It's a miracle she got here without being killed. They must have followed her.

"We'll be out of here soon," he told her.

"Hmm-mm," she said non-committally, pulling his jacket around her shoulders. Did she realize that she took a step away from him?

He ran his hands up and down her arms and across her back, willing the cold away. The top of her turtleneck was sopping wet, as were the hems of her jeans. The rest was relatively dry.

They held each other in silence, tense and uneasy. He was alert to every sound – the flickering of the torches; the skittering of rats; her breathing, her pulse. She was so frightened.

He pulled one of the torches out of its holder and handed it to her. Then he took the other one.

"We should gather some things to burn," he told her. "We need to keep these going."

He didn't tell her that his great-grandmother Abigail had been burned as a witch. No one knew that. Back in the day, when he had married Moira, he should have told her. He'd been too afraid she'd refuse him. After his Change, he hadn't known there really were witches – now called the Gifted. It was Andrew who told him about them. New York City had been a neutral zone, where no Gifted were allowed to live or work their magic. But the House of the Phoenix had moved in, and a good thing too, with all the troubles.

Claire stayed close beside him as he began to search. The tunnel floor was slick with moss and rat droppings, but little else to feed the flames. The tunnels were familiar, despite all the years since he and the nest had lived in them. Where would they be now, if Andrew hadn't led them out, taken them to live in luxury? He felt a terrible sense of loss, and he grieved.

Time passed; he didn't know how much, but he was beginning to get hungry. He had to assume she was, too. The torches were dwindling into stubs maybe a foot in length. He could see in the dark, but she wouldn't be able to. It would be bad for her when the torches finally went out.

They came to a T-intersection. He scented the exit route the nest had used and took that one. A rat ran over the tip of his boot and he thought briefly about catching it. He might do well to take a moment away from her, find a rat or two, and drink. His stomach turned at the thought. He would be mortified if she saw him do it.

But I can't get too hungry, he thought anxiously.

At the end of a tunnel was a metal door, closed and locked. He felt the barriers of holy objects – communion wafers and crosses – on the other side. For reasons unknown even to Andrew, Christian symbols deterred vampires, even though vampires were not evil in the traditional Christian sense.

"Can you open it?" she asked hopefully.

"I want to check it out first," he replied.

He thought about breaking down the door anyways, enduring if he could and taking on whatever comers were there. Now, while he still had his strength.

He turned his head and saw a hole of blackness. It was a small sort of room, with what appeared to be a small pile of leather near the wall. Entering the space, he smelled Sanguine, Jack and Dianne, his confederates. Upon closer inspection, he realized the leather was three jackets. They had dropped them for him on the way out. For her.

He was moved. And he had hope.

He led her into the room and pointed to the jackets.

"These are from my allies. I want you to rest here. Stay warm. I'm going to explore a little."

"Don't leave me," she begged, reaching out a hand.

"I'll be back soon," he promised, squeezing it. He handed her both the torches. "Keep the torches going. If you have to burn the jackets to do it, do it."

She licked her lips, nodded, watching him as he went back to the tunnel proper and re-examined the door.

Then something in his head whispered, *No*.

"What?" he asked aloud, turning half around. "Claire?"

But he knew she hadn't called him.

He put his hand on the door. The barriers on the other side of the door tingled against his palm.

*Go back to her. Be with her.*

He jerked his hand away and took a step backwards. What the hell was going on?

Frowning, he whispered, "Who are you? Where are you?"

It had to be her Gifted housemates. It had to be help on the way.

There was no answer. He stood still, cocking his head, listening. Nothing more came to him.

He crouched down and pressed along the bottom edge of the door. His fingers stung.

"Claire, I heard something. Someone," he called to her. "A voice inside my head."

He walked back into the little room to find her on her feet. The torches were propped against the wall, and she was unzipping her jeans. Her face was serious, the colour in her cheeks high. His gaze dropped to the roundness of her hips, the tiny square of fabric covering her sex, as she pushed her jeans over her hips, down to her knees.

Her eyes were shiny with emotion as she slipped his jacket off her shoulders and allowed it to gently fall to the ground. She gazed at him steadily and gathered up the edge of her red turtleneck sweater.

"Maybe it's the same voice I heard, telling me to make love to you," she whispered. And then she took off her sweater.

"No, it's so cold," he said, rushing to her. He meant to embrace her, warm her, but his mouth came down on hers. His fangs were much smaller than any other vampire he had ever known; carefully, he slipped his tongue into her mouth and found the sweet taste of her there. Slowly they sank to the floor, on the pile of jackets left by his comrades. He kissed her hungrily, splaying his hands over her back as she reached to the front of her bra and unhooked it, drawing it away from her breasts.

Then he knew with every fibre of his being that they were meant to make love now, that it was the best thing they could do to save themselves.

*To say goodbye*, said the voice.

"No," he rasped under his breath.

She moaned as his right hand cupped her breast and he ran his thumb over one taut nipple and then the other. Her jeans were down around her knees. He moved swiftly to her wispy thong, and moved it aside, pleasuring her sex, his finger over her clitoris, the shell-lip, glistening pink.

He slipped his finger inside her, feeling the wetness, the warmth. Wanting to be there.

Then his need shifted and he felt himself hungering for her as only a vampire could, hungering for human blood. He panicked, drawing away, but she held him tightly as his finger stayed inside her. His body was reacting, hard and thrusting; so, too, were his fangs, aching to bury themselves in her veins. She was in terrible danger.

Part of his mind registered that she was unzipping his trousers and moving her hand inside. Her fingers grazed his sex, then wrapped around it. He reared, engorged. He groaned like an animal; he hissed and writhed.

"Get away from me," he pleaded. "Claire, run."

She didn't seem to hear him. She moved her hand up and down, kissing his mouth, the sides of his mouth, the hollow of his cheek.

"Holy Mary, leave me," he begged again, as his mouth crashed over hers. He pulled her up in his arms, as she madly pushed her own jeans further down, and then his.

"Do it," she urged him.

"Lass, lass," he groaned, his Irish brogue thickening. He felt years fall away from him. He was so young again. Ireland was there, shamrock green and purple, and the sea and seabirds calling him to go afar. *Take your loved ones and go. You'll be back someday.*

But they had never gone back. They were dead.

But Claire is alive. Keep her alive.

Then they were joined, one to one, and the sensation that roared through him blazed a white-hot heat from the base of his spine to his sex and into his chest, where his heart did not beat. Where his heart . . .

Then he saw her: his ancestress, walking in the heather. Old Maggie Cadogan, the witch, bending beside the cairn on the hill, her lips moving. And then Maggie at the stake, the fire rising, smoke filling her lungs. He heard her words: "Such as mine will carry my blood until the dark days; and it will boil in their veins and give them powers such as you have never seen—"

It was her voice inside his head.

Liam's blood was boiling now, steaming away the Change until he felt a terrible thumping in the cage of his ribs, in the veins that were as cold and empty as the tunnels. His lungs filled with air for the first time in over one hundred years.

"Oh, God, oh my God," Claire whispered. "Your skin . . . it's warm. And your heart . . ." She flattened her left hand against his chest. "It's *beating*. Liam, it's beating!"

He wanted to tell her, to speak to her. But the flames inside him were rising higher. He was a *man*, and not just a man but a man of witch-blood born. He was deep inside Claire and he pushed her backwards onto the jackets and took her, hard. More energy surged through him and more heat. Blurry kaleidoscopes of colours, sounds and smells rushed through him. He could no longer see or smell or taste; he could only feel. He was rocketing through the sky. He was a comet, on fire.

"Sex magic," she whispered. "The Gifted—"

He was Gifted. He hadn't known it; no one had. He'd been Changed and now changed again. He took her hard, allowing ecstasy to mount within him. He felt her constricting around him, weeping with excitement and wonder. Her smooth, heated core; his woman, his living woman, his darling . . .

Oh, my God, I'm not alone any more, he thought, as tears streamed down his face for his lost loved ones, for all the hopes dashed and the anger and hatred that had consumed him.

Like a windstorm, his body gathered its forces, and hovered for one last moment before he poured his joy and his life into her. He climaxed in a river of energy, of magic. He was soaring and floating; he was loved and he was new.

"Liam, Liam," she cried. She was with him, riding the throes of her own passion as she clung to his shoulders. For a moment he thought they were flying, floating in delirious joy.

Back down to earth, back down inside the tunnel, they rested in each other's arms, silent and weeping, both of them. He had no words; he clung to her, gasping, feeling his body live.

"What . . . how," she began, and then fell silent as she covered his face with soft kisses. And then more kisses.

She was dazed. He dressed her quickly, like a little child, and put Sanguine's jacket and then his own on her, for warmth. He put on another leather jacket – it belonged to Jack – and picked her up in his arms.

He didn't know what was going to happen, but he could save her now. He knew it. He would take on all comers, battle all monsters and men and vampires. He would have Andrew's head on a pike before dawn if it came to that.

But he would not lose another beloved woman.

Moira, he thought. Seamus, Saraid, Emilie, his children. And then, Maggie Cadogan, help me. He strode back to the metal door and willed it to open. And it would open. He could see it in his head as he prepared himself for the holy water and crosses on the other side. Instead, the door immediately collapsed in a heap of rust.

On the other side was a meadow, covered with heather. Beyond, a hill, rolling with shamrocks, and above the blue sky, banked with clean, fluffy clouds and a golden sun.

Ireland.

He turned back to face the tunnel. It was gone. Instead, the grey and green glistened and rolled, cresting with foam, and single little seal, riding the swells. Seabirds wheeled above. He blinked, then gazed down at Claire in his arms, and kissed her like a man who had not seen the sky in 100 years and more, like a man who had nearly lost his soul.

And she kissed him back, like a woman whose every dream had been answered. Warm lips, hands, skin; eyelashes, soft tendrils of hair.

"Sex magic," she whispered against his temple. "The strongest kind there is among the Gifted – among your people. It brought us here."

He nuzzled her cheek, her neck. His fangs were gone. His heart was beating like the crashing of the waves. "Nay, Claire, love brought us here."

A seabird cawed as Liam lifted his head and saw an old grey-haired woman dressed in an old-fashioned kirtle and a grey woollen shawl standing at the top of the hill. There was a pile of stones beside her – the cairn of his vision. She raised a hand in greeting and leaned against the rocks with a self-satisfied air.

"*Sonas ort*," he called to her. Thank you.

She gestured for him to come closer. As he began to walk towards her, small sod houses appeared in the meadow. Smoke came from holes in the roofs. Pipes played over the rush of a breeze.

Children laughed.

*Children*, Maggie Cadogan whispered in Liam's ear.

Secure in his arms, blessedly safe, Claire gazed around in wonder and awe. "To be gone from that hell . . ." Her voice caught, and she gazed up at him again. "Liam, will love keep us here?"

He lowered his head over hers and kissed her like her man. Like her protector.

Like her husband.

"Aye," he promised. "It will."

# A Stand-up Dame

## Lilith Saintcrow

When a man wakes up in his own grave, he sometimes reconsiders his choice of jobs.

If he's smart, that is. Me, I'm as dumb as a box of rocks and my skull felt like a cannonade was going off inside. The agony in my head was rivalled only by the thirst. Aching thirst in every nerve and vein, my throat scorched and my eyes hot marbles. It was raining, but the water from the sky falling into my open mouth did nothing for the dry nails twisting in my larynx. I struggled up out of clods of rain-churned clay mud, slick and dirty as a newborn pig. My clothes were ruined and the monster in my head roared.

I fell backwards, still trapped to my knees in wet earth, padded hammers of rain smashing along the length of my body, and screamed. The spasm passed, leaving only the parched desert plains inside every inch of me.

A few moments of effort got me kicking free, the last of the wet clay collapsing in a body-shaped hole now that the body was above ground. I opened my mouth, rain beating my dirty face, and got only a mouthful of muck.

Coughing, gagging, I made it to hands and knees. My head was a swollen pumpkin balanced on a thin aching stick, and the headache receded between waves of scorching, unbearable, agonizing *thirst*.

There were pines all around me, singing and sighing as the sodden wind slapped them around. It took me two tries to stand up, and another two tries before I remembered my name.

*Jack. Jack Becker. That's me. That's who I am.*
*And I've got to find the dame in the green dress.*

Outside the city limits and I'm a duck out of water. The mud wouldn't dry, not in this downpour; it just kept smearing over the ruin of my shirt and suit pants. Even Chin Yun's laundry wouldn't be able to get out the worst. Slogging and slipping, I made it down a hill the size of the Chrysler Building and found the dirt road, turned off the highway, and there was a mile marker right there.

Twelve miles to the city. Cramps screamed from my empty belly. Maybe getting shot in the head works up a man's appetite. Every time I reached up to touch my noggin it was tender, a puckered hole above my right eye full of even more mud.

I wasn't going to get far. The idea of stumbling off the side of the road and drowning in a ditch was appealing – except for the dame in the green dress.

*Think about that, Jack. One thing at a time.*

Thunder rumbled somewhere far away. Miss Dale would be at home, probably talking to her cat or making a nice hot cup of tea. The thought made my insides clench like they were going to turn into a meat grinder, and my breath made a funny whistling sound through my open mouth. My nose was plugged and, in any case, I was gasping for air. Sometimes it rains hard enough to drown you out here.

That was when I saw the light.

It was beautiful, it was golden, it was a diner. Not just any diner, but the Dentons' Dandy Diner, eleven miles from the city limits. I couldn't go in there looking like this. It took me a while to fumble for my wallet and I nearly ended up in the ditch anyway, my feet tangling together.

The wallet – last year's Christmas present from Miss Dale – was still in my pocket and held all the usuals, plus nineteen dollars and twenty cents. They hadn't taken any money. Interesting.

*Think about that later, Jack.*

My shirt was wet enough to shed the mud, my suit jacket nowhere in evidence. Stinging pellets warned me the rain was turning to ice.

But the crazy thing was, I wasn't cold. Just as thirsty as hell. Maybe the idea of the dame in green was warming me up.

Neon blinked in the diner's windows. It was closed, goddammit, and just when I could have used a phone. I could even *see* the phone box, smearing my muddy mitts on the window and blinking every time the COLD DRINKS sign blinked as well. The phone was at the end of the hall, right near the crapper.

My legs nearly gave out.

*This is turning out to be a bad night, Jackie boy.*

I found a rock I could lift without busting myself and heaved it. The glass on the door went to pieces, and I carefully unlocked it. The long slug trail of mud I left going towards the phone might have been funny if I'd been in a grinning mood.

A man like me knows his secretary's home number. Any dame dumb enough to work for a case like me probably wouldn't be out dancing at a nightclub. Dale didn't have any suitors – not that she talked, of course. She was a tall thin number with interesting eyes, but that was as far as it went.

Not like the dame in green, no sir.

I hung on to the phone box with fingers that looked swollen and bruised. Dirt still slimed my palms. Under it I was fishbelly white, almost glowing in the dim lighting. The Dentons were going to find their diner not quite so dandy in the cold light of dawn, and I was sorry about that.

"Hello?" She repeated herself, because I was trying to make my mouth work. "Hello?"

"Dale," I managed through the obstruction in my mouth. Sounded like they'd broken my jaw, or like I was sucking on candy.

"Mr Becker?" A note of alarm, now. "*Jack?*"

"You got to come pick me up, doll-face." I sounded drunk.

"Where have you—? Oh, never mind. Where are you?" I could almost see her perched on her settee, that cup of tea steaming gently on an end table, and her ever-present steno pad appearing. "Jack? Where are you right now?"

"Denton," I managed. "Dandy Diner, about eleven miles out of the city. You got the keys to my Studebaker?"

"Your car is impounded, Mr Becker." Now she sounded like the Miss Dale I knew. Cool, calm, efficient. Over the phone she sounded smoky and sinful, just like Bacall. I might've hired her just for that phone voice alone, but she turned out to be damned efficient and not likely to yammer her yap off all the time, which meant I paid her even when I couldn't eat.

You don't find secretaries like that every day, after all.

"Never mind, I'll bring my car. Denton's Dandy, hm? That's west out of town, right?"

"Sure it is." My legs bucked again, I hung on to the box for all I was worth. "I'll be waiting out front."

"I'm on my way." And she hung up, just like that.

What a gal.


The pain in my gut crested as Miss Dale peered over the seat. I'd barely managed to get the door open, and as soon as I was in the car she took off; I wrestled the door shut and the windshield wipers made their idiot sound for about half a mile as I lay gasping in the back seat.

The car smelled like Chanel No. 5 and Chesterfields. And it smelled of Miss Dale, of hairspray and powder and a thousand other feminine things you usually have to get real close to a dame to get a whiff of. It also smelled like something else.

Something warm, and coppery, and salty, and so good. The windshield wipers went ka-thump ka-thump, and her Ford must've had something going on with the engine, because there was another regular thumping, high and hard and fast. My mouth wouldn't close all the way. I kept making that wheezing sound, and she finally risked another look over the seat at me.

"I'm taking you to Samaritan General," she said, and I stared at the sheen of her dark hair. "You sound terrible."

"No." Thank God, it was one word I could say without whatever was wrong with my mouth interfering. "No hospital." The slurring was back, like my jaw was broken but I wasn't feeling any pain. As a matter of fact, now that the headache was gone, the only thing bothering me was how *thirsty* I was.

Another mile squished under the tyres. She turned the defroster up, and that regular thumping sounded like her car was about to explode, it was going so fast. "Mr Becker, you are beginning to worry me." She lit a Chesterfield, keeping her eyes on the road, and, when she opened the window to blow the smoke out, the smell of the rain came through and I realized what that thumping was.

It was Miss Dale's pulse. I was hearing her heartbeat. And the tyres touching the road. And each raindrop smacking the hardtop. The hiss of flame as she lit the cigarette showed the fine sheen of sweat on her forehead and I realized Miss Dale was nervous.

"Don't worry, doll-face. Everything's fine. Take me . . ."

*Where can you go, Jack? The lady in green knows your office, and if she thinks you're dead . . .*

"Take me to your house." Only it was more like *hauwsch*, like I was a goddamn German deli-owner, and when I ran my tongue along the inside of my teeth everything got interesting. My tongue rasped, and I lost whatever it was Miss Dale would have said because the taste of copper filled my mouth and I suddenly knew what I was thirsty for.

The knowledge might have made me scream if I hadn't gone limp against the seat as if someone had slapped me, because it was warm and the twisting in my gut receded a little bit, and because goddammit, after a man claws his way up out of his own grave and breaks into a diner, he deserves a little rest.

*The green dress hugged her curves like the Samaritan freeway hugs the coast, and, under the little veil on her hat, those eyes were green too. She even had green gloves, and she accepted a light from me with a small nod and raised eyebrows, settling her emerald velvet clutch purse in her lap.*

*"You come highly recommended, Mr Becker." A regular Bryn-Mawr purr, over the sound of Miss Dale typing in the front. The lady kept her back as straight as a ruler and the lamp on my desk made her out to be pale, not one of those sun-bunnies.*

*Miss Dale stopped typing.*

*"Glad to hear that." I made it non-committal, as casual as my shoes on the desk. It was five o'clock and already dark, the middle of winter, and I was behind on the rent.*

*"Mr Becker?" Miss Dale stood tall and angular in the doorway. "Will you be needing anything else?" Her cat-tilted dark eyes met mine, and she had a sheaf of files in her capable, narrow hands. If she got a little more meat on her, she'd be a knockout. If, that is, you could chip through the ice.*

*Right now she was giving me the chance to say we were closing and the dame in green could come back another time. I waved a languid hand. "No thanks, Miss Dale. I'll see you in the morning."*

*"Very good, sir." Frosty as a Frigidaire. Miss Dale spent a few moments moving around the office, locking the files in the front cabinet, and the dame in green said nothing until my secretary left, locking the door behind her and her heels click-tapping down the hall, as efficiently as the rest of her.*

*The sign outside my office window blinked. We were up over an all-night lunch counter and news-stand, and the big neon arrow drenched the room with waves of yellow and red after dark once Miss Dale turned the lights off. The couch opposite my desk looked inviting, and it would have looked even more inviting if I hadn't been looking eviction in the face, I suppose.*

*"So what do you want me to do, Mrs . . . ?" I made it into a question.*

*"Kendall. Mrs Arthur Kendall. Mr Becker, I want you to follow my husband."*

It smelled like Chanel and dirt. And even though I was under a pile of blankets, I was lying on something soft and I shot up straight, swallowing a scream. It was the sound a bullet makes when it hits a skull, the explosion that was death.

My fingers were around something soft, but with a harder core. My other hand flashed up, catching Miss Dale's other wrist as she tried to slap me. Silk fluttered – she was dressed in a wrapper, a red kimono with a sun-yellow dragon breathing orange fire.

She yelped, and I realized I was half-naked, only in a pair of mud-crusted skivvies. Someone had undressed me and put me in a bed made of pink fluff, pillows spilling over the edges. The Chanel was her, and the dirt? That was me, stinking up a nice dame's bed.

"Mr Becker," she said, and it was my imperturbable secretary again, the belt of her kimono loosened enough to show a strap of her – well, I'm only human, of course I looked. "Mr Becker, let go of me at *once*."

The nightmare receded. I let go of her wrists. She retreated two steps, bumping her hip against a bedside table loaded with a jar of cold cream and a stack of big leather-bound books that looked straight out of Dr Caligari's library, as well as a lamp with a frilly pink shade and an economy-sized box of Kleenex. We stared at each other, and the fine, damp texture of her skin looked better than it ever had.

She rubbed at her right wrist, the one I'd grabbed first. "You were screaming," she whispered.

For once, I had no smart-aleck thing to say. Of course I'd been screaming.

Miss Dale drew herself up, tightening her kimono with swift movements. She was barefoot, and her dark hair wasn't pinned back. It tumbled down to her shoulders in a mass of curls, and it looked nice that way. She folded her arms and tried her best glare on me, and if I hadn't been lounging half-naked in what I suspected was her bed, it might have worked.

"I'm sorry." It was all I could say.

"You'd better be. You're wanted for murder."

I closed my mouth with a snap and started thinking furiously.

"You disappeared three days ago, Mr Becker. The police tore apart your office. I am sad to report they also took your last three bottles of Scotch. They questioned me rather extensively, too."

My throat was dry. The thirst was worse than ever, and that distracting sound was back, the high hard thumping. It was her pulse, and it sounded like water in the desert. It sounded like the chow bell in basic training.

Her heart going that fast meant she was terrified. But there she stood, high colour on her cheeks, arms folded and shoulders back, ready to take me to task once again.

*Three days?* "Murder?" I husked.

"The murder of Arthur Kendall, Mr Becker. His widow identified you as the killer." Hung on the bedroom wall behind her was a Photoplay page of Humphrey Bogart in a fedora, leering at the camera like the bum he was. I was beginning to suspect my practical Miss Dale had a soft spot for leering bums.

"The Kendall job." It was difficult to think through the haze in my head and the sound of her pulse, calming down a little now, thank God.

There was something very wrong with me.

"The Kendall job," she echoed. "Naturally I have an extra copy of the file you prepared. And *naturally* I didn't mention it to the police, especially to Lieutenant Grady. I think you are many things, Mr Becker – a disgraceful drunk and an immoral and unethical investigator, just to mention a few. But a murderer? Not the man who does widow cases for free." She rubbed at her right wrist.

*So I'm a sucker for dames with hard stories. So what?* "I didn't kill anyone." It was a relief to say it. "You've got the file?"

"*Naturally.*" She dropped her arms. "I would appreciate an explanation, but I'm only your secretary."

"You're a stand-up doll," I managed. "The Kendall job went bad, Miss Dale. I didn't kill him."

Being that practical type, she got right down to brass tacks. "Then who did, Mr Becker?"

Even though the thirst was getting worse by the second and the sound of her pulse wasn't helping, I knew the answer to that one. "Get me that file, Dale. And while you're at it, can I have some clothes or am I just going to swing around like Tarzan?"

If she'd muttered something unladylike under her breath as she swept from the room I wouldn't have blamed her.

I cleaned the rest of the mud off in her pink-and-yellow bathroom. She had an apartment on the seedier side of Parth Street, but everything was neat and clean and prim as you'd expect from the woman I'd once caught alphabetizing my incoming mail. She even had a suit hanging on the back of the door for me, one of mine. The door didn't shut quite tight, and I could hear her moving around the kitchen, and hear that maddening, delicious, irresistible thumping.

I looked like I'd been dug up that morning. Which, if you think about it, I had. There was an ugly flushed-red mark over my right eye, a divot I could rest my fingertip in. It was tender, and pressing on it made my whole head feel like a pumpkin again. The back of my skull was sore too, seamed and scarred under my short wet hair. There were bruised bags of flesh under my eyes, and my cheeks had sunken in, and I looked yellow as a jaundiced Chinaman.

I peeled away my shirt collar and looked. A fresh bruised mark above the collarbone, two holes that looked like a tiny pair of spikes had gone into my throat. The bruise was fever hot and when, I touched it, the rolling thunder of a heartbeat roared in my ears so loud I grabbed at Miss Dale's scrubbed-white sink and had to fight to retain consciousness.

*What the hell happened to me?*

The last thing I remembered was Letitia Kendall wiping her mouth and the skinny, nervous red-headed guy putting the barrel of the gun to my forehead. Right where that livid mark was, the one with speckles of dark grit in an orbit around its sunken redness. Then that sound, like an artillery shell inside my skull . . .

. . . and waking up in a cold, cold grave. Wanting a drink, but not my usual drink. Not the kind that went down the gullet like liquid fire and detonated in the belly, wrapping a warm haze between me and the rest of the world.

*You're insane, Jack. You got shot in the head.*

The trouble with that was, I shouldn't be insane. I should be *dead.*

But I had a pulse too. Just like Miss Dale. Who was starting to smell less like Chanel and more like . . .

Food.

A sizzling sound drifted down the hall. I tied the shoes she'd thoughtfully left right outside the bathroom door and saw her front door, and the warm light of the kitchen, a square of yellow sanity. She had her back turned and was fiddling with the stove, and a steak waited on a plate on the drainboard. She poked at the pan with a fork, and I was moving up quietly, just as if I was going to slap her.

Three steps. Two.

She never even turned around.

I reached out, saw my hand, yellow in the yellow light, shaking as it brushed past Miss Dale's hip . . . and fastened on the plate with the steak.

She jumped, the fork went clattering, and I retreated to the table. If I hadn't been so cold I would have been sweating buckets. I dropped down in one of Miss Dale's two straight-backed, frill-cushioned chairs next to her cheap gold-speckled kitchen table, and I found out why my mouth hadn't been working properly.

It was because the fangs had grown, and I licked the plate clean of bloody juice before burying my teeth in the raw meat and sucking as if it was mother's milk.

Dale's hand clapped over her mouth. She pinched so hard her cheeks blanched white from the pressure of her fingers, and her cat-tilted dark eyes turned as big as the landlord's on rent day. The pan sizzled, I sucked and sucked, and the two sounds almost managed to drown out the thunder of her pulse again.

Her free hand shot out and jerked the pan from the stove. The gas flame kept burning, a hissing circle of blue, and Miss Dale stared at me, holding the pan like she intended to storm the barricades with it.

I kept sucking. It wasn't nearly enough, but the thirst retreated. *This* was what I wanted. When it was as tasteless as dry paper, I finished licking the plate clean and dropped the wad of drained meat down.

I looked at Miss Dale. She looked at me. I searched for something to say. Dames on her salary don't buy steak every day. She must've thought I'd be hungry.

"I still need a secretary, doll-face."

Her throat worked as she swallowed. Then she put the pan down on an unlit burner. She peeled her fingers away from her mouth, the bruise still a dark bracelet on her right wrist. It took her two tries before she could get the words out.

"There's another steak in the fridge, Jack. It's . . . raw."

Winter nights last forever, and the rain was still coming down. Dale's wrist was swelling, but she wrapped it in an Ace and told me in no uncertain terms she was fine. She drove the Ford cautiously, the wipers ticking, just like her pulse. I spread the file out in my lap and checked for tails – we were clean.

Down on Cross Street, she parked where we had a good view of the Blue Room, and I paged through the file. Pictures of Arthur Kendall, millionaire, who had come back from Europe with a young wife who had begun to suspect him of fooling around.

*If I hadn't been so interested in the dollars she fanned out on my desktop, I wouldn't have taken the job. Divorce jobs aren't my favourites. They end up too sticky.*

*This one had just gotten stickier. Kendall wasn't just a million-aire, he was as dirty as they come. I'd been careful, sure, but I'd gotten priceless shots of him canoodling with the heavies in town – Lefty Schultz, who ran the prostitution racket, Big Buck Beaudry, who provided muscle, Papa Ginette, whose family used to run gin and now ran dope. Big fan of tradition, Papa Ginette.*

*I'd thought I was just getting into a dicey situation until I snapped a few shots of Kendall and his wife at a pricey downtown joint where the jazz was hot and the action was hotter. The Blue Room had a waiting list ten years long, but money talks – and it was Willie Goldstein's place. If Goldstein hadn't owned more than half the cops in town, he'd have been in Big Sing years ago.*

*Another late-night appointment, and the dame in green waltzed in my door just as Miss Dale was waltzing out. I spread the shots out and told her Kendall wasn't cheating. She'd married a dirty son of an unmentionable, but he wasn't hanging out with the ladies.*

*Those green eyes narrowed and she picked up the glossy of the crowd outside Goldstein's. There they were, Kendall and the missus and the red-headed, rat-faced gent who followed Kendall like glue. He wasn't heavy muscle – his name was Shifty Malloy, and he had a dope habit the size of Wrigley Field – but he was dapper in a suit and lit Kendall's cigarettes.*

*Mrs Kendall set the photo down again, and smiled at me. She crushed her cigarette out in the ashtray and I glanced down at the pictures again. Something very strange occurred to me.*

*I remember thinking that for a dame who wore green so much, she had awfully red lips. I remember snapping the shot, and I remember the flash of white calf as she turned to follow her husband past the velvet ropes and into the restaurant.*

*There in black-and-white was Kendall, and Malloy, and a crowd of other schmucks thinking it was hot stuff to pay five bucks for a steak and ogle the other rich schmucks, and there was a space where the dame in green should have been.*

*But Letitia Kendall wasn't in the picture. She was sitting across the desk from me, the last ghost of her cigarette rising in the air, and her face suddenly shifted under its little green veil. She came over the desk at me like a feral tiger, and everything went black . . .*

'There he is,' Dale whispered. 'The redhead.'

And sure enough, there was Shifty Malloy, dapper as ever in tails, getting out of a shiny new Packard. The Blue Room had a long awning to keep the rich dry, but the rat-faced bum actually unfolded an umbrella and held his hand out to help a lady out of the back seat. Miles of white, white leg through a slit in her dress, and she rose up out of the back of the car like a dream. Only she wasn't in green. The dame was in mourning like midnight, her red lips a slash on the white powder of her face, and I wondered how long it would take people to catch on that she liked to sleep in all day. I wondered if anyone would know her hands were as cold as ice cubes under the satin gloves, and I wondered if anyone would guess how Arthur Kendall gurgled when she had her teeth in his throat.

Because if I hadn't killed him, that only left one suspect, didn't it?

*It was cold. I lay on the floor and looked at the shapes in front of me – a wall full of splinters and long handles ending in metal shapes. It was the type of shack you have when you've got a pool and a garden and you need somewhere to store all the unattractive bits needed to keep it clipped and pretty – a lawnmower, shovels, all sorts of things.*

*"You'll do as I say," Letitia Kendall said.*

*"Aw Jesus," Shifty Malloy whined. "Jesus Christ."*

*Then a dainty foot in a green satin pump stepped into view. I blinked. Felt like I'd been hit by a train, throat was burning,*

*couldn't take a deep breath, and I couldn't even squirm. My hands
were tied back and my feet felt like lead blocks. She bent down, the
dame in green, and she wasn't wearing her pretty face any more.
The smear of crimson on her lips was fresh, and she wiped at it with
one white, white hand as her other hand came down, snagged a
handful of my suit coat and shirt, and hauled me up like I weighed
nothing.*

*"You have to cut off the head," she said. "It's very important.
If you don't, you won't get any more."*

*Malloy was sweating. "Got it. Cut off the head."*

*"Use a shovel. They do well." Her head tilted a little to the side,
like a cat's considering its prey. "It is very important, Edward, to
cut off the head."*

*If I could have opened my mouth, I might have said that asking
Shifty Malloy to decapitate someone was like asking a politician to
be honest. I knew the bum. Malloy might shoot a man in the back,
but he was squeamish about cockroaches, for Christ's sake.*

*"All right, already." Malloy stepped into view, and his ridi-
culous little pasted-on moustache was as limp as a dead caterpillar
with sweat. He raised the gun, a serviceable little derringer, and
put it to my forehead. "You might wanna put him down. This is
going to make a mess."*

*"Just do it." Letitia gave me an impatient little shake. My feet
dangled like a puppet's. "I have a party to attend tonight."*

*When I came back from the war some bum asked me what the
worst thing about it was. I told him it was the goddamn food in the
service. But the worst thing in the war was the not knowing, in the
smoke and the chaos, where the next bullet was coming from.*

*The only thing worse than that is knowing where it's coming
from, and when that gun is to your head and nothing comes out of
your crushed and dry throat but a little sound like nuh-nuh-muh.*

*Then the world exploded.*

"Wait until I get around the corner," I said, handing her the
file. "Then go home. You're a stand-up dame, Dale."

"For Christ's sake." She slid down in the seat, as if afraid
someone would see us parked here. "Call me Sophie, Jack. How
long have I worked for you?"

"Three years." *Kept me on time and kept that office from going under, too.*

"I deserve a raise." Her pulse was thumping again. Like a rabbit's. The thirst was back. It scorched the back of my throat like bile from the worst hangover ever, and it smelled her. Chanel and softness and the steak she'd cooked, and my fingers twitched like they wanted to cross the air between us and catch at her dress. It was a pretty blue dress, high in the collar and tight in the waist, and she looked good.

Never noticed before how easy on the eyes Miss Dale was. Yeah, I'm an unobservant bum.

"Go home, Sophie." It was getting hard to talk again, the teeth were coming out. *Shophie*, I mangled her name the first time I ever said it. "You're a doll. A real doll."

"What are you going to do?" She had never asked me that before. Plenty of questions, such as "Where did you put that file?" and "Do you want coffee?" and "What should I tell Boyleston when he calls about the rent?" But that particular one she'd never asked.

"I'm going to finish the Kendall job."

I slid out of the car and closed the door softly, headed down the street. She waited, just like I'd told her, for me to reach the corner. Then the Ford's engine woke and she pulled away. I could hear the car, but the biggest relief came when I couldn't hear her pulse any more.

Instead, I heard everyone else's. The drumbeats were a jungle, and here I was, the thirst burning a hole in me and the rain smacking at the top of my unprotected head. I flipped up the collar of my coat, wished like hell a bottle of Scotch could take the edge off the burning, and headed for Chinatown.

You can find anything in Chinatown. They eat anything down there, and I have a few friends. Still, it's amazing how a man who won't balk when you ask him to hide a dead body or a stack of bloodstained clothes might get funny ideas when you ask him to help you find . . . blood.

That's what butchers are for. And after a while I found what I was looking for. I had my nineteen dollars and the twenty in pin money from Miss Dale's – *Sophie's* – kitchen jar. She said I was good for it, and she would take it on her next pay cheque.

I would worry about getting her another pay cheque as soon as I finished this. It might take a little doing.

After two bouts of heaving as my body rebelled, the thirst took over and I drank nearly a bucket of steaming copper, and then I fell down and moaned like a doper on the floor of a filthy Chinatown slaughterhouse. It felt good, slamming into the thirst in my gut and spreading in waves of warmth until I almost cried.

I paid for another bucket. Then I got the hell out of there, because even bums will stop looking the other way for *some* things.

It's amazing what you can do once a dame in a green dress kills you and pins you for murder.

The next thing I needed was a car. On the edge of Chinatown sits Benny's Garage, and I rousted Benny by the simple expedient of jimmying his lock and dragging him out of bed. He didn't know why I wanted the busted-down pickup and twelve jerrycans of kerosene. "I don't want to know," he whined at me. "Why'd'ja have to bust the door down? Jeez, Becker, you—"

"Shut up." I peeled a ten-spot off my diminishing bankroll and held it in front of him, made it disappear when he snatched at it. "You never saw me, Benny."

He grabbed the ten once I made it reappear. "I *never* goddamn see you, Jack. I never wanta see you again, neither." He rubbed at his stubble, the rasp of every hair audible to me, and the sound of his pulse was a whack-whack instead of the sweet music of Sophie's. How long would his heart work through all the blubber he had piled on?

I didn't care. I drove away and hoped like hell Benny wouldn't call the cops. With a yard full of stolen cars and up to his ass in hock to Papa Ginette, it would be a bad move for him.

But still, I worried. I worried all the way up into Garden Heights and the quiet manicured mansions of the rich, where I found the house I wanted and had to figure out how to get twelve jerrycans over a nine-foot stone wall.

The house was beautiful. I almost felt bad, splishing and splashing over parquet floors, priceless antiques, and a bed that smelled faintly of copper and talcum powder. There was a whole closetful of green dresses. I soaked every goddamn one of them. Rain pounded the roof, gurgled through the gutters, hissed against the walls.

I carried two jerrycans downstairs to the foyer – a massive expanse of checkered black and white soon swimming in the nose-cleaning sting of kerosene – and settled myself to wait by the door to a study that probably had been Arthur Kendall's favourite place. I could smell him in there, cigars and fat-headed, expensive cologne. I ran my hands down the shaft of the shovel while I waited, swung it a few experimental times, and tapped it on the floor. It was a flathead shovel, handily available in any garden shed – and every immaculate lawn needs a garden shed, even if you get people out to clean it up for you.

I'm good at waiting, and I waited a long time. The fumes got into my nose and made me light-headed, but when the Packard came purring up the drive I was pouring the last half of a jerrycan. I then lit a match and a thin trail of flame raced away up the stairs like it was trying to outrun time. Even if her nose was as acute as mine she might not smell the smoke through the rain, and I bolted through the study, which had a floor-length window I'd been thoughtful enough to unlock. Around the corner, I moved so fast it was like being back in the war again, hardly noticing where either foot landed as long as I kept moving. The shovel whistled as I crunched across the gravel drive and then smacked Shifty Malloy right in the face with it, a good hit with all my muscle behind it. He had gotten out of the car, the stupid bum, and he went down like a ton of bricks while Letitia Kendall fumbled at the door handle inside, scratching like a mad hen.

The house began to whoosh and crackle. Twelve jerries is a lot of fuel, and there was a lot to burn in there. Even if it was raining like God had opened every damn tap in the sky.

She fell out of the Packard, the black dress immediately soaked and flashes of fish-belly flesh showing as she scrabbled on gravel. Her crimson mouth worked like a landed fish's, and if

I was a nice guy I suppose I might have given her a chance to explain. Maybe I might have even let her get away by being a stupid dick like you see in the movies, who lets the bad guy make his speech.

But I'm not a good guy. The shovel sang again, and the sound she made when the flat blade chopped three-quarters of the way through her neck was between a gurgle and a scream. The rain masked it, and she was off the gravel and on the lawn now, on mud as I followed, jabbing with the shovel while her head flopped like a defective Kewpie doll's. I chopped the way we used to chop rattlers back on the farm and, when her body stopped flopping and the gouts and gouts of fresh steaming blood had soaked a wide swatch of rain-flattened grass, I dropped the shovel and dragged her strangely heavy carcass back towards the house. I tossed it in the foyer, where the flames were rising merrily in defiance of the downpour, and I tossed the shovel in too. Then I had to stumble back, eyes blurring and skin peeling, and I figured out right then and there that fire was a bad thing for me, whatever I was now.

She was wet and white where the black dress was torn, and the flames wanted to cringe away. I didn't stick around to see if she went up, because the house began to burn in earnest, the heat scratching at my skin with thousands of scraping gold pins, and there was a rosy glow in the east that had nothing to do with kerosene.

It was dawn, and I didn't know exactly what had happened to me, but I knew I didn't want to be outside much longer.

Of course she hadn't gone to sleep. As soon as I got near her door, trying to tread softly on the worn carpet and smelling the burned food and dust smell of working folks in her apartment building, it opened a crack and Sophie peered through. She was chalk white, trembling, and she retreated down the hall as I shambled in. It was still raining and I was tired. The thirst was back, burrowing in my veins, and my entire body was shot through with lead. The pinpricks on my throat throbbed like they were infected, my skin cracked and crackled with the burning, still, but the divot above my right eye wasn't inflamed any more.

I shut her door and locked it. I stood dripping on her welcome mat and looked at her.

She hadn't changed out of the blue dress. She had nice legs, by God, and those cat-tilted eyes weren't really dark. They were hazel. Her wrist was still bruised where I'd grabbed her; she had peeled the Ace off and it was a nice dark purple. It probably hurt like hell.

Her hands hung limp at her sides.

I searched for something to say. The rain hissed and gurgled. Puddles in the street outside were reflecting old neon and newer light edging through grey mist. "It's dawn."

She just stood there.

"You're a real doll, Sophie. If I didn't have—"

"How did it happen?" She swallowed, the muscles in her throat working. Under that high collar her pulse was still like music. "Your . . . you . . ." She fluttered one hand helplessly. For the first time since she walked into my office three years ago and announced the place was a dump, my Miss Dale seemed nonplussed.

"I got bit, sugar." I peeled my sodden shirt collar away. "I don't want to make any trouble for you. I'll figure something out tomorrow night."

Thirty of the longest seconds of my life passed in her front hallway. I dripped, and I felt the sun coming the way I used to feel storms moving in on the farm, back when I was a jug-eared kid and the big bad city was a place I only heard about in church.

"Jack, you ass," Sophie said. "So it's a bite?"

"And a little more."

Miss Dale lifted her chin and eyed me. "I don't have any more steak." Her pulse was back. It was thundering. It was hot and heavy in my ears and I already knew I wasn't a nice guy. Wasn't that why I'd come here?

"I'll go." I reached behind me and fumbled for the knob.

"Oh, no you will *not*." It was Miss Dale again, with all her crisp efficiency. She reached up with trembling fingers, and unbuttoned the very top button of her collar.

"Sophie—"

"How long have I been working for you, Jack?" She undid another button, slender fingers working, and I took a single step forwards. Burned skin crackled, and my clothes were so heavy they could have stood up by themselves. "Three years. And it wasn't for the pay, and certainly not because you've a personality that recommends itself."

Coming from her, that was a compliment. "You've got a real sweet mouth there, Miss Dale."

She undid her third button and that pulse of hers was a beacon. Now I knew what the thirst wanted, now I knew what it felt like, now I knew what it could do . . .

"Mr Becker, shut up. If you don't, I'll lose my nerve."

Sophie is on her pink frilly bed. The shades are drawn, and the apartment's quiet. It's so quiet. Time to think about everything.

When a man wakes up in his own grave, he can reconsider his choice of jobs. He can do a whole lot of things.

It's so goddamn quiet. I'm here with my back to the bedroom door and my knees drawn up. Sophie is so still, so pale. I've had time to look over every inch of her face and I wonder how a stupid bum like me could have overlooked such a doll right under his nose.

It took three days for me. Two days ago the dame in the black dress choked her last and her lovely mansion burned. It was in all the papers as a tragedy, and Shifty Malloy choked on his own blood out in the rain too. I think it's time to find another city to gumshoe in. There's Los Angeles, after all, and that place does three-quarters of its business after dark.

Soon the sun's going to go down. Sophie's got her hands crossed on her chest and she's all tucked in nice and warm, the coverlet up to her chin and the lamp on so she won't wake up like I did, in the dark and the mud.

The rain has stopped beating the roof. I can hear heartbeats moving around in the building.

Jesus, I hope she wakes up.

# Untitled 12

## Caitlín R. Kiernan

As it turns out, *finding* her was the easy part, as easy as falling off a log, as easy as pie, as easy as you fucking please. I spent so many years preparing myself to begin looking – years and years and finally a whole decade seeking out those frightened old men hoarding secrets, the mad women guarding forbidden and forgotten books, years committing all the usual indiscretions and blasphemies that might finally make me suitable in her eyes, *if* I could ever find her. But I doubted I ever would. I would search, I thought. I would search as diligently as anyone had ever searched for anything, holy or unholy. I would likely search my entire life away and, as with all the others before me, I would only find hints and rumours; there would be times when I'd come so, so close that it would seem some capricious agent must be leading me, surely, coaxing me, feeding me the right leads only to steer me astray at the very last moment. That's what I expected, more or less, because that's what I'd been told to expect, and that's what I'd read in the books – *Unaussprechlichen Kulten*, *De Vermis Mysteriis*, *Livre d'Eibon* and so on and so forth – pages too brittle and stained to read, riddles too oblique to fathom, all of it spiralling deeper into the certain despair that I was only an idiot chasing a myth that had never possessed more substance than the ramblings of schizophrenics and liars. And then, one night, *she* found me. Weeks after that I don't recall, darkness until I woke somewhere unfamiliar, sick and sweating in half-light and shadows, sick as a junky going cold turkey; the high walls, bare masonry, bricks and mortar, fire doors scabbed with rust, the

constant sound of water dripping somewhere. I lay naked on a
bare mattress soaked through with blood and piss and mildew,
realizing, slowly, that I'd been beaten almost to death, maybe
more than once, that there were broken bones and missing
teeth. The pain made me want to climb back down into the
numb, insensible darkness. But she crouched nearby, watching
me with her ebony eyes. Those secret, ravenous eyes to match
the black holes waiting at the centre of galaxies, eyes to devour
stars and planets and even time, eyes to devour souls, and when
she smiled blood spilled from her mouth and pooled on the
concrete floor. "It's not a game," she said and licked at her lips.
"I never thought it was," I replied, dizzy and slurring the
words.

She nodded her head. "Just so we understand one another.
Just so *you* understand *me*. Just so you know it ain't—" "—a
game," I interrupted, and for a moment I thought she might
take my head off.

She crawled a few feet nearer the mattress, moving across the
floor more like some reptilian thing than a woman, and the
faintest, furious spark glinted in her dead eyes. "Are you
hungry?" she asked and more blood leaked from her mouth.
"Do you know what I've done to find you?" I said, instead of
answering her question. "Do you think that matters? Do you
think that's why you're here? I asked you a question."

"I'm sick," I told her.

She nodded her head. "You'll get a whole lot sicker," she
said. "Especially if you don't eat." Then she vomited, a sudden
gush of the darkest red across the concrete and the edge of the
mattress. It spattered my bare skin, speckling me with half-
digested blood. She wiped her mouth and sat down.

"That's how you start," she said.

I stared at the cooling puked-up blood for a moment or two,
and then lay back down on the mattress and stared, instead, up
at the ceiling of the place, which seemed far, far away. There
was glass up there, a skylight, and I could see it was night. I shut
my eyes and wondered what it would take to get her to kill me.
"You should hurry. It's better warm," she said. "Can I still say
no?" I asked. "Can I change my mind?" There was a long

moment of silence. Maybe she was surprised. Maybe she wasn't. I doubt I'll ever know. "It's not too late," she said, finally. "I'll kill you, if that's all you want. It seems a shame, though." Her voice – I wish I could find the language to describe her voice. It has to be heard, I think. It made me want to scramble away on my shattered limbs and hide in some dark hole where she would never be able to follow. It made me *want* to die. "It doesn't really matter to me," she said. "There will be others. There always are. They will never stop coming." "I didn't come," I said. "I don't even know where I am. You . . . *took* me."

"Is that how it was, little girl?" She laughed, licking some of the regurgitated blood from her fingertips. "Well, that's not how I remember it." And then she brushed the sweaty hair back from my eyes, her hand as cold as ice across my brow, arctic air against fevered skin, and I shivered so hard my teeth clacked together. "Don't look for monsters if you don't want to find them," she said. What *had* I expected? Some glorious fallen angel, some beautiful Byronic being of light and shadow? Had I really thought she would be *beautiful*? I'd read enough to know better. But I'd been unprepared for *this*, this *gargoyle* squatting there before me, smeared with blood and gore, dirt and shit, her salt-and-pepper hair pulled back into a matted crown, her lean, boyish body a road map of scars and half-healed injuries. At some point, her left nipple had been torn entirely away. "What? Am I not pretty enough for you?" she asked and bared her teeth like a spiteful child. Somewhere overhead, a bird fluttered about in the criss-cross of steel girders before the skylight. "I thought you were a *learned* woman," she snarled. She stood up. And I saw the organ hanging down between her legs. It almost looked like a small penis, almost, a stunted penis sheathed in bone or horn, barbed and ridged and misshapen. "The books," I said, unable to take my eyes off the thing between her legs, "the books were mostly a waste of time. The men who wrote them . . . they didn't know . . ." "They never do," she said, stepping over the cooling pool of bloody vomit. Then she stood above me, glaring down with those hungry eyes, and she began to squeeze the sharp end of the penis thing between her fingertips. "They hide in their rituals and incanta-tions, too afraid to confront what they truly desire. You're not like that," she told me. "I'm not? Are you certain about that?" "No," she replied. "I'm *never* certain. But we'll see. Soon, we shall see, little girl."

She knelt down, straddling me, and that hard prong, grown stiff now and slightly larger, pressed hard against my belly. She bent down and kissed me, her tongue darting quickly past my teeth, and I tasted the blood of whatever or whomever she'd killed that night. The taste of blood was nothing new to me. My earlier depredations had seen to that. But there was something more, something beyond the rich, faintly metallic flavour, something like biting down on aluminum foil, something that tasted of mould and molasses and dried thyme. She breathed into me then, a sudden etheric rape, storm wind blown off a tideless pack-ice sea, her rancid, sweet breath pouring down my throat and filling my lungs. She withdrew immediately, and I gasped, coughed, gagged and almost threw up. "Don't you dare let that go," she warned. "Don't you fucking dare."

Then she pressed one hand into the sticky-dark pool she'd left for me beside the mattress and smeared it across my breasts. There were bruises there, bruises and cuts and maybe broken ribs, and I shuddered at the pain and the cold of her touch but managed not to cry out. She was smiling as she painted my chest. "It isn't in the blood," she said with a smirk. "That's what they all think, I know. But they're all wrong. It isn't in the blood. Aren't you hungry yet?" I looked up towards the sky-light again, fifty or sixty feet above the floor. Where was that sky? What constellations gazed down on us? Maybe we were no longer even in a world with stars. Perhaps, she'd dragged me away to somewhere else, somewhere the starshine was too afraid to follow. Some decaying ante-room of one or another lesser hell. I shut my eyes and tried to let it all go, every thought that stood in-between me and the demon I'd spent so long trying to find. I had come looking for her, and she had found me. I opened my eyes as the thing between her legs slid into me. There was pain, but not so much as I'd expected. "Yes," she sighed, grinding her hips against mine. "You're still here with me, little girl. Maybe you'll stay after all. Maybe you're what you always thought you were." And then she leaned closer, her spine arching like the back of a cat, like the spine of nothing human, and her long, rough tongue began licking away the blood on my breasts, taking little bits of skin with it. Her breath in me, taking me more surely than any mere sexual act, taking me and taking me apart. Cunningly altered molecules of oxygen and hydrogen splitting the cells of my body, carbon dioxide, nitrogen, mundane gases rendered impossibly exotic to divide mitochondria from their DNA, to drive the nuclei of my body to supernova. I wrapped my legs around her as her organ probed deeper, tearing me up inside. This was utter dissolution, alchemy too sublime and mercurial for crude earthly chemistries. The rupture of membranes to release floods of cytoplasm as she had her way with me. I could feel those barbs, digging in so deep I'd never get her out. No going back now, and nowhere left to go back to, because I'd gone looking for her, and she had noticed. "What's happening to me?" I asked her, the guttural grunt of some animal escaping my lips, almost but not quite forming words. "Don't you know? Lead into gold," she whispered. "Water into wine. Isn't that what you wanted?" I closed my eyes. Isn't that exactly what I'd wanted? The concrete below me crumbled and fell away, or it only seemed to, and I was tumbling into some pit for which a bottom had never seemed necessary. Crossing distance that was not space or time, and she was still inside me. She would always be inside me. She kissed me again and blood flowed from her mouth into mine. Her short nails dug into my sides, puncturing skin and muscle and scraping bone, and an instant later her lips were pressed to my left ear. There were words – promises, threats, taunts, but none of it as important as her voice. The words themselves were irrelevant, mostly, only there because the voice had to take some form. It was the voice of this consuming pit, and in it I heard the aeons and saw the feral creature for what she was, saw the primordial forests she'd stalked, the glacial wastes and caverns, the necropolises and catacombs of vast cities gone to dust 10,000 years before the coming of mankind. She was there through it all. She is the constant. She is the rising of the sun and the setting of the moon. Her jaws clamped tightly about my throat, her long canines and incisors opening up new wounds, releasing more of me into the chasm rising up around us. "No doubt," she whispered, the wind and darkness tearing her words away almost before I could hear them. "No doubt ever again." "We're going to fall forever," I replied, surprised at the resignation in my voice. I'd never been so sure of anything in all my life. "That's up to you, little girl," she said with a laugh, and there was only a moment's confusion before I understood exactly what she meant.

She thrust her hips again, that pulsing shaft of flesh and horn between her legs becoming suddenly an unlocking key, becoming now the holy grail to divide my last resistance, and the deep places of this nowhere rumbled and echoed as we began to rise. The angry, cheated abyss, oblivion's dragon that much more empty for our retreat, and then we were lying on the mattress again, and I could hear the steady, determined drip of water. She kissed me once, her lips softly brushing mine, then withdrew and crawled away into the gloom. But I could still see her. With these new black eyes, this new flesh, she could never go so far that I would be unable to see her.

I lay there for a time, until the sun began to rise, shining in dusky cathedral shafts through the skylight, throwing chiaroscuro bands across the concrete. We would have to sleep soon, but first I rolled over onto my belly and licked away the blood she'd left for me on the floor.

# Author Biographies

**C. T. Adams and Cathy Clamp**
Award-winning *USA Today* bestselling authors C.T. Adams and Cathy Clamp have written nearly a dozen paranormal romances. They are the authors of the Sazi Shapeshifter series, as well as the Thrall Vampire trilogy.
www.ciecatrunpubs.com

**Keri Arthur**
Keri Arthur publishes books in both the paranormal romance and urban fantasy fields, and is the author of nineteen novels, including the *New York Times* bestselling Riley Jenson, Guardian series.
www.keriarthur.com

**Amanda Ashley**
*New York Times* and USA *Today* bestselling writer, Amanda Ashley, is the author of over fifty books and is a pioneer of vampire romance.

**Jenna Black**
Jenna Black writes paranormal romance for Tor (the Guardians of the Night series), and urban fantasy for Bantam Dell (the Morgan Kingley series). www.jennablack.com

## Karen Chance

*USA Today* and *New York Times* bestselling author of the Cassandra Palmer series from Penguin. Her new series, beginning with the novel *Midnight's Daughter*, starts this year.
www.karenchance.com

## Delilah Devlin

Award-winning author of erotic, paranormal romance, including the My Immortal Knight series from Ellora's Cave.
www.delilahdevlin.com

## Barbara Emrys

Barbara Emrys teaches creative writing at the University of Nebraska.

## Sherri Erwin

*Naughty and Nice*, the sequel to Sherri Erwin's first paranormal romance *To Hell With Love*, is published this year by Zebra.
www.sherribrowningerwin.com

## Colleen Gleason

Bestselling author of The Gardella Vampire Chronicles from Signet.
www.colleengleason.com

## Raven Hart

Raven Hart is the author of the Savannah Vampires series from Ballantine books.
www.ravenhart.com

## Nancy Holder

*USA Today* bestselling author of the Gifted series (Silhouette), co-author of the Wicked series (Simon & Schuster) and author of many novels tied into the *Buffy the Vampire Slayer/Angel* universes.
www.nancyholder.com

**Dina James**
Dina James is a first-time writer addicted to all things paranormal. She lives in Astoria, Oregon.

**Caitlín R. Kiernan**
Caitlín R. Kiernan is the author of seven novels, including the award-winning *Silk* (winner of the International Horror Guild Award for Best First Novel and a finalist for the Bram Stoker Award for Best First Novel) and Threshold. She writes science fiction and dark fantasy works, comic books, short stories, novellas and vignettes.
www.caitlinrkiernan.com

**Jenna Maclaine**
Her first paranormal romance novel, *Wages of Sin*, is published by St Martin's Paperbacks this year.
www.jennamaclaine.com

**Alexis Morgan**
Alexis Morgan is the bestselling author of seventeen books, including two contemporary paranormal romance series for Pocket Star (the Paladins of Darkness series and the Talions series).
www.alexismorgan.com

**Vicki Pettersson**
*USA Today* bestselling author of The Signs of the Zodiac series, which is set in her hometown of Las Vegas, Nevada. After ten years with the Tropicana's Folies Bergere, she still knows all about what really happens behind the scenes in Sin City.
www.vickipettersson.com

**Kimberly Raye**
*USA Today* bestselling author Kimberly Raye is the author of the Dead End Dating series from Ballantine, featuring the vampire matchmaker Lil' Marchette.
www.kimberlyraye.com

## Savannah Russe

Bestselling author of the vampire series The Darkwing Chronicles from Signet Eclipse, and the upcoming Sisterhood of the Sight series.

www.darkwingchronicles.com

## Lilith Saintcrow

Lilith Saintcrow is the creator of the Dante Valentine series from Orbit. Her new Jill Kismet series begins this year.

## Susan Sizemore

Award-winning author Susan Sizemore always seems to be writing about vampires. Among her efforts are the dark fantasy Laws of the Blood series and the romantic Primes vampire series from Pocket Star.

## Rachel Vincent

Urban fantasy author Rachel Vincent writes the Werecat series for Mira Books.

www.rachelvincent.com

## Shiloh Walker

Bestselling author of the vampire Hunter's series from Berkley Sensation.

## Rebecca York

Award-winning *New York Times* and *USA Today* bestselling novelist, Rebecca York (aka Ruth Glick) is the author of more than 100 books. She writes the romantic-paranormal Moon series for Berkley and romantic thrillers for Harlequin Intrigue.